The
CHARM
Offensive

The
CHARM
Offensive

— a novel —

ALISON COCHRUN

ATRIA PAPERBACK

New York   London   Toronto   Sydney   New Delhi

ATRIA
PAPERBACK

An Imprint of Simon & Schuster, Inc.
1230 Avenue of the Americas
New York, NY 10020

First Atria Paperback edition September 2021

ATRIA PAPERBACK and colophon are trademarks of Simon & Schuster, Inc.

For information about special discounts for bulk purchases, please contact Simon & Schuster Special Sales at 1-866-506-1949 or business@simonandschuster.com.

The Simon & Schuster Speakers Bureau can bring authors to your live event. For more information or to book an event, contact the Simon & Schuster Speakers Bureau at 1-866-248-3049 or visit our website at www.simonspeakers.com.

Interior design by Jill Putorti

Manufactured in the United States of America

11

Library of Congress Cataloging-in-Publication Data

Names: Cochrun, Alison, author.
Title: The charm offensive : a novel / Alison Cochrun.
Description: First Atria paperback edition. | New York : Atria Paperback, 2021.
Identifiers: LCCN 2021001980 | ISBN 9781982170714 (paperback) | ISBN 9781982170721 (ebook)
Subjects: LCSH: Dating shows (Television programs)—Fiction. | Gay men—Fiction. | GSAFD: Love stories. | Humorous fiction.
Classification: LCC PS3603.O2933 C48 2021 | DDC 813/.6—dc23
LC record available at https://lccn.loc.gov/2021001980

ISBN 978-1-9821-7071-4
ISBN 978-1-9821-7072-1 (ebook)

*For Heather, Meredith, and Michelle—because
everyone knows the female friendships are the best part*

The
CHARM
Offensive

THE FIRST NIGHT OF FILMING

Dev

Dev Deshpande knows the exact moment he started believing in happily ever after.

He is ten years old, sitting cross-legged in his living room, staring up at the television in awe at *Ever After*. It's like the stories he reads before bed, tented under *Star Wars* sheets long after his parents have told him to turn out the lights—stories about knights and towers and magic kisses. It's like the movies he watches with his babysitter Marissa, stories about corsets and handsome men with dour faces and silent dances that say everything. Stories that make his heart feel too big for his small body.

Except *Ever After* is better than those stories because it's *real*. It's reality television.

On-screen, a beautiful blond man extends a jeweled tiara to a woman in a pink dress. "Are you interested in becoming my princess?"

The woman sheds a single tear as music swells in the background. "Yes. Yes!" She claps her hands over her mouth, and the man rests the crown on the woman's head, gold against her golden hair. The golden couple embrace with a kiss.

He's mesmerized by this world of horse-drawn carriages and ball gowns and big romantic gestures. The foreign travel destinations and the swoon-worthy kisses against brick walls while fireworks go off in the distance. This world where happily ever afters are guaranteed. He watches, and he imagines himself as one of the women, being waltzed around the ballroom by a handsome prince.

"Turn off that anachronistic, patriarchal bullshit," his mother snaps as she comes into the house carrying two grocery bags, one under each arm.

But Dev didn't turn off that anachronistic, patriarchal bullshit. In fact, he did the opposite. He joined it.

"A toast!" he declares as he sloshes the rest of the champagne into the glasses held in eager, outstretched hands all around him. "To beginning the quest to find love!"

He is twenty-eight years old, sitting in the back of a limo with five drunk women on the first night of filming a new season of *Ever After*. There's a former beauty queen, a travel blogger, a medical student, a software engineer, and a Lauren. They're all beautiful and brilliant and masking nerves with copious amounts of limo champagne, and when they finally arrive at the castle gates, the women raise their glasses excitedly. Dev takes an obligatory sip of champagne and wishes for something slightly stronger to dull the current aching of his too-big heart.

For the next nine weeks, these are the contestants he'll coach for the cameras, guiding them through Group Quests and Crowning Ceremonies, helping to craft their perfect love stories. If he does his job right, in nine weeks one of these women will receive the Final Tiara, the proposal, the happily ever after.

And maybe then Dev will forget that in his own life, happily ever afters are never guaranteed.

He plasters on his best producer smile. "Okay, ladies! It's almost time to meet your Prince Charming!" A chorus of shrieks fills the limo, and he waits for it to die down. "I'm going to go check in with our director. I'll be right back."

On cue, a production assistant opens the limo door for him. He steps out of the car. "Hey, babe," Jules says condescendingly. "How are you doing?"

He slings his handler bag over his chest. "Don't patronize me."

She's already pivoted and started her brisk march up the hill toward the castle. "If you don't want to be patronized, I guess you don't need *these*"—she pulls a bag of mint Oreos out from under her arm—"to stave off your crippling depression."

"*Crippling* is a bit much. I like to think I'm sort of dabbling in depression."

"And how many times have you cried while listening to the same Leland Barlow breakup song in the past twenty-four hours?"

"Fair point."

Jules smacks the Oreos against his chest without breaking stride. Then she shoots him a sideways glance, almost like she's searching for evidence of his epic cryfest in the shower three hours ago—and again in the Lyft on the way to the hotel ballroom to pick up his contestants. Her eyes fall to his outfit. He's wearing his standard first-night uniform: cargo shorts with deep pockets, a T-shirt—black, to mask the pit stains—comfortable shoes to get him through a twelve-hour shoot. "You look like an Indian Kevin James in an 'after' weight-loss photo."

He puts on his charming Fun Dev smile and plays along with this little game. She's wearing corduroy overalls and a Paramore concert T-shirt with her giant Doc Martens, a fanny pack across the front of her chest like a sash, and her thick hair in its usual topknot. Jules Lu is every twenty-four-year-old LA transplant with mountains of student debt, settling for something less than her delusions of Greta Gerwig grandeur. "You look like the sad old person at a Billie Eilish concert."

She flips him off with both hands while walking backward through the security gate. They both flash their badges to the guard before immediately having to dart to avoid a golf cart carrying two set runners. They skirt the jib, which captures establishing shots from twenty feet up, and run directly into the first assistant director, who accosts them with pink revised call sheets. Dev has always been a little bit in love with the chaos and the magic of the first night of filming.

Jules rudely slams him back into reality. "You sure you don't want to talk about it?" she asks. By "it" she clearly means his breakup three months ago and the fact that he's about to see his ex for the first time since they divided up their assets, Ryan taking the PS5 and the apartment and all the real furniture, Dev keeping the Disney collectible mugs and the DVD box sets. "It" being the fact that Dev has to work side by side with Ryan for the next nine weeks.

Talking about "it" is the last thing Dev wants, so he stuffs three Oreos into his mouth. Jules tilts her head and stares up at him. "I'm here for you, you know. If like . . ." But she doesn't finish the sentence, can't fully commit to her offer of emotional support. Instead, she reverts to their usual teasing. "You let me know when you're ready for a rebound. I've got at least four dudes at my gym I could set you up with."

"Oh, sweetheart, don't pretend like you've ever stepped foot in a gym."

She punches his arm. "I'm trying to be a good friend, asshole."

Jules is a great friend, but you don't just rebound from a six-year relationship, and the thought of dating again makes him want to crawl back into bed for another three months. He doesn't want to go on awkward first dates with fit, well-groomed, West Hollywood queer men who won't be able to look past his scrawny physique, his Costco-brand jeans, and his very uncool prescription glasses.

He thought he was done with first dates.

"I think I'm going to take a man-sabbatical," he tells Jules with rehearsed indifference as they continue their march toward Command Central. "Just focus on scripting other people's love stories."

Jules detours them by the crafty table for cold-brew refills. "Yeah, well, you're going to have your work cut out for you this season. Have you met Mr. Charming yet?"

"No, but he can't possibly be as bad as he sounds in the group chat."

"He's *worse*." She claps her hands together to dramatically punctuate each word. "He. Is. A. *Disaster*. Skylar says he's season-ruining. *Career*-ruining."

Dev would be more concerned if Skylar Jones weren't always apocalyptic on the first night of filming. "Skylar thinks every season will be our last. I highly doubt Charles Winshaw is going to topple a twenty-year franchise. And Twitter is sufficiently twitterpated about the casting."

"Well, apparently the prepackage shoot was awful. They took him to the beach, and he almost fell off his white horse."

Dev could admit that didn't sound *great*. "Charles is an outsider. He probably just needs some time to adjust to the cameras and the lights. It can be overwhelming."

Jules rolls her eyes. "Bringing in an outsider isn't going to convince anyone these Instagram influencers came on this show for *love*."

"They're not Instagram influencers," he insists. Another Jules Lu eye roll. "*Most* of them are not Instagram influencers. And of course they're here for love."

"And never to promote their line of funky festival headbands on Etsy," she snaps. "The only people who actually come on this show for love are so brainwashed by the wedding industrial complex, and so convinced their self-worth is tied to matrimony, they literally convince themselves they're in love with a person they've spent all of ten total hours with."

"It's so sad to see such cynicism in one so young."

"And it's so sad to see such blind idealism in one so old." He throws an Oreo at her, even if she sort of has a point. About Charles Winshaw, not about love and marriage.

In the six years Dev has worked for *Ever After*, the new star has always been chosen from the crop of fan-favorite rejects of the previous season. Except recently, this pattern has caused some vocal critics within the Fairy-Tale Family to cast doubt on the show's romantic realism. Instead of coming on the show to find love, some people were coming on the show to become the next star. So their showrunner, Maureen Scott, decided to bring in an outsider for the new season to shake things up.

Charles Winshaw—the enigmatic, millionaire tech genius with an inexplicable eight-pack—is good for ratings, regardless of whether he can stay mounted on a horse.

Dev pulls out a copy of *People* magazine from his shoulder bag. It's the issue with their new star on the cover, the words *Silicon Valley's Most Eligible Bachelor!* splashed across the front.

Blond curls and a broad jaw and a chin dimple. A perfect Prince Charming.

As they turn away from the crafty table, the sun is beginning to dip behind the castle's twin turrets, dappling everything on set in soft, orange light. Strands of twinkle lights shine from the trees like stars, and the air is fragrant from the bouquets of flowers, and it's exactly like the fairy tales Dev imagined as a kid.

"It's a shitstorm, Dev! A fucking shitstorm!" Skylar Jones shouts as they enter the Command Central tent. She's already halfway through a roll of Tums, which is never a good sign this early in the night.

"Why is it a shitstorm, exactly?"

"Because this season is completely and epically fucked!"

"I'm very sorry to hear we're somehow fucked before we've started." Dev slots in his earpiece as Jules hands him a walkie-talkie from the charging station. "Is this about him almost falling off the horse?"

"I wish he *had* fallen off the horse," Skylar seethes. "Maybe if he'd been trampled, we could've cast a Jonas Brother or a subpar Hemsworth."

"I think all the Jonases and Hemsworths are married."

"Oh, is that why we're stuck with a constipated computer nerd?"

Dev knows better than to laugh at his boss. As a queer Black woman, Skylar Jones did not become the lead director of a reality television juggernaut by having chill. When she developed early female pattern baldness before forty from the stress of this job, she simply began shaving all her hair off.

"How can I help, Sky?"

"Tell me what you know about Charles Winshaw."

"Uh . . . Charles Winshaw . . ." Dev closes his eyes, pictures the spreadsheets he compiled from network background checks and Google searches in preparation for this season, and rattles off facts rapid-fire. "Has the brains of Steve Wozniak and the body of a Marvel superhero. Graduated high school at sixteen when he won a coding contest and a full-ride scholarship to Stanford. Launched his tech startup, WinHan, with his dorm mate Josh Han before his twentieth birthday. Left his company at twenty-six and now runs the Winshaw Foundation as a twenty-seven-year-old millionaire. Has graced the cover of both *Time* and *GQ* but has been notoriously private until now, so little is known about his dating history. But—"

Dev shakes out his arms. This is what he does. "Based on what we know, I would guess Charles is looking for a woman between the ages of twenty-five and thirty, no taller than five foot six. Athletic, but not particularly outdoorsy. A woman who is grounded and ambitious, who has her life together and clear goals for the future. Intelligent, but not more intelligent than him, family-oriented and outgoing. He'll say he's looking for someone passionate with a great sense of humor, but what he really wants is someone easygoing and agreeable who will happily adapt to his life in San Francisco. Given this profile, I've already prepared folders on the women most likely to make top three."

Skylar gestures to the rest of the tent. "And this, folks, is why Dev is the best."

Dev does a little mock bow in the direction of a sound mixer. Skylar claps him on the back. "Here's what you're going to do, Dev. Hustle down to the west gate to meet Charles's car and get him to his mark."

As much as Dev loves a good hustle, especially on the first night of filming, he doesn't move. "Shouldn't Ry—I mean, shouldn't Charles's handler get him to his mark?"

"You're Charles's handler now. This is me reassigning you. And unless you want this show to go the way of *Average Joe*, I suggest you stop standing there with your mouth hanging open and *really* fucking hustle."

Dev still doesn't move. "I'm sorry, but I don't understand. I'm a contestant handler, and . . . Ryan is the prince's handler."

Ryan Parker is good at douche-bro camaraderie and Dev is good at coaching women. As the entire crew recently learned after their public breakup at Dev's twenty-eighth birthday party, they were never good for each other.

"Except Ryan couldn't get the shots at the prepackage shoot, so now he's being moved to supervising producer, and you're taking his prince. Listen." Skylar cups Dev's face in her hands in a flagrant disregard of recent network memos about workplace boundaries. "You're the best handler we've got, and it's gonna take the best with this guy."

The only thing Dev loves more than this show is being flattered about his abilities as a producer on this show. "If we're going to make this season work, I need Dev 'Truly Believes in Fairy Tales' Deshpande coaching our star. Can you do that for me?"

He doesn't think about his own failed fairy tale. He simply says what his boss wants to hear. "Of course I can."

"Excellent." Skylar turns to Jules. "Go find Charles's folder and bring it to Dev. You'll work as his PA for the season. Help him with Charles. Go, both of you. It's almost sundown."

Dev can't even enjoy the repulsed look on Jules's face at being named his personal production assistant because all he can think about is seeing Ryan for the first time in three months now that he has stolen his job.

There is no time to dwell on that right now. He does what he was ordered to do. He *fucking hustles* down the flagstone path toward the west gate, where the town car is waiting with their star.

And maybe this is good. Maybe this is better. Dev can coach women in his sleep, but Charles Winshaw will be a challenge, the kind of thing he can throw his entire mind and body into, getting lost in the bright lights and the beautiful stories.

He barrels toward the town car, reaches for the back door handle without pausing, and perhaps, in his enthusiasm, wrenches open the door with more force than is strictly necessary, because their Prince Charming comes spilling out of the car in a mess of limbs and lands squarely at his feet.

Charlie

"Do we think the crown is a bit much?"

Maureen Scott doesn't look up from her phone or in any way acknowledge he's spoken.

Charlie shifts awkwardly in the town car backseat, the tux pulling across his chest in all the wrong ways. His body hasn't felt like his own since they waxed it and tanned it and drenched it in very pungent cologne. The least they could do is let him remove the crown, so he doesn't look like Stripper Prince William. He even had to double-check the tux wasn't a tear-away.

(It's not. However, there were enough nudity clauses in his contract to raise legitimate concern.)

He looks down at the magazine lying casually on the seat between them and experiences the cognitive dissonance of seeing photos of himself. If he could look in a mirror right now, he knows his face would be sweaty and red, pinched together anxiously at the corners of his eyes and the corners of his mouth. But the man on the magazine cover isn't anxious about anything. His face is smooth, his eyes friendly, his mouth casually tilting in the corner. The man on the magazine cover is a stranger.

The man on the magazine cover is a *lie*—a lie he has to live for the next two months. He's made a deal with the proverbial devil, and he can't control much about his circumstances at the moment, but at the very least, he can take off this stupid plastic crown. He reaches up.

"Don't do that, dear," Maureen Scott snaps, eyes still on her phone.

Even with the *dear*, there is an edge to her words, and his hands fall limply at his sides. He's stuck with the crown, then.

Or . . . he could jump out of the moving vehicle and abort this foolish, misguided publicity stunt right now. He tests the door handle, but of course it's locked. He's been labeled a flight risk, which is why the show's creator is personally escorting him from the studio to the set.

Two days ago, *Ever After* took him to a beach where they expected him to ride a white horse for the intro package, like the Prince Charming he's supposed to be. Prince Charmings are supposed to intrinsically know how to ride horses. They're definitely not supposed to be *afraid* of horses. Instead of looking strapping and manly, he kept slouching and delaying production and grimacing with every uncomfortable jostle of the saddle until the sun was gone and everyone was generally pissed with the shots. The bald woman running set called him "fucking uncoachable."

Which sounds about right, honestly.

He tries to remember what his publicist said before he left: "You're Charlie *fucking* Winshaw. You built a billion-dollar tech company before you got your braces off. You can handle *Ever After*."

"But I lost my company," he had muttered in response. Parisa pretended not to hear him. She knows what he lost. That's why he's *here*. This is his last chance to get it all back.

He feels the pressure of it weighing down on him, and before his generalized anxiety turns the corner into full-blown panic attack, he runs through his coping strategies: three deep breaths; count to thirty in seven languages; tap out the Morse code for "calm" thirteen times on his knee.

Maureen Scott stops jabbing her thumbs against the phone screen and looks at him—*really* looks at him for the first time all evening. "What are we going to do with you?" she muses, her voice sickly sweet.

He wants to remind her *she* is the one who sought *him* out. She's the one who pestered his publicist for months until he agreed to do the show. He says nothing.

"You need to relax," she drawls, as if telling someone to relax has ever once in the history of human beings yielded that outcome. Maureen's silver-gray bob swishes stylishly as she shoots him a threatening look. "All of our futures are riding on this. You need some personal rebranding, for obvious reasons. The show does too. Don't fuck this up for everyone."

He would like the record to show he does not fuck things up on purpose. He would very much like to be a not-fucking-things-up sort of person. If he were that sort of person, he wouldn't be the new star of a reality dating show.

Maureen narrows shrewd eyes at him. "Stop looking so gloomy, darling. You get to date twenty beautiful women, and when it's over, you will propose to whoever is left standing. What's so awful about that?"

What's so awful about dating on television when he has not gone on a real date in two years? What's so awful about getting fake-engaged to an almost-stranger on the slim promise he might be able to work again when this is over?

Nothing. Nothing at all. He feels great about all of this.

In other news, he's probably going to vomit.

"And who knows," Maureen says cloyingly. "Maybe you'll even find real love by the end."

He won't. That's the one thing he knows for absolute certain.

The car comes to a smooth stop, and Maureen pockets her phone. "Now, when we get out, you'll meet Dev, your new handler, and he'll coach you through the entrance ceremony."

Charlie wants to ask what was wrong with his old handler, but the driver turns off the engine, and without another word, Maureen gets out of the car and disappears into the night. He's not sure if he's supposed to follow her, or just sit in the car like a pretty puppet until someone shows up to pull his strings.

He chooses the former, refusing to relinquish every ounce of his free will as he embarks on this two-month journey through reality television hell. He dramatically throws his weight against the door . . . which gives with suspicious ease.

Because it turns out someone is opening the door at that exact moment. He's thrown off balance. In one fluid motion, he lands facedown at someone's feet.

"Shit. Are you okay?"

Suddenly, there are hands on him, hoisting him into a stand-ing position exactly like a pretty puppet. The hands belong to a tall man with dark skin whose Adam's apple is at Charlie's eye line. There is something disconcerting about having to look up that drastically at another person. He looks up. Dramatic cheekbones and intense eyes behind plastic-framed glasses and an amused mouth. The man gripping the front of his tux (Dev?) slides his fingers into Charlie's hair to adjust the crown, and it's too much.

Too much touching.

Too much *everything*, too quickly.

The anxiety hijacks his brain, and in a panic, he throws himself backward against the car door to break contact. The new handler raises a single eyebrow in response. "So, no touching, then?" He flashes Charlie a crooked smile, like this is all a big joke.

Touching is never a joke to Charlie. He doesn't hate it as a general rule, but he does prefer advance warning and for hand sanitizer to be involved. He knows he signed up for this show where touching is required, so he attempts to explain. "You can touch me anywhere you like," he starts.

And he realizes he's phrased this inelegantly when the man's other eyebrow shoots up.

"Wait, no, what I meant was . . . I don't mind being touched by you, but if you could just . . . uh . . . if you could wash your hands first? Not that I think you are unclean. I'm sure you are very clean. I mean, you smell clean, but I have a thing about germs, and if you could maybe warn me? Before you touch me?"

This is what he gets for attempting verbal communication with a stranger. At first, his handler simply stares at him in open-mouthed silence. Then . . . "No!" he says firmly. "Get back in the car."

Dev yanks the door back open and kicks at Charlie's legs with the toe of his Converse. Charlie's reentrance into the car is about as graceful as his exit two minutes before. He tries to scoot backward to make room for the very tall man who is now halfway sitting on top of him.

Dev asks the driver to get out. "I'm sorry," Charlie blurts. Apologizing always seems like a good idea when he doesn't understand a social situation, and he has absolutely no idea what's happening right now.

"Please *stop talking*!" Dev plunges his hands into a gigantic shoulder bag and pulls out a tiny bottle of green hand sanitizer. He lathers his hands, and Charlie is weirdly moved by the gesture. Then, when he realizes the hand sanitizer means more touching, he is weirdly freaked out by the gesture.

"Lean forward," Dev orders.

"Uh . . ."

"Hurry! Lean forward!"

Charlie leans and this total stranger reaches around his back and untucks his shirt, warm fingers sliding across his skin. And yes, in the past few days, he's learned LA types are very weird about both personal space and naked bodies, but Charlie is not an LA type. He's not accustomed to being groped in cars by men wearing truly hideous cargo shorts.

Dev's fingers feel like pinpricks every time they make contact as he fondles the nude-colored mic belt wardrobe put on Charlie back at the studio. After fifteen excruciating seconds, which Charlie counts out one Mississippi at a time to stop himself from spiraling, Dev pulls away and slumps back against the seat. Charlie finally exhales.

"Holy shit, dude. You were hot."

"I—*what?*"

"Your *mic.*" Dev points to the place where Charlie's shirt is now untucked in the back and then points to his own earpiece, where someone is presumably shouting things. "Someone left your mic on from earlier, and you're back in receiver range. Always be wary of a hot mic. Consider this the first lesson from your new handler: anything you say can be taken out of context. Your soliloquy about letting me touch you could easily be inserted into a very different kind of scene."

"Oh." He's suddenly reminded it's June in Southern California, and he is sweating without the air-conditioning. "Right. Okay, right. Yeah. Sorry."

From two feet away, his new handler studies him carefully behind his glasses. Charlie holds eye contact for *one Mississippi, two Mississippi,* then looks down and nervously adjusts his cuffs.

"Did you get hurt? When you fell out of the car?" Dev asks softly. "You look like you're in pain."

"Oh. Uh, no."

Dev dives back into his shoulder bag. "I've got pain killers and Tiger Balm and Band-Aids. What do you need?"

"N-nothing," he mutters. "I'm fine."

Dev is cradling an entire first-aid kit in his arms. "But your face. It's all pinched together like you're in pain."

"Um. That's just. My face."

At that, Dev throws his head back and laughs. One of Charlie's chief failures in life is his inability to understand when someone is laughing *with* him versus laughing *at* him. Nine times out of ten, it's the latter.

"It's confusing," Dev notes in a tone that almost makes Charlie think he's laughing with him, "because you look like the guy in a fancy cologne commercial, but you're distinctly acting like the guy in an IBS medication commercial."

"I can be both of those guys simultaneously."

"Not on this show you can't." Dev pulls the *People* magazine out from under him and jabs a finger at the face on the cover. "If this whole thing is going to work, you've got to be *this* guy for the cameras."

Charlie stares at the magazine version of himself, fumbling for a way to explain. *I'm not that guy. I don't know how to be that guy. This was a huge mistake.*

"I . . ."

The car door behind Dev opens. He manages, quite easily, not to fall out.

"Dev! What the fuck are you doing in here? We're behind schedule, and Skylar is going to demote us to casting if we don't get the prince to his fucking mark this fucking instant."

The petite foul-mouth shoves her arm toward Charlie. "Jules Lu. Nice to meet you. I'm your production assistant. It's my job to make sure you're where you're supposed to be when you're supposed to be there. And you are not where you're supposed to be right now."

"Sorry." He stares at her hand but doesn't take it. "Uh, you . . . also meet."

"Does he think that was a sentence?" Jules asks Dev. "God, we're screwed."

Jules yanks Dev out of the car, and Dev yanks Charlie out of the car, and anything Charlie was going to say to Dev gets swallowed up by the madness all around them. They head up a path toward the set, which is supposed to look like a fairy tale. The castle is lit up in the distance, and the show's host, Mark

Davenport, waits in front of an ornate fountain. There are twin-kle lights and flowers and a horse-drawn carriage ripped straight out of *Cinderella*.

It *should* look like a fairy tale, but the castle is actually just a millionaire's house in Pasadena, and there are crew members dressed in black, shouting and vaping. Mark Davenport screams at his assistant about kombucha until she cries.

So, like, *not quite* Walt Disney's vision.

"Stand here for me." Dev motions to a little tape *x*, and he warns Charlie before he slides his hands around Charlie's back again to click on his mic. Charlie tenses. This is it. He can't undo it, can't back out, can't hide. If he thinks too hard about the past year and all the things that led him here, to this single act of desperation, he knows he won't be able to keep it together.

"Remember," Dev says low and close to his ear, "everyone in Command Central can hear you now."

Charlie swallows the lump forming in his throat.

"You look miserable."

"Oh, that's probably because I *am* miserable."

"*Mic.*"

"I'm . . . ah . . . miserably happy to be here."

"*Very* convincing save. You're a natural at this."

Charlie smiles despite himself, and Dev explodes with an en-thusiastic, "*Yes!* Yes!" He turns his fingers into a box and squints one eye like he's lining up the shot. "Just like that! Smile just like that when the cameras are on."

Unfortunately, Charlie's smile collapses in on itself as soon as Dev draws attention to it.

"Well, now you look like you're going to vomit."

"I probably am."

"You're not going to vomit! You're about to meet twenty women who are all here on a quest to find love with you!" Dev seems to think this is a delightful prospect, as if all of Charlie's fairy-tale dreams are about to come true. As if Charlie has fairy-tale dreams. "This is going to be amazing!"

Dev forgets the advance-notice-for-touching rule, and his hand folds around Charlie's bicep, burning through the layers of his tux. Charlie isn't sure what's happening to his body right now, but it's not good. It's maybe very, very bad.

Dev leans in even closer. His breath is hot on Charlie's cheek. He smells like sugar and chocolate and something else Charlie can't quite place. "I know you're freaked out right now, but at the end of all of this, you're going to find *love*," Dev whispers. "In nine weeks, you're going to have a *fiancée*."

And that's when Charlie truly does vomit, all over Dev.

Dev

There is vomit on his Chucks.

Granted, there is always vomit on his shoes the first night of shooting, but it usually happens at dawn, not dusk, and the vomit typically belongs to an overserved contestant, not to Prince Charming himself.

Then again, it turns out Charles Winshaw is no one's definition of a Prince Charming, no matter how much he might look the part. And he really does look the part. Broad-shouldered, with the tux doing little to conceal his muscular build. Straight-nosed and square-jawed and sweet—it's the sweetness that caught Dev off guard when Charles fell out of the town car. All the men who come on this show are handsome. None of them have ever been sweet.

Then again, none of them have ever been quite *this handsome*. Charles Winshaw is somehow the most beautiful man Dev's ever seen in real life, even with vomit in his chin dimple. Even talking absolute nonsense. Even with all the nervous sweating.

(Maybe especially with all the nervous sweating.)

"I . . . I'm s-so, so, so sorry," he sputters.

Any annoyance Dev feels about the vomit disappears when he looks up into Charles Winshaw's enormous eyes. He's like a terrified baby bird. Like a two-hundred-twenty-pound baby bird with crippling anxiety and a fairly intense germ phobia who can't navigate his way through a complete sentence.

A man from set design comes over with a hose to casually clean the puke off the pavement and douses Dev with a burst of cold water, which is pretty par for the course on his night so far.

"I . . . seriously . . . so sorry," Charles says again as the makeup team swoops in to fix his face without missing a beat.

The vomit is cleared from his chin, the lights are adjusted, and from somewhere in the dark, the first AD shouts, "Final checks, please!" whether Charles is ready to become Prince Charming or not.

He's definitely not. He looks gray and sickly, and Dev wants to stay by his side, but the AD calls to lock it up, and Dev jumps out of frame at the last second.

They're rolling. The sound of horse hooves on wet flagstone fills the now-silent set, and then the carriage comes into view, rolling up to the fountain where Charles is waiting. Camera one stays trained on Charles, while camera two films the door open-ing. A woman in a blue dress steps out: big blue eyes to match her dress, blond beach curls, slender figure. She smiles shyly when she sees Charles, a cross necklace framed in her plunging neckline.

Her name is Daphne Reynolds, and she's the former beauty queen from Dev's limo. It's no surprise Maureen sent her out of the carriage first. Quite frankly, she looks like someone fed a 3-D printer the algorithm for creating an *Ever After* winner. Dev knows from her file she has a college degree *and* her father's a reverend, which means she perfectly straddles the line of catering to the show's large conservative fan base without alienating its even larger feminist fan base, which claims to watch ironically.

"Hi," Daphne says, her heels now clacking on the stones. Charles does not say hi back. Charles does not move. He stands by the fountain, his arms stiff and awkward and maybe not attached to his body, and he does not react to the beautiful woman approaching him. No smile. Not a flicker of lust.

Perhaps in response to his indifference, Daphne hesitates as she gets closer. Sputters, stops, and briefly looks like she's contemplating a leap over the gate. She takes another step forward, and her silvery heels either catch the hem of her dress or an especially wet stone, and she slips, topples forward directly into the immovable, stoic wall that is Charles Winshaw. It's almost a perfect—albeit unconventional for this show—meet-cute, except instead of putting out an arm to rescue Daphne, Charles flinches backward at her physical contact with his chest. She manages to right herself without his help.

"Stop! *Stop!*" Skylar screams. The director bursts out of the Command Central tent and into the shot, even though the cameras never stop rolling on *Ever After*. "What the hell was that?

How can two sexy people be so offensively *un*sexy together? Take it again!"

Daphne's handler escorts her back to the carriage, and they take the scene from the opening of the door. This time, Daphne doesn't trip, but Charles still looks disinterested, and they shake hands like this is a board meeting. So they film the scene again. And again. By the fifth take, Jules is turtling into her overalls from secondhand embarrassment, Charles looks like he might vomit again from the stress, and Skylar is screaming profanities into everyone's earpieces.

Dev has to do something before the season actually *is* epically fucked. He waves his hands in front of the camera to get Skylar's attention back at Command Central and requests a five-minute break. Then he darts across the courtyard toward the first limo, where the contestants wait for their carriage ride.

"Ladies!" he greets as he slides inside. "How's it going in here?"

They've all had another two hours' worth of limo champagne fed to them by their new handler, Kennedy, who looks slightly shell-shocked by their sudden, unexpected promotion. The women hoot and holler in response. They seem to be in the middle of a dance party. Dev briefly mourns the fact that he's not going to be spending the next nine weeks with these amazing women. "Sorry I abandoned y'all, but they've got me working with your Prince Charming. He's a little bit nervous about meeting so many beautiful women."

A collective *aww* ripples through the limo. *Perfect.* "I think he needs y'all to help him loosen up."

Dev turns to Angie Griffin, the medical student, and the next woman out of the carriage. Angie has a beautiful, heart-shaped face framed by a pretty Afro and bearing a mischievous smile, which suggests she's the perfect candidate for loosening up their tech nerd.

"Here's what I'm thinking: Angie, what if you go out there and get him dancing a little bit?" Dev shimmies his shoulders demonstratively.

Angie appears to weigh the risk of potential humiliation on national television against the thrill of dancing with Charles Winshaw and slams back the rest of her limo champagne. "Let's do it!" she says excitedly, and Dev knows it will be perfect. That part is done.

He climbs back out of the limo and jogs back to Charles for part two.

"I'm going to touch you again," Dev warns, and good Lord— Charles *blushes* as Dev reaches up and adjusts his blond curls beneath the crown. Dev can't imagine how he's going to survive nine weeks of being groped by the women. "Okay. I need you to turn it on now."

"Turn it on?" Charles repeats each word slowly, turning them over on his tongue. Dev watches his mouth puzzle it out, watches him press his tongue against the back of his very white, very straight teeth. Dev gently reminds himself to stop staring at this man's mouth.

"Yes. Become the cologne ad guy. Whatever you used to do when you had to perform in front of crowds at WinHan. *Turn it on.*"

The expression on Charles's face would be comical if it weren't so thoroughly pathetic, and if this man weren't at risk of ruining their entire show. "You can do this," Dev says without evidence or proof that he can. But he's good at putting faith in things other people are quick to dismiss. "I believe in you."

Dev slides back out of the cameras' view.

When Angie comes out of the carriage a few minutes later, she sambas over to him, and Charles doesn't look repulsed when he sees her. He lets Angie put her hands on his hips and tango him around the courtyard, and he smiles genuinely for the cameras. It's reality television gold. Skylar sounds pleased in Dev's earpiece.

After that, Charles relaxes more with each woman he meets. When the contestants make bold choices for their entrances, like coming out in a kangaroo costume because they're Australian or wearing a pregnant belly because they want to be the mother of his children, he takes it all in stride. He makes it through all twenty carriage exits without vomiting again, and everyone is impressed with Dev's coaching, because apparently that is where they've set the bar.

"You're doing fucking spectacular!" Dev tells him as the cameras get ready to move inside for Charles's welcome speech to the gathered women. Charles blushes and smiles down at his feet in response, like this is the nicest thing anyone has ever said to him.

Dev temporarily worries this *is* the nicest thing anyone has ever said to Charles Winshaw. He swoops in to adjust Charles's hair. "So, based on first impressions, which of the women would you describe as your type?"

Charles arches away from Dev's fingers. "Uh, none?"

Annoyance spikes in Dev's chest. "What about Daphne? You're both shy and a little . . . awkward."

"Which one was Daphne, again?"

"Blue dress. First out of the carriage. We filmed the scene *five times.*"

"Oh . . . I . . ." End of sentence.

A camerawoman is nearby, and Dev lowers his voice. "I can't coach you if I don't know what you're looking for in a partner."

In response, Charles does an elegant sidestep that almost ends with him facedown in a succulent. "A partner? With a woman *here*? B-but . . . I mean, I'm not. That's not why I . . . But this show is *fake*."

The crackle of annoyance shifts to a full-blown wildfire inside Dev's stomach. "What do you mean, *fake*?"

His eyebrows are scrunched in confusion. "I mean, the show—it's not really about *love*."

Charles Winshaw is standing in front of him, but all Dev can see is Ryan six years ago when Dev first joined the crew, fresh out of USC. Ryan Parker: leather jacket, dark hair falling in front of his eyes, apathy perfected. "*This show isn't really about love*," Ryan said as he gave Dev a tour of the castle. "*We aren't here to help people find happily ever after. We're here to help Maureen Scott make interesting television*."

And Dev was already so smitten—with Ryan and with this show and with the idea of being behind the cameras, making the stories come to life—all he'd said in response was, "There's nothing more interesting than love."

Ryan never misled him. Dev can give him credit for that, even now. From their first night together, Ryan told him he didn't believe in soul mates or fairy tales or loving one person forever. Dev willingly threw away six years on a man who told him from the beginning exactly how their love story would end.

Now Dev is going to throw away nine weeks on another man who thinks this show is fake. He's about to fly around the world with a man who isn't here for love; he's about to spend every waking minute next to a man who is clearly only here to use the romantic expectations of twenty women for his own selfish needs.

On this show, in this world, happily ever after is supposed to be a guarantee.

So what is he supposed to do with the fact that Charles Winshaw doesn't want a happily ever after?

Charlie

He's not sure how he went from "fucking spectacular" to fucking it all up, but he can see it in Dev's expression. Charlie doesn't understand.

He just met twenty women and forgot the names of twenty women, and he doesn't have much mental capacity for understanding anything beyond the fact that the front of his tux is somehow covered in glitter.

He considers apologizing again, but Dev stomps off toward the giant white tent across set. Jules swoops in, her bun bobbing like an Adam's apple. "Come on, Charles. I'll take you inside for your welcome speech to the women."

He tries not to obsess over what he did to anger Dev. Naturally, he obsesses over it.

He obsesses over it throughout the generic speech his former handler wrote for him, about how he's "excited for his quest to find love" and how he's "sure his future wife is in the room." He obsesses over it as the cameras shift again for the social hour. Then a blond woman grabs him by the wrist, and he can't obsess about anything but the unwanted touching.

"Can I steal you away?" the woman purrs. He thinks her

name is Megan. She tugs on his wrist and drags him outside to the patio. Charlie hears the producers whispering to contestants as they pass:

"Wasn't that forward of her?"

"I guess *someone* is here to win."

"You're so much prettier than her."

Megan drags him to a small bench beside the pool where cameras are already waiting. She proceeds to sit too close to him, touch him too much without permission, and drone sweet nothings in his ear about her YouTube channel where she posts exercise videos. People have always told him he has terrible social awareness (usually while firing him, or dumping him, or trying to ring up his groceries), but he isn't *totally* oblivious. He's aware of how he looks and of the effect his looks have on some people. Particularly women. Particularly *this* woman, who is putting her hands all over his thighs.

He clenches his jaw and tries to listen to her stories about working as a spray-tan technician in Tampa until they're interrupted by another blonde who comes to confront Megan about hogging Charlie's time. Soon, the two women are yelling at each other. He tries to de-escalate the unexpected tension, then quickly learns the tension is not so much *unexpected* as it is carefully coordinated by producers with headsets who poke and prod the women into these little altercations.

There are some okay moments. He talks to a software engineer named Delilah who starts a jokey argument about spaces versus tabs, and it's the first time all night he feels like he knows what's going on. A woman named Sabrina tells interesting stories about her travel blog. At one point, when attempting to dodge a very assertive woman who won't stop touching his ass, he finds Daphne (the first woman out of the limo, he remembers now) and Angie (the woman who danced with him, he could never forget) sharing a bottle of wine behind a generator. They kindly offer him a top-off of pinot and let him know half of his shirt buttons are open, which is kind.

Soon it's two in the morning, and he has a raging headache, indigestion, and an unsettling pit of anxiety metastasizing in his chest. Worse, he feels the horrible certainty of knowing this was a mistake. He never should've deluded himself into thinking he could handle this. He never should have let Parisa convince him this was the right move.

He'll back out—pay for the money lost in production himself. Yes, all of America will hear the rumors about how Charles Winshaw had a breakdown on a reality television show. Yes, he will never work in tech again. But maybe that's for the best. Perhaps he's better off hiding in a secluded cabin in the Sierra Nevada mountains away from all other humans. Perhaps he'll learn to whittle.

"You've almost survived the worst of it," Jules reassures him on a break as she brings him a bottle of water. Another woman fixes his hair. Dev, he notes, is nowhere to be found.

"Just one more contestant to talk to," Jules continues, "and then you'll need to choose four women to send home in the Crowning Ceremony."

He wants to tell Jules about his new plan to send *himself* home at the Crowning Ceremony, but she's already leading him to the place set design has arranged for his meeting with Kiana. They chat for about a minute before Charlie notices a large white man with bulging muscles and neck tattoos walking toward them. Two cameras follow, along with two security guards.

Kiana follows Charlie's gaze, a look of unguarded horror flashing across her symmetrical features. "Oh God. No."

"What the hell, slut?"

"What is happening?" Charlie asks, maybe of the man shouting horrendous derogatory terms. Maybe of Kiana, who is being shouted at. Maybe of the cameras, or the crew members, or the little half-circle of contestants who've gathered around to watch this scene.

"Are you the dude dating my girlfriend?" the man growls as he jabs a finger against Charlie's chest. And first, *ouch*.

Second: Kiana had a boyfriend back home *and they brought him onto the set to scream at her?* What's worse, no one steps in to stop it. Four cameras, and no one intervenes when the man gives Charlie another shove.

"Roger, it's not his fault!" Kiana cries.

"Shut up, slut!"

Something about the second "slut" triggers the panic inside him, and Charlie can feel himself hurtle toward the brink of an episode. And he can't have an episode right now. Not in front of all these cameras. Not when he came on this show to prove to the world that he's the sort of man who doesn't have triggers or episodes, the sort of man who never breaks down, who keeps it all in, keeps it all together under pressure.

Charlie looks at Kiana, her expression a mixture of sadness and shame, and the only thing more potent than the anxiety attack clawing at his chest is his outrage. He turns to the boyfriend. "It's not acceptable to talk to her that way," Charlie says.

Or that's what he *intends* to say, before he is promptly punched in the face and says nothing at all.

Dev

"Put me back on contestant duty."

"Dev—"

"Please, Sky. *Please*. I cannot spend the next nine weeks standing in that man's shadow. He's cold and awkward and he called the show *fake*."

Skylar finishes ordering camera one to pivot so the audience won't see how bored Charlie looks talking to Kiana; then she turns to Dev. "This show *is* fake."

"It's *produced*. Sure, we set things up, create the perfect ingredients for romance, but people truly fall in love." Dev points at the monitor as Charles stifles a yawn. "He didn't come here for love."

"I hate to be the one to tell you this, but neither did most of your girls."

"My *women* are decent human beings. Charles isn't."

Dev thought Charles had a sweetness to him, but he is obviously a poor judge of character.

Skylar shakes out another antacid. "You know you're the best producer we've got."

"If I'm the best, I shouldn't be saddled with an uncoachable mess."

"Dev, it wasn't my call to put you on prince duty, so if you're pissed about your reassignment, take it up with Maureen—*What the fuck is this?*"

Camera three has cut to an assistant producer and a security guard escorting what seems to be the anthropomorphic embodiment of toxic masculinity.

"Who the *hell* is this? Who brought this man onto my set?"

The answer to these questions becomes clear when the stranger confronts Kiana and Charlie. Kiana had a boyfriend back home, and Maureen brought him to set. "*Shit.*"

Dev books it out of the Command Central tent, down the sloping driveway to where Maureen is coordinating this scene with another producer. "Cut! You've got to call cut! Charles isn't ready for this! You've got to get him out of there!"

"Relax," Maureen Scott says with a dismissive flick of her hand. "America loves a man who fights back. Our new prince might surprise us."

Dev knows he won't. "Seriously, I don't think—"

"Chill, D," the other producer says, because the other producer is Ryan in his new supervising producer position. Dev's ex is standing on Maureen's other side looking, as always, like a mystifyingly attractive combination of grunge rocker and yacht club enthusiast. Ryan's wearing cuffed khakis and boat shoes, a flannel tied around his waist, brown hair pulled back in a tight bun. The sight of him hits Dev squarely in the solar plexus.

He's spent weeks agonizing over seeing Ryan again. He's rehearsed how he'd come across as aloof and unaffected, still Fun Dev, doing fine. Yet, of course, the reality is Ryan gets to be the one standing there looking casual and indifferent, and Dev is the frantic, emotional one. Ryan Parker: always making Dev feel ridiculous for caring. Across the set, the boyfriend starts poking Charles in addition to shouting misogynistic things.

"This will be great for ratings," Ryan says coolly, refusing to meet Dev's gaze. "And we've got security right out of frame."

But Dev knows security will only break up a fight after it starts, not prevent good television before it happens. As much as he resents Charles and this reassignment, violence is not part of Dev's fairy tale. He's two seconds away from barreling into the scene himself, even if it means ruining the shot. The show has legal permission to use any footage he accidentally ends up in, but producers aren't supposed to appear on camera. Still, he's about to do it when a hand grabs his elbow. It's Ryan, anticipating his next move.

"Let it play out, D."

So Dev lets it play out, which means, thanks to Ryan Parker, he watches Charles Winshaw get punched in the face from thirty feet away.

Because Dev is *truly* a terrible judge of character.

"Well, the good news is, the nose isn't broken," the set medic announces to the cramped back room full of producers and cameras. Charles is sitting on a table with blood down his shirt and two cotton tubes shoved up his nostrils. "The bad news is, he's definitely going to have some bruising, and he needs to sit here until the bleeding stops."

"Shit," Skylar snaps. "We're already behind schedule, and we needed to start filming the Crowning Ceremony ten minutes ago!"

The medic shoots her a glare.

"Which is not as important as his health, obviously," Skylar corrects herself. "I'll just go arrange some establishing shots of the contestants on the risers."

Skylar pushes her way past two cameras as Maureen slinks over to Charles.

"Listen, dear, I hope you don't think we invited that man onto set."

They definitely did.

"He showed up unexpectedly demanding to speak to Kiana. We had no idea what he was going to do."

Oh, they definitely knew.

Maureen places a manicured hand on Charles's shoulder. "I am so sorry this happened."

She most definitely is not sorry.

Ryan was right: a physical altercation on night one is going to be amazing for ratings. Dev can't even blame her for it; Maureen Scott is only doing what she has to do. The only thing audiences want more than a happy ending is drama.

Charles says nothing in response, and Maureen drops her hand and turns to the medic. "Ten minutes?"

"Ten minutes should be sufficient to stop the bleeding, but—"

"Ten minutes," Maureen says firmly before she follows Skylar out the door.

The medic hands Charles two cold compresses and shoves acetaminophen at Dev. "Have him keep the ice packs in place for ten, then take out the gauze and give him six hundred milligrams of this."

At the medic's exit, Jules takes her cue to round up the cameras and lingering crew members. Then Dev is alone with the star he hates on the show he loves, unsure of how to proceed. Charles has a cold compress under each eye, bloody gauze dangling from his nose.

"You look ridiculous."

Apparently, *that* is how he's proceeding.

"Well, you smell like vomit," Charles snaps back.

"And whose fault is that?"

Charles tries to smile, but the pain turns it into a wince. He pulls the cold compresses away from his face to reveal the bruises already forming under his eyes. "Are you also going to try to convince me Maureen didn't pay that man to come on the show?"

"She didn't have to pay him," Dev clarifies. "Men like that come on this show for free."

Charles looks wounded, which is sort of his default expression since his face is 90 percent eyes. His eyes are storm-cloud gray, the color of the sky during the North Carolina thunderstorms of Dev's childhood. Charles licks his lips nervously. "Have I . . . upset you, or—?"

"You said the show is fake." The words come out harsher than he intends, and he bites his lip. Yelling at Charles isn't going to help. Besides, Skylar is right. Dev is the best. Unless they want this entire season to be an uneditable sequence of their star getting the literal and metaphorical shit beat out of him, Dev's got to step up.

He takes a deep breath. "I know a lot of people believe this show is fake, but I don't. I think if you open yourself up to this process, you could find real love in the next nine weeks. I could help you find love."

Charles kicks his legs, which don't quite reach the floor from where they dangle over the edge of the table. "I'm not really looking for love."

"Then why did you come on this show?"

"To have my ass kicked in front of twenty million viewers, apparently."

That startles a laugh out of Dev. Charles tries to smile again. This one sticks, and *shit*. He's kind of adorable. The women are probably half in love with him already.

"Don't worry," Charles grumbles back into his lap, "I'm not going to be the star much longer."

Dev crosses the room and stands two feet in front of Charles on the table. "What do you mean?"

"I . . . I thought I could do this, but I was wrong. Maureen can recast me."

"No, she can't. We've already announced you publicly as the star."

"I can pay for the cost."

"Will you be able to pay millions of dollars after the network sues you for violating your contract?"

"I mean," he looks vaguely embarrassed, "yes, probably."

Dev takes a minute to remove his glasses with one hand and scrub his face with the other. "Look, can we maybe start over?" He sticks out his hand. "Hi, it's nice to meet you. My name is Dev Deshpande."

Charles allows one of the compresses to fall into his lap so he can shake Dev's hand. His fingers are freezing against Dev's palm. He shivers. "It's nice to meet you, too. I'm Charlie Winshaw."

"Charlie?"

He does a little half shrug, too careful to commit to a full one. "Charles is the cologne model. I'm just Charlie."

"Charlie," Dev repeats, testing the lightness of it. "Charlie, why did you come on this show, if not to find love?"

Unsurprisingly, this question still gets no answer. Charlie fidgets, and the cold compress in his lap slides to the floor. Dev scoots closer to pick it up. "Here, let me. . . ." He gestures with the ice pack and slots it in place under Charlie's left eye. Charlie tenses at the contact, then settles into it, letting Dev help, each of them holding onto one ice pack. It's a perfect metaphor for Dev's job on *Ever After*.

He tries one more time. "Why did you come on this show?"

Charlie takes three slow, deep breaths. His chest strains against the buttons of his tux. "Before I, uh, resigned as my company's CTO, I developed a reputation for being . . . *difficult* . . . to work with. A liability. I . . . I haven't been able to get a job in tech since, and my publicist accepted Maureen's offer for me to come on the show because she thought it might help me salvage my reputation. I'm starting to see the inherent flaw in the theory, though. . . ."

Dev wants to call bullshit. A reputation of being difficult isn't enough to blacklist you from any industry when you're as white and male and traditionally handsome as Charlie, not to mention a certifiable genius. But this is the most he's said all night—multiple grammatically correct sentences in a row—so Dev doesn't call him out on it. "Why don't you just start a new company?" he asks instead.

Charlie gives another half shrug. "I don't have a mind for business. That was always Josh's role. And I don't exactly have people clamoring to be my business partner."

"Okay, then why work at all? You've apparently got enough fuck-you money to pay off the network. Why not just run your charity and swim in your piles of gold like Scrooge McDuck?"

Charlie scrunches up his face. "I want to work," he says. "It's not about the money. It's about the *work*. I'm good at the work."

Dev can relate to the rush that comes with being damn good at something. "So you need me to help you look hirable, then?"

Charlie nods slowly.

"I can definitely do that," Dev says, "but for *my work*, I need to write your love story, and if I'm going to help you with your reputation, you've got to help me, too. I need you to try to make it work with the women. And I need you to be *on*. Cologne Charles, whenever the cameras are rolling."

Charlie takes exactly three breaths again. "Being on is really hard for me. It drains me emotionally, and sometimes I'll need time. To recalibrate my mind. Or else I'll, um . . . I'm not sure . . . does that make sense?"

Now Dev is the one who stumbles over his words. "Uh, yeah, actually. It makes perfect sense."

Dev can *really* relate. When they're filming, Dev can throw himself into it completely, feeding off the energy of it all, giving his busy brain the perfect outlet for all its extra. For nine weeks, he flies through twelve-hour days on a steady diet of coffee and cookies and feels no need to ever stop moving. But invariably, after they film the Final Tiara Ceremony, he crashes. The energy bottoms out, creating a vacuum inside his head. He climbs into bed and stays there for a week until he can recalibrate.

It's how he's always worked. In college, it would come in huge bursts of creative energy. He would spend two weeks writing a script—open up his heart and pour it all onto the page—and then, out of nowhere, he would sort of wake up, realize every word was shit, climb into bed, and watch *The Office* until he could face the real world again.

For some inexplicable reason, he almost tells Charlie Winshaw about the coffee and cookies and dabbling with depression, about his busy brain and his too-big heart. The urge to confide in him makes no sense, except he feels like he's been living this night for *years*—like he's stuck in a very unfunny *Groundhog Day* of his own personal hell, haunted by cute boys who don't believe in love.

Dev swallows down the confession rising in his throat. "It sounds like we have a deal."

He reaches for Charlie's hand.

"Deal," Charlie echoes, and his enormous hand squeezes Dev's. Charlie doesn't pull away immediately, so they remain with their hands frozen between them for a beat too long. Dev ignores the way his skin hums at the touch, because they're finally making progress, and Dev isn't going to screw that up because a pretty man with a weak understanding of socially appropriate handshake lengths is touching him.

When it becomes clear Charlie is *never* going to let go of his hand, Dev pulls away first.

"It's probably been ten minutes. Should we assess the damage?"

They lower the ice packs, and somehow, Charlie makes a nose injury look exquisite, his cheeks a crisp pink from the cold compresses and his large gray eyes circled in light purple.

"Yikes," Dev says.

"Is it bad?"

"You might as well scrap this face completely and start over from scratch."

"Ah, well, no great loss. People don't like me for my face. They generally prefer my sparkling personality."

Dev laughs again. Charlie's kind of funny when you can get him to speak without stammering. Dev shakes out three Tylenol and reaches for Charlie's water bottle. "So you're not going to quit on us? You'll stick it out as our Prince Charming?"

Charlie swallows the pills. "If . . . if you really think I can do this?"

"*We* can do this."

Charlie stares up at him, a question twisting the corner of his mouth. "You," he tries, eyebrows bunched together, "you think you can make me *actually* fall in love with one of these women, don't you?"

Charlie is more perceptive than Dev gave him credit for.

Charlie Winshaw didn't come on the show for love, but he's about to spend the next nine weeks going on extravagant dates in beautiful places with amazing women. Dev might have been completely wrong about what Charlie is looking for in a woman, but he can still find him a soul mate. He always does.

He gives Charlie a breezy smile. "I *know* I can make you fall in love."

Story notes for editors:

Season 37, Episode 1

Story producer:

Dev Deshpande

Air date:

Monday, September 13, 2021

Executive producer:

Maureen Scott

Scene: Opening montage of contestant confessionals about Charles Winshaw

Location: Shot pre-carriage exits at the Beverly Hilton's ballroom

Lauren L., 25, Dallas, professional cat cuddler: When I heard Charles Winshaw was going to be the next *Ever After* prince, I knew I had to audition to be a contestant. He is literally everything I've been looking for in a man. I mean, he's strong, but you can tell he's also sensitive.

Megan, 24, Tampa, spray-tan technician: Why did I come on this show? I'll give you *eight* reasons, and all of them are Charles Winshaw's abs.

Delilah, 26, Los Angeles, software engineer: Charles Winshaw is a legend in the tech world. This will be like dating the Michael Jordan of app design. You know, if Michael Jordan were notoriously private and mysterious. My friends are going to be so jealous.

Lauren S., 23, Little Rock, former student: I've had my heart broken in the past, but I'm older and wiser now. I'm ready to find love again. I'm ready to be a wife. I'm ready to be a mom.

Whitney, 31, Kansas City, pediatric nurse: Did I think I'd already be married at thirty-one? I mean, yeah. But it's given me extra time to get to know myself. I've spent years taking care of sick babies. Now I'm ready to take care of a man.

Sabrina, 27, Seattle, travel blogger: My life is pretty rad, honestly. I'm just looking for a partner to make it even radder.

Daphne, 25, Atlanta, social worker: Why did I come on this show? Gosh, um, you know, the same reason as everyone else. I'm here for love—the kind of love you see in movies and hear about in songs.

Love that changes you, love that conquers all. Everyone talks about that kind of love, so it must be real, right?

Maureen's note to editors: Please create the bio chyron for each contestant based on the provided details.

WEEK ONE

Charlie

Deep breath.

He sweeps his arms overhead for his sun salutation until he's staring up at the ceiling of his bedroom.

Well, it's the ceiling of the guesthouse bedroom where he lives at the moment. The guesthouse thirty yards from the *Ever After* castle where sixteen women are waiting to compete for the chance to marry him. The guesthouse where he will live for the next three weeks with Dev, who showed up with a duffle bag and moved into the second bedroom like it's summer camp. Dev, who is currently banging around in the kitchen, blasting trashy pop music from his portable speaker so loudly Charlie can hear it over the sound of his yoga app. *At seven in the morning.*

When Charlie agreed to do the show, he didn't realize it would require cohabitation with a total stranger. He obviously didn't know what to expect at all.

He's under constant surveillance. Because he needs constant coaching. Because he's a fraud, a mess of a man masquerading as a Prince Charming, and it's only a matter of time before everyone realizes—

But no. He catches himself mid-spiral.

These are not appropriate morning-yoga thoughts. He tries to refocus on things that calm him: Excel spreadsheets, quiet libraries, one-thousand-piece jigsaw puzzles, 90-degree angles.

Deep breath. He bends forward and presses his nose to his knees, palms flat on either side of his feet.

Deep breath. He's halfway between plank and downward dog when the meditation app is interrupted by the chirp of Face-Time. He swipes to accept the call without losing his balance. "Good morning."

"*Oh. My. God.* Is that Charlie Winshaw?" his publicist squeals, and there is nothing calming about it. "The hunk? The dreamboat? The object of my masturbatory fantasies?"

He swings into a cross-legged position on the bedroom floor. "Please stop."

Parisa Khadim never stops once she commits to a comedic bit, and her faux-fangirling crescendos when she cups her hand around her mouth and shouts, "Take your shirt off, Hot-Ass!"

"I will not tolerate being objectified in this manner," he responds primly. He can see from the view of the bay out her window she's in her San Francisco office. "Is this the reason you're calling? To sexually harass me in your workplace?"

"I didn't know I needed a reason to call my sugar daddy."

He snorts. "Sugar daddy" is an absurd way to describe their dynamic. Parisa earns every dollar he pays her ten times over by dealing with the nonstop PR clusterfuck that is his life. "I just wanted to check in and see—*wait a minute*." She slams her open palm onto the desk. "What happened to your face?"

"It's fine." He picks up the phone and disconnects his Bluetooth headphones so that her voice now fills the entire bedroom, competing with the sound of Dev's music. Usually, the star of *Ever After* is not allowed to keep his phone, but Parisa negotiated it into his contract. He can't be cut off from her.

"It does not look *fine*. Tell me who I need to sue!"

"There is no one to sue, because you forced me to sign a contract making it nearly impossible for me to bring litigation against anyone affiliated with *Ever After*."

She does some elaborate pantomime of innocence. "Did I? Hmm . . ." And then she promptly changes the subject away from his two black eyes. "So how was it? It would seem you survived the first night. Mostly."

"It was . . ." *Exhausting? Demoralizing? Briefly painful and consistently confusing*? "Fine."

"Use your words, Charlie."

"I don't know. It was . . ."

She sighs dramatically. "What are you doing today, then?"

"Something called a Group Quest. It's this thing where they divide the remaining contestants into two teams, and—"

She interrupts. "Charles, I'm a human woman. I've seen *Ever After* before. I know about the vaguely fairy-tale-themed Group Quest challenges and the Courting Dates and the Crowning Ceremonies."

The phrase *Crowning Ceremony* is mildly triggering. That was the name of the awful process that didn't end until eight Sunday morning after a twelve-hour shoot. He called the names of contestants one at a time, placed a cheap tiara on their heads, and asked the dramatic question, "*Are you interested in becoming my princess?*"

They all said yes. Obviously.

"Parisa, how can you describe the concept of this show with a straight face?"

She points accusingly at him. "Don't you dare infantilize the show simply because it's made for women, by women, and is about women."

"Most of the people who work here are definitely male—"

"And *do not* act dismissive toward the women on the show, do you understand me? You are not better than them because you went to Stanford and care about fracking."

"*Jesus*, Parisa, I wasn't—"

"You were."

He thinks about Megan and her exercise videos. He kind of was.

"You're the one who told me these women aren't really here to find love." He bristles. Then he thinks about Dev, his crooked grin at four in the morning. *I know I can make you fall in love.*

Charlie shakes off the dread of that thought. "You said that's why it's morally justifiable to use the show. Because the women are all here for shameless self-promotion, too."

"I'm sure most of them are," Parisa concedes, "but that doesn't give you permission to condescend them like a sexist a-hole. Also, are you listening to Leland Barlow right now?"

"It's not me. It's my new handler. Dev."

"*Dev?*" Parisa smooths out her perfectly smooth ponytail and pushes her round face close to the screen. "Is your new handler cute?"

"Why . . . why would it matter if he was cute?"

"Because I'm thirty-four and single and these things matter to me."

He sighs. "You can't date my handler, Parisa."

"Because you'd be jealous?"

"What? *No*. Why the heck would I—*jealous*?"

She preens in front of her camera. "Because you're secretly in love with me. That's why you're blushing right now."

"Yes, you caught me," he says, the strange tension easing from his shoulders. "I have spent the last four years secretly pining for you, and I've only rejected your drunken proposals of marriage because I'm playing hard to get."

"I have only drunkenly proposed to you *twice*, and I assumed you rejected my offers of a marriage of convenience because you intend to fall madly in love with a former Miss Alabama."

"That . . . will not happen."

"Because there is no former Miss Alabama on this season? Seems unlikely."

"Because I'm not exactly lovable." He means to say it jokingly, but the sentence sags in the middle, becomes heavy and tinged with sadness. Shit.

"*Charlie*." Parisa stops her teasing instantly, her voice tender and sweet.

"You are so lovable and so *deserving* of love," she insists.

Dev yells his name from the kitchen over the sound of his blaring music. "I . . . I need to go."

"I just want you to be happy. You know that, right?"

"I know, but not everyone needs a romantic partner to be happy."

"So you're happy now, then?"

"I *will* be happy, when I can work in tech again."

"Makes sense, given how happy you were at WinHan before."

"Goodbye, Parisa."

"Just remember, you have the world's biggest heart and the world's finest ass and—"

He doesn't hear what she says next. He's already hung up.

"I made flash cards!" Dev shouts in lieu of a morning greeting when Charlie enters the kitchen dressed in salmon-colored shorts, boat shoes, and an oatmeal V-neck. Dev, meanwhile, is wearing a slight variation of his first-night outfit: tragic cargo shorts, an oversize T-shirt, and the same sneakers Charlie vomited on. He's got a breakfast burrito in one hand and a coffee thermos in the other, and Charlie barely has time to grab the index cards off the kitchen counter before Jules is shoving a plate of craft services food into his other hand and ushering them both into a town car. On the drive to set, Charlie reads through Dev's study tool. On one side of each card is a photo of a woman next to her name. On the back is Dev's handwritten commentary in a sloppy script, little asides to Charlie.

Angie Griffin, the first card says, with a photo of the woman who danced with him. *24, San Francisco; Australian cattle dog named Dorothy Parker; starting medical school at UCSF in September. Hella smart. Almost made you laugh once.*

He flips to the next card and sees the woman in the blue dress. *Daphne Reynolds, 25, Atlanta; social worker and former Miss Georgia runner-up; loves (in no particular order) Jesus, her parents, romantic comedies starring Meg Ryan, and chicken wings. We filmed the scene five times, so help me God if you forget her again.*

Sabrina Huang, 27, Seattle; travel blogger; tattoo sleeve on her left arm; used to play bass in a punk band; too cool for you? Probably.

Megan Neil, 24, Tampa; is probably the villain, which means you will have to keep her for at least four weeks.

Lauren Long, 25, Dallas; blond. That's. . . it? I know nothing else about her. Goal for today: learn one fact about Lauren L.!

Overwhelmed and mildly nauseated, Charlie hands the cards back to Dev and presses his forehead against the cool glass of the car. Dev proceeds to explain the setup for the first Group Quest: Sixteen grown women will beat each other senseless with foam noodles in a historically inaccurate pantomime of a jousting tournament to determine his future bride.

Dev doesn't explain it in those *exact* words, but Charlie gets the gist.

The town car pulls up to a UCLA soccer field that's been ever-so-slightly Ren faired for the occasion. He is immediately whisked away by the makeup artist, then a hairstylist, then Dev again, who positions him on one edge of the field. From across the way, the women are gathered together by their handlers, and when Skylar Jones gives the signal, all sixteen women rush at Charlie, leaping into his arms ecstatically in greeting.

He hugs each woman in turn, counts his Mississippis, feels his forced smile strain at the corners. Between scenes, Dev pulls him aside under the guise of fixing his crown. He hand-sanitizes and warns Charlie in advance. "Are you okay?" Dev whispers, his fingers winding through Charlie's hair.

One Mississippi, two Mississippi. "Uh . . . ?"

"Do you need a minute to recalibrate?"

Recalibrate. He forgot he used that word. He doesn't often try to explain his mind to other people. On the rare occasions he does, other people don't tend to listen.

"No." He sighs. "I'll be fine."

He is, mostly, fine.

He stands on the sidelines for most of the day. The women are divided into two teams, and the producers line up each woman's individual opponent based on what they believe will lead to the most drama. Intimidating-looking Sabrina (with her arm tattoos and her facial piercings and gravelly voice) is pitted against waifish Daphne with the intent of clearly turning Sabrina into a villain by having her injure the woman who most looks like a Barbie doll come to life. Except it turns out Daphne has secret upper body strength and Sabrina has a secret fear of being smacked in the face with a pool noodle. They sprint at each other chanting battle cries that quickly dissolve into a fit of giggles as Sabrina chickens out at the last minute, and she and Daphne somehow end up on their backs on the grass, laughing hysterically like old friends.

Most of the contestants make a joke out of it except Megan, who loudly declares to the cameras—a little too on the nose—that she intends to win more time with him, not bond with the other women. She succeeds magnificently at the latter goal, plunging her lance into the throats of her opponents until three different women cry.

When med-student Angie squares off against Megan in the final round, Megan charges across the field with unnecessary aggression. At the last second, Angie swerves to avoid being lanced in the face, and she trips, reaches out for balance with her free hand, and catches the edge of Megan's shirt. They both go down hard.

Producers and medics rush the field while Charlie watches uselessly from the sidelines.

"*Ow!*" Megan cries out, clutching her arm. "I think it's *broken!*"

Angie has already pulled herself off the grass. "I'm so sorry! I panicked and tripped!"

"You *attacked me on purpose*!"

"I didn't!"

Megan quivers her lip into the nearest camera. "That was not an accident!"

"*Go comfort her*," Dev hisses as he appears at Charlie's side.

"But it was obviously Megan's fault," he hisses back.

"*Mic*." Dev nudges Charlie forward with a sharp elbow, and he stumbles toward the carnage. Awkwardly hovers over the woman pretending to be injured.

Then Dev is at his side again, demonstrating how to do this. Dev crouches down next to Megan, and Charlie follows, squatting beside him, shoulder to shoulder. Dev whispers, "Hold her hand."

The words tickle the sensitive skin behind Charlie's ear, and he feels heat rise to his cheeks as his fingers intertwine with Megan's.

"You're going to be okay, Megan," Dev says breezily. He's so effortlessly good at all of this. Charlie feels miserably out of place attempting to play the part of the concerned boyfriend. Megan leans into Charlie, cries into the front of his chambray shirt.

Charlie thinks, if they edit Dev out of these shots, it will be a nice moment between him and Megan. He might even seem like a decent prince.

"You know Megan wasn't really injured at the Quest, right?" Lauren S. tells him. Or maybe it's Lauren L.? "That whole thing was just for attention."

"Hmm." He nods and pretends to take a sip of his glass of chardonnay.

She takes a gulp of her gin and tonic. He mentally adds *copious amounts of free alcohol* to the list of things he didn't expect. "I'm glad her team didn't win just because she pitched a fit."

"I think . . . our time is up," he attempts, and a producer steps in, escorts one woman out and another woman in. They call this the social hour, though it's actually a period of *several hours* where he's poured into a Tom Ford suit, escorted to a closed bar, and plunked down on a couch to talk to contestants one-on-one.

Or, more aptly put, they talk *at him*.

As soon as Rachel is brought in, she says she has something to confess to him, and promptly launches into a rehearsed speech about her recently broken-off engagement to a man she dated for two months. Becca shows him pictures of her dog, who suffers from arthritis, and a woman named Whitney, who he swears he's never seen before this moment, talks for twenty minutes about her parents' divorce when she was three.

Not a single one of the women asks him a personal question about himself. They *tell* him a lot about himself—about how he's so handsome, so smart, so ambitious, and so generous. Delilah, the software engineer, announces that they have similar values. He almost asks her to cite her sources. He thinks about his phone call with Parisa, her insistence that he's lovable. He can almost see the early stages of love in the sparkly eyes of these women. But they're infatuated with some *idea* of him. Charles Winshaw: millionaire tech wunderkind philanthropist with a slight addiction to physical exercise. In their eyes, his silence makes him mysterious, and he's filled with dread thinking about what will happen when the Cologne Charles guise begins to slip.

A little before midnight, it's finally Angie's turn, and Dev suggests Charlie take her outside for a stroll. The show has shut down the street in front of the bar, and Angie takes Charlie by the arm. With her other hand, she reaches up to press her fingers gently to one of his black eyes, concealed beneath the layers of his makeup. He flinches. "Does it still hurt?" she asks, pulling her hand away.

"Uh, not really, but I—"

Angie doesn't wait for him to puzzle his way through the sentence. She grabs his arm and tugs him forward until his body falls against hers, so he's pinning her back against a brick wall.

"Sorry!" Charlie scrambles. "Sorry, I didn't mean to—"

"No, *I* meant to," Angie says with a smile. Charlie doesn't understand her tone. He moves away from the wall.

"What the fuck?" Ryan bellows from behind the camera, breaking the illusion of the scene. "Why did you pull away like that?"

Dev also emerges from the dark along with Angie's handler. "Ryan, please don't yell at my talent."

"Then talk to your talent, D! We've only got another ten to do the kiss shot, and then—"

Kiss shot.

The words are like a bullet tearing through what's left of Charlie's ability to hold it all together. His skin flushes hot, then cold, becomes itchy and ill-fitting inside his suit as he struggles to take a deep breath.

Dev takes a step closer. "You okay?"

Charlie tries to speak, fails, shakes his head, tugs at his collar. Why is his collar so tight all of a sudden?

And then Dev is gently guiding him down an alley away from Angie, who's now being coached by her handler on proper kissing technique for the camera angles. Warm fingers are on his back as Dev clicks off the mic belt. Underneath the mounting panic, Charlie is dimly aware he might vomit again.

"What's wrong, Charlie?"

"I . . . I can't kiss Angie. I don't even know her."

Dev nods in slow understanding. "Right, but you're getting to know her, and kissing is part of this whole process. You knew kissing was going to be required when you came on this show, right?"

He did know. Abstractly.

Dev is looking at him like he's trying to learn the language of Charlie's eyebrow furrow.

"Tell me what you need in order to make this work."

Ryan shouts, "Come on, D. We don't have all night!"

But Dev shrugs his shoulders, like they do have all night, like they're not going to do anything until Charlie's ready. He manages a deep breath. It's just kissing. Maybe if he tells himself it's *just kissing* over and over again, he'll start to believe it. "It's fine," he tells Dev. "I'll be fine."

This time, he is unequivocally not fine. Dev arranges him against the brick wall, Angie's soft body pinned beneath him. "Sorry," Charlie tells her before they begin filming again.

"Sorry for what?"

"For absolutely all of it."

Angie reaches up for the back of his neck and pulls him down. Her mouth is soft. She tastes like mints and smells like lavender shampoo, and for a second, it all seems okay. Not exactly enjoyable, but okay.

But then he thinks *okay* is probably not good enough, because everything hinges on Charlie selling this kiss so he can get his old life back. So he tries to kiss Angie like it means something, and he waits for the feeling he generally associates with how kissing another person *should feel*. He waits, and he waits.

He doesn't feel anything at all.

He pulls away from Angie. "I need air."

"We're outside," she says, but he's already stumbling away from her, past the sidewalk barricade closing off the set. He tries to take his three deep breaths, but it feels like there are shards of glass in his lungs.

It's a panic attack. You're having a panic attack. Panic attacks cannot kill you.

But cars can, and he's so deep in his spiral, he steps off the curb and is only spared from being flattened by a Prius when Dev grabs a handful of his blazer and pulls him back onto the sidewalk. "Come here, Charlie. Sit down, sit down."

Dev keeps pulling until they're both seated side by side on the edge of the curb. "So, what just happened?" he asks patiently.

Charlie searches for something logical amidst the spiral to offer Dev as an explanation. "It's been a while. Since I've dated."

"How long is a while?"

He pretends to think about it—pretends like he doesn't remember the night he had a similar panic attack in the bathroom of a Mediterranean restaurant with self-punishing clarity. "Two years."

"Okay . . . but before that? You've dated, right?"

"Not much." Charlie taps out Morse code against his thighs.

"Why don't you date?"

"I don't know." And that's usually all it takes. Usually if Charlie stutters and sweats enough, people stop pushing him.

"You don't know why you don't date?"

Why won't Dev stop pushing him?

"I . . ." He manages to seize a deep breath. "I don't want to think about this."

"But you're on a reality dating show. You can't spend the next nine weeks *not* thinking about it." Dev reaches over for Charlie's hand, which is still tapping out the pattern on his leg. He moves slowly, so Charlie has time to avoid contact if he wants. Charlie doesn't avoid contact, and Dev's warm fingers come over his like a weighted therapy blanket.

"I'm here to help you through this, Charlie, but you've got to talk to me."

Dev squeezes his hand, and it feels different than the way holding Megan's hand did before. It reminds Charlie of the other night, when they shook hands, and he forgot to let go.

He stands up and tugs his blazer across his chest. "There's nothing to talk about. I'm not here to find love, remember?"

Dev

"It can't be done. We can't salvage this." Skylar Jones stares at the monitor. "He's just too awkward."

Dev watches the footage over Skylar's shoulder. It's a relayed video of what's happening two rooms over, where Charlie is spending his first Courting Date with Megan. Since the Kissing Catastrophe with Angie three nights ago, Charlie has somehow only gotten worse at being Cologne Ad Charles in front of the cameras. At Wednesday's Quest, he walked directly into a lighting kit when Daphne tried to hold his hand, and yesterday, while the women were competing in a literal quest (with treasure maps and shovels) Charlie sat down in the dirt to put his head between his knees in the middle of moderating a fight between Megan and three other women.

So naturally, Maureen rigged it so Megan could earn the first solo date with Charlie. After three Group Quests, Megan was named the week one champion, and it caused drama all through the castle. Charlie looks violently ill on his date as Megan places a flirtatious hand on his arm over their untouched salmon.

Charlie does not react to her attempt at flirting. Dev is pretty sure Charlie Winshaw doesn't know what flirting *is*. Hence the need for an emergency production meeting.

"We can't edit this into something romantic!"

Dev washes down his fifth Costco oatmeal raisin cookie with a swig of cold brew and tries to reassure Skylar. "Our editing team can splice together footage of anything."

"But the women aren't going to want to date a man who freaks out every time they touch him!" she continues. "The contestants are going to pick up on how awkward he is, and then this whole thing is going to fall apart!"

"Oh, *please*. The guy is a millionaire with an eight-pack and a tight ass. The women will see what they want to see. He's a blank canvas for their romantic delusions." This is Ryan's contribution to the conversation. Ryan seems entirely unperturbed by the working-with-his-ex situation, which is Ryan Parker in a nutshell. Hence Dev's need for copious amounts of sugar and caffeine.

Ryan pushes the hair out of his eyes and continues. "We should be far more concerned with what happens when the show airs and all of America sees Charles nervous sweat in high def."

"I think you all underestimate the power of Dev's charm offensive," Maureen Scott says from her place at the front of the room. "He can coach anyone. Remember that time he convinced a Southern Baptist to do the naked mud bath?"

This isn't quite the positive encouragement Maureen thinks it is. Dev is not especially proud of that moment. Besides, he's already giving everything he has to this season. Maureen has him working twenty-four-hour days, staying in the guesthouse so he can coach Charlie before and after filming. He's pretty sure he's not getting paid overtime for literally living on set, but that's the cost of making this show work. If he complains, there are hundreds of other film-school grads waiting in the wings for an opportunity like this.

"Let's focus on the girls." Maureen gestures to her iPad, where she's pulled up the contestant profiles. "Daphne seems like the obvious candidate for either the winner or the next princess. She's practically got singing birds shooting out her ass."

Jules plunks herself down on the arm of Dev's camp chair. "I like Angie for a possible next princess. In her initial interview, she talked about bisexual representation and—"

"You think our next princess is going to be biracial *and* bisexual?" Maureen crosses her arms. "It would never sell. Besides, we did a bisexual storyline on that one season of *Ever After: Summer Quest*."

"Yet we've done thirty-seven seasons of hetero storylines," Jules mutters, loud enough for only Dev to hear.

Maureen taps her manicured nails against the inside of her arm, considering. "I suppose we could use Angie's sexuality as an obstacle. Have Charlie question her loyalty. . . ."

"As a bisexual woman, I'm going to vote hard no on that one."

Maureen glares at Jules. "I don't remember giving you a vote."

Skylar attempts to redirect the meeting. "I also think we should be cautious of vilifying one of the few women of color this season. The whole confrontation with Megan already felt like baiting an angry-black-woman trope."

"Tropes exist for a reason," Maureen says as innocuously as possible in her usual high-pitched, saccharine voice. Skylar flinches in response, and the room goes painfully quiet.

Dev respects his boss, he really does, and he knows she didn't mean that the way it came out. When Dev was studying television at USC, Maureen Scott was one of his idols. At forty, she was a single mother winning daytime Emmys for her work on soaps while struggling to date as a woman who was "too old" by LA standards. That was when she had an idea for a show. It was a quarter satire, a quarter reality competition, and one half good old-fashioned fairy-tale romance. She was laughed out of every pitch meeting until she found a network that would give her a little bit of money and a terrible Sunday time slot. From there, she built it into one of the most successful franchises in reality television. While other showrunners might cash in and disengage, Maureen is here in the trenches with them. It's her show.

And yes, the image in front of the cameras hasn't changed much over the years, and it definitely doesn't reflect the image *behind* the cameras, but that's not Maureen's fault. She has the network and the advertisers to appease, and both are breathing down her neck about this season.

The thing Dev can't figure out is why Maureen Scott would bring Charlie on the show in the first place. Sure, his face can sell magazine covers, but if they're trying to revitalize the romantic realism of the show, why would Maureen bring in a man who isn't here to find love?

But it's not Dev's place to question Maureen Scott.

Ryan is the one who speaks up. Maureen always listens to Ryan, which is how he managed to fail his way into a senior story producer job. "Forget Angie. I think Megan is our best bet for a villain. She's already borderline, so it'll only take a few nudges from her handler to get her to go full crazy."

The cookies and cold brew turn on Dev, churning unpleasantly in his stomach.

Maureen claps her hands together. "It's settled, then. Ryan, get the handlers to focus on the villain narrative. Skylar, have the cameras shift their attention to the girls until our star gets a little more comfortable. And Dev . . ." His boss looks at him, her tone losing a bit of its usual sweetness. "*Charm him.*"

"Are you okay?" Jules asks as they stumble out of the meeting.

"Of course I'm okay," he says automatically, even as the words *go full crazy* rattle around in his head. "I'm always okay."

Jules doesn't push it. She follows him down a short hallway toward the museum showroom where Megan and Charlie are eating dinner amidst a collection of contemporary sculptures. As soon as Charlie spots them behind the cameras, he makes a *get me out of here* face at Dev, like he thinks this is a normal date, and Dev can text him with some fake emergency about his cat.

"What are we going to do, Jules?"

"Sit back and watch it burn?"

He shakes his head, scrubs a hand up and down his face, almost knocking off his glasses. "I know I can find a way to make him fall for one of these women if I can just get him to loosen the fuck up. I just need . . . I need . . . I don't know. Something to . . . *argh*. It's not usually this hard."

Jules tilts her head and peers up at him with her usual look of concern. She opens her mouth, closes her mouth, then sighs. "Okay, fine. You want my actual advice on how to crack him?" She takes a dramatic pause. "Exposure therapy."

"Which is . . . *what*, exactly?"

Jules points to Charlie and Megan. "Somehow, that fine-ass man sitting over there becomes an anxiety-ridden mess every time he's in a high-pressure social setting. It's as if the concept of dating triggers all his neuroses. And what do you do to treat an anxiety disorder?"

"I think he's already on meds." Jules raises an eyebrow. "*What?* I maybe went through his things in the bathroom. I'm his handler."

"You're unscrupulous is what you are. And no. I mean, I'm sure the meds help, but that's not all."

"I'm a therapy dropout. Just tell me the answer."

Jules adopts a condescending tone. "You gradually expose the patient to the source of the anxiety to desensitize them. Charlie needs to go on dates *without* the stress of the cameras. He needs to be exposed to non-stressful dating scenarios."

"Okay, I am not sure any of this is psychiatrically sound, but also, it's kind of genius."

She shrugs. "I know."

"We have him go on practice dates," he says, excited now, because *yes*, this could work. Charlie can't date the contestants without the cameras, but they get time off after each Crowning

Ceremony. "Jules, you could take him out on a date Sunday, just the two of you. Help him get more comfortable. Teach him how to relax."

"Oh, I can't be his practice girlfriend." Jules pointedly adjusts her nonexistent breasts inside her crop top. "I'm too hot."

"Not sure how that's relevant."

"It would be a Kate Hudson rom-com situation," she says with a straight face. "He'd fall in love with me while we're fake-dating. The season would be destroyed, and we'd both get sued. Is that what you want, Dev?"

He laughs, but when they look over at Charlie again, he makes eye contact with Jules and blushes, ducking his head toward his plate. So maybe she's not entirely wrong.

"Shit," is all Dev says. Because it *is* a good idea. And because Dev is the one who's supposed to charm him.

Story notes for editors:
Season 37, Episode 2
Story producer:
Ryan Parker
Air date:
Monday, September 20, 2021
Executive producer:
Maureen Scott
Scene: Week-one Crowning Ceremony
Location: *Ever After* castle

Mark Davenport: [*Medium shot of M.D. approaching from the left.*] Maidens, there is only one tiara remaining. If your name is not called, that means your quest has ended.

Charles Winshaw: [*Close-up of his hands picking up the last remaining tiara; cut to footage of Megan, Sarah, and Amy, the only remaining women without tiaras; cut back to Charles; hold the moment for five seconds.*] Megan. [*Cut to shot of Megan stepping down off the risers.*] Megan, are you interested in becoming my princess?

Megan: Of course.

[*Cut to confessionals after the C.C.*]

Megan: I wasn't really worried he wouldn't pick me. We have insane chemistry. These other women just don't have that kind of connection with Charles.

Amy: I can't believe I'm going home at the end of week one. I feel like Charles didn't give us a proper chance. I know we'd be perfect together. We have so much in common.

Producer [off camera]: What's something you and Charles have in common?

Amy [muttering over the sound of her sniffles]: You know, we're both, uh, blond. And I know I could've made him happy if he'd given me that chance. Why doesn't any man want to give me a chance? [*Stay tight on her crying for three seconds.*]

Maureen's note to editors: Make a moment of this woman's pathetic desperation.

WEEK TWO

Dev

"I was thinking we could go get brunch together this morning."

Charlie pauses in the diligent peeling of his banana and looks up all wide-eyed and startled. "Um. Why?"

Dev leans back against the kitchen counter. "It's our day off. I figured it might be nice to get away from set for a bit. I know this brunch place just down the hill."

"But why?"

Charlie's eyebrows are knotted anxiously, and Dev fights the urge to smooth them out with his thumbs even though there aren't any cameras around to capture his constipated face. "I thought it could be fun to hang out and get to know each other better."

"You want to hang out," Charlie repeats slowly, "with me? *Why?*"

"Jesus, Charlie!" Dev explodes, abandoning his attempts to play this off casually. "Look. I thought it might be helpful if I took you on a . . . *practice* date."

"A practice date?"

If Charlie repeats his words as a question one more time, Dev is going to smash banana in his beautiful face. "Yes, a practice date. To help you get a little more comfortable on your dates on camera. Work up toward the dates with the women."

Charlie is quiet for a second. Then: "With you?"

Dev throws his arms up. "Just meet me outside in five."

Thankfully, five minutes later, Charlie meets Dev in front of the guesthouse wearing navy shorts and a gray short-sleeve button-down that matches his eyes, looking like the douchey frat bro of Dev's nightmares. He borrows Jules's car, and they drive through the streets of Pasadena in awkward silence. Dev fiddles with the aux hookup until he's playing Leland Barlow's debut album, and Charlie nervously clings to the handgrip in the door and pumps an invisible brake pedal with his right foot every time Dev careens toward a stop sign.

Junipers restaurant is a crew favorite thanks to its proximity to set and its bottomless mimosas, and when they're finally seated, the outdoor patio is packed with clusters of twentysomethings rehashing their Saturday night revels and thirtysomethings with strollers refusing to give up their old way of life. Dev loves the sunny, clamorous crowdedness of it all. The hostess leads them to a tiny table tucked in the corner. As they sit down, their knees brush. Charlie dramatically swings his aside to break the contact.

"Isn't this place great?"

Charlie reaches carefully for a menu, his face pinched again. Dev cannot understand how such an attractive man can do such unattractive things with his face.

"What's wrong?"

"Uh, nothing. It's just . . . I'm gluten-free and vegan," Charlie says, still frowning down at the single-sided menu.

Charlie Winshaw is everything Dev is trying to avoid by not dating, and Dev's current state of hunger makes it more difficult to deal with Charlie in general. "This is LA. I'm sure you can find something gluten-free and vegan."

"Yes, but it's all French toast and waffles."

"I don't see the problem."

The waiter weaves his way to their table, offers them an indifferent greeting as he flips through pages in his little pad, and then finally looks up, his eyes falling on Charlie. "*Oh*," he breathes in surprise. It's not an *I recognize you* kind of surprise—he can't be older than twenty and probably doesn't subscribe to *Wired* magazine, nor is he in *Ever After*'s target demo. No, it's a *holy shit I just looked up and saw the most beautiful human being alive* kind of surprise. Dev witnessed this look on the faces of twenty women the first night of filming.

The waiter blushes and blusters, "What can I do to you? I mean, *for* you? I mean, get you? I mean—"

Charlie is oblivious. He orders a cup of tea, a side of fruit, and two veggie sausages. Dev orders the crab eggs Benedict, a side of bacon, and a side of sourdough toast; he intends to eat all his gluten and animal by-products robustly. He tries not to think about how the women are all probably drinking Bellinis in the hot tub on their day off. Dev should've been coaching them.

"So," he attempts begrudgingly, "tell me about yourself."

Charlie is studying his fork. "Um . . . what do you want to know?"

"How about your family? What are your parents like? Siblings?"

"Well, see, it's . . . We're not close," he stammers. "I mean, *I* am not close. With the rest of my family. We don't really—"

"Speak?" Dev tries.

Charlie coughs.

The waiter comes back with the tea and coffee. "Excuse me, but could I please get a new fork? This one is dirty."

"Oh my God, yes. I'm so sorry. I'll take care of that immediately." The waiter comes back thirty seconds later with four different forks for Charlie to choose from.

Dev takes a slow, deep breath and tries to remember he's supposed to be *charming* Charlie into going along with the show. Still, his voice comes out irritated. "You know, it's a customary part of dating to ask questions to get to know each other better."

"In my limited experience, the women aren't very interested in getting to know me."

"Well, maybe not Megan, but the producers will probably rig it so your next Courting Date is with Daphne, and she'll definitely ask you questions about yourself."

The group one table over erupts in a loud laughter, and Charlie winces. "I . . . I don't want to talk about myself."

Dev grinds his teeth. "Okay. Then, why don't you practice asking me a question about myself?"

Charlie's mouth falls open. "Like what?"

"I don't know, Charlie!" He knows he's losing his temper again, and he knows that means Charlie will only continue shrinking into himself, but he can't help it. The more Charlie retreats, the more Dev wants to advance. He wishes he could get back to the brief understanding they struck after Charlie got punched, when Charlie let him hold one ice pack and peeled back the tiniest corner of himself.

The waiter arrives with their brunch in unprecedented time for Los Angeles food service, and they both look grateful to have something to occupy their hands and mouths. After a torturous silence in which Dev inhales four slices of bacon without breathing, he snaps, "What are you so afraid of, Charlie?"

Charlie spears a piece of cantaloupe with his sterilized fork and hovers the fruit in front of his open mouth, brushing it against his bottom lip. (And for practical purposes, Dev will have the rest of this conversation with Charlie's left ear.) "What do you mean?"

Dev mops up some excess Hollandaise sauce with his sourdough. "Why can't you just say what's on your mind?"

"I . . . I have a tendency to, uh . . . say the wrong thing."

"How so?"

"I just . . ." Charlie flails his left hand. "I . . . I . . . am not good with words, or with trying to communicate my thoughts. People always think I'm weird, so it is easier if I never talk."

"Well," Dev says after a long pause. "That's the saddest thing I've ever heard."

Charlie sits up straight in his chair, like he's attempting to project confidence Dev knows he doesn't have. "No, it's fine, really. Some people have strong emotional intelligence. Interpersonal skills." He gestures vaguely at Dev. "I don't. But my brain is really good at other stuff, and if I keep my mouth shut, I'm not even abnormal by Palo Alto standards."

Dev shifts in his chair, and their knees brush under the table again. This time, Charlie doesn't immediately move, so neither does Dev, and it's the first night handshake all over again but with knees. "Plenty of people struggle with social anxiety," Dev tells him. "You're not abnormal by any standards."

"Says the guy who told me I have to be the cologne ad version of myself."

Dev pushes aside his plate. He feels like an asshole. It's obvious whatever abnormalities Charlie is convinced he has, people have been historically unkind about them. "You're right. That was a bullshit thing for me to say. You shouldn't have to change yourself for love."

Behind them, a group gets up to leave, and Charlie scrunches his shoulders, becomes as small as possible to avoid being bumped by their swinging purses. Under the table, Charlie's leg presses even more firmly against Dev's, and he can feel Charlie trembling in the place where their bodies meet. He thinks about the crowded patio and the noise and all the germs. Under the table, Dev reaches out and puts a hand on Charlie's knee to steady him. He can feel Charlie relax by a few degrees beneath his fingers.

"You hate eating at restaurants, don't you?" Dev asks gently.

"I don't *hate* it," Charlie starts unconvincingly, beads of sweat gathering around his hairline, "but it can be tricky for me, on bad days. Days when I'm already anxious."

Dev understands bad days, and now he's back to feeling like an asshole, because he's gone about this whole practice-dating thing all wrong. Of course it's been an unmitigated disaster. It didn't even occur to him to ask Charlie what he would want to do on a date, even though the entire point of this exercise is to help him feel more comfortable.

Incidentally, Charlie isn't the only one who is out of practice when it comes to first dates. "Come on." Dev smiles. "Let's get out of here."

Dev removes his hand from Charlie's leg and waves over the waiter, who is never more than ten feet away from Charlie's gravitational pull. Dev asks for the bill. "Before we go, a quick experiment, okay?"

Charlie looks skeptical but nods. "Okay."

"I want you to say exactly what's on your mind at this moment."

Charlie folds his lips into a thin, worried line and stares down at his empty plate.

"No self-censoring, no worrying about saying the wrong thing, no overthinking it," Dev orders. "Just say what's on your mind this exact instant."

"Um—"

"You're *overthinking*."

Charlie makes sudden, unexpected eye contact, and Dev forgets his previous commitment to only staring at Charlie's ear. He's now confronted with the whole image of Charlie's face—the stormy gray eyes with their faint bruising and the blond curls and the chin dimple, and it's a lot, and Charlie keeps staring at him, and when Charlie opens his mouth, Dev feels something drop in his lower stomach.

"You have Hollandaise sauce all over your face!" Charlie blurts.

The tension in Dev's chest uncoils. "Well," he says, reaching for a napkin, "I guess that's a start."

Charlie

"*This* is your idea of a romantic time?"

"I never claimed to know anything about romance," Charlie clarifies from his cross-legged position on the floor of the guesthouse living room, "but I enjoy a good puzzle, yes."

Dev is sitting on the opposite side of the coffee table slowly sorting out the edge pieces while trying to watch the television show playing on his laptop. After the disastrous brunch full of germ-related crises and verbal idiocy and far too much leg touching, Dev asked Charlie what he would do with his ideal afternoon. So now they're working on a jigsaw puzzle while watching the first season of *The Expanse*, because Dev has never seen it.

"The fascinating thing about this show is," Charlie explains, "in most science fiction, they totally ignore the physiological repercussions of FTL."

Dev looks the opposite of fascinated. "What's FTL?"

"Faster-than-light travel."

"Right. Okay, so to recap"—Dev points to the actors on-screen—"the hot skinny guy, the hot buff guy, the hot maybe-Indian guy, and the hot lady just fly around in the ship solving mysteries like Scooby-Doo in space?"

"That's not remotely the premise of this show. Are you even paying attention?"

"Any of these hot dudes ever going to hook up with each other?"

"No . . ."

"Then what is even the point of it?"

"The *science*!" Charlie says, perhaps a little too passionately.

Dev does this infuriating crooked smile, and Charlie understands they're playing a different game, in addition to the puzzle, with Dev trying to coax out little tidbits of who Charlie is, the things he usually keeps tucked away so they can't be used against him.

Charlie falls silent, and for a while Dev does too, his tongue tapping his front teeth as he concentrates on the image displayed on the front of the box. With Dev, silence never lasts long, though. "Would you say you're looking for a lady to puzz with you on a Saturday night?"

"I do not believe that is the correct verb form of *puzzle*. Just organize your edge pieces."

"I haven't puzzed since . . . shit, middle school trips to Nag's Head with my parents, maybe? I don't usually sit still for this long."

"I haven't noticed that about you."

"Was that sarcasm? What, you're capable of sarcasm now?"

"My system must have upgraded."

Dev throws a puzzle piece at him. It bounces off his nose and it slides under the couch.

"I swear, if we get to the end of this thousand-piece puzzle and we're missing one—"

"I'll get it." Dev crawls across the floor, twists his body, and sticks his arm under the couch. His black T-shirt rides up to reveal his dark brown stomach, a trail of black hair disappearing into the waistband of his cargo shorts. "Ha!"

Dev sits up triumphantly, brandishing the puzzle piece. His T-shirt is still bunched in the corner. Charlie looks away.

"I was serious before," Dev says, the silences shortening. "Is this how you picture your life with a partner? Puzzling and watching nerdy sci-fi shows?"

"I've honestly never pictured my life with a partner. We weren't all indoctrinated into the cult of fairy-tale love at a young age."

"Don't quote Jules at me while I'm trying to puzz."

Maybe because he's so caught up in his intense focus on the puzzle—or maybe because Dev never stops pushing, and Charlie knows his usual evasive strategies won't work—he speaks without filtering. "When you can barely make it to a third date with a woman, it's hard to imagine another person permanently in your life."

"But you look like *that*." Dev gesticulates wildly, upending the puzzle box from its display stand. "I don't get how you're bad at dating."

"You could only spend *thirty minutes* on a practice date with me because you had such a thoroughly miserable time."

"Excuse you, we're still on that practice date, and I just connected *five* pieces in a row." He snaps another puzzle piece into place. "I'm having a fucking incredible time."

Charlie smiles down at the table. "Well, no one has ever said that about a date with me before." He doesn't explain that he never enjoyed those dates either, that he hated the pressure to be perfect, to conform to the assumptions people made about him based on how he looks. He doesn't explain how the dates were something he did out of obligation, because dating was something he was *supposed* to do. He doesn't explain how they always felt wrong, like Charlie was putting on a costume that didn't fit quite right.

"Plus *this*"—Charlie adopts Dev's frantic hand gesture—"this is for my mental health. All the exercise, I mean. I don't do it because I care what my body looks like. I do it because I care how my brain feels."

Dev looks up from the picture they're assembling on the coffee table. He has a geometric face—the sharp V of his chin, the 90-degree angle of his jaw, the straight line of his nose—but his expression softens entirely when his eyes lock onto Charlie's. Charlie prepares himself for Dev to make a snide comment about his mental health.

Instead, he cocks his fist and punches Charlie in the arm. "*Bro.* That was awesome! You opened up to me about something!"

"Ouch," Charlie mumbles.

"Sorry, I got a little overexcited." Dev winces apologetically and reaches out to massage Charlie's bare arm. *One Mississippi. Two Mississippi.* "But that was really good! That's the kind of thing you should share with the women on your dates."

Dev's hand is still on Charlie's skin, just below the cuffed sleeve of his shirt, hot fingers kneading into Charlie's bicep.

Three Mississippi. Four Mississippi. "You think the women want to hear about my mental health?"

"Yes!" Dev shouts enthusiastically. *Five Mississippi.* "They want you to open up."

This didn't seem to be true. The women he went out with *said* they wanted him to open up, be vulnerable, let down his guard. Yet whenever he showed even a smidge of real emotion, they were turned off completely. They mostly confirmed what his father always used to say: real men don't cry, and they definitely don't talk publicly about their self-care.

Dev's fingers encircle Charlie's bicep completely, his thumb brushing the inside of Charlie's arm. Charlie loses count of his Mississippis. "The women want you to be your true self," Dev says, before his hand falls away. He turns back to the puzzle.

"We made good progress," Dev says as he slots together a few more pieces. "Emotionally and puzzlely. You know, I think this is the best practice date I've had."

Charlie doesn't tell Dev it's the best date he's had, period.

"Practice dates?" Parisa repeats during their video call late Wednesday night. "What the hell is a practice date?"

"Like a fake date. To help me feel more comfortable on the real dates. With the women."

Parisa pokes at her lavender-and-seaweed-extract mask, staring at her own face inlaid in the corner of her phone screen. They're both doing facials, per their usual tradition. In Charlie's normal life, every two weeks or so, Parisa shows up unexpectedly at his apartment with a bottle of expensive wine and face masks. She usually invents some excuse for needing to talk to him—something terrible happened at work; something terrible happened with her meddling extended family; something terrible happened with her current girlfriend or boyfriend or whoever she's hooking up with at the moment—but Charlie knows the truth. Parisa pops over whenever she hasn't heard from him in a while. She comes over to make sure he's okay. When she packed his things for the show, she stuck a dozen face masks in his bag so she could have a pretext for these conversations. He was happy to let her.

"And what exactly do you do on these practice dates?"

"We mostly work on puzzles after filming and watch *The Expanse*. Sometimes we talk about stuff."

"*You* talk about stuff? What kind of stuff?"

He shrugs. "Stanford stuff. WinHan. The work I do at the foundation. You, obviously."

"I'm both flattered and confused. You say words? Out loud? Entire sentences? Is this Dev fellow some kind of wizard?"

"No, he's just good at making people feel comfortable." Because that is literally his job, and Dev is kind of amazing at his job. "He's super into the whole fairy-tale thing, and he gets angry if you call the show fake, and he washes his face with hand soap, but I think you'd like him."

"Hmm." Parisa reaches for her glass of wine. "And he's pretending to like puzzles and *The Expanse*? He either takes his job very seriously, or he's secretly trying to fuck you."

Charlie's blush is conveniently concealed behind the lavender cream. "Dev is not trying to—" He stops, wonders if Dev is still awake on the other side of the wall. He probably is. Dev is always awake. "He's not trying to do anything with me. *Jesus*, Parisa."

"I promise you, at least half the people you meet are secretly trying to fuck you, Charles. You're just too innocent to notice."

"You know, the other nice thing about Dev is that he doesn't mock me incessantly."

"Not to your face, anyway."

"That's fantastic for my self-esteem, thank you."

"Oh, you love it when I mock you."

"I cannot imagine what has led you to believe this about me."

Parisa throws her head back and laughs. The mask cracks in lines around her mouth. "Okay, okay. So are these practice dates helping?"

He thinks back to the Group Quests the past two days. "Well, I held Daphne's hand yesterday, and then I kissed Angie without having a panic attack about it, so yes?"

"Guard your hearts, ladies! Casanova is on the loose."

"You can't help yourself, can you?"

"Do you like any of the women?"

"I like most of the women, honestly."

Parisa makes a highly suggestive hand gesture. "Not like that," he snaps. Then, evasively, "I should go. I need to wash my face."

"Take me with you," she demands. He huffs and carries the phone into the bathroom. "You don't have crushes on any of the women?"

He props the phone behind the sink and turns on the water. "I didn't come here for *crushes*. I came here to show the world I'm nice and normal so I can work again. Work is what matters."

While he splashes handfuls of water in his face, Parisa says, "Believe it or not, there is this newfangled thing where people have careers *and* romantic relationships."

"I'm sorry to destroy your romantic delusions, but I don't have those feelings for any of the contestants here."

"Yeah, but would you know if you did?"

He pauses in the middle of pat-drying his face. "What do you mean?"

She switches to her gentle, coaxing voice. "I mean, you haven't seriously given dating a chance. Do you know how to recognize it, when you're interested in someone? The butterflies and the stolen glances and the feeling of wanting to be near them?"

"I . . . I don't—"

"Who are you talking to?"

Charlie jumps, drops the towel, and turns. He left the bathroom door open, so Dev stands leaning against the doorframe in plaid pajama bottoms and a USC Trojans T-shirt.

"Nothing. No one." Charlie jabs at the screen of his phone, hears Parisa shout, "*Don't you dare hang up on me Charles Michael Winshaw,*" before he manages to end the call.

"It was just Parisa," he tells Dev. He knows there is no way to conceal his blush now. He just doesn't know why he's blushing.

Dev steps into the bathroom. "You've got a bit of . . . just there." Dev gestures to the side of Charlie's face, and Charlie frantically tries to wipe the cream on the back of his hand.

"Here. Do you mind?" Dev bends over to pick up the towel Charlie dropped, and his shirt slides up in the back, revealing the sharp points of his spine. He stands, and his bare skin disappears again. Dev turns on the sink to wet the corner of the towel, then reaches up to dab the lingering face mask from Charlie's temple.

Charlie holds his breath. Remains as still as possible.

"You smell good," Dev says when he's done, setting the towel next to the sink. "Like . . ." He gets close to Charlie's face and sniffs. His nose grazes the edge of Charlie's jaw, and Charlie feels a nauseous lift below his rib cage, as if someone released a thousand balloons inside his stomach. "Lavender," Dev declares.

"Oh. Yeah. It's the face mask."

Dev props himself against the counter. "So, you were great today. On the Group Quest. I almost believed you were into it when you flirted with Megan."

"Almost," Charlie says, staring down at his socks.

"Almost."

He glances up and sees Dev smiling at him. Balloons again.

"Tomorrow, you're going to ask seven Maidens personal questions about themselves, right?"

"Three," he attempts to barter.

"Six."

"Five?"

Dev's smile widens. "Okay, five. But I get to choose which five."

"Deal."

Dev pushes away from the edge of the counter. "You should probably get some sleep." He steps into Charlie's reach and lifts a hand, and for one fleeting, foolish moment, Charlie thinks Dev is about to cup his cheek. Which would have been weird. And unwanted, obviously. Instead, he ruffles Charlie's hair, the way an affectionate older brother might. The way Charlie's actual older brothers never did.

"Good night, Charlie," Dev says as he walks out of the bathroom.

"Good night, Dev."

Dev

"They have to collect frogs and *kiss them*?" Charlie asks, horrified, as they wait for the contestant handler to prep the women across the field. "Who even comes up with these Group Quest ideas?"

"Sadistic misogynists in preproduction," Jules answers, "and this one has an added layer of animal cruelty."

Cynics, the pair of them. "I think the Frog Actors Guild ensures safe working conditions."

"Well, I heard the show was casting toads to work around the frog union rules," Charlie teases. Because teasing is something he does now, thanks to the wonders of practice dating. Dev reaches over to tousle Charlie's hair slightly, so it falls over his forehead. "Just go make your meaningful connections with five women like we rehearsed."

Filled with dread, Charlie does a slow march across the field they've stocked with frogs, and he turns his head over his shoulder to look back at Dev like a nervous child being forced to go play with kids his own age. Dev can picture little Charlie being that kid—the kid who begged to stay inside with the teacher at recess, the kid who tried to hang out with the grown-ups at birthday parties, assuming little Charlie got invited to any birthday parties. Little Charlie, always looking over his shoulder for a way out.

"You two seem to be getting close," Jules observes as they watch Charlie join a small cluster of women.

"Thanks to your plan. And he's not so bad to hang out with. He's kind of . . . sweet."

Jules cocks her head to stare up at him.

"What?"

Jules shrugs. "Nothing."

Dev rakes his hands over his three-day stubble. "He'll open up a bit when we're alone, and he's doing better for the cameras, but I'm not sure it's *enough*." Charlie grows more comfortable with the women every day, but he's still holding back, still holding his breath. It makes Dev feel itchy and restless. "I still don't know what he's looking for in a woman, or how to make him fall in love."

"You're doing the best you can, Dev. You've got to make sure you're taking care of yourself, too, yeah? It's bad enough Maureen is making you stay at the guesthouse." She reaches up to give his arm puppy scratches, which is the Jules Lu answer to all situations that require emotional intimacy. "Have you been sleeping?"

Across the field, Charlie smiles warmly as Daphne Reynolds shows him a frog. "I'll sleep when Charlie Winshaw is engaged."

"Isn't it strange that they spend all this time preparing decadent food," Daphne asks, "but we're not allowed to eat any of it?"

Charlie stares down at his plate of risotto. "It does seem criminally wasteful," he agrees, and they both shoot overt glances toward the cameras. "And I am a little hungry after that hot-air balloon ride."

Daphne defiantly picks up her fork. "I say we just do it."

Charlie picks up his fork, too, and they clink their utensils before they dig into the risotto. Dev waits for someone to yell in his earpiece. There are reasons the talent isn't supposed to eat on these Courting Dates. No one—not even Charlie Winshaw—looks cute while chewing, and the mics often pick up the sound. Not to mention, the entire purpose of these one-on-one dates is to *talk*, which they can't do while masticating.

Still, Skylar never screams cut, because it's actually a cute scene between Daphne and Charlie, the two of them eating, their heads conspiratorially bowed together. It was no surprise Daphne Reynolds "won" the week-two Courting Date; Maureen has already decided she's a front-runner. Plus, Daphne's fear of heights made her the perfect candidate for the hot-air balloon ride. She freaked out and Charlie had to comfort her. Sympathetic is a good look on him.

Now, though, Dev needs Charlie to take his relationship with Daphne to the next level. "It's week two," Dev told Charlie before the dinner, "which is typically the time for emotionally vulnerable conversations about past relationships. Ask Daphne about her dating history."

"Do I have to?"

He does "have to" as if they're going to sell this love story.

Charlie looks up from his plate to find Dev in the corner of the room, and Dev makes an impatient gesture with his hands. Charlie clears his throat. "I . . . uh . . . have you . . . I mean, I was wondering, in the past, before the show, if you, uh—"

"Are you trying to ask me about my last relationship?" Daphne supplies. "My handler prepped me on what to discuss, too."

They both laugh, and there's an inarguable chemistry between them, two shy, awkward people stumbling in circles around each other. Dev sucks in his cheeks and watches it unfold.

"I haven't dated much in the last few years," Daphne continues, "at least not seriously. I can't seem to find what I'm looking for. How about you?"

Charlie nods. "Yes, um. Same."

"What *are* you looking for?"

Charlie chokes on his food. "Hmm?"

"What are you looking for in a partner?"

"Oh. Well. I . . . ." Charlie stammers, then stops, like he thinks he can just get out of this conversation by simply tapering off. Dev scrubs his face and waits for Charlie to pick the sentence back up. "I am, well, I'm into puzzing," he finally says.

On Dev's left, Jules snorts. In front of the cameras, Daphne looks offended. "Is that a sex thing?"

"No!" Charlie nearly drops his wineglass. "No, I meant puzzling. I enjoy puzzles."

"That's what you're looking for in a woman?" Daphne asks slowly. "A puzzle?"

"No." Charlie sweats. He dabs his forehead with his napkin. "That would be nonsensical."

"So what are you looking for in the women on this show?"

Charlie is clearly three seconds away from regurgitating his risotto all over Daphne's dress. He pushes back from the table and his chair tips over, thudding against the marble floor. "Will you . . . ah . . . excuse me for a moment?"

Charlie bolts for the nearest exit, but Dev is already after him, following him outside the estate to a small garden bench. Charlie drops his head between his knees.

"Sorry. I'm so sorry." Charlie apologizes to the floor while he struggles to breathe. "That was bad. That was really bad."

Dev sits down on the bench next to him. "Yeah," Dev agrees. He puts a hand on Charlie's back and rubs comforting circles through the layers of his suit.

Charlie sits up abruptly. "*Yeah?* Aren't you supposed to say something to make me feel better?"

"I'm not sure there's any way to spin what just happened. I can't believe you said *puzzing*."

"So you admit this entire thing was your fault, then? For the bastardization of the word *puzzle*?"

"I admit to no such thing."

Charlie releases a puff of air that almost sounds like a laugh. Dev keeps rubbing his back. "Do you think Daphne hates me now?" he asks, like he cares about the answer. Like he cares about *Daphne*. Dev's chest tightens with hope.

"I think Daphne is a kindhearted person who just wants you to open up to her," Dev says, "to be yourself with her. Why didn't you tell her the stuff you told me while we were puzzing?"

"I don't know. It's easier with you." Charlie nudges his shoulder against Dev's and leaves it there. It's knees under the Junipers table; it's shaking hands on night one. For someone who hates touching, Charlie Winshaw is always leaning in and not leaning away. He smells like risotto and the organic oatmeal body wash Dev sees in the shower, and Dev doesn't really want to lean away either.

"What the fuck?" Ryan comes stomping outside with Jules right behind him. "Charles, get back out there. We need to reshoot that entire conversation!"

"He needs a minute."

"Well, it's been a minute, and now he needs to stop being such a head case and get back to his date."

Charlie visibly shrinks. "I'm sorry."

And Dev just *snaps*. "You're being an insensitive dick right now, Ryan."

Everything goes silent. Then Jules inserts her tiny body between Ryan and Dev. "Why don't I take Charlie to get his makeup fixed?" she says calmly. Charlie shoots Dev one last look before the pair vanishes, and then it's just Ryan and Dev. Alone. For the first time since the breakup.

He's been so busy coaching Charlie, he hasn't had time to

think about his own problems, but now they're standing right in front of him: five feet nine inches of Dev's insecurities in human form.

"What the hell?" Ryan seethes. "You can't talk to me like that in front of the talent."

"You can't talk to my talent like that," Dev rages right back. "He's not a head case."

Ryan snorts and folds his arms across his chest. "Look, I'll give it to you, D. You've done more with him in two weeks than I could have, so I'm glad it's you and not me, but"—Ryan squares his shoulders—"the dude is crazy, and it's total bullshit that we have to deal with his antics because Maureen made a bad casting choice."

"Jesus, Ryan, he's not *crazy* because he sometimes needs a minute to collect himself. Did you think *I* was crazy?"

Ryan drops his hands to his hips. "What?"

"When we were together, all those days I couldn't get out of bed . . . did you think I was crazy?"

Dev needs Ryan to admit this is such a shitty thing to say. He needs Ryan to recognize why it is so personally offensive to Dev to hear his ex-boyfriend of six years casually call a man *crazy*— why it makes Dev feel infinitesimal and defensive and angry. He needs Ryan to apologize.

Ryan rolls his eyes. "Oh, come on. You know I didn't mean it like that. Don't be so sensitive."

Dev feels flattened. One-dimensional. A cardboard cutout of himself. He stares at Ryan and tries to figure out how he spent *six years* thinking he and Ryan were a perfect fit.

"What's your deal with this guy, anyway?" Ryan asks. "Are you *into* Charles?"

Dev scrapes his fingers painfully through his hair. "*Shit*. No. That's not what this is about—"

"Then why are you taking this so personally?"

He wants to find a way to explain it to Ryan, but he knows it's pointless. He broke up with Ryan because he finally realized Ryan was never going to understand Dev—not his too-big heart or his too-busy brain—and as much as it hurts, the beauty of the breakup is Dev no longer has to try.

"It's nothing," he finally says.

But it doesn't feel like nothing.

Charlie

Something is wrong with Dev.

First he screamed at Ryan. Then he didn't talk to Charlie for the rest of the shoot, which Charlie chalked up to the disastrous conversation with Daphne. But now Dev sits in the backseat of the town car angrily working his jaw. Jules hitched a ride back to set in an equipment van, probably because she didn't want to deal with Dev's sulking, so there's no buffer between Charlie and Dev's stormy mood.

He tiptoes cautiously toward the problem. "Are you . . . upset?"

"No," Dev snaps. Sounding very upset.

"Okay, but uh . . . you don't seem like yourself."

Dev keeps his eyes on the window. "I'm so sorry my bad mood is ruining your night," he says in a clipped tone. "I will try to only be Fun Dev from now on."

Charlie is somehow screwing this up in record time, and he desperately tries to save it. "I don't need you to be Fun Dev, but if you're upset about what happened with Daphne, I'm sorry."

Dev finally turns his head toward Charlie, his face damp in the passing street lamps. Dev *is crying*. "It's not you. It's Ryan. Ryan and I sort of dated . . . for six years. We broke up three months ago."

"Oh," Charlie says.

Oh, Charlie thinks, something important about Dev clicking into place. Something he probably should've pieced together sooner. So he asks, inelegantly: "Wait, are you gay?"

The tension in the backseat of the town car breaks, and Dev starts laughing. "Yes, Charlie! *Oh my God.* How did you not know I'm gay?"

Honestly, the possibility hadn't even occurred to him. "In my defense, you're obsessed with helping straight people find love, and your cargo shorts are heinous."

"The way I dress has nothing to do with the fact that I like dick."

Charlie flinches involuntarily.

Dev groans and runs his fingers through the stubble on his angular jaw. "Please don't be awkward about this. Don't be one of those straight guys who acts like every gay dude wants to date you. I'm not trying to get in your pants."

"Eh, I mean . . . *obviously*."

"You're going to be awkward about this, aren't you?"

"Of course not."

"Are you going to freak out every time I touch you now?"

"I already freak out when you touch me."

Dev's mouth slides open before promptly snapping shut.

"That . . . that came out wrong. I didn't mean . . ." Charlie feels the sweat gather on the back of his neck, and he pivots, hard. "Why did you and Ryan break up?"

"Because he bought me a girl's T-shirt for my birthday."

"I know I don't have a lot of relationship experience, but *what?*"

Dev sighs. "For my twenty-eighth birthday, Jules threw me this huge surprise party with half the crew at my favorite bar, and Ryan showed up with a *Goonies* T-shirt still in the brown paper Target bag as his gift. I'm not materialistic, but we had been together for *six years*, and he bought me a novelty T-shirt for twelve bucks in the girls' section at Target. It was clear he had forgotten my birthday and picked it up on the way to the party. And it was an XXL, so it didn't even fit me. It was like a wide crop top, and not in a sexy, *A Nightmare on Elm Street* kind of way."

"Well, I mean, do you like *The Goonies*?"

"Of course, I like *The Goonies*! That's not the point! The point is . . . *that* is what our relationship was worth to him: a twelve-dollar T-shirt that didn't fit. I wanted marriage and babies, and he didn't even care about me enough to know my shirt size. And the worst part is . . ." Dev sucks in his cheeks, making the geometric angles of his face even more dramatic in the dark car. "The worst part is, I knew going into the relationship that Ryan didn't want any of those things, but I thought I could change his mind. I thought that if I were good enough and fun enough, Ryan would want to be with me forever."

Dev pauses for a second, his breath catching on the rough edge of tears again, and Charlie panics, unsure of the protocol here. He thinks about Dev on the sidewalk, Dev on the bench, Dev always comforting Charlie when he needs it. Charlie reaches over to put a hand on Dev's knee. "I'm sorry," Charlie says.

Dev looks down at Charlie's pale fingers on his dark skin. "Actually, the worst part is, I threw away six years on someone who only loved me when I was Fun Dev."

"What's so special about Ryan?" Charlie isn't sure why this is the first question that springs to his mind.

"Well, I mean, you've seen him. He's *hot*. Like way out of my league."

Charlie would politely disagree; Ryan looks like a pirate who is going to try to upsell you rental car insurance, some befuddling blend of scruffy and preppy that almost disguises the fact that he's rather boring to look at. Dev's face is never boring. "And, I don't know. . . ." Dev shrugs. "He liked me? He laughed at my jokes? He usually enjoyed my company?"

"That seems like a low bar. I thought you were a hopeless romantic."

"I am. When it comes to other people's romances."

The car goes quiet for a minute as the driver pulls onto the winding road that leads to the *Ever After* castle. Dev drops his eyes back down to Charlie's pale fingers, still sprawled out on Dev's knee. Charlie isn't sure if he moves his hand first, or if Dev pulls back his knee first. All he knows is they suddenly aren't touching anymore. "Enough feeling sorry for myself," Dev announces. His face is all mischievous shadows, that crooked, amused smile. "You know what we should do tonight?"

Charlie's mouth goes dry. "Um . . . what?"

"Practice date. But with bourbon."

As soon as they get back to the guesthouse, Dev heads straight for the cupboard above the refrigerator and stands on his tiptoes to reach for the bottle of bourbon he's stashed in the back. Charlie watches his white T-shirt ride up and his cargo shorts strain against his backside as he pulls the bottle down.

"Sit down," Dev says, his back still to Charlie. "It makes me nervous when you hover."

Charlie obediently shrugs out of his blazer, loosens his tie, and sits on one of the stools at the counter. Dev pushes a glass into his hands, and the first sip burns the whole way down, cutting a path of fire through his body.

Dev leans back against the adjacent counter, and the silence unspools in the small distance between them. Charlie isn't sure what happens next. It feels like they should be talking, but instead they're just staring, and any second now, Dev is going to realize Charlie is a terrible drinking buddy.

Charlie wants to say something—to find a way to keep Dev here, lazily propped against the counter, long limbs fluid like tributaries, but the longer the silence stretches, the more his anxiety mounts, and the harder it becomes to fill it, until Charlie blurts again, "Tell me about how you got into reality television."

"Why?"

"Oh, I'm sorry, I thought you wanted me to practice asking personal questions," he says in a rush. "We can just get drunk in awkward silence if you'd prefer."

Dev's mouth falls open. "*Wow.* A little bit of hard alcohol, and you're already sassing me. I should've gotten you drunk a long time ago."

The conversation hiccups for some reason, and they both take another sip. "I just loved movies and television as a kid," Dev starts. "I'm an only child and my parents were both college professors who worked a lot, so I was practically raised on TV. When I was, like, seven or eight, I started writing scripts. My parents are indulgent, so they bought me a camera and editing equipment, sent me to film camp every summer, drove me thirty minutes to east Raleigh every day so I could go to art school."

Dev smiles, but it's not his usual amused grin, twisting the corner of his mouth. This smile is larger and fuller. Realer, maybe, causing ripples on either side of his lips, a dozen parabolas stretching up to his ears. "My parents used to host these premieres every time I finished making a movie, and I don't know. . . . Writing for movies and television is all I ever wanted to do."

"So you decided to work in unscripted television?"

Dev glares, but it doesn't have any bite. "Yeah, I mean, I love this show, and I lucked into an internship with the network right out of USC. The experience I've gained these past six years has been incalculable."

Charlie senses an ellipsis. Dev's limbs are restless, fluttering at his sides the way they do when he's got something to say. "But . . . ?"

Dev reaches for the bottle to top off their glasses. "*But* sure. Yeah. Someday I would love to write. I have a script, like everyone living in LA, but it's a queer rom com that takes place on the set of a Bollywood movie—kind of like what *Jane the Virgin* did for telenovelas—so the entire cast is Desi, which is not something studios are seeking out right now. Which obviously sucks, because there aren't exactly a lot of American movies where people look like me." Dev gestures from his wide shoulders down to the sharp, narrow points of his hips. "Maureen said she would help me get the script to an agent, but she's busy."

Charlie takes another long sip of bourbon, lets it warm him from the inside out. "Can I read it?"

"Read what?"

"Your script."

Dev pushes his glasses up the bridge of his nose with two fingers. "Why would you want to read it?"

"Because you wrote it."

Dev adjusts his glasses again, and Charlie realizes it's a nervous gesture. Dev is *nervous*. Dev, who is always so confident, so charming, so *extroverted*, is nervous at the thought of letting Charlie read his work.

"I don't have a printed copy of the script."

"I can read things digitally."

Dev squirms. "It's . . . it's super personal. The script is a lot of *me*. It's, like, *all of me*. I put all of myself into it, and if you hated it, it would be like . . ."

Charlie isn't sure what to do with the knowledge that Dev Deshpande cares what he thinks of him. "I won't hate it."

"Okay." Dev nods once, twice, seven times, shaking loose his nerves. "Yeah, okay. Fine, I guess you can read it."

He sets down his bourbon on the counter in front of Charlie and grabs his laptop off the coffee table. "If you do hate it, just . . . don't tell me."

Dev comes back to the counter and stands so close, Charlie gets a noseful of his deodorant, Tide laundry detergent, and something else, something smoky and sweet. Charlie inhales and tries to place the scent before he realizes . . . it's just Dev's skin. Then he realizes he's smelling Dev and should probably stop. He takes a gulp of bourbon.

"What's your email address?" Dev asks. Charlie reaches across Dev to type it in for him and presses send before Dev can change his mind. Charlie's phone buzzes in his pocket ten seconds later. He pulls it out.

"No, don't read it now! Don't read it in front of me!" Dev lunges dramatically to shove Charlie's phone aside. Dev's hand brushes Charlie's hand, then his thighs brush Charlie's knees on the stool, then they're touching in so many places, Charlie doesn't know what to do. Dev stands in between Charlie's open legs, hovering over him. Dark brown eyes and body heat and that distinctly Dev smell.

Something churns in Charlie's lower stomach—panic, probably, from the closeness. From the touching. He doesn't like touching, and he definitely doesn't like the feeling of Dev's entire body pressing against his. Charlie's skin is on fire.

Dev finally pulls away. "Sorry," he mumbles, eyes on his bourbon as he takes an unsteady sip, spilling some down the front of his white shirt. In an instant, Charlie's brain does an impressive one-eighty, no longer able to panic about the touching, now fully panicking about *the stain*.

There's a giant stain down the front of Dev's shirt. Charlie's fingers itch to soak it before it fully sets. Dev starts talking again, but Charlie can't make out the words. A thick, buzzing sound has filled his ears, and his eyes are unable to look at anything—*think about anything*—but the stain on Dev's white shirt.

(This is definitely about the stain and only the stain, and not about what happened before the stain, when Dev stood between his legs, and Charlie's entire body ignited.)

He knows the stain isn't literally getting bigger, but it feels like it is. It's getting bigger and bigger and bigger, and Charlie's skin is getting tighter and tighter. He tries to revert to a coping strategy, count to thirty in German, but the spiral is too strong, and he is unable to latch onto any thought but *stain*.

Stain stain *stain*.

If he doesn't do something about it *right now*, he'll peel off his own skin.

Without thinking, he reaches out for the bottom of Dev's white T-shirt and pulls. "Take off your shirt!"

Dev

Charlie's fist is knotted in the fabric of his shirt. Dev takes another large step backward until it's not. "Excuse me?"

Dev knows, professionally speaking, getting drunk alone with Charlie Winshaw is maybe not the smartest thing he's ever done, but it felt so good to finally open up to someone about everything with Ryan—to have someone *listen*, to have someone give him permission to let go of the Fun Dev mask a tiny bit. Just for a minute.

In his defense, he could not have predicted Charlie would start demanding he remove articles of clothing.

Charlie springs off the stool. "You need to take your shirt off so we can soak the stain." He rushes into the small kitchen, flings open cupboards, pulling things down violently. "Why is there no white vinegar in this house?"

"Well, it's a fake house. . . ."

"Dish soap will have to work."

It isn't until Charlie has filled a bowl with warm water and Dawn dish soap that Dev realizes what's going on. "It's just a shirt, Charlie. They come in Costco three-packs. Don't stress about it."

"I can't just not stress about it!" Charlie's fists slam onto the countertop. "My mind doesn't work that way!"

And *oh*.

Until this exact moment, Dev assumed Charlie's social awkwardness was the product of generalized anxiety and too many Friday nights spent in front of a computer screen instead of out in the world with other humans. It hadn't occurred to him it could be something else.

Briefly, viciously, Ryan's "head case" creeps back into his mind. But then he's thinking about Charlie's constant fear of saying the wrong thing, and Charlie's fear of letting other people get close, and Dev wonders if maybe there isn't something very specific Charlie Winshaw doesn't want other people to see.

The anger fades from Charlie's posture as quickly as it appeared, and Dev crosses the kitchen and puts a cautious hand on Charlie's shoulder. "Okay," he says quietly. "We'll soak the shirt."

Dev pulls the T-shirt up over his head, and Charlie's eyes travel the distance between his clavicle and his hipbones before they fix themselves back on the bowl of soapy water. "Um, we should soak it for fifteen minutes." Charlie sets the timer on his phone. "And then put it in the wash."

"Okay," Dev says again. He knows the signs of Charlie's anxiety now—the way his shoulders rise up to his ears, the way his eyebrows compress together, his mouth a painful grimace, his eyes hazy. Dev starts tapping a pattern over and over again with two fingers onto Charlie's shoulder.

Charlie watches Dev's fingers. "How do you . . . ?" He seizes an awkward breath. "It's Morse code. For 'calm.' "

"Is it? Huh." Dev keeps drumming the pattern. His voice is low, quiet. *Calm.* He's not sure where the *calm* is coming from, but calm is what Charlie needs, so Dev pulls it up from some secret wellspring he didn't know he had. "I've seen you do this on set when you're anxious. When it gets like this, how can I help?"

Charlie swallows. "No one has ever asked me that before." He looks back at Dev, and his eyes linger this time. They're close enough for Dev to smell his oatmeal body wash and feel the way Charlie tenses, tightens a bit beneath Dev's fingers. Dev is always so careful to not look at Charlie fully, but Charlie's right here, in freckle-counting range, letting Dev help him through this, and Dev is overwhelmed by how desperately he wants to help.

"Take your deep breaths," Dev whispers. Charlie takes three breaths—always exactly three—whenever he needs to calm down, and he takes a shaky one now and holds it in.

"Exhale." Charlie does, and they're so close, Charlie's breath is humid on Dev's throat. "Again."

Charlie takes another slow, painful breath, and Dev can see it strain against the buttons on Charlie's shirt.

"Last one."

Charlie takes his third breath, deep and clear, and Dev slips his fingers into Charlie's hair as he waits for the exhale. He teases apart Charlie's thick blond curls, massaging his scalp. In this moment, it feels like Charlie is wide open for him. A week of puzzle pieces, sci-fi shows, and the smallest hints of a hard childhood, but at two in the morning in the guesthouse kitchen, it almost feels like he's glimpsing Charlie Winshaw in his entirety—anxious and obsessive and still so fucking beautiful—leaning into Dev like there's some secret part of Charlie that wants to let other people in but doesn't know how. "I'm sorry I'm such a . . . burden."

That word opens a fissure inside Dev's chest. *Burden*. The way he felt as a kid every time his mom got off work early to take him to therapy; the way he felt every time his dad just wanted to spend a fun Saturday together, but he was too restless or too lethargic, too loud or too quiet, spontaneously crying in front of a Rodin sculpture at the North Carolina Museum of Art. The way he felt every time they sat him down and begged him to *just tell them what was wrong*, and even though he loved words—loved using words to build stories and escape hatches from the real world—he could never find the right ones to help his parents understand his heart and his mind.

"You're not a burden, Charlie. Let me take care of you. It's my job."

For one more second, he does. Charlie exhales and arches into Dev's hand. Just as quickly, he pulls away, tripping into the cabinets behind him.

"Are you okay?"

"Uh, yeah. *Yes*. No, that helped, so . . . thank you. But I should . . . bed."

"What about the shirt?" Dev points to the bowl on the counter, but Charlie's already out of the kitchen, rushing into his bedroom.

Dev stands there staring at the closed door for a long time after Charlie's locked himself away behind it.

Charlie

He doesn't sleep. He twists himself into a thousand anxious knots between starched sheets that aren't his, in a bed that's not his, in a room that's not his. He stares up at a popcorn ceiling in the dark and counts dots into the thousands. He hasn't had an episode that severe in years.

As a kid, long before he knew what the term *compulsion* meant, he would get stuck in these patterns he couldn't explain. He would sit on the swings at recess, reciting the same storybooks from memory over and over again until he got it just right; he would have to spit up his saliva into tissues because he was terrified if he swallowed he would choke on it; he would have to do every school assignment *perfectly*, even if it meant spending hours on a single hand turkey for Thanksgiving. Being perfect was the only way to ensure everything was safe and everything was healthy.

Then he grew up. He had good teachers who took a vested interest in his intelligence. His good teachers found him good therapists, who provided him with good treatment and good meds, and for the most part, his intrusive thoughts and compulsions haven't controlled his adult life. Not in a long time. Not until he lost his damn mind over two drops of bourbon on a white T-shirt.

He had an episode in front of Dev, and now Dev's going to act differently. People always do.

Except . . . Dev tried to understand, which people almost never do.

Let me take care of you.

Charlie punches his pillows, trying to get comfortable, but it's no use. His brain is a runaway train, and he's never going to sleep. He does calculus in his head until it's an acceptable hour to get up. Then he does the most strenuous exercise video he can find on YouTube as punishment for the Bourbon Stain Incident, for the way he can't seem to keep it all together, even now, when it matters the most.

When exercise doesn't help, he calls his therapist to schedule an emergency session, takes a Xanax, and throws himself into the shower. He puts off facing Dev for as long as he can, then forces himself to go into the kitchen to deal with the fallout.

He finds his roommate dancing to Leland Barlow in front of the stove. Something is burning. "I'm making brunch," Dev announces, flinging his spatula like a baton. "And yes, the pancakes are vegan and gluten-free. Do you want blueberries in yours?"

"Um . . ." Charlie doesn't know what to make of this scene. Is Dev's plan to butter him up with baked goods before he stages a mental illness intervention? (It wouldn't be the first time—Josh once bought him a new micro soldering kit before he told Charlie he couldn't do interviews on behalf of the company anymore.)

"I'm taking that as a yes," Dev says, sprinkling blueberries into the batter on the skillet. "Do you need help deciding who you're going to send home at tonight's ceremony?"

Dev deposits a plate of dark brown pancakes in front of Charlie. "Uh, what?"

"You've got to send home two more contestants tonight, and I think it's between Shawna, Emily, and Lauren S."

"Who is Shawna again?"

"Exactly."

Charlie picks up his fork and knife and begins cutting his pancake into meticulous little squares, waiting for Dev to pull the rug out from under him, waiting for Dev to act less Dev and more like people do whenever he has a breakdown.

"How are the pancakes?"

Somehow both burned *and* raw in the middle. "Delicious."

"Be honest, Charlie."

"I think I already have food poisoning."

Dev laughs, and Charlie stares at his mouth. He doesn't understand what's *happening*. Why isn't Dev being awkward around him like his colleagues at WinHan used to be after an episode, avoiding eye contact like they were embarrassed for him, skirting him in the halls like he was a bomb set to go off? Why isn't Dev confronting him about the Bourbon Stain Incident? Why isn't he looking at Charlie with the mixture of pity and fear he memorized on Josh's face?

"Well, this was a failure," Dev says, grabbing the plate and sliding the contents straight into the trash. "Should I send Jules to get takeout? I'm thinking breakfast burritos."

Charlie stares at Dev in his hideous cargo shorts and his ill-fitting T-shirt, toothpaste in the corner of his mouth, and he finally accepts Dev is never going to pull out the rug.

Charlie hasn't met many people like this—people who don't make assumptions about you when they discover your brain doesn't work like theirs; people who don't judge you; people who simply stay with you and ask what they can do to help. People who trustingly hand you all of themselves in PDF form.

"You're staring at me. Do I have something on my face?"

"Literally always," Charlie says, and Dev laughs again, louder this time. Charlie feels the sound unlocking all his twisted fears. "I have OCD," he says before he can't.

Dev props an elbow on the countertop and leans into his hand. "Okay."

"Real OCD. Not the thing where people think it's cute that they're anal about organizing their pen cup."

"Yes, I figured."

"And I have generalized anxiety. And a panic disorder."

"Okay," Dev says again. Like it truly is *okay*.

Charlie feels a loosening in his chest, an unburdening. He's only ever talked about this with Parisa, but she always looks at him like he's a rare, exotic bird living in her attic, and she's hoping he'll one day fly out an open window into the world.

Dev is looking at him like he's a man sitting on a kitchen stool who didn't like his pancakes. It's as if nothing has changed.

Charlie takes only one breath. "Okay."

Dev comes around the counter toward Charlie on the stool. For a second, he stands close, like he did last night, crowding between Charlie's legs. Charlie becomes hyperaware of his skin against the seams of his clothes. Dev reaches up to ruffle Charlie's hair again, but he's got a pained look on his face. "You know you still deserve to have this love story. Right?"

Charlie swallows a weird lump forming in the back of his throat. Dev's fingers are still resting in his hair, and Charlie looks up.

"You deserve love," Dev says again, "and I honestly think Angie and Daphne are both good fits for you. I think both of them will love you, Charlie. Just as you are."

Dev steps back. Charlie closes his legs. "Angie and Daphne," he repeats.

Dev nods. "Oh, yeah. It's definitely going to come down to the two of them. So, breakfast burritos?"

Charlie tries to smile. "Breakfast burritos."

Story notes for editors:
Season 37, Episode 3

Story producer:
Ryan Parker

Air date:
Monday, September 27, 2021

Executive producer:
Maureen Scott

Scene: Daphne, Angie, and Sabrina debrief Daphne's Courting Date
Location: Poolside, *Ever After* castle

Daphne: The date was going great. He was so sweet when I panicked about the hot-air balloon, and then I ruined it by pushing him at dinner.

Angie: It sounds like *he* ruined it by being unable to answer a fairly basic question.

Sabrina: It's not unreasonable to expect a man you're dating to be able to articulate what he's looking for in a partner.

Angie: And if he's looking for a Thomas Kincaid thousand-piece jigsaw, we should all know that now.

Daphne: [*Cut to the close-up of her nervously pushing her hair behind her ear.*] He obviously gets . . . I don't know . . . *anxious* sometimes.

Sabrina: I don't think you're allowed to talk about things like that on *Ever After*.

Angie: [*Shot of Angie reaching out to put a hand on Daphne's thigh.*] Girl, don't take on the blame for this. You didn't do anything wrong, and you shouldn't beat yourself up.

Daphne: I shouldn't have expected him to talk about serious stuff on our first real date.

Angie: Honestly, *men*. This is why it's so much easier dating women.

Sabrina: You're definitely not allowed to talk about *that* on *Ever After*.

Daphne: [*Close-up of her staring down at Angie's hand on her thigh.*] You've dated . . . women?

Angie: What, they don't have bisexuals on the Georgia pageant circuit?

Maureen's note to editors: Cut this entire scene and replace it with the one of Megan and Delilah shit-talking the other women in the hot tub.

WEEK THREE

Pasadena—Wednesday, June 23, 2021
12 Contestants and 46 Days Remaining

Charlie

He can't sleep again. He hasn't been able to sleep in days.

It's one in the morning, and he's tried meditation, tried journaling, tried calling Parisa in the hopes the sound of her familiar voice might soothe him to sleep, but none of it has worked.

He should be exhausted, both emotionally and physically. At today's Group Quest, the women competed in a relay race to rescue him from a tower (*Ever After*'s answer to feminism, apparently), and when Daphne won again, half the women revolted, with Megan leading the mob, claiming the game was rigged. (Which, obviously, it was.) Angie and Sabrina defended Daphne, and Charlie spent most of the day trying to mend fences and prevent an all-out war. The producers loved every minute of it.

There's no point in counting asbestos dots in the dark for the third night in a row, so he climbs out of bed, clicks on the light, and fishes out his iPad. He hasn't opened the email Dev sent since the Bourbon Stain Incident, but he opens it now and climbs back in bed. He starts to read Dev's script.

It is definitely all of Dev.

As he reads the dialogue, he can hear Dev's voice, almost as if he's lying on the bed next to Charlie, reading it aloud to him. He doesn't know a damn thing about screenplays, and jargon like *MCU* and *EXT* means nothing to him, but somehow, he can imagine the world Dev is creating with his words all the same. The protagonist, Ravi Patel, *is* Dev: a hopeless romantic who has been unlucky in love but is still convinced of its almighty power.

There is a meet-cute, as Dev would call it. A miscommunication. An enemies-to-lovers trope Charlie remembers from his days of reading *Star Trek* fanfic on his home-built laptop. About halfway through the script, Charlie realizes he has never read a story about two men falling in love before.

He pushes himself back against the headboard and draws his knees up to his chest. There is a foreign pressure in his stomach, but he ignores it, completely engrossed in Dev's story. The screenplay ends the only way it could, with an epic kiss and a happily ever after, and when it's over, Charlie stares at the blank white space at the end of the PDF for a long time. Even though it's the middle of the night, he feels compelled to talk about it. Right now.

He follows this urge all the way to Dev's bedroom door.

Dev's awake, sitting cross-legged with his laptop, wearing a loose-fitting T-shirt featuring a young man's face surrounded by rainbow starbursts. When he looks up and sees Charlie, he smiles. "Hey. What are you doing awake?"

Charlie steps into the room, then pauses when he notices the white fingerprints down Dev's shirt. "Are you eating white cheddar popcorn in your bed at three in the morning?"

"Did you come in here at three in the morning to judge me?"

"No." Charlie sits down on the edge of Dev's bed. He gestures to Dev's shirt. "Did you get that at a Leland Barlow concert?"

Dev plucks at the image of the man's face on his chest. "What? Oh, no. I missed him when he was in LA last year. Tickets were expensive, and I *thought* Ryan was going to get them for me for Christmas, but he bought a PS5 instead. Jules ordered me the shirt online."

"Do you like video games?" Charlie asks, but he already knows the answer.

"It was more a household present. Look, is this why you came in here? To once again remind me that my ex-boyfriend never really cared about me?"

"I read your script."

"Oh. You did?" Dev pushes up his glasses with two fingers. "What did you think?"

Charlie smiles. "I *loved* it."

Dev doesn't let himself smile back, like he's afraid to let Charlie see how much those words mean to him. Only the tiny curl in the corner of his mouth gives him away. "You did?"

"It's so good. It's *better* than good. It's fucking amazing!"

"I can't believe you just said *fuck*. . . ."

"You don't need Maureen's help. You should totally sell your script."

"Well, in order to sell a script, you sort of have to let other people read it."

Charlie shifts on the bed so he's sitting cross-legged, like Dev, their knees forming two corners of a parallelogram. "Who's read it?"

"Well, there's you." Dev holds up one finger to count it off. "And then there's you."

He's still holding up one finger.

Charlie is the only person Dev has let read his script. He doesn't know what to do with that revelation. He's not the person people open up to—he's not the person you trust with *all of yourself.* He feels this frantic need to deserve Dev's trust. "Parisa, my publicist, works for an agency with offices here in LA, and a bunch of their clients are industry types. I bet she could get your script to an agent."

"No, you don't have to—"

"I want to. It should be a movie. People should see it. I've never—" He realizes what he's about to say just before he says it, and not quickly enough to *not* say it. "I've never read a story about that before."

"You mean a romantic comedy?"

Charlie pulls at a loose thread in Dev's comforter. "No, about, um—"

"Gay people?" Dev supplies.

He starts to stand up. "Sorry."

Dev reaches out for his legs to pin him in place, and something hot comes to life deep in his stomach, like he's taken a shot of bourbon. "Why are you sorry? Sit back down."

Charlie should not sit back down. He never should have come in here, and he feels weirdly vulnerable in his oversize Stanford T-shirt and a pair of sweatpants, sitting on Dev's bed, so close to Dev. "No, I should just . . . I should—"

"Charlie," Dev says, holding those two syllables on his tongue like they're breakable. "Why did you come bursting into my room at three in the morning?"

"Because . . . because I finished your script."

Dev leans forward and the loose collar on his Leland Barlow shirt slides to reveal the slope of his neck where it meets his swimmer's shoulders. The dip of his clavicle looks deep enough to swallow Charlie's whole hand. "And why were you reading my script at three in the morning?"

"I couldn't sleep."

"Why couldn't you sleep?" Dev asks. It's a dangerous question. Dev's hands are still on his legs. "Are you stressed about the show?"

"Oh. *Yes*. The show. Definitely. I can't sleep because I'm stressed about the show."

Dev nods in understanding. "It seems like you're connecting more with the women. Don't you think?"

He considers it. In some ways, yes. He enjoys talking about tech stuff with Delilah when she's not provoking drama with Megan, and he enjoys Sabrina's stories about her travels, when she's not intimidating the shit out of him. He likes spending time with Angie, who is smart and clever and makes him laugh, and he likes spending time with Daphne, who is patient and kind and understanding. But it's like he told Parisa—he likes the women, but he doesn't *like them*. He isn't here for that.

"Sort of," he says carefully.

"Do you see yourself developing real feelings for anyone?"

"I . . . uh . . ."

"Come on, Charlie. You can talk to me about this stuff. Not just as your producer, but as your friend."

He falters. "Are . . . are we friends?"

"I'm pretty sure I'm your only friend."

"I have other friends."

"Besides your publicist?"

"I have *one* friend," he corrects. Dev laughs, and the combination of Dev's laughter and his sleep deprivation makes Charlie feel drunk.

Dev leans even closer. "I'm going to say this as your friend. I think you've gotten really good at talking yourself out of your feelings."

Dev places his hand across Charlie's chest, and a trapdoor appears just south of his sternum. Charlie's heart falls through, crashing into his stomach. *One Mississippi.* Dev talks quickly like he's afraid Charlie is going to pull away.

(Charlie isn't going to pull away. Dev's hand is on his chest, and he's not about to pull away.)

"Try listening to your heart. You have some amazing women left on this show, and you deserve happiness."

Dev's still got his hand pressed to Charlie's chest, burning him through the thin layer of his T-shirt. *Two Mississippi.* Dev swallows, and his Adam's apple hitches. *Three . . .* Charlie follows the swallow down the elegant column of Dev's throat, imagines following it all the way down the length of Dev's torso, to the patch of hair on his stomach visible in the place where his T-shirt has bunched at the waist. He's not sure why he's thinking about Dev's stomach, or how he knows Dev's shirt has crept up in the corner.

Except.

Except he does know. He knew as soon as he read Dev's script. A slow, sinking realization that only became clear when he saw it mirrored back to him on the page.

The way he feels when Dev touches his hair, the way he feels when Dev touches his hand, the way he feels *every single time* this man touches him. Those feelings didn't make sense because he's never felt them before. Now they make perfect sense, and *God*—he wishes he could go back to his ignorance.

He wishes he could stop thinking about all of this, wishes he could stop thinking about tracing the imaginary line from Dev's slightly parted lips down the length of his body, and he wishes just *picturing* doing so didn't bring the pressure back to his lower stomach in a way he now understands too well. He leaps off the bed, positioning his body away from Dev's view.

"I should let you sleep."

"It's fine, Charlie."

It's definitely not *fine*.

Charlie throws himself into his own bedroom, slams his door, and leans back against it. His heart hurls itself against his chest so loudly he's convinced Dev can hear it from his room. He never should have asked to read Dev's script, never should have gone into Dev's room, never should have come on this show.

Because things were fine before, when he was not feeling things, when all his feelings were stashed away, unexamined.

He's still leaning against his bedroom door, and his heart is still thrashing violently, and his body is still . . . doing body-like things. It won't *stop* doing body-like things. He wants to alleviate the pressure, but he can't, because it's Dev, and Dev is his *handler*, and his friend, apparently, and he's right on the other side of his bedroom wall.

But then he's thinking about Dev on the other side of the wall. Shirt loose around his throat. White cheddar popcorn dust on his fingers. And Charlie decides, just this once. Just to get rid of these feelings before they devour him. He thinks about Dev's script, and what Dev's voice would sound like reading the script aloud to him, close to his ear, breath on Charlie's throat as he pushes aside the waistband of his sweatpants.

And *holy shit*—Dev's knees and Dev's mouth and Dev's Adam's apple. He tries thinking about Daphne's pretty blue eyes instead, but he can only see Dev's dark ones, peering intensely at him behind his glasses. He tries to conjure the image of Angie's soft body, but it's superimposed with Dev's wide shoulders, the slenderness of his hips, the sharp points and the beautiful brown skin and the smell of him.

He doesn't let himself think about what it means, or why he feels this way. He imagines Dev beside him—Dev's hand instead of his own—and that's all it takes to send him over the edge. He shoves his mouth into the crook of his left elbow, so he doesn't make a sound.

An hour later, after he's showered, he enjoys the first night of good sleep he's had in days.

Dev

He shouldn't have pushed.

Dev paces at the foot of his bed. *Why does he always have to push?*

Things have been good. He's gotten Charlie to open up *just enough*—enough for the occasional flash of sarcasm and gentle teasing; enough for compound-complex sentences; enough to start taking his antidepressants every morning in front of Dev; enough for smiling (sometimes) and laughing (like, twice). Just enough for Dev to feel a little wild with wanting more, so that when Charlie came into his bedroom in gray sweatpants, complimenting his script, Dev pushed. And Dev spooked him.

Dev grabs another handful of white cheddar popcorn and resumes his anxious pacing. Of course Charlie freaked out when Dev pushed him on his feelings about the women. Charlie has probably spent his entire life thinking he doesn't deserve love, to the point that he's taken it off the table completely. Dev thinks Charlie's probably never let himself fall in love, out of fear of rejection, so how could he recognize the feelings he has now for Daphne?

Maybe Dev should go into his room. Check on him. Talk to him.

Next door, he hears Charlie go into the bathroom and turn on the shower.

Or . . . yeah, Dev should probably just go to sleep instead.

He doesn't sleep, though, and when he goes into the kitchen the next morning feeling half-dead, Jules is already there with a bag of breakfast sandwiches from crafty. Charlie is shoving a load of clothes into the washing machine.

"The assistants can do your laundry for you," Dev says as he comes up behind him.

Charlie nearly jumps out of his skin. "It's fine. I . . . I can—" He cuts off and doesn't bother trying to resuscitate the sentence.

Jules hands Charlie his breakfast. "Charlie, you look like you're auditioning to be the thirteenth Cylon on *Battlestar Galactica*," she teases.

Charlie blinks. "Sorry."

Apparently Dev pushed so hard he shoved Charlie all the way back to night-one awkwardness.

Jules and Dev try to draw him out of his shell on the drive to set, but he refuses to be baited, even when Dev loudly declares *Westworld* the greatest science-fiction show of all time. At set, when Dev reaches to adjust Charlie's crown, Charlie pulls away so violently, he trips backward over an equipment crate. He's jittery with the women, too, confusing the Laurens and overtly rolling his eyes when Megan pulls him aside to tell him Daphne isn't here for the right reasons.

"What the hell is wrong with your boy?" Jules asks as they watch Charlie literally duck out of an oncoming kiss from Delilah.

"I have no idea."

Jules puts her hands on her hips and cocks her head up at him.

"Okay, well, maybe Charlie came into my room late last night. . . ."

"Oh, he *did*, did he?"

"What?"

"What?"

"Charlie came into my room, and we talked about his connections with the women."

"Oh."

"What did you think I meant?"

She assumes a casual position. "That. Obviously."

"I was trying to help him realize his feelings for Daphne, and—"

Jules cackles. "Wait. You're serious? You actually think Charlie has feelings for *Daphne*?"

"Yeah. Why?" He chews on his thumbnail. "Do you think Angie is a better fit for him?"

Jules sighs and reaches over to scratch his arm. "Sure, Dev. That's what I think."

Every season, at the end of week three, before they winnow the contestants down to ten and winnow the crew down to essential personnel for the travel portion of the show, they always host a gigantic "ball" before the Crowning Ceremony. Twelve women competing to dance with *one* man. It's *always* a shitshow.

When the town car pulls up to the Peninsula Beverly Hills, Charlie is a bundle of nerves, which means Dev is a bundle of nerves, though his anxiety is at least in part caused by the Sour

Patch Kids and nitro coffee he had for dinner. While Charlie is whisked away into hair and makeup, Dev distracts himself from his restless worrying about Charlie by checking on the women. They're gathered together in a conference room that's been converted into a dressing space. They're all strapped into Disney-inspired ball gowns with cinched waists and tulle skirts.

He finds Angie, Daphne, and Sabrina huddled in the corner surrounded by a surplus of fabric and In-N-Out drive-thru bags smuggled in by Kennedy, the handler who replaced him. They've all got napkins shoved down the front of their dresses like bibs. It's charmingly adorable.

Charlie's already decided which two women he's sending home tonight, so in addition to these three women, it's Delilah, Lauren L., Becca, Whitney, Rachel, Jasmine, and Megan—whom Maureen insists on keeping for a few more weeks—who will be flying on to New Orleans with them tomorrow.

"Well, if it isn't our future husband's keeper." Angie raises an animal-style burger at him in greeting. "How's our boyfriend doing?"

"He's . . ." Dev pulls a Charlie and doesn't bother finishing that sentence.

Daphne also pulls a Charlie and furrows her brow intensely. "He's seemed upset about something all week. Is there anything we can do to help?"

He shakes his head. If Dev knew how to help get Charlie back to where they were before, he would've done it already.

"Hey, Daphne, I was wondering," Megan says as she stomps over in a dress clearly inspired by Maleficent. The wardrobe department is not subtle. "Are you going to ask Charlie to dance at the ball, or are you hoping Angie asks you instead?"

Daphne turns the same color pink as her *Sleeping Beauty* gown, and Angie throws a French fry at Megan. "Fuck off, you homophobic twat."

Megan wheels around to Dev. "Did you hear what she just said to me?"

Dev points to his ear, like someone is shouting in his headset, so he doesn't have to openly acknowledge her casual homophobia. Then someone actually *is* shouting in his headset. It's Ryan. "Dev, get over here. We have a problem."

As out of shape as he is, it only takes thirty seconds for him to sprint across the hotel to Charlie's wardrobe room. Still, in those thirty seconds, Dev imagines dozens of horrible scenarios involving Charlie. What he finds is worse than anything he could've envisioned.

Charlie is standing in the middle of the room wearing nothing but his plastic crown and the smallest pair of black boxer briefs. He is basically *naked*, the muscles of his abdomen all funneling down to a V pointing toward his crotch like a neon flashing arrow. The sight is, in a word, pornographic.

Dev shouldn't look but he does. At all of Charlie. So much tan skin, strong thighs, faint freckles along his collarbone, muscles reduplicating down his abdomen, and still, those big gray eyes, so innocent and sweet and contradictory to everything else.

Ryan conveniently steps in between Dev and his view of Charlie's obliques. "He's refusing to wear the Prince Charming suit!" Ryan screams, as if Charlie isn't there to explain himself.

Charlie chokes. "I'm sorry. I'm so . . . so sorry."

"If you're sorry, *put on the suit!*"

"It's wool. I'm sorry, but I just can't . . . I don't wear wool."

Charlie's deep into a spiral about this, and Dev pushes aside his thoughts about the nakedness so he can tap out Morse code against Charlie's bare shoulder. Then he turns his attention back to Ryan. "It sounds like you need to get Charlie a new suit."

"We're filming in thirty minutes. How the *fuck* do you propose I get a new suit that quickly?"

Dev shrugs. "You're the supervising producer on set. You'll figure it out. It's in Charlie's file that he doesn't wear wool. It's also *June.*"

Ryan grinds his teeth and violently grabs his walkie-talkie. "We need a new suit, pronto," he snaps as he storms out of the wardrobe room with a PA on his heels.

Then they're alone in the dressing room, and Dev realizes he hasn't really been alone with Charlie since the 3 a.m. conversation.

"Thank you," Charlie manages, his eyes on the ground. "For sticking up for me."

"You never have to thank me, Charlie. This is my job."

"Your job," Charlie echoes slowly. Dev wants to push. He wants to poke and prod. He wants to grab Charlie by both shoulders. *Come back to me,* he would scream. *Don't lock yourself up again.*

Skylar bursts into the room, and Dev takes a step back. "What is this about a new— *Son of a bitch.*" Skylar stops short when she sees Charlie. "Jesus Christ. Can someone please get this man a robe?"

A different PA materializes out of thin air with a plush hotel robe, and Charlie sticks his arms inside but doesn't tie it at the waist, like he thinks the robe is to keep him warm. It hangs open, his body still on display. Dev adopts a comical, vaguely British accent, because surely laughing about this will make it easier for Dev to stop staring at Charlie's body. "Oh, love"—Dev fastens the front of the robe himself—"you clearly don't know what you look like."

Charlie lifts those huge gray eyes to Dev's face. A splotchy pink blush has spread across his throat, and the absolute last thing Dev does is stare at any part of Charlie that is blushing right now. "What do I look like?" Charlie asks innocently.

The door to the wardrobe room opens again, and this time Maureen Scott swans in. "What seems to be the holdup?"

"The suit for the ball was made out of wool, and Charlie doesn't wear wool," Dev explains. "We're finding him a different suit."

"Oh, are we?" Maureen asks, her tone barely hinting at the layers of anger simmering beneath her affable surface. "And who authorized this?"

"I did," Ryan says as he comes rushing back carrying a plastic dry-cleaner bag.

"Well, let's hope our little diva finds this suit acceptable," Maureen says with a smile. Charlie is wrestled into a suit an assistant purchased off a hotel guest, and Maureen watches him with a single raised eyebrow, her manicured nails tapping her forearm.

"Lovely," she says when Charlie's dressed. She grips him too tightly by both shoulders. "Don't you look like the perfect Prince Charming ready for his ball?"

Quite predictably, it's a shitshow.

Charlie doesn't recover easily from the drama with his suit, and Megan doesn't recover easily from her confrontation with Angie. It's obvious the producers are spurring her along; in real life, away from the cameras and the pressure to win, Megan is probably a mostly decent person, if somewhat emotionally immature. But maybe because of her emotional immaturity—or maybe because she's desperate to promote her YouTube channel by any means necessary—Megan gives in to the show's worst impulses when it comes to pitting women against each other. At the start of the evening, she throws a fit, screams at Angie, then locks herself in the dressing room until Charlie is forced to come console her.

Daphne doesn't recover from the earlier confrontation easily either, and in the middle of the ball, she unexpectedly makes a huge show of asking to speak with Charlie privately.

Angie is there, grabbing Daphne's arm, hissing, "You don't have to prove anything to anyone, Daph."

She lightly nudges Angie away, takes Charlie's hand, and guides him into a tiny space next to a bathroom. Dev, Jules, and Ryan all cram themselves in behind the two cameras.

"Is everything okay?" Charlie asks Daphne as they sit side by side on a bench.

"Yes, of course. I just wanted to . . . talk." Daphne clears her throat. "We haven't had much time tonight, and I want to make sure you know how much I like you."

"Oh." Charlie visibly relaxes. "I like you, too, Daphne."

She pushes her hair behind her ears. "I wanted to *show* you how much I like you," she says, like she's trying so hard to sound brave. She puts her hand on Charlie's thigh, and Dev understands exactly what's about to happen. He has a weird impulse to shout *cut*. To intervene. To rescue Charlie and Daphne both.

But then Daphne is pulling him into a passionate kiss, and Charlie doesn't look like he needs to be rescued. He meets every ounce of Daphne's fervor with his own. They're moving too quickly; she slides her hand up to his groin; he pulls her on top of his lap. His hands are in her hair, around her waist, up the front of her pink dress.

"Finally"—Ryan exhales quietly—"these two are giving us something we can sell."

Cut, Dev wants to scream. *Someone call cut.*

Four days ago, he told Charlie to listen to his heart, and here Charlie is, doing just that, and it's good. It's *right*. It's the way things are supposed to be. Charlie is their prince, and Daphne is the perfect princess, and this is all how it's supposed to go. So why does Dev feel like everything is terribly wrong?

Jules reaches over and gives Dev's arm puppy scratches.

This is good.

"Wait, sorry . . . just . . . " Charlie ducks his head away from Daphne's, hands on her waist, sliding her off his lap.

Daphne looks confused as she adjusts her clothes. "What's wrong?"

"I'm sorry, but I . . ." Charlie clears his throat. He has lipstick in his chin dimple. "I was trying, but I don't think I . . . I'm sorry, but—"

"But you *what*?" Daphne pushes impatiently. "You were trying to *what*, Charlie?"

Sweat coats Charlie's hairline, and he turns to find Dev behind the cameras. Daphne turns to look at Dev, too, and it's an obvious fourth-wall break, but no one calls cut. Daphne reaches up for Charlie's face to pull his gaze back to her. "I'm trying, too," she says. "Just talk to me. What's wrong?"

"I can't." Charlie snaps, and he's off the bench, lunging forward, lunging toward Dev. Confused, one of the cameras swings around as Charlie catapults into Dev's arms, and then Charlie's weight is propelling them both backward, toward a single-stall bathroom. They trip, half fall, and then Charlie's slamming the bathroom door closed behind them, cutting them off from the cameras. Charlie tries to claw at his mic belt to turn it off, but his entire body is shaking. He turns to dry-heave into the sink.

Dev has seen Charlie build toward a dozen panic attacks, but he's never seen him like this. Dev is paralyzed, with no idea how to help.

Outside the bathroom, someone pounds on the door, and Daphne's voice floats through. "Charlie! Come out! Talk to me!"

Dev ignores the knocking, and Daphne, and Ryan screaming in his earpiece. All he can see is Charlie, shaking, choking, heaving. He finally springs into action. "Breathe," he whispers as he puts a hand on Charlie's back.

"Don't touch me, Dev!" Charlie explodes in a voice Dev's never heard before.

Dev pulls back as if Charlie burned him. "Okay. I'm sorry."

Charlie drops his head. "Wait. No, I'm sorry." He tears at his hair. "I'm so sorry, Dev. Shit, I'm sorry."

"It's okay. We're okay." Dev puts one hand tentatively on Charlie's shoulder, then another. "Tell me what you need."

"I . . . I need . . . I need . . ."

"Take your deep breaths," Dev says, quiet but firm, and they take three perfectly synchronized deep breaths together. "Tell me what you need, Charlie."

"I need . . ."

He fumbles for words, and when he can't seem to find any, he falls forward until his chest bumps against Dev's. He doesn't right himself. Instead, he grabs onto the back of Dev's T-shirt with both hands, presses his forehead into Dev's throat, telling Dev what he needs in the only way he can communicate right now. He needs to be hugged. Held.

Charlie is heavy, but Dev wants to be able to hold him up. That's his job. To help Charlie. To support him through this in whatever way he can.

He wraps one arm around Charlie's wide shoulders and with the other winds his fingers into Charlie's hair, massaging his scalp until Charlie relaxes against him. Every bit of tension that leaves Charlie's body somehow ends up in Dev's, until he's standing there rigid and stiff-limbed, muscles shaking from the effort, but it's fine. He can bear it.

"I'm screwing everything up," Charlie pants against Dev's clavicle.

"Oh, love, you're not screwing anything up," he says, and he means for the *oh, love* to come out in the same patronizing, joking tone he used earlier, but the situation is too different, and the words *feel* too different. Charlie shifts in his arms so he's looking up at Dev—gray eyes and freckles, too pretty and too close.

"I *am* screwing it up," Charlie whispers. "Worse than you know."

"Well, then, we'll figure it out together. But you can't close up again, okay?"

Charlie nods.

"You've been so far away all week." Dev has no idea what drives those words out of his mouth, except it's week three, and he's so desperate to make this season work, so desperate to help Charlie find love, so desperate for this story to have the right ending. The ending Charlie *deserves*.

He thinks about Charlie on the kitchen stool, telling Dev he has OCD like that somehow makes him less worthy; Charlie sitting cross-legged on his bed at three in the morning, so terrified of feeling his feelings. Charlie wearing nothing, asking *what do I look like?* And Charlie right here, right now, in his arms, being so vulnerable, and quite suddenly, it's Dev who is noticeably *feeling his feelings*. His feelings are pressed firmly against Charlie's waist.

Charlie freezes, and Dev freezes, and then Dev unfreezes, trying to disentangle their limbs without giving away how utterly humiliated he is—because he's *twenty-eight, not fourteen*—but Charlie doesn't make it easy, hand still pressed into the small of Dev's back, and Dev prays that means Charlie hasn't noticed.

There's a loud click of metal on metal, a shout on the other side of the bathroom door. The door swings open, and Charlie and Dev spring apart. A hotel employee is holding a key, having unlocked the door from the outside, and behind him: two cameras, Daphne Reynolds, Jules Lu, Skylar Jones, Ryan Parker, and Maureen Scott.

Charlie doesn't look at Dev as he steps out of the bathroom, and Dev doesn't look at his bosses, his ex, or Charlie's girlfriend. He can barely concentrate on anything but the blood pumping in his own ears as Charlie apologizes to Daphne for his behavior. They shift back to the ballroom, to the Crowning Ceremony, where Charlie passes out his ten tiaras, asking each woman if she is interested in becoming his princess. The two women who are sent home both cry, clinging to the front of Charlie's suit the way Charlie clung to Dev in the bathroom.

Dev tamps down all feelings associated with what happened in the bathroom until filming is over. Until the crew starts deconstructing the set. Until Dev can vanish to the hotel bar, order himself a whisky neat, and forget about this entire night.

Story notes for editors:
Season 37, Episode 4

Story producer:
Maureen Scott

Air date:
Monday, October 4, 2021

Executive producer:
Maureen Scott

Scene: Pre–Crowning Ceremony ball, one-on-one confessionals with contestants

Location: Shot on location in and around the Peninsula ballroom

Producer [voice off camera]: ~~What do you think about the other women in the castle?~~

Megan: I literally don't think about the other women at all.

Producer: ~~What about Daphne? Does she act arrogant at the castle when the cameras aren't around?~~

Megan: Daphne ~~isn't arrogant. She~~ is insecure. That's why she felt the need to pull Charles away in the middle of the ball.

Producer: ~~What do the other women think about Daphne?~~

Megan: The other women all buy into her whole wide-eyed, innocent Disney princess routine. I'm the only one who sees through her bullshit fakeness.

Producer [voice off camera]: ~~What do you think of Megan?~~

Delilah: Oh, she's straight-up crazy. Fun, but definitely not wife material. And it's insane to think Charles would choose someone like her. He needs someone who is more on his level, intellectually. Like me.

Producer [voice off camera]: ~~What do you think about Megan?~~

Angie: ~~Is this about what happened in the dressing room? With Daphne? I'm not going to apologize for what I said to her, and I'm not going to discuss it in front of the cameras.~~

Producer: ~~Megan told the cameras Daphne's insecure and fake.~~

Angie: God, Megan is such a bitch.

Producer [voice off camera]: ~~Would you describe Megan as crazy?~~

Sabrina: I don't use the word *crazy*. It's offensive and derogatory. Megan just happens to lack emotional intelligence. She could also use a punch in the face.

Producer [voice off camera]: How would you describe your relationship with Megan?

Daphne: I like all the women in the castle.

Producer: Is it true about what Megan said to you before the ball started?

Daphne: I like all the women in the castle.

Producer: Don't you want to know what Megan said about you behind your back?

Daphne: I like all the women in the castle.

Maureen's note to editors: Use this script to help splice together the footage.

WEEK FOUR

New Orleans—Sunday, June 27, 2021
10 Contestants and 42 Days Remaining

Charlie

As he sits in a plush first-class seat somewhere over Arizona, he closes his eyes and pretends like closing his eyes can erase the past twelve hours. He would especially like to erase the part where he kissed Daphne Reynolds like kissing Daphne Reynolds could solve all his problems.

Kissing Daphne Reynolds solved exactly zero problems.

All kissing Daphne did was verify he does not enjoy kissing Daphne. And not enjoying it induced a panic attack, which forced him to confront the reality that he very much does want to kiss someone else.

"Look at this!" Dev points to his knees, points to the back of the seat in front of him, points to his knees again. There is a three-inch gap between his legs and the chair. "Do you know the last time this happened on an airplane. *Never!* I've never had enough legroom in my whole life. Is this what it's like to be rich? You always have room for your whole body?"

As a contestant handler, Dev usually travels economy, so he excitedly orders his free mimosa while Skylar and Jules both sleep across the aisle. It's just the four of them. A travel crew has been in New Orleans setting things up for the past two weeks, and Skylar will meet with them as soon as they land. The rest of the crew and his ten contestants are flying out later tonight, but they wanted to give Charlie extra time to settle in.

His only consolation at the moment is that Maureen Scott doesn't travel with the show. She remains in LA with the editing team splicing together the first few episodes. For the next four weeks, she won't be around to haunt him with her fake-sweet voice and her overt manipulation of the women.

The flight attendant hands Dev a hot towel, and he looks thoroughly confused by its existence. He reaches over and drapes it across Charlie's forehead. For the length of two wild, frantic heartbeats, Dev's fingers are on Charlie's face. He shoves them away. "Stop. I'm trying to sleep."

"*Sleep?* How can you *sleep* right now?"

Dev has an inexplicable level of energy for someone who, based on the sound of his anxious pacing through the wall, didn't sleep last night. Dev jostles his knee and impatiently beats his fingers against his armrest and gets up to walk around when the seatbelt sign clicks off, presumably just for the hell of it. Charlie will take whatever Dev-reprieve he can get.

Not that distance from Dev actually helps. He tried that.

He tried avoiding Dev; he made sure they were never alone together; didn't look at him, didn't touch him. Charlie still couldn't stop thinking about him.

Then, when they were alone together last night in the bathroom, Charlie tried to dry-hump Dev mid–panic attack.

The terrifying thing is, he doesn't know what any of it *means*. He's pretty sure he's never been attracted to a man before. He's not bothered by this turn of events, though he wishes he could've chosen a *different man* for this particular sexual awakening, one who isn't his producer.

No, it's more that he can't quite wrap his brain around being attracted to *anyone*. He can appreciate the aesthetic beauty of other people, and he's had intellectual crushes on women—he's admired women, respected them, had a vague desire for an intimacy and a closeness he's never been able to achieve. But he's never really *wanted* a woman before, and his sexual fantasies about women are usually vague and abstract. They're not usually even about him.

But this—this is something else entirely. This feels wild and intoxicating, and all of his fantasies involve Charlie himself. Charlie *and Dev*.

If that were always the issue, though—if the reason he could never make things work in his relationships was simply because he was dating the wrong gender—then isn't that something he would've figured out about himself by now? It's not like he hasn't had *opportunities* with men. He's generally hit on by people of all genders equally, and he's been told on several occasions by well-intentioned men that he would make a very successful gay (whatever that means).

The first time Parisa told him she was pansexual, she said she always *knew* but repressed it for a long time. And that's not his situation. He hasn't been repressing anything.

Well, technically speaking, he's repressed a lot of things, but not *that thing*. He hasn't been subconsciously suppressing being attracted to men. *Has he?*

An image rises to the surface of his mind. He's sixteen, meeting Josh Han in their dorm room for the first time, lingering on a handshake. Then he thinks about his brothers, the names they used to call him when he cried about dirt and germs, the hateful words his father used to say, until he learned to only cry on the inside, and maybe he learned to repress it before he ever knew what "it" was.

"Whoa." Dev slides back into his seat. "What are you spiraling about right now?"

"I'm not spiraling."

"I know your spiral face."

"Well, *stop* knowing my spiral face."

"Can't. It's too distinct." Dev reaches over and grabs grabs one of Charlie's AirPods right out of his ear and inserts it (disgustingly) into his own. "Huh . . . I would not have pegged you for a Dolly Parton fan."

"Everyone loves this song," Charlie says as "Jolene" reaches the chorus. Dev nods in agreement and slumps down in his seat. If Charlie were judging by Dev's behavior alone, he would never guess that twelve hours ago, this man had held him through a panic attack. He would never guess Dev had stroked his hair and called him *love* and—no, he'd probably only imagined that last part, because Dev is acting like nothing happened at all. And if *that* had happened while they were hugging, Dev wouldn't be acting so cavalier. Except sometimes . . .

Sometimes Charlie wonders if maybe, maybe these wild feelings aren't completely one-sided. If maybe, beneath Dev's burning desire to make Charlie fall in love with Daphne Reynolds, there isn't something else.

When "Jolene" ends, Dev syncs the AirPods over to his Spotify, and Leland Barlow's "Those Evenings of the Brain" cues up.

"Can I ask, what is it about Leland Barlow? He seems like

just another generic, early-twenties British pop star with a cute face."

Dev sits up too quickly. "Excuse you. He's not just a generic British pop star! How many pop stars are openly bisexual and second-generation Indian and have achieved Leland's level of fame? And *this song*"—Dev shakes his phone—"this song's title comes from an Emily Dickinson poem, and it's a metaphor for depression. Leland is super outspoken about destigmatizing mental illness, and he manages to work that into his music while also writing, like, legitimately *amazing* pop songs. Songs that make you *feel*."

Dev works himself up into a frenzy of passion, his arms flailing and his eyes shining brightly. In this moment, in this light, his eyes remind Charlie of the dark wood Mendini violin he played in his high school orchestra, almost black around the strings, a well-loved umber brown on the edges of the lower bout. He loved that secondhand violin.

"So, yeah," Dev says, his shoulders deflating a bit. "That's why I like Leland Barlow so much."

From across the aisle, Jules throws a neck pillow at them, and the other first-class passengers glare. "Will you idiots shut up? I'm trying to sleep so we can party tonight, and y'all would be wise to do the same."

Dev plucks up the pillow and puts it on like a necklace.

"Are you going out tonight?" Charlie asks.

"*We* are going out tonight. Drinks and dancing with Skylar and Jules. It's a crew tradition to take the star out the first night of travel."

Charlie swallows down his sudden panic.

Drinks and *dancing* and *Dev* sounds like an unbelievably dangerous combination.

Dev

New Orleans is the perfect first destination for the travel portion of the season because it has a heady, frenetic energy that matches Dev's current need for distraction. The hired driver snakes through the crowded streets of the French Quarter on the way to the hotel, and Dev rolls down the window and sticks his head out.

Even though it's only four-thirty in the afternoon, and it's a Sunday, people spill onto sidewalks in bright-colored clothing, visibly drunk. There's music coming from an unknown source, and as they drive past a group of women wearing "Bride's Entourage" sashes, they all holler obscene things at him. He loves everything about it.

Skylar has to meet up with the travel crew for a few hours, but she promises to join them at the bars later. Dev *needs* this night out. He needs a day off from the cameras and the crowns. He needs a night of heavy drinking with good friends.

Also, he needs sex.

Which is clearly his problem—the reason for all his restless energy and the disastrous *oh, love* and the even more disastrous semi-hard he shoved at the hetero star of their show. It's been almost five months since he's had sex. He needs a rebound. He needs to get this energy out of his system.

His plan is simple: he's going to have a night of casual sex with a random hookup he finds at a bar on his night off work. He'll end his sex drought, and then the smell of Charlie's oatmeal body wash won't mess with his mind so much. He'll have sex and get his head screwed on straight so he can help Charlie fall in love and write him a happy ending.

The show has Charlie and the production team staying at the Hotel Monteleone, on the top floor, and the women will be downstairs when they arrive later tonight. Jules and Skylar both have rooms on one end of the hallway, and Charlie and Dev have adjoining rooms on the other end. As soon as Dev gets to his room, he takes a long, hot shower, shaves, and shakes out his duffle bag onto his king-size bed, searching for the right outfit that says, "Gay dude looking for mutually enjoyable, non-committal sex."

Unfortunately, most of his clothes seem to say, "Straight dude actively trying to die alone."

He kicks the adjoining door until Charlie opens it, half asleep, pillow lines already formed on his cheek from an afternoon nap. Dev pushes his way into the room. "I need to borrow a shirt."

Charlie stares at his bare chest, at the waistband of his boxers, his eyes sliding all the way down Dev's legs. There's something about Charlie's enormous gray eyes that makes Dev's skin come to life under his gaze.

Charlie closes his eyes, covers his face with a giant hand, and groans. "God, why are you *naked*?" He sounds repulsed, and the tone returns Dev's skin to its normal, dormant state.

"Because I need to borrow a shirt."

Charlie gestures to the armoire, where he's already unpacked all his things. "You can borrow whatever you want, but it's all going to be big and short on you."

"*Big?* I'm not that much skinnier than you."

Charlie drops his hand from his eyes and stands directly in front of Dev in a wordless display of their respective widths. And yeah, okay. Charlie is twice his size. He could cover Dev like a duvet.

And that thought—*that thought right there*—is why Dev needs to have sex tonight.

He goes to the armoire and begins rifling through Charlie's expensive things. Charlie's clothes are beautiful, but none of them really scream *Dev*. None of them really scream *Charlie*, either. Charlie's fancy clothes are another protective layer he puts on every day. Except.

"Oh my Lord, is this a jean jacket? Why do you have a jean jacket? I've never even seen you *in jeans*. It's *glorious*."

Dev grabs one of Charlie's hundred-dollar T-shirts and throws the jean jacket on over it. He swims in both. "Honest assessment: am I rocking this jean jacket, or does it make me look like a twelve-year-old trying to get into a bar while wearing his father's suit?"

"You look really good."

Dev punches his arm. "Thanks, man. Now get dressed!"

Dev goes to put on a pair of skinny jeans while Charlie gets up to brush his teeth. Charlie's in the process of choosing from his many possible colored-shorts-and-short-sleeved-chambray combinations when there's a double knock on the door, and Jules comes bursting in holding two mini bottles of vodka she pocketed from the plane. She's released her hair from its usual topknot prison, and black curls spill down her back in beautiful waves. In place of her usual T-shirt, she's wearing a jean skirt and crop top and *mascara*. "Shit, Jules! You look hot. Like a Chinese, 'Sometimes'-era Britney Spears."

She tosses him a mini bottle. "You look like an Indian, *Growing Pains*–era Leo."

"I think that's the nicest thing you've ever said to me."

Charlie settles on periwinkle shorts and a cream-colored chambray with little flowers stitched into the fabric. Jules snorts. "Charles, you look like a stockbroker vacationing in Martha's Vineyard, as always."

"Well, you look very beautiful," Charlie says with the same sincerity.

His earnestness seems to dissolve some of her usual cynicism. Jules shyly looks down at her feet. "Thanks, Charlie."

Something unpleasant in Dev's chest, but he swallows it down with vodka, puts on a smile. "Shall we?"

Charlie

There's an undercurrent of panic beneath his skin—a tiny, nagging voice that says, *Maybe this isn't a good idea. Maybe don't get drunk with Dev tonight.* But the voice is buried beneath an overwhelming thrum of anticipation as Jules leads them out of the hotel and into the chaos of the French Quarter.

It's all the things he usually hates: too many people, too many smells, too much noise. But for some reason, all Charlie can see and smell and hear is Dev. Dev laughing at something Jules says; the smell of hotel shampoo as Dev brushes against him, pulling them along toward the bar where they're meeting Skylar; Dev strutting around, wearing Charlie's clothes. The sight of Dev in his oversize jean jacket makes Charlie feel . . . *something* he can't quite name.

It takes them an hour to walk three blocks because Jules wants to eat at every food stand, and Dev wants to talk to every stranger, and Charlie wants to read every historical plaque.

When they finally meet up with Skylar outside a gay bar, she looks nothing like her usual high-strung-director self, and every bit like a happy fortysomething woman. She hugs Jules and Dev, shakes Charlie's hand in greeting, and then they're all stuffing themselves around a tiny table, knees banging together. "We are getting belligerent tonight, yes?" Skylar asks with a formal air.

"Indubitably," Jules agrees.

Charlie doesn't say anything. He watches Dev press the pad of his thumb against his bottom lip. Charlie imagines *his* thumb, Dev's lip, and the gentle pressure it would take to coax his mouth open. He's losing it a bit, and they haven't even started drinking.

"Can we get four of your house margaritas and a round of tequila shots?" Dev asks the server.

Jules rubs her hands together, getting down to business. "Okay, Dev. Let's find you a man."

Charlie's stomach folds in half.

"A man?" Skylar asks.

"Dev is finally ready for his post-Ryan rebound. We are on the prowl for a one-night-stand candidate. Oh, how about that Joe Alwyn–looking dude by the bar?"

The server deposits the drinks on the table. Charlie doesn't reach for his shot. He was stupid, so stupid to think Dev might—

"A one-night stand? *Dev?*" Skylar snorts after she's thrown back both her own shot and Charlie's. "Mr. *Happily Ever After?* I doubt it."

Dev is immediately defensive. "There is nothing wrong with believing in happy endings."

"Isn't there, though, when statistically, you know half of those endings are actually divorce?" Jules sucks on a lime. "Shouldn't orchestrating love stories for our crappy show spoil the magic for you a bit?"

"No! Never!" Dev is ridiculously cute when he's passionate. Charlie stares down at his coaster. "Look, I know in real life relationships are complicated, but on our show they're not. It's as simple as two people liking each other enough to try. And then we put them on a boat in St. Thomas, and they fall in love, *because who can resist falling in love on a boat?*"

Skylar snorts again, but Dev plows on. "The situations are dramatized, sure, and the emotions are heightened to the point of absurdity for ratings, and in most cases, people don't fall in love in two months. *But sometimes they do!* Sometimes, you meet someone, and you just *know*. That happens on our show two seasons per year! How is that not magic?"

Skylar grins. "Tell me again how you're looking for a one-night stand?"

Dev flips her off across the table. "Charlie, why aren't you drinking?"

He wasn't ready for anyone to address him, so he stumbles through some vowel sounds in response to Dev's question.

Dev puts a hand on Charlie's knee under the table and leans in close. "Let go a little. You're safe with us."

He doesn't feel safe. He feels exposed and ridiculous, even though no one knows how profoundly disappointed he is. And it's all so silly, because of course Dev wanted to go out tonight so he could flirt with other men. Whatever weird friendship they've formed is friendship at best, and Dev being damn good at his job at worst. When this is over, they won't stay in contact. Dev will be busy prepping the next princess and Charlie will hopefully be busy with his new job. Too busy to think about repressed feelings or Dev's mouth.

Besides, Charlie *wants* Dev to find someone else. Maybe if he sees Dev with someone else, he'll stop picturing Dev with him.

Dev's hand is still on Charlie's knee when he flags down the server again. More shots land on the table. Dev's fingers fall away. "Charlie, can I see your hand for a minute?"

"My hand?"

Dev's fingers, cooled from his margarita, slip around Charlie's wrist, and then Dev is bringing Charlie's hand up to his mouth. For a fraction of a second, he thinks Dev is going to kiss his hand, like a noble prince in one of the fairy tales he loves so much.

Dev *licks* Charlie's hand instead. Dev's tongue. The side of Charlie's hand. Saliva and germs and *Dev's tongue*. That's all it takes for Charlie's whole body to go rigid. Then he's thinking about the bathroom, Dev's arm around his shoulders, Charlie's hand pressed into the small of his back, Dev hard against his hipbone. There's an ache in the back of his throat, and he can barely focus on the salt being poured along his hand, Dev forcing him to lick the salt, Dev positioning the shot glass against his lips.

"You're taking this shot with us, Charlie," Dev says. "It's crew tradition."

He already feels drunk as Jules counts it down. "*Three . . . two . . . one!*"

Dev tilts the glass. The tequila slides down Charlie's throat, and then there's a lime. Dev slots the lime between Charlie's lips, his thumb pressed to the corner of Charlie's mouth. "Suck, Charlie."

Charlie sucks on the lime slowly, trying to live in this moment of tequila and Dev's fingers for as long as he can. Another round appears on the table, and Charlie takes this one without any part of Dev touching him. Charlie *needs* Dev touching him. Everything beyond Dev goes quiet and blank. Radio static. Panic and longing and a third shot.

Charlie needs to be touching Dev, and soon he's too drunk to stop himself, so his hand finds Dev's sharp knee under the table. Dev lets him keep it there, and Charlie doesn't know what it *means*.

He isn't sure when they end up leaving the first bar or how they arrive at the second, a club where drag queens perform onstage. He only knows the feeling of his shoulder pressed into Dev's arm as they walk, the back of Dev's hand brushing his. Dev's mouth on Charlie's ear, lip and earlobe and hot breath: "Let me buy you another drink."

Dev leaning against the edge of the bar. Long limbs and sharp points, so beautiful and so *not his*.

Dev

"So . . ." Charlie starts. He props himself against the bar while they wait for their drinks. In Charlie's mind, he must think this little lean he's doing looks casual. It does not.

Drunk Charlie is an absolute mess. Dev is kind of obsessed.

"You're looking for a man-shaped person to share the night with?" Charlie asks primly.

Dev laughs. "Yeah, I guess I am. I think it's time, after Ryan."

The bartender sets their Sazeracs on the napkins in front of them, because when in New Orleans, mix hard alcohol like you're not twenty-eight and prone to heartburn, Dev thinks.

"Tonight, I'll be the handler," Charlie says while his tongue struggles to find his straw, "and you be the Prince Charming. I'll find you someone to love."

Dev laughs again, and Charlie reaches for a passing person with a bright blue pompadour and sequined top. "Excuse me?" Charlie sounds vaguely European and looks distinctly cross-eyed. "Can I introduce you to my friend Dev?"

Sequins's eyes never make it past Charlie. "Are *you* Dev?"

Sequins doesn't wait for Charlie's answer, but latches onto the front of Charlie's shirt and pulls down his ear. Whatever Sequins whispers makes Charlie blush from hairline to collar. "That's a very nice offer," Charlie says. "But I am currently dating ten women on a reality show, so I will have to pass."

Sequins pouts, then disappears into the crowd. Charlie by-passes the straw to take a large gulp of alcohol. Dev laughs again. Dev feels like he'll never stop laughing—like there's a bottle of champagne bubbles stuck in his throat.

"Come on!" He grabs Charlie's free hand and pulls them through the pulsating bodies until they find Skylar and Jules. It's Lady Gaga night at the club, and all the drag queens are dressed in costumes from various music videos. "Poker Face" Gaga is performing onstage right now, and Dev swings his hips in time to the music.

"Dance with us, Charlie!"

The request is met with some horrible hetero head-bob, knee-locking combo from Charlie.

"Good Lord, Jules! Make it stop!"

Jules takes Charlie's hands in hers and tries to correct his robotic moves, tries to loosen his hips. "Bad Romance" comes on, and Jules and Skylar teach Charlie a bastardized version of the choreography, and Dev is all champagne bubbles and a second Sazerac and the perfect feeling of a bass thumping through his bones.

Men flock to Charlie, and Charlie tries to introduce the men to Dev, but it's impossible to see anyone else when Charlie's around, hulking and blond and sweating in the flashing lights. Dev loses track of how many drinks he's had. He loses track of everything except for Charlie's curled lips, his white teeth, strobe lights. He wonders how many nights like this Charlie Winshaw has had in his life. Permanent smile, completely out of his head, not worried about being weird and being totally, unapologetically weird as he thrusts his hips to Lady Gaga.

Has Charlie *ever* had a night like this? Has he ever just let himself *be*? Charlie dances like his skin is a pair of stiff jeans he's finally broken in, like for the first time, he *fits*. Dev wishes Angie and Daphne were here right now, wishes all the women could witness this, because it would be impossible not to fall in love with this version of Charlie.

"You're not dancing!" Charlie screams in his face. He grabs Dev's waist and pulls him toward where Jules is grinding on someone wearing fishnets and nothing else. Skylar's in her own world, arms vertical, completely free from her usual stress. It really is a perfect night.

"I was just watching you enjoy yourself."

"*What?*" Charlie shouts over the music.

"Nothing!" Dev laughs, but for the first time all night, it doesn't feel funny. Charlie's hands are massive on his narrow hips, like bookends holding him upright. Charlie pulls him even closer, knees brushing knees.

"You're too nice to me," Charlie shouts.

"No one can ever be too nice to you, Charlie."

"No. *No.*" He closes his eyes and shakes his head. He looks so serious, carved in florescent, flashing light. "I'm worried you don't know."

"Don't know what?"

"I'm worried you don't know what you deserve." He grabs Dev's shoulders. "Six years is a long time to stay."

For a second, Dev isn't sure if Charlie is talking about his six years with Ryan or his six years with *Ever After*. Charlie's hands are on the back of his neck, and he pulls their foreheads together. Dev can taste the alcohol on Charlie's breath with every exhale. "You're too amazing to settle for *Goonies* T-shirts and a PS5."

Ryan, then. "Thanks, Charlie."

Charlie leans back just enough to reach out for a man dancing close by. He pulls the man into their little hug-circle. "This is my friend Dev," Charlie tells the stranger. "You should love him."

The man is drunk enough to roll with this moment. "Okay," he says, winking at Dev.

"No, *listen*." Charlie's got one hand on the back of Dev's neck, one hand on the back of this other man's. "Dev is the best there is. The *absolute best*. He's so fucking beautiful. Look at him."

And then Charlie is looking at him. It's the same horrible combination of Charlie's eyes and Dev's skin as before. "Isn't he the most beautiful man you've ever seen?"

"I think *you* are the most beautiful man I've ever seen," the stranger tells Charlie in a husky voice, and Dev detaches himself from the triangle of limbs, pushing himself away from Charlie. He needs more alcohol. Or maybe less alcohol. Or air. Or *something*.

"Hey!" Jules follows him to the fringes of the club, to a dark corner where the music isn't tangled in his heart, where Charlie isn't tangled in his body. "Are you okay?"

"Yeah." He manages an easy smile. "Of course! It's just . . ." He points to where Charlie is still talking with the man. "He's a human cockblock."

"I'm not sure what you expected. He's gorgeous."

Dev feels that same tug in his chest from earlier. "Careful, Jules. Your crush is showing."

She rolls her eyes. "*My* crush?"

"What?"

"*Dev.*"

"Seriously, what?"

"Dude." Her voice cuts through the noise of the club. "If you really wanted to find a random hookup tonight, you would have done it."

"It's not my fault no one even notices me with Charlie around."

"You could try *not* being around Charlie."

"It's my job to take care of him."

"You're not working tonight."

He feels like his brain is trying to swim upstream through a powerful current of Patrón as understanding reaches him. This is his career and his professional reputation she's questioning. He conjures drunk flippancy, strives for humor. "Gay men can be platonic friends with straight men, Jules. This isn't some non-hetero *When Harry Met Sally*."

"I am sure gay men and straight men *can* be friends. But I am also seventy percent sure you and Charlie *aren't.*"

Dev needs to find the right thing to say, the right line of dialogue, because what Jules is suggesting is not an option. It would be wrong on a million different levels. On a professional level, and a friendship level, and a too-old-to-crush-on-a-straight dude level. On every level, feeling anything toward Charlie other than professional regard would be catastrophic, and he doesn't. He can't.

Strobe lights and music and bodies pressing in on all sides, and he can't find the right thing to say to Jules to convince her she's wrong, so wrong. "I just broke up with Ryan."

"I thought you were ready for a rebound?"

He sucks in his cheeks. "Charlie is our *star*."

"Okay," Jules says with a casual shrug, as if they both didn't sign contracts forbidding fraternization with the talent. As if the entire future of their franchise isn't hanging in the balance, depending on Dev helping Charlie fall in love *with a woman*. "But if it makes a difference, I think he's into you, too."

Dev can't afford to think about that. "I'm going to head back to the hotel."

"Dev, wait!" Jules calls after him as he turns toward the exit, but he doesn't stop until he's outside. And air . . . air is what he needs. He takes greedy gulps of it as he stumbles past the bouncers and a line of clubgoers and a twenty-one-year-old puking her guts out on the curb. Dev makes it a good twenty feet before he collapses against a brick wall.

He's too drunk and too hot inside the jean jacket to process all of this. He searches for an emotion and lands on anger. How *dare* Jules accuse him of having feelings for Charlie?

He cares about Charlie, of course. Because Charlie is their Prince Charming, and it's Dev's job to care. And because Charlie is *Charlie*. Sure, he might be *attracted* to Charlie, but only because Charlie is objectively attractive, and Dev is objectively lonely.

And then he's thinking about what Charlie said about him in the club. *He's so fucking beautiful.*

No one has ever told him he's beautiful before. High school boyfriends and college boyfriends and Ryan, and how is Charlie Winshaw the first person to ever say that to him, blackout drunk in a dance club surrounded by Lady Gagas?

But he already knows the answer. Hell, Charlie Winshaw somehow knows the answer.

I'm worried you don't know what you deserve.

Charlie

Dev was here. Dev is now not here.

Charlie's fairly certain he has an exceptional brain—he's maybe even won awards for it—but right now, it doesn't seem capable of understanding where he is or what he's doing. He thinks there are hands on him. He thinks he's dancing. He thinks someone gave him another drink. He *knows* Dev is gone.

His legs feel numb as he moves through the crowd like a puppet on bad strings, weaving in and out. Bodies and arms and low voices in his ear and hands that glide across his chest. Where's Dev?

Jules. He catches his fingers on Jules's tiny shoulders, sharp like Dev's. "Dev?"

"He went back to the hotel."

Charlie stumbles toward the door. "Wait!" Jules shouts over the music. "I'll find Skylar, and we'll all go!"

He keeps walking. Beyond the door, the air is warm, muggy. Charlie swims in it. "Dev?"

"Charlie?"

Dev. He's leaning against a brick wall up ahead, his long legs spilling into the sidewalk. Dev is ten feet tall, and his face is wet. "You're crying," Charlie yells. "Hey, you're crying."

"Shit." Dev pushes tears around his face. "Sorry. It's nothing. I'm just . . . I'm really drunk."

"You're crying," he says again, quieter now. The music is gone, and Dev is right here, two feet in front of him. He probably doesn't need to yell. "Why are you crying?"

Charlie reaches up and catches a tear on his thumb. He blows on it. *Make a wish*. Or is that eyelashes? Charlie's so drunk, he doesn't know anymore. Dev pushes past him and starts walking up the busy sidewalk.

"Where are you going?"

"Back to the hotel."

"Dev." Charlie reaches out for Dev's jacket—*his jacket*—to hold him in place. "Did I do something wrong?"

Dev laughs and looks down at his sneakers, the same ones Charlie barfed on—was that just three weeks ago? "No. You didn't do anything wrong."

"Then tell me."

"I *can't*." Dev's voice breaks. Charlie wants to put it back together.

Dev tries to walk away again, and Charlie doesn't let him. He had Dev. He had Dev in his hands and in his arms on the dance floor. He had Dev *right there*, and he's far away again.

Charlie grabs two fistfuls of Dev's jacket. "Why do you always pull away from me?"

"What are you talking about?"

"Let's play a game," he hears himself say. He's drunk, so drunk. "Let's see who pulls away first."

And then he shoves Dev's back against the brick wall again, harder than he intends, but it's fine, because Dev is here. Dev is *right here*. Charlie's holding him in place, and Dev's knee is on Charlie's thigh, and Charlie's knee is brushing Dev's skin. This is what he wanted. This is what he's wanted for *days*, and now Dev is here, and Charlie realizes he has no idea what happens next. Dev usually scripts these sorts of things for him.

"What the hell, Charlie?"

He grabs tighter to the front of Dev's jacket. He's not sure what to say.

He says, "Can I please kiss you?"

Dev

First Charlie shoves him against a brick wall, and then he asks permission to kiss him, and the stark juxtaposition between that act of aggression and the thoughtful question of consent might be the sexiest thing that's ever happened to Dev, overriding any logical thought. He says something. It might be "okay."

But Charlie Winshaw isn't going to kiss him. It makes no sense. None of this makes any sense. Charlie's pinning him against this wall with a wild look in his eyes, and Dev wants to pull away; Dev never wants to pull away. But Charlie isn't going to kiss him, and Dev doesn't want Charlie to kiss him. Because he doesn't have feelings for Charlie.

Then Charlie's thumb is on Dev's lower lip, brushing it tenderly, and then *Charlie's mouth is on Dev's lower lip.* And *fuck.*

The Prince Charming on the show *Ever After* is kissing him against a brick wall, so hesitantly, his mouth soft and tasting of salt. For a second, Dev thinks about the camera angles and the music they would add in postproduction, and then he doesn't think about anything, because Charlie's hands are on his hips, sliding their bodies together as his tongue teases Dev's mouth apart.

Charlie Winshaw tastes better than mint Oreos, and Dev definitely wants this. Which is why he has to stop.

"I'm sorry." Charlie exhales as soon as their mouths fall apart.

"Charlie, you're drunk." It's almost impossible to get those words out, especially with Charlie six inches away, mouth half open. Dev clings to all his logical reasons for not doing this. The moral questionability of kissing your straight friend when he's drunk. Not being a straight boy's experiment at twenty-eight. *Losing his job.* "You don't want to do this."

"Dev," Charlie slurs. "I really want to do this." And he grabs him by the back of the neck again. There's nothing soft about the way he shoves them back together, teeth first, and then tongue, and then hands. Heat—messy, sloppy *heat.* Charlie's fingernails scrape the small hairs on the back of his neck, and even as Dev's body dissolves at the touch, his mind gets stuck on an important thought: *Charlie hates kissing.*

Charlie hates kissing, so why is he kissing Dev like his whole life depends on it?

Charlie is *straight*, so why would he want to kiss Dev?

Charlie is *Charlie*—beautiful, brilliant, carefully guarded Charlie—so why would he want to kiss *Dev*?

Dev needs to push him away again. Dev is going to push Charlie away again. In, like, five seconds, he will totally stop this.

But then Charlie grinds his hips against Dev's, and Dev can feel Charlie harden through his shorts, and *nope.* Dev's not going to do a damn thing. He's going to live and die in this moment. He'll happily quit *Ever After* in shame and never work in Hollywood again if it means one more minute against this brick wall with Charlie Winshaw.

And once he determines this kiss is worth destroying his entire life for, he decides to make it count. He grabs a fistful of Charlie's curls—and he knows with absolute certainty every time he grabbed Charlie's hair before now, *this* is what he really wanted—and he snaps him around so that Charlie's back is against the wall.

Once Dev's running the show, there are more hands and more teeth. What Charlie lacks in skill and experience, he eclipses with raw enthusiasm. Charlie's hands find his ass, the inseam of his pants, his stomach beneath his shirt. Charlie touches Dev like he doesn't know where to start, like he's overwhelmed by his options; Dev touches Charlie like he knows this is his only chance. He touches Charlie like Charlie is going to disappear at any second.

Dev runs his teeth along Charlie's strong jaw until he arrives at the chin dimple and bites, and Charlie shivers in response. Dev feels that shiver in every inch of his body, the want gathering in him like something dangerous, until he hooks his leg behind Charlie's and grinds down against him. Charlie exhales a shy moan into Dev's mouth, and Dev fills his lungs with the sound of Charlie wanting him.

All at once, he comes to his senses. They're in public, on a street in New Orleans, where anyone could stumble upon the star of *Ever After* kissing a man.

He pulls away. Beneath him, Charlie slumps against the wall, breathing heavily, his cheeks pink.

"Thank you," Charlie eventually whispers into the space between them.

"Did you just *thank me* for kissing you?"

Charlie presses two fingers to the corner of Dev's smile. "I did."

Dev shakes his head and laughs. "That is a little weird."

"I think you like that I'm a little weird," Charlie says in a new, confident voice—a voice that scrapes along his skin like Charlie's fingernails did before—and Dev *has* to kiss him one more time, one last time before he can never kiss him again. Dev grabs Charlie's chin, and Charlie meets him so gently, his hands hooking around the back of Dev's neck, his thumbs on the side of his jaw. Charlie sucks on Dev's bottom lip, and Dev wishes he could keep this moment somehow. He wishes he could preserve it in the grooves of a vinyl record and fall asleep listening to the song on repeat.

"Dev, last night . . ." Charlie's mouth finds his ear. "In the bathroom. Were you hard for me?"

Dev groans in embarrassment. He's already decided to destroy his entire life, so he says, "Yes, Charlie. *God*, yes."

Charlie melts against him.

The door to the club opens twenty feet away, and "Telephone" streams outside. Charlie jerks away.

"Skylar, come *on*." Jules's voice is so clear through the chaos of the night, it feels like a sobering bolt of lightning tearing through everything else. "Those drunk idiots could be dead somewhere!"

By the time Jules spots them on the sidewalk, Charlie is five feet away from him, and Dev's not openly panting anymore. "Hey, we found you," Skylar says. "And look, Jules. They're not dead."

Dev isn't convinced this is true.

"What are you guys doing?"

"Nothing," Dev says too quickly, avoiding Charlie's gaze at all cost. If he looks at Charlie for even a second, Skylar will know. If Dev looks at Charlie, his face will telegraph every damn feeling competing for room inside his chest, and everyone will know.

"Charlie," Skylar says, "you don't look so good."

"Um . . ."

Dev turns toward Charlie then, to see if he's okay. He gets a brief glimpse of Charlie's expression—an expression he should recognize from night one—before Charlie hunches over and vomits all over Dev's legs. Just like he did on night one.

Somehow, it's still the best night Dev's had in a long, long time.

Charlie

Oh, he thinks with a sinking realization. *I'm dead.*

Death is waking up in a strange bed with a railroad spike drilled into his brain and lead for limbs and a very shaky understanding of the past twelve hours.

He has *never* been this hungover.

He tries to sit up in the hotel bed and immediately vomits on himself. He goes to the bathroom to clean off the vomit and proceeds to vomit again into the toilet for an undetermined length of time. Jules arrives while he is sitting on the floor of the shower under the hot water, still wearing his outfit from the night before.

"Yeah . . ." Jules sets tea and a bottle of Excedrin on the counter for him. "This looks about right."

"Did I do anything to humiliate myself last night?"

The night is nothing but a blur of Lady Gaga songs and tequila. So, so much tequila.

Jules takes a while in answering. "Depends on your definition of humiliating . . ." Was she faking her shots? She looks perfectly perky, and she's exactly half his body weight. "You got shit-faced drunk and danced to a lot of Lady Gaga in a drag club. Does that sound humiliating?"

"The way I dance? Probably."

Jules sits down on the closed toilet seat and pulls out her phone. On her Instagram story, there is a video of Jules and Skylar teaching him the moves to "Bad Romance." It actually doesn't look humiliating at all. It looks kind of fun. He looks like he's having *fun*.

"You also spent a lot of time trying to pimp Dev out to random gay dudes."

Dev.

It all comes back to him. Dev's tongue, and Dev's hips under his hips, and Dev against that brick wall, and Dev—

Oh, shit. What did I do? What did I do?

Charlie curls into the fetal position inside the shower. This is what regret tastes like: regurgitated tequila and dirty cotton balls.

As if Charlie's shame is strong enough to summon Dev, he walks in through the open bathroom door wearing sunglasses and carrying the world's largest cup of coffee. "We've got to get downstairs to film the greeting scene with the contestants. Are we ready to go?"

"Charlie is sitting fully clothed in a shower, so no."

"Get it together, Charles. We have work to do," Dev says condescendingly. He then casually turns and throws up into the sink.

"*Gross!*" Jules screams.

"You were sitting on the toilet seat! What was I supposed to do?"

Jules covers her nose and mouth, rushing from the bathroom, and Dev blots vomit from the corner of his mouth, looking as dignified as possible. They're alone, both of them smelling like vomit and each refusing to speak first. Charlie stares up at him through the shower water. Dev stares down at him through his sunglasses. Charlie has no idea what's going on inside Dev's head.

Maybe Dev forgot?

"How . . . how much do you remember of last night?" Dev finally asks.

Everything. He remembers every damn second.

Charlie kissed Dev last night. He kissed Dev, and it was what kissing is *supposed* to feel like. He enjoyed kissing Dev in a way he's never enjoyed kissing anyone. He's overwhelmed by the clarity of this fact, and he's overwhelmed by the confusion of what happens next. He kissed Dev, but he knows he can never kiss him again, not without ruining this season and Dev's entire career. Not without hurting the ten women who are still on this show to date him and not without destroying his chance to rebuild his reputation.

It was a mistake. He made a huge mistake. But Dev is standing there handing them an *out* with this question—a way to undo what happened—and Charlie doesn't think about what he wants. He thinks about what he needs to do.

"I don't remember much." Charlie swallows the sick rising in his throat. "I can remember getting to the dance club, and that's . . . it."

"Okay." Dev's face is unreadable behind the sunglasses. "Okay."

Then he marches out of the bathroom, calling, "*Jules!* Will you please get him dressed?"

Jules comes back into the bathroom and tries to hoist Charlie into a standing position. He immediately vomits again. She smirks. "Today should be fun."

*   *   *

Absolutely none of it is fun.

He's so hungover he can barely film the welcome scene with the contestants in the French Quarter. Even by Tuesday's Group Quest, he doesn't feel wholly recovered. He meets the ten remaining women at Mardi Gras World, and they receive a tour where they learn about the history of the parade. Then they're taken to a warehouse where the women are divided into two teams tasked with building their own Mardi Gras parade floats, even though it's June.

The producers want him to mingle with the women while they work on their floats, and he gravitates toward Daphne first before he remembers they also have awkward, kiss-related drama. "Uh, hey," he starts.

Daphne smiles shyly up at him. "Hey. I've been hoping to talk to you." She leads him—and by extension, two cameras—across the warehouse to where the other women won't overhear. "I just really wanted to apologize about the ball," she says, fiddling with her braid. "I shouldn't have, um, thrown myself at you like that."

"It takes two to consensually dry-hump," he attempts.

Daphne doesn't smile. Her mouth worries itself into a grimace. "Megan said something to provoke me, and I maybe had a few more glasses of wine than normal, and Maureen told me I should. . . . I made a silly, drunken decision."

He swallows. "I can maybe relate."

Daphne nervously unbraids her blond hair, then rebraids it, then sighs. "The thing is, I really do like you, Charlie. I feel like we have a lot in common, and we have fun together."

Everything she's saying is true, and when he looks at Daphne in her cute overalls, he feels tenderness and affection for her. But he doesn't feel any particular impulse to push Daphne up against a brick wall and shove his tongue down her throat.

"So I think we should trust our bond," Daphne is saying, "and not feel any need to rush the physical aspects of our relationship."

"Agreed," he says too quickly.

Daphne opens her arms with a tentative offer to hug, and Charlie accepts, tucking her slender body against his. It's actually sort of lovely.

"Hey!" Angie pops up holding a dripping paintbrush. "Did y'all have a postmortem on your cringey make-out?"

Daphne blushes. "Um, yes. Thank you for phrasing it like that."

"Awesome! Group hug!" Angie wedges herself into the circle of their embrace and splatters paint all over Daphne's overalls. "Oops! Sorry, Daph!"

To which Daphne responds by swiftly marching across set, picking up a paintbrush, and running it down the front of Angie's romper. Angie half gasps, half laughs, nothing like the usual fights that break out between the women on set. "How dare you? You're buying me a new romper!"

"That's *my* romper! You stole it out of my luggage!"

Then both women turn to him with very grave expressions, paintbrushes outstretched. Charlie holds up his hands. "You know, I'm really not feeling well today, and I think you should strongly consider your chances of receiving a tiara if you ruin these shorts—"

It's a useless plea, and they both flick him with drops of paint until it covers the front of his T-shirt, his legs, his face. "You're both going home immediately," he threatens, but the women just laugh hysterically, loud enough for the other contestants to wander over. And from there, the float-making competition quickly devolves into an all-out paint war.

The producers don't intervene on anyone's behalf as the women run around like children, covering each other in paint. Sabrina dips Daphne's braid in blue paint and uses it like a brush across Delilah's crop top and Lauren L.'s skirt. Charlie tries to protect Jasmine from a paint bomb concocted by Becca and ends up with paint drenched down the front of his shirt. So, he takes off his shirt.

"Big mistake," Angie tells him. "Now we know what we have to do to get you naked."

Someone—Whitney, he thinks—has the bright idea to add glitter to the mix, and even Megan bonds with the rest of the contestants as they all become human Mardi Gras parade floats. Charlie has never laughed this much or this hard in his entire life.

Ryan is livid. "They're all *covered* in paint and glitter!" he shouts when they finally call cut. "We can't take them to the restaurant like this for the social hour!"

"Ryan, this is the best footage we've gotten all season," Skylar argues. "It's the most likeable Charlie has ever been."

"But what are we going to do with them now? We need at least ten minutes' worth of footage for tonight's social hour."

Dev, who has been keeping his distance from Charlie all day, raises his hand. "I might have an idea."

They forget about the competition and the social hour and haul the cast back to the hotel. The women and Charlie go to their respective rooms to shower and change into their pajamas. Then everyone rendezvouses in Charlie's hotel room, where the cameras and lights are set up. They order massive amounts of takeout, and for the first time all season, Charlie and the contestants are just allowed to *be* together. The previous bonding of the day has created some temporary illusion that makes the women forget they're here to compete against each other. Instead, they sit on the floor with wet hair, eating jambalaya and passing around bottles of rosé.

When he's not feeling pressured to kiss them, Charlie really likes all of these women. That realization is quickly chased by guilt.

Charlie knows, realistically, that most of these women are not here for him, just like he's not here for them. Megan is here to promote her exercise videos, and Sabrina is trying to get more hits on her travel blog. Rachel wants to brick-and-mortar her food truck, and Jasmine is trying to expand her brand as the former Miss Kentucky. And all of them want more Instagram followers.

Still, it seems impossible that he's going to get through the next five weeks without hurting one—if not all—of these wonderful women.

"Have we entered the hotel dance party stage of the evening yet?" Angie asks the room, and Lauren L. immediately cues up an upbeat Leland Barlow song on her handler's phone and grabs Sabrina's hand to pull her into a tango. Charlie instinctively looks for Dev. He's standing in the doorway between their adjoining rooms, hiding behind a camera, and their eyes meet across the budding dance party. Charlie tells himself to look away. But he doesn't.

"I think we should discuss your relationship trajectories with the remaining contestants before the next Crowning Ceremony," Dev says a little after midnight, when the contestants have gone back to their rooms and the production team has finished cleaning up the mess.

"Everyone knows you and Daphne are like identical blond wedding-cake toppers, and you have amazing chemistry with Angie, though I get the impression Angie Griffin would have amazing chemistry with a cactus. But Lauren L. was a real surprise today, and I think we've been sleeping on Sabrina." Dev is holding a bag of Double Stuf Oreos, and he sits down on Charlie's bed beside him. "What are your thoughts?"

At the moment, his thoughts are about how close Dev is sitting next to him. "My thoughts are solely preoccupied by you brazenly eating Oreos in my bed."

Dev leans over, so when he takes a bite, little black Oreo crumbs fall into Charlie's lap.

"You're a monster."

"As I was saying . . ." Dev continues to talk about the contestants while absentmindedly brushing crumbs out of Charlie's lap. Charlie feels his entire body seize up: Dev's fingers and Dev's smoky-sweet smell and Dev's body close to his on his bed like it's nothing. Which is why Charlie has to keep pretending the kiss never happened, even though the secret churns his stomach every time he thinks about it. Because the kiss clearly meant nothing to Dev—he can ignore it, let it vanish into the drunken ether, carry on being friends like normal.

Charlie isn't sure what he wants the kiss to mean, but he knows it wasn't nothing.

On the day of his Courting Date with Lauren L., Charlie turns twenty-eight years old.

He's done everything in his power to conceal this information from cast and crew alike because he hates his birthday. He hates the attention and the pressure to do something memorable and the feeling he's failing at life. Another year has passed, and he's still the same old Charlie.

(Except now he's a Charlie who was brave enough to kiss a person he likes but is still too much of a coward to admit it.)

Birthdays are always a twenty-four-hour anxiety trap, and he would happily pop a Xanax and sleep through the whole day if he didn't have to get up for filming.

He wakes to a Bitmoji of Parisa throwing confetti. He receives a few messages on social media from old Stanford acquaintances and women he barely knows. He doesn't hear anything from his family and doesn't expect to. It's fine.

He goes down to the hotel gym and exercises through the birthday blues, then showers while Jules kindly lays out his pre-approved outfit for the day. When he gets out of the shower, the door between his and Dev's room is open.

"Charlie, get dressed, and come help me with something!"

He's in no hurry to be alone with Dev, so he takes his time putting on his mustard-colored shorts and the beautiful floral-patterned shirt Jules picked out for him.

"Charlie, *now*. Get over here right now."

Charlie sighs, goes into the adjoining room, and promptly freezes in horror in the doorway. Dev's hotel room is full of *Ever After* crew members. Skylar Jones has a party hat on her shaved head, and Ryan Parker blows into a noisemaker, and even Mark Davenport is there. Charlie has never seen the host off camera, but he's here now, lounging on Dev's bed. Jules stands in the middle of the room holding a cake.

"Happy birthday!" Dev shouts, and the woman standing next to Dev throws a literal armful of confetti into the air.

"Surprise, bitch!"

It's Parisa.

Real-life Parisa Khadim, standing in Dev's hotel room in New Orleans, wearing a power suit with her hair pulled back in a tight ponytail. Dev's got his greasy, unwashed hair shoved under a baseball cap. Charlie's brain can't fully process the image of *Parisa* standing next to *Dev*, of these two people from two different parts of his life existing in the same physical space.

"What are you doing here?"

"Your handler convinced the show to let me travel with you for the next week as a birthday surprise!" Parisa claps Dev on the back, and Charlie's head explodes. "Get over here and give me a hug, Hot-Ass."

He takes a few shaky steps forward and lets her pull him into a hug. She wraps her round arms across his shoulders, and he collapses into the softness of her chest. He's so unbelievably happy to see her. His real family doesn't give a shit about his birthday, but Parisa—Parisa gives a shit about everything, and she's *here*.

"*Happy birthday to you*," Mark Davenport begins in an absurd falsetto, and the whole crew launches into an off-key rendition of "Happy Birthday." Jules holds up the cake, and he blows out the candles, and Skylar starts cutting it into pieces, serving it on paper plates at nine in the morning. "Dev had me go all over town to find a gluten-free carrot cake, and honestly . . ." Jules eyes the cake skeptically. "I'm not sure it's any good."

Dev. Charlie turns to find him in the corner of the room, already massacring a giant slice of cake. "Thank you," he says when he stumbles over to him. "Thank you for this. This is the nicest thing anyone has ever done for me on my birthday."

The depressing thing is, he means it. No one has ever thrown him a surprise party, let alone flown his best friend across the country for him. But of course Dev would.

Dev stabs at his cake with a plastic fork. "Yeah, sorry if it's . . . a lot. I planned the party before, uh, well . . ."

Before.

"Before what?" he asks seamlessly.

"Before nothing. Never mind."

"Well, thank you," Charlie says again.

More cake plates are passed around, and they eat quickly so they can head downstairs to where the vans await to take Charlie and Lauren L. on a swamp tour. Parisa falls into step with him as they leave.

"I can't believe you're here," he tells her.

"I wouldn't miss the chance to see you on your birthday." Parisa watches Dev jog ahead to call the elevator. "So . . . that's Dev, huh? He's kind of cute."

An irrational stab of jealousy lances through him. "He's gay, Parisa."

"I didn't say he was cute *for me.*"

Charlie whips his head around to see her knowing grin. *Does she know?* As his best friend, can she look at his mouth and automatically *tell* that three days ago, Dev's tongue traced his lower lip?

And if she knows, what does she think?

If Parisa knew, she would probably be furious. She got him on this show so he can triage his reputation. She did not get him on this show to exchange illicit kisses with pretty boys on Bourbon Street.

But Dev is *so pretty*. Sometimes Charlie forgets, and then he sees a glimpse of Dev, and the perfect geometry of his face catches Charlie unaware, like it's the first time he saw him. Like he's falling out of a car at this man's feet over and over again.

Up ahead, Dev presses the elevator button, lets the rest of the crew go first. Dev in his stupid baseball hat, Dev with his greasy hair, Dev with his cargo shorts, Dev with frosting on his face. Dev, who flew his best friend across the country for his birthday. Dev, who thinks Charlie deserves love.

Dev, who he kissed and can never kiss again.

Dev

They're pretending the kiss never happened.

Or at least Dev is pretending. Charlie couldn't draw a timeline of Sunday night if his life depended on it, so he has no idea he grabbed Dev's waist and said those words.

Can I please kiss you?

Which is fine. It's better than fine, actually. It's great.

If Charlie remembered the kiss, Dev would be fired by now. Sometimes he thinks he should resign anyway, out of guilt. Most of the time, he feels eternally grateful that his lapse in judgment was kindly expunged by a benevolent universe and multiple tequila shots.

Charlie doesn't remember, so now they're able to sit five feet apart on a bed, and it's not weird at all. There are only six minutes left of Charlie Winshaw's twenty-eighth birthday, but Parisa is requiring him to stay up until midnight, even if he refuses to drink any wine and keeps dozing off.

Parisa reclines on her throne of pillows at the head of Charlie's hotel bed, Jules nuzzled in at her side. She's only been here a day, but Jules is already obsessed with her, perhaps because there aren't a ton of women on set who are not contestants or her bosses. All day, Parisa and Jules huddled conspiratorially by the crafty table, whispering and snickering.

For Dev's part, he's not sure if Parisa Khadim is the coolest person he's ever met or the most terrifying. She wears her hair in an intense business ponytail, and her suit looks like it cost as much as his rent. Her size is proportionate to the amount of attention she demands; she's tall, with broad shoulders and wide hips, and Dev thinks if Charlie were having a really bad panic attack, Parisa could probably carry him. Dev never could.

"Can I please go to bed now?" Charlie asks, his arms thrown up over his face.

Parisa kicks him. "No. We still have five more minutes of celebrating your prodigious birth."

"If you really wanted to celebrate me, you'd let me sleep."

Charlie rolls out of range of Parisa's feet before she can kick him again, and Dev is too distracted by his wine to care about how Charlie's shirt rides up in the back when he does this.

"But I need to take a shower before bed," Charlie whines. "Can I spend the last five minutes of my birthday washing swamp stank out of my hair?"

"Absolutely not." Then Parisa turns the weight of her intense gaze to Dev. "So, Dev. Charlie tells me you wrote an amazing screenplay."

His face heats up. From the wine. "I don't know about *amazing*—"

"It is absolutely amazing," Charlie corrects. There's something about the tone of his voice that makes Dev imagine Charlie's mouth against his throat. He crosses his legs on the bed.

"Charlie said you want me to get your script to an agent?"

"Charlie misspoke. It wouldn't be professional for me to hit up our star's publicist for networking help." Of course, it would hardly be the least professional thing he's done recently. He doesn't look over at Charlie sprawled out on the bed. "Besides, it's a queer rom com."

Parisa looks unaffected. "I'm queer. I like rom coms."

"No, I mean, at best, we get like one studio queer movie a year if we're lucky, and they're usually about two white people. My movie is not marketable, and I don't want to waste your time."

Dev can feel Charlie's eyes on the side of his face, can almost sense the way he wants to argue but doesn't. Parisa just shrugs.

"All right, friends," Jules announces, passing Dev the wine bottle. "I've got to get up early tomorrow for a production meeting, so I should probably head back to my room."

"Boo!" Parisa shouts after Jules as she heads out.

"And I'm getting in the shower," Charlie says, rolling off the bed and stumbling exhaustedly toward the bathroom.

"Double boo!"

Neither Dev nor Parisa move off Charlie's bed, probably because they both understand you don't leave half a bottle of wine at the end of the night. Dev tops off his cup and passes Parisa the rest.

Parisa waits until they hear the sound of the shower running before she speaks. "Thanks for doing this for him."

"Yeah. Of course, he's . . ." Dev awkwardly peels back the lip on his paper cup. "It's his birthday."

"Yeah," Parisa says with an understanding nod. "He's pretty special."

"You and Charlie. Have you ever . . . ?"

Parisa immediately catches his meaning. "No. Never. It's not like that with us."

He looks at this beautiful, confident, self-possessed woman who clearly recognizes how amazing Charlie is, just as he is. "Can I ask *why*?"

Parisa crosses her legs and tucks the bottle of wine between them. "I mean, I've thought about it. I have *eyes*, and when we first met, before he hired me, I thought . . . *maybe*."

"Why didn't maybe happen?"

"Because he's Charlie. Because *maybe* never even occurred to him," Parisa says matter-of-factly. "And I'm glad. The dude is a great friend, but he'd be a disaster of a boyfriend. He doesn't know the first thing about how to be in a relationship."

"Why did you send him on this show, then? Were you actively trying to humiliate him?"

"Of course not. He wants to work in tech again, and I want him to be happy. Maureen Scott promised she could help reboot his image, so . . ." Parisa's eyes cut toward the closed bathroom door, and she lowers her voice. "If I tell you something, can you *promise* it stays between us?"

Dev nods.

"This spring, one of my cousins got married, and Charlie went with me to the wedding as my plus-one. My Pinterest-obsessed cousin decides to have the only Muslim wedding with a signature cocktail, and it turns out Charlie *loves* blackberry mojitos. He chugged, like, six of them, and you have to understand, when Charlie gets drunk—"

"Oh, I've met Drunk Charlie, actually."

Parisa raises a perfectly arched eyebrow. "Imagine Drunk Charlie interpretive dancing to Whitney Houston at a wedding with a guest list of two hundred. He looks over at my cousin with her new husband and he points at them—I mean *points*, like noticeably across the dance floor, people were staring—and he says to me: 'I want that.'" Parisa pauses in her story and lets the weight of Charlie's words wash over Dev. "Maureen Scott had been hounding me to let Charlie do the show for months, and there Charlie was, drunkenly admitting that some part of him wants a relationship, so I just thought . . ."

"Wait. Your ulterior motive for sending Charlie on this show is *the actual purpose of this show*?"

Parisa smooths down her ponytail. "Well, yeah. Maybe it sounds ridiculous to think he could fall in love with a woman on this show, but—"

"It doesn't sound ridiculous at all. Not to me."

They both sip wine in the silence for a minute. "Has he told you anything about his family?" Parisa asks, her voice even quieter.

"Not really."

"He hasn't told me much either. Just bits and pieces over the years. From what I've put together, the Winshaws are a bunch of pricks who can all burn in hell for the way they treated him."

Dev decides Parisa is definitely the coolest person he's ever met.

"His family didn't deserve him. Charlie is wonderful, and they made him feel like shit growing up because his beautiful brain works a little differently sometimes." She pauses again, and when she speaks, her voice is gentle. "I can't really imagine what it would be like if the people who were supposed to love me unconditionally didn't, but I think maybe if I'd grown up like that, I might have a hard time thinking I deserve love, too."

The shower shuts off, and they both startle as if they've been caught. Dev unfurls his legs. Parisa slides off the bed.

"He considers you a good friend, and I'm glad," she says as she downs the rest of the wine. "Platonic love is important, too. Night, Dev."

The hotel door closes behind Parisa, and Dev collapses under the weight of this new guilt. Parisa sent Charlie on this show to find love, and in five weeks, Charlie can have what he wants: a fiancée and a job in tech. If Dev doesn't screw it all up, Charlie could have everything.

The bathroom door opens, and the humid sweetness of Charlie's oatmeal body wash rushes into the room before Charlie steps out and freezes. He stands by the bathroom door, no shirt, navy sweatpants slung so low on his hips, they're practically inconsequential. Dev is still sitting on the bed with his wine, and he gives himself exactly thirty seconds. Thirty seconds to lament the injustice of a world where a man who looks like *that* kissed him and doesn't remember it.

He doesn't even like muscles, really. Usually.

"Sorry," Dev finally says. "I was just about to head back to my room."

"It's fine," Charlie replies, but his voice sounds oddly strained.

Dev sets his cup on the bedside table next to Charlie's lotion. "Did you have a good birthday?"

Charlie smiles. "I had a perfect birthday. Thank you, Dev."

Dev wonders if he'll ever be able to hear Charlie say the words *thank you* without imagining him wrecked and wanting against a brick wall, thanking him for a kiss. A furious blush spreads over Charlie's face, almost like he's remembering the same thing. But Charlie doesn't remember. "I meant, *thank you* for the birthday. For Parisa and the cake and stuff. That's all I meant."

"Yeah, I figured. . . ."

Charlie starts suspiciously fidgeting around the room like a caged bird. "I really need to go to bed now, actually, so . . ."

Charlie doesn't remember. There is no way Charlie *remembers*. But. "The other night, outside the club—"

"Please," Charlie cuts him off with a strangled syllable. "Let's just go to bed and talk about this tomorrow."

Charlie fucking remembers.

Dev should let them both live in their little bubble of false ignorance, but he can't, because *Charlie remembers*. He remembers, and he knows Dev remembers, and he's just left him alone with the knowledge of the kiss all week.

Dev leaps up from the bed. "Okay," he snaps. "You can go to bed. But first, let's play a quick game." He grabs Charlie by the drawstring of his pants and pushes him back against the wall beside the bed, hard. "Let's see who pulls away first."

He only means to call Charlie's bluff—to force him to admit he remembers and is pretending not to for reasons Dev doesn't want to think about too deeply. Because those reasons are probably in the regret-and-shame family. Yet as soon as Charlie's body knocks against his, the joke of it dissolves, because Dev is reminded what it feels like to have Charlie there, tucked up just beneath his chin. It feels so good.

Dev fights to keep his amused grin, the grin that says *this is just a game, now admit you remember*. Charlie reaches up and presses two fingers to the corner of Dev's smile like he did that night, and Dev takes it as proof. "You liar, why did you—?"

And then Charlie presses his mouth to the corner of Dev's smile, and Dev's anger no longer feels relevant. Charlie pushes, then pulls back with some hint of reserve before he throws himself completely into the momentum of the kiss. It all comes back to Dev—he didn't imagine it outside the club. Kissing Charlie feels different than kissing anyone else. Maybe because it's new, or maybe because it's a little awkward, or maybe because it's Charlie, whose hands feel enormous on Dev's cheeks and the back of Dev's neck as Charlie folds himself around Dev exactly like a duvet.

Dev gives himself one minute. One minute to wrap his arms around Charlie's waist. One minute to pretend this is a thing they can keep doing. Then he pulls away.

"We can't. You're drunk."

Charlie's eyes snap open. "I'm not drunk at all. I didn't drink anything."

"Oh. Right."

Charlie releases Dev and stumbles over to the bed. "I'm sorry. I'm so, so sorry." He drops his head into his hands. "Shit. I am sorry."

"Which part are you sorry about?"

"The kissing-you part," Charlie whimpers into his hands. Dev didn't know adult men were capable of whimpering, but it's Charlie, so he whimpers majestically. He's whimpering over the thought of kissing Dev. It hurts more than it should.

"Kissing me just now?" Dev bites out, "or kissing me on Sunday and pretending you were blacked out?"

"*Dev.*" Charlie looks up, tears streaming down his face.

Well, *shit*. Dev can't fixate on his bruised ego when Charlie's crying. He sits down next to him on the bed. "Hey. Hey . . . it's fine. It's all fine." Dev puts a hand on Charlie's knee.

Charlie's entire body tightens at the touch. "How is it fine, exactly?"

It's not. It's the absolute opposite of fine. He kissed the person he's been assigned to handle *twice*, and now the star of their show is crying shirtless in a hotel room on his birthday. But Dev has a history of willing things into existence on the basis of sheer tenacity, so maybe if he keeps saying it's fine, it will become fine, eventually. Not for him, but for Charlie.

"I only meant . . . it's not a big deal."

Charlie slides his leg so he breaks contact with Dev's hand. "Not a big deal?"

"Yeah." He shrugs so nonchalantly, he almost convinces himself. "If I had a dollar for every time a straight dude kissed me on a lark, I'd have . . well, like, five dollars."

Charlie doesn't laugh. His brow is furrowed into his constipation face. It is maybe Dev's favorite face. "It's . . . it's a big deal to me, Dev."

"What do you mean?" Dev fears the answer—fears the shame and regret Charlie's about to put into words.

"I mean, I like you. Or I like kissing you. Or I don't know." A beautiful blush climbs up Charlie's neck, spreads across his cheeks. "But I get it. You don't want me to kiss you, and it's inappropriate for me to keep throwing myself at you."

Dev feels slightly untethered from his body. "You . . . you like kissing me?"

"I sort of thought that was obvious after the other night." Charlie gestures awkwardly to his body, and Dev remembers the feeling of Charlie pressed against him outside the club. He wants Charlie against him *right now*, but he knows he can never have that again.

"I thought you weren't really into kissing."

"Yes, this is sort of a new development for me," Charlie admits quietly. The confession lands somewhere south-southwest of Dev's sternum.

"Maybe that means you're becoming more comfortable in your own skin," Dev says. He's not sure who he's trying to convince. "Maybe as you continue developing genuine emotional connections with the women, you'll find that you can enjoy kissing them, too."

"Yeah." Charlie swallows. "Maybe."

They sit hip to hip in awkward silence. Dev should get up and leave. He should close the door between their adjoining rooms, close the door on this entire impossible moment. He should not reach over and touch Charlie's knee again. But he does.

He runs through his logical arguments: his job is to help turn Charlie into the perfect prince so he can fall in love with one of the contestants, and he's *so close*. Charlie is becoming an amazing star when the cameras are rolling, and he bonds with the women more each week. With more time, Dev knows he can help Charlie get his happily ever after. But not if he keeps doing this.

They're both staring at Dev's fingers on Charlie's navy sweatpants, and when Dev looks up, he realizes Charlie's face is only six inches away. "Dev." Charlie's voice is thick and close.

"It could be like practice dating," Dev hears himself say. Desperately, pathetically, so full of longing, he's convinced he might choke on it. "To help you feel more comfortable with it?"

Charlie nods and keeps nodding until his mouth meets Dev's in the small space between them on the bed. It's a soft kiss, hesitant, like Charlie's afraid he might be quizzed on it later. Dev tries to focus on the *practice* part of practice kissing, but as soon as Charlie's hand touches his waist, his sentient skin overrides all his logic and drives him up into Charlie's lap.

He stares down at Charlie as he straddles him. "Is this okay?" Dev asks. "Um, for practice purposes?"

"Yeah." Charlie's voice trembles. "Okay."

Dev scrapes his fingers through Charlie's damp hair. "Is this okay?"

Charlie swallows. "Definitely okay."

He leans forward, his mouth hovering next to Charlie's jaw. "Is this okay?"

Charlie makes an unintelligent sound of consent before Dev kisses his jaw, once, twice, three times, until he arrives at Charlie's ear. As soon as Dev takes Charlie's earlobe in his mouth, Charlie goes rigid beneath him, and he grabs onto Dev's thighs for support. "Okay?" Dev breathes as he scratches his teeth along the skin behind Charlie's ear.

"Dev," Charlie says. Or sort of *moans*.

Dev doesn't know if the moan means *stop* or *don't stop*, so he stops. "Okay?"

Charlie's hands are shaking when he takes Dev's face in his giant hands. "Yes. Very yes."

He arches up, meets Dev's mouth halfway, and Dev pushes Charlie back onto the bed.

Charlie's temerity gives way to something else. He snakes his hands up the front of Dev's shirt. Dev wishes he could bottle the feeling of Charlie's fingers on his stomach, use it as body wash. It would smell like oatmeal and taste like very intense toothpaste. *Focus, Dev. Practice kissing.*

"It's important to know what you like, Charlie," he says as he moves to find Charlie's earlobe again.

"I like that."

"I can tell." Dev likes it, too, likes the way Charlie's body responds to Dev's touch like a finely tuned instrument. He traces his fingertips over the absurd undulations of Charlie's biceps, and Charlie bites down on his bottom lip. "It's okay to create boundaries with the women, and it's also okay to ask for what you want."

"I want . . ." Charlie starts, inhales sharply. "I want to take your shirt off, please," he declares with perfect politeness. Charlie starts to remove Dev's shirt, but he does it so clumsily, it's like he's never taken off an article of clothing before.

"You could help instead of laughing at me," Charlie suggests.

"I literally cannot. You realize my arm is stuck, yes?"

Then the shirt's gone, and Charlie is staring at Dev's neck, his collarbone, his stomach. Dev stops laughing.

"You're so fucking beautiful," Charlie whispers.

It's the same thing Charlie said at the club, but he'd drunkenly shouted it at a stranger then. Now he says it quietly, almost shyly, and the words are only for Dev.

This is just practice, Dev reminds himself.

Charlie slides both hands up Dev's chest, one hand pausing over Dev's heart. He counts the seconds as the heartbeats drum against Charlie's fingers. "I think I really like you," Charlie says, even quieter, and the confession is like nitro and Sour Patch Kids consumed intravenously. Dev's too-big heart strains inside his chest, pushing against Charlie's hand, and he tries to hold back all the feelings he's not entitled to feel.

Because that's not how *Ever After* works.

In thirty-seven days, Charlie will get engaged to Daphne Reynolds. That's the story they've been crafting since night one. That's how Charlie gets his happy ending.

In thirty-seven days, Charlie will kiss Daphne Reynolds like this, but tonight Dev is going to lose himself in practice kisses, get carried away by Charlie's hands, the push and pull of Charlie's body, even though he knows how badly it's going to hurt tomorrow.

Charlie

He doesn't want to miss a second of this. Kissing Dev. Dev kissing *him*.

His sober brain wants to memorize every detail this time, so when Dev pulls away again, he'll have something to hold onto, something to remind him it was real. That once, he kissed someone he liked, and they kissed him back. Even if it's only for practice.

Dev is definitely going to pull away again. Charlie can feel it, even as he shifts beneath Dev so that Dev's hips slide down against his own, their mutual desire straining against flimsy sweatpants. Dev groans into his mouth as he rubs himself against Charlie's body. Charlie wants to eat that sound, pour it like sugar over fresh strawberries.

Dev is going to pull away, and Charlie needs to stay in this moment, to record it for posterity.

The smoky sweetness of Dev's skin this close; Dev's sharp knees and sharp elbows and sharp hipbones, all digging into him; the confidence of his tongue and the sureness of his kisses; the heat of his skin as his thumbs brush across Charlie's nipples, and *oh*. That's not something he knew his body could do, but it's like Dev knows everything about his own body and Charlie's. Charlie wants to remember that feeling most of all—the feeling of Dev bringing to life parts of himself he didn't know were there.

"Do you like that?" Dev's voice, against his throat. Dev's thumbs, circling his chest.

"Um, obviously."

Dev laughs, and then it's his tongue circling Charlie's skin, his mouth on Charlie's chest, sucking as he slides lower down his body, and—

"Dev." Charlie catches both of Dev's hands and stills him. "I think we should probably . . . stop. I need to . . ."

Dev understands and slides off Charlie. Charlie pecks Dev clumsily on the cheek and barely makes it to the bathroom. It doesn't take much to finish; he's almost there already. All he has to do is imagine what it would have been like if he'd been brave enough to let Dev keep going.

When he comes out of the bathroom, he can hear the sound of the shower running next door. He puts on a shirt and wanders into Dev's room, sits down on the edge of his bed. He leans over. The whole bed *smells* like Dev.

"Are you sniffing my pillow?"

Charlie jerks up and sees Dev standing five feet away, hair wet, in a different pair of basketball shorts. "No, I was *inspecting* your pillow. For . . . dirt."

Dev smiles, and something immense shifts inside Charlie's chest, something he doesn't understand, something he can't name.

"Yes, I was sniffing your pillow."

Dev laughs and comes over to the bed. "You really are kind of a weirdo."

Charlie opens his legs so his knees can bracket Dev's knees. "You smell good. That's hardly my fault."

Dev's fingers wind into his hair, and Charlie catches his hand. He kisses the soft skin on the inside of his wrist. Dev pitches forward a little. He looks like he wants to fall into Charlie's lap again, but then he forces himself not to. Holds back. "We should go to bed."

"Okay," Charlie says, and he starts to lie down.

Dev throws his head back and cackles. Charlie didn't know he was funny until Dev Deshpande started laughing with him. "In separate beds, sir. Come on."

Charlie lets Dev haul him off the bed and drag him toward the door between their rooms. "Good night, Charlie."

Charlie looks back at him one last time. "Good night, Dev."

"I'm going to kiss you now."

Angie Griffin leans in close to him on the fainting couch, and Charlie responds (quite composed, he thinks) with, "Cool."

Cool. It's totally cool he's sitting in the parlor of some ridiculous estate outside of New Orleans before a Crowning Ceremony where he'll send home two more women and keep eight—eight women who theoretically want to *marry him.* It's totally cool he has to sit here kissing Angie when all he wants to do is kiss Dev instead. It is totally cool Dev has to stand there *watching* him kiss Angie. Though he's not really sure how Dev feels about any of the kissing.

"*Cut!*" Skylar shouts from the other room, mercifully ending the awkward make-out session. Charlie and Angie both get up off the couch and head toward the main ballroom, where a different camera is filming Parisa.

Apparently, the only way Dev could convince Maureen Scott to let Parisa travel with the show was to have Parisa actually appear on the show. Charlie introduced her as his best friend for the cameras, and before the Crowning Ceremony, she's supposed to grill all the remaining contestants about their intentions. Parisa is clearly more intimidating than Dev realized, so everyone is regretting the arrangement at this point.

"I said be *tough*," Ryan tells Parisa. "I did not say make them cry."

Charlie shifts his gaze and sees that Daphne Reynolds is crying. Quite hard.

"I was asking her a simple question!" Parisa shouts back. "I didn't know she was going to crack so easily. Jesus."

Skylar calls for a ten-minute break, and Dev wanders outside through a pair of French doors. Charlie counts to thirty and follows him. It's a little after ten, but the air is still warm with Southern summer thickness and loud with cicadas. Dev stands on the far side of the courtyard, staring at a bush. "Hey," Charlie says, bumping him with his shoulder.

"Hey," Dev says back. When he smiles, it's a shadow of his normal one. "Your best friend is terrifying."

"She's just protective," Charlie says with a half shrug. "She wants what's best for me."

Dev nods, and he seems weirdly far away. Charlie needs him closer. He reaches out for his hand and tugs, pulling them into the maze of manicured shrubbery where no one will see. It's dark, but Charlie finds Dev's mouth anyway, teeth catching on his lip. Charlie's forehead bumps Dev's glasses, and Dev laughs into the kiss.

"We shouldn't—" Dev tries. But Dev said they shouldn't this morning when Jules texted she was bringing breakfast to their room in ten, and Dev still pushed Charlie back against the bathroom counter anyway. He said they shouldn't in the dressing room when he was helping Charlie put on his tux, and he still kissed Charlie until his knees buckled. Now he's saying they shouldn't, but he keeps pushing them deeper and deeper into the garden. Charlie would let Dev push him anywhere—he feels reckless with wanting him, and he'll happily accept whatever part of Dev he's willing to give him.

"I'm sorry about kissing Angie," he says when they finally pull apart.

Dev laughs hollowly. "That's literally the entire point of the show, Charlie."

"I know, but I wish it weren't. I don't want to kiss Angie and Daphne." He takes a deep breath. "I only want to kiss you."

Dev tightens in his arms. "Is that supposed to make me feel better?"

"I don't know," Charlie fumbles.

Dev doesn't say anything, and Charlie wishes Dev could give him *something*. He's told Dev he *really likes him*. He's told Dev he's fucking beautiful. He sniffed his pillow, for Christ's sake. It's obvious, so painfully obvious, that none of this is practice for Charlie. But Dev still looks at him like he's mentally planning his wedding to Daphne Reynolds.

"Dev," he says, "please tell me what you're feeling."

In the dark, Dev's thumb finds the corner of Charlie's mouth. "I don't think you need practice, Charlie."

"What does that mean?" he asks, even though he already knows.

"It means you should go inside and kiss Angie," Dev says. And then he pulls away, just like Charlie knew he would.

Story notes for editors:
Season 37, Episode 5

Air date:
Monday, October 11, 2021

Story producer:
Ryan Parker

Executive producer:
Maureen Scott

Scene: Post-paint fight during the Mardi Gras Group Quest, confessional with Daphne Reynolds

Location: Shot on location at the float warehouse, New Orleans

Daphne: [*Close-up of her smiling face, covered in yellow and purple paint.*] It was a great day! I had a great day! It was good to get the chance to talk to Charlie and clear the air between us. I shouldn't have thrown myself at him like that back at the ball. I . . . I let things . . . I let what other people thought . . . Anyway, we're fine now. Charlie gets it. Not everything has to be about physical connection. Charlie and I get along really well. So what if I'm not . . . if I don't want to . . . all that matters is getting the happily ever after in the end. Right?

WEEK FIVE

Charlie

"Dev! Come on!" Parisa pounds on his hotel door. "We're ready to go!"

"There's strudel!" Jules adds. "You love strudel!"

Charlie fists his hands and shoves them into his raincoat pockets. It's July, but it's *raining*. "Maybe Dev doesn't want to come with us," he mumbles.

Jules's head tilts at him. "Why wouldn't he come with us? We said we were going to explore the city together on our day off."

Charlie grinds the toe of his shoe into the hotel carpet outside of Dev's room. "Maybe he just . . . maybe we should go without him?"

Jules tries calling his phone, and Parisa tries knocking, but neither attempt gets any response. So, they explore Munich without him.

Dev hasn't talked to Charlie at all since the garden, hasn't even looked at him, and Charlie shouldn't be surprised. He shouldn't be hurt. What did he think was going to happen? Did he think they would *be* together in secret for the rest of the season? Did he honestly think Dev would want that? When he made it so clear everything was for practice, so Charlie could be a better version of himself for the cameras?

Charlie doesn't want that either. He didn't come on this show for the stupid fairy tales it sells to gullible people. He doesn't want a relationship or romance. He doesn't want someone who kisses him numb and calls him love. He doesn't.

Charlie tries to enjoy the Glockenspiel and the strudel and this precious time with Parisa, but even as his body wanders up and down the halls of the Residenz, his mind is behind that closed door with Dev.

Tuesday morning, the crew meets in the hotel lobby for the first Munich Group Quest, which, to Charlie's infinite delight, will involve horses. Dev is late.

Dev has never been late for filming, and when he finally shows up, he's wearing black sweatpants and a wool beanie. He hasn't shaved, apparently hasn't showered. In the van on the way to set, Dev keeps his headphones in so he doesn't have to talk to anyone and silently eats chocolate-dipped biscuits from the Aldi down the street from the hotel. Jules pokes at him for a bit, tries to draw him out, but even she gives up eventually.

When they arrive at the shoot out in the Black Forest, Dev coaches Charlie robotically. He doesn't joke with Charlie, doesn't touch Charlie unnecessarily. He won't even look him in the eye.

The horses make everything a thousand times worse, especially because Skylar won't let him wear a helmet, and he's pretty sure he's going to fall off this massive beast and get concussed. With any luck, he'll end up with selective amnesia, and he won't remember what Dev was like before Munich, so he won't have to miss Dev so much when he's standing right there.

"Is Dev okay?" Angie asks during her and Charlie's one-on-one time. "He doesn't seem like his normal self."

Charlie doesn't know what to say, but he must look thoroughly pathetic, because Angie reaches up and takes him by the chin. "Oh, sweetheart. Are *you* okay?"

"Not really, no."

"What is it?"

He knows he can't tell her, but he wishes he could; as the only openly queer contestant, she might understand. He wishes he could tell *someone* that for one night, Dev felt like *his*, and now he feels like someone else entirely. "I . . . I just want Dev to be okay again."

Angie looks up at him with a soft expression. Then, she pulls him in close, brushes kisses along his forehead. "Sweetie, I know. I know."

Charlie looks at Angie. *Really* looks at her. At her beautiful hair, which she wears pulled back today. At her dark brown eyes, framed with pretty lashes. At her heart-shaped face, which comes to a lovely point at the chin, kind of like Dev's.

Angie is smart and funny and kind. She listens to him, and she respects him, and he thinks maybe he could learn to love her, at least platonically, at least if he really tried. He wonders if loving Angie would fix things with Dev.

By Wednesday morning, the panic has started to settle on Charlie's skin, which is prickling and restless.

Dev has told the production team he has the flu, and he uses this as an excuse to get out of crew breakfast and crew dinner and crew nightcaps in the *bräuhaus* across the street from the hotel. He's literally willing to lie about being sick to avoid seeing Charlie.

For his part, Charlie has tried to distract himself by forcing Jules on long, punishing runs with him in the rain; he lifts every night in the hotel gym until his body goes numb. It fixes nothing.

Wednesday's Group Quest is out near Neuschwanstein Castle, its Romanesque white turrets rising out of the fog on the hill. It's the real-life inspiration for *Sleeping Beauty*'s castle, and therefore half the inspiration for this godforsaken show, but based on Dev's disinterest, it might as well be a Lego castle constructed by a six-year-old.

The contestants compete in a medieval-style obstacle course with the castle perfectly framed in the backdrop of every shot. Charlie tries to focus on spending time with the contestants— with Lauren L., who successfully manages to give him a piggyback ride when Sabrina dares her to; with Angie, who cheers him up by telling dad jokes; with Daphne, who is perfectly pleasant as long as Parisa is twenty yards away.

Instead, all he can focus on is why Dev is curled up in a camp chair half-asleep on the edge of set. By his lunch break, he's in so many knots about it, he knows only one thing can help him. One *person*.

Charlie finds Parisa shouting at a producer, which is pretty much what she does every time she comes to set. "Don't stand there and tell me *Ever After*'s perpetuation of internalized misogyny is unintentional, Aiden! If I were running this show, I would— Oh, hey, babe." Her face immediately softens when she sees him.

"Do you want to go for a walk with me?"

Parisa follows him up the muddy path toward the castle. "You okay, Hot-Ass?" she asks when they're out of earshot of the crew.

"Yeah, I just . . ." He takes three deep breaths. Parisa is his best friend. His *pansexual* best friend, who is unlikely to be scandalized by this news. "I need to talk to you about something."

"Finally," is what Parisa says. She tugs him over to a damp bench on the side of the path, and they sit on their coats. "I'm ready."

He takes three more deep breaths before he can say it, and still, it comes out as a question. "I maybe, sort of, have feelings for Dev? And, like, maybe kissed him?"

"Oh my God, really?" she asks in a monotone. "I am totally shocked by this unexpected revelation."

"So, you knew, then?"

She shrugs. "I suspected."

"How?"

"You talk about him *a lot*, and when you look at him, your whole face relaxes," she says so matter-of-factly, Charlie feels like he might as well be ass-naked on this bench, completely exposed to the world. "Plus, as soon as I saw him, it just made sense. He's your type."

"You think my type is six-foot-four skinny dudes with unfortunate haircuts?"

"I can't really explain why, but yes."

"And you're not mad at me?"

"Mad? Hot-Ass, you know I don't legitimately want to marry you, right?"

"I do, but you also sent me on this show to get engaged to a woman, so . . ."

"Quite frankly, you kissing your producer is the most interesting thing that's ever happened on this heteronormative cesspool of a shitty television show."

He waits for her to pull out the rug, waits for the other shoe to drop. He waits for her to tell him he needs to keep this new development hidden away. But of course she doesn't. "That's . . . it? That's all you're going to say?"

"I don't see the need to have a whole sexual identity crisis about it," she says, dismissively waving her hand in the direction of a tour group of loud French teenagers. "Unless you *want* to have a sexual identity crisis about it. Are you freaking out about being attracted to dudes?"

"Not really," he says. "Besides, I'm not really sure I *am* attracted to dudes. Like, plural."

"Are you sexually attracted to women?"

"I don't know. . . . I don't think so, no. I never have been before." Then he collapses against her soft side. "What do you think that means?"

"So, you *do* what to have a whole sexual identity crisis about it? Okay. Do you think you might be asexual?" She asks it so simply, without any judgment or pressure, and he can't believe in four years of friendship, they've never had this conversation. He wonders how many times Parisa wanted to initiate it and was patiently waiting for him to open the door just a crack.

"I've never really considered . . . but based on recent developments, no, I don't think I'm asexual," he finally says. "I'm definitely not sex-repulsed."

"Not everyone who is asexual is. Asexuality is a spectrum." Parisa holds her hands two feet apart like she's measuring for a very small Ikea bookshelf. "On one end, you have allosexual people, or people who experience sexual attraction, and on the other end you have asexual people, who do not. But there is a whole range between those two things."

"Very informative."

"I'm just saying, you might be into dudes but also demisexual, which means you need emotional connection to feel sexual attraction. Or you might be demiromantic or graysexual or—"

He cringes. "I don't know if the specific label is important to me."

"It doesn't have to be," she says, "and you're not obligated to figure it out, or come out, or explain yourself to anyone, ever. But also"—she drops her hands from their spectrum and tucks an arm around his shoulder—"labels can be nice sometimes. They can give us a language to understand ourselves and our hearts better. And they can help us find a community and develop a sense of belonging. I mean, if you didn't have the correct label for your OCD, you wouldn't be able to get the treatment you need, right?"

He stares out at the muddy road winding up to the castle. "That's just it. I feel like I've been shoved into different boxes with different labels my whole life. I don't know if I want more boxes."

He can feel Parisa nod against him. "That's fair, and look, for me, sexuality is fluid, but I want you to know, you're allowed to have whatever feelings you have toward Dev, even if they don't fit into some fairy-tale idea of what relationships are supposed to be. You're allowed to want the romance parts without the sex parts. Or the sex parts without the romance parts. All of those feelings are valid. You're deserving of a relationship in whatever form you want it."

He holds his breath like he's trying to hold Parisa's unquestioning acceptance, her unwavering love, inside his chest for a little longer. "That means a lot to me, but . . ." He puffs out his cheeks and just says it: "What if I maybe *do* want both parts with Dev?"

"*Oh.*"

"But Dev doesn't want either part with me."

"Seems highly improbable."

He tells Parisa everything—about practice dates and practice kisses, about the script and realizing what he felt at three in the morning, about the Bourbon Stain Incident and tequila shots and Lady Gaga. "And now he's pretending to have the flu to avoid me because he doesn't feel the same way."

"How do *you* feel?"

"What?"

"You said Dev doesn't feel the same way. So how do *you* feel?"

He wants to slowly back away from that question like it's a bomb about to go off in his hands. "I feel *so much*," he hears himself say, running toward the bomb, opening himself up entirely to the injury of it. "I think about him *constantly*. I always want to be talking to him, or touching him, or looking at him, and I want him to look at me in a way I've never wanted anyone to look at me before. That doesn't . . . make sense."

"Yes, it does," she says, her words a quiet invitation for him to keep talking.

"I can't explain it, but when I'm kissing Dev, I'm not in my head about it. I don't feel the pressure to make it work. It just *works*. And I don't have to force myself to feel anything. I feel *everything*."

He stops himself and cuts his eyes to Parisa on the bench beside him. She's making her soft, gooey face, and she reaches up to brush his hair off his forehead. He continues. "And I've got these eight women, who are actually all kind of spectacular, but I just don't want to kiss any of them. And I signed a contract that requires me to propose to one of them at the end of this. And I'm stuck here on this show with Dev for another four weeks, and he doesn't want me." His voice cracks at the end, and he tries to disguise it as a cough.

Parisa doesn't buy it. "And you asked him that? Directly? You asked Dev if he wants you, and he said no? Like, to your beautiful face?"

"Well, not exactly . . ."

"Has it occurred to you that Dev also had to sign a contract to work on this show, and that his legally precludes kissing you?"

"Uh . . ."

"That *kissing you* is probably going to get him fired from a job he loves so much?"

"I mean, I considered—"

"And don't you think there is a good chance Dev's current depression was triggered by the fact that he likes you, too, and that it's literally his job to help you fall in love with someone else?"

"Dev doesn't have depression," he corrects.

"Take it from someone who has been in a committed relationship with Lexapro and cognitive behavioral therapy since she was eighteen," Parisa says, "your handler is in the midst of a major depressive episode."

Charlie shakes his head. She's wrong. Dev doesn't struggle with his mental health. Dev is *Dev*. He's always happy, always smiling, always thinking about other people. He usually thrives on set, fluttering around to everyone, helping and chatting and feeding off the energy of it all. He's the most charming person Charlie's ever met. That's not the description of a depressed person.

And yeah, maybe he loves Leland Barlow because he sings about mental illness, and maybe sometimes he gets sad—like after his fight with Ryan, or outside the club in New Orleans— but that's not the same thing as being depressed. Just because he hasn't been his usual Fun Dev self lately . . .

Charlie remembers what Dev said in the town car, about Ryan only ever wanting Fun Dev, and it hits him. "Oh, shit. Dev struggles with depression."

Parisa claps him on the back. "Knew you'd get there eventually."

He's not entirely sure what you're supposed to do when you discover your sort-of friend who you also like to kiss might have clinical depression, but he figures he could start by talking to Dev. Except when he and Parisa get back to set, Dev is nowhere to be found. Ryan informs him that Dev's gone home sick with Jules. Charlie has to wait until they're done filming for the day.

When they get back to the hotel, he goes straight to Dev's room, where the "Do Not Disturb" sign hangs on the doorknob. Jules answers, looking her usual combination of annoyed and exhausted, with a twinge of sadness tucked away in the corners of her eyes. "He won't talk to me about what's wrong."

"Let me try."

He steps into the room alone. The air is stale and thick with the scent of unwashed things, and a kick of anxiety rockets through him at the filth. But then he sees Dev cocooned on the bed, the comforter sealed tight above his head, and he's able to push aside those thoughts.

Charlie opens the window before he climbs onto the bed and tries to pull back the comforter. Dev stubbornly holds on tight, but Charlie's stronger, and he yanks the blanket away from Dev's face. The sight makes Charlie's throat close up: unwashed hair, no glasses, curled up in a tight ball.

"Leave," Dev grunts into his pillow.

"Tell me what you need."

"I need you to *leave*."

Part of him wants to. The more powerful part of him reaches out to push Dev's hair off his forehead. "Please tell me what you need."

Dev opens his eyes and looks up at Charlie. They're the color of his perfect violin and filled with tears, and he's the most beautiful person Charlie's ever seen, even now. "I need you to leave. I . . . I don't want you to see me like this."

Charlie thinks about all the times he's pushed someone away because he didn't want them to see his anxiety and his obsessiveness, and he thinks about what he really wanted all those times people took him at his word. He climbs back onto the bed and reaches out for Dev. Dev pulls away, fights him off, eventually curls down against his chest, and holds on tight. Dev sinks deep into Charlie, crying into the folds of his oxford shirt. Charlie tries to hold Dev like Dev held him that night in the bathroom, carrying his weight.

Most of the time, Dev is like a human bonfire walking around generously warming everyone with his presence. But burning that bright and that fiercely must be exhausting; no one can sustain it forever. Charlie wishes he could tell Dev it's okay to flicker out sometimes. It's okay to tend to his own flame, to keep himself warm. He doesn't have to be everything for everyone else all the time.

Charlie wishes he could cup his hands around the feeble Dev flame, blow on its embers to keep him going before he burns himself out completely.

"Do you get like this a lot?"

A few quiet sobs dislodge from Dev's throat. "I get like this sometimes, yeah," he whispers. "Little funks. But I bounce back. I'll bounce right back."

"How can I help when it gets like this?"

Dev folds himself tighter against Charlie, all those lovely sharp points digging in. "You can just stay," he says, at last. "No one ever stays."

As Dev falls asleep on his chest, Charlie understands so clearly that Dev has spent four weeks trying to convince Charlie he deserves something Dev doesn't believe he himself deserves. That whatever these little funks are—these evenings of the brain— they've convinced Dev he doesn't deserve someone who stays. Charlie wishes he could find the words, find a way, to show Dev what he's worth, even if this thing between them is already over. Even if it was only ever practice.

But Charlie doesn't know how you show someone they're worthy of being loved. So he just stays.

Dev

It was his seventh therapist—or maybe his eighth?—who asked him to describe it once, the way it feels when the depression is at its worst. Dev told her it was like drowning from the inside. Like his brain was filling with water. Like sitting on the bottom of the deep end of the west Raleigh public pool the way he would as a kid, letting the silence and the pressure crush him until he couldn't stand it any longer.

That is how he feels when he opens his eyes Thursday morning, so it takes a while to figure out when he is and where he is and why Charlie Winshaw is sitting on the edge of his bed tying his shoes. Relief sweeps across Charlie's face. "You're awake."

Dev clears his throat. "You stayed."

A shy smile tugs at the corner of Charlie's mouth. "How are you feeling?"

Like I almost drowned but didn't. "That question is a little too much to handle pre-coffee."

"You get in the shower, then, and I'll go find some coffee." One more smile, then Charlie climbs off the bed. Dev watches him move to the desk chair, watches him slip on his coat, watches him grab the hotel room key off the desk.

Charlie turns to look at him again, propped up against the headboard. He takes two uneasy steps toward the door. Hesitates. Pivots. Then he takes three determined steps toward the bed. Charlie grabs Dev's face and kisses him firmly in the middle of the forehead. "I'll be right back, okay?"

And then he's gone.

When the door clicks shut behind Charlie, Dev takes a deep breath, gathers up what little energy he has, and gets out of bed. He takes an exceptionally long shower, trying to make up for the four days he didn't shower, for the days he could barely get out of bed at all. He lathers the soap between his hands and imagines he can scrub off the days of fog, the days of never feeling fully awake, the days of climbing deeper and deeper into that place where he feeds the darkness with his self-loathing, his loneliness, his feelings of inadequacy. The depression has a special knack for listing all his shortcomings, and this time, it had his epic mistake of kissing Charlie to throw in his face.

Kissing Charlie—and coming to terms with the fact that he needs to stop kissing Charlie—shouldn't have been enough to trigger his depression, but unfortunately, that's not how his depression works. It's not logical or reasonable. It doesn't need some catastrophic tragedy to turn the chemicals of his brain against him. Tiny tragedies are more than enough.

"I couldn't find black coffee, but I got you a large Americano," Charlie says as soon as Dev gets out of the bathroom. "Jules texted, and call time is in an hour."

"Thanks." Dev reaches around for the paper cup and Charlie startles.

"You shaved," Charlie announces. He lifts his hand, like he's about to touch Dev's cleanly shaven cheek, but then he clasps both hands around his tea instead. "I . . . I missed your face."

It's a surprisingly honest thing to say. He doesn't know what to make of Charlie saying sweet things to him, or of Charlie kissing him before he left, or of Charlie holding him all night, even after Dev gave him every reason to leave. Dev is usually the one who takes care of people. No one ever takes care of him. "Um, thanks for the coffee."

He sits back on the edge of the bed. Charlie leans against the desk across from him. In the three feet between them is the kissing and the not kissing and Charlie holding him while he cried. "Do you want to talk about it?" Charlie asks.

"By 'it,' you mean my depression?" He means for the words to come out flippantly, but he's still half-submerged, so he sounds bitter instead. Charlie doesn't say anything. "I . . . I don't really like to talk about it. Sunil and Shameem made me go to a dozen different therapists for 'my moods' as a kid, and I just got sick of discussing it to death. It's not even a big deal."

"Are you in therapy now?"

"I said it's not a big deal."

Charlie hesitates, then crosses the room and sits beside Dev, their thighs lined up against an ugly hotel comforter. Charlie doesn't say anything, but it's not his usual awkward silence. It's silence as invitation. He reaches for Dev's hand. Interlaces their fingers.

"They're just little funks," Dev insists, "and I don't usually get this way during work."

Charlie squeezes Dev's hand. "You . . . you know night one, after the boyfriend punched me in the face, when you asked me why I came on the show?"

Dev isn't sure where this is coming from, but he nods.

Charlie takes three deep breaths. "The truth is, I got fired from WinHan. From my own company. I had a breakdown. Well, I had a lot of breakdowns, actually, but one really big breakdown at our quarterly board meeting. I started to have a panic attack, and I tried to excuse myself from the room, but Josh blocked the door and wouldn't let me leave, because they needed my vote for some expansion he'd had proposed. You've seen how it is when I have a panic attack. It was . . . Rumors started going around, that I was unstable. *Crazy*."

Charlie takes an unsteady breath, and Dev knows he shouldn't. He does it anyway. He winds his free hand into Charlie's hair, teases apart the curls until Charlie leans into the comforting touch. "Anyway, Josh was worried my reputation was going to cost him investors. There was an emergency vote of no confidence, and I was removed as CTO. Parisa tried to spin the story, bury the reason I was removed from the company, but it didn't matter. The rumors still got out."

He pauses, and Dev explodes. "That's such *bullshit*! There are so many people who have done *actual terrible things* who are actively working in tech! Mark Zuckerberg exists! And firing someone for having OCD—that's got to be illegal. I'm surprised Parisa didn't sue."

"Josh never knew about my OCD," Charlie says quietly. "It's not something I want people to know about. Which is to say, I get it. I get not wanting to talk about your mental health with most people. But you can talk about it with me. If you ever want to. Okay?"

Dev doesn't know what to do with what Charlie is offering him.

"You know, you're good at this," he jokes. "A conversation like this in front of the cameras, with one of the contestants, would go a long way to earn you sympathy. Of course, we'd have to switch 'mental health' for 'relationship trauma' or something, but—"

Charlie smiles, but it doesn't reach his stormy eyes. Charlie has shared something huge and private. He's flung his doors wide open and he's inviting Dev to do the same. Dev thinks about the darkness, about drowning, about tiny tragedies. He pulls away his hands. "I really am fine."

Story notes for editors:
Season 37, Episode 6

Story producer:
Ryan Parker

Air date:
Monday, October 18, 2021

Executive producer:
Maureen Scott

Scene: Pre-Crowning Ceremony conversation between Mark Davenport and Charlie Winshaw

Location: Shot on location at the Justizpalast in Munich, Germany

Mark: Well, here we are. Over halfway through your quest to find love. How are you feeling?

Charlie: Hungry and tired, mostly.

Mark: Fair enough. You're about to send home two more women, which means you'll be down to your top six. Do you know who you're sending home?

Charlie: It's a difficult choice. All of the women here are so incredible, and I've loved my time with all of them.

Mark: Be honest, Charlie. You were skeptical of the process when we started.

[*Wide shot of both men laughing in their leather chairs.*]

Charlie: Maybe a bit. It was hard for me to imagine being able to get to a place of emotional intimacy that quickly with another person. I think you can't really understand this process if you haven't experienced it yourself—you're together all the time. You're going through stressful situations together, and it bonds you in this unique and intense way. Add to that meeting someone who understands you, who *sees* you.

Mark: Do you have a specific *someone* in mind?

Charlie: Maybe.

Mark: Can you see yourself falling in love by the end of this?

Charlie: Absolutely.

WEEK SIX

Charlie

"Did you know that South Africa has eleven official languages?"

"I did know that," Jules groans as she jostles forward in the horrendous customs line at the Cape Town airport, "because you already told me. On the plane. *Twice*."

"And fun fact—"

"Ten bucks says the fact will not actually be fun," Parisa interjects, because she clearly chose to extend her trip with the ulterior motive of mocking him on a new continent.

"*Fun fact*," Charlie says louder. "South Africa has three capital cities, and Cape Town is one of them."

"Told you. Where's my ten bucks?"

"No one bet against you," Jules snaps. "*No one* thought the fact would be fun."

There's nothing quite like a twelve-hour flight to turn the entire *Ever After* crew into a bunch of grumpy zombies, sniping at each other over travel arrangements and bickering about permits and paperwork. Charlie only really cares about *one* grumpy zombie, though, and he's standing quietly next to him in line, his shoulders stooped forward like he's carrying an impossible weight.

He's not. Charlie's been carrying Dev's duffle since they got off the plane. He wishes he could carry Dev, too, wishes he could scoop him into his arms. But Skylar is right in front of them, and Ryan is right behind them, and everywhere Charlie looks, there are reminders of all the reasons he can't hold Dev through the rough parts. So, he says, "Another fun fact: did you know locals call the cloud coverage over Table Mountain the *tablecloth*?"

Dev looks up and rolls his eyes. Charlie will take it. It's a reaction, at least.

For all Dev's talk about "bouncing back," and his insistence that he's fine, the last few days in Munich were difficult. Dev's recovery was more recursive than linear—more two steps forward, followed by a catatonic collapse back. Long stretches of silence, bursts of irritability, little crying spurts. But when Charlie asked what he needed, Dev would tell him, mostly, even if all he needed was space.

Charlie knows there is no magical cure-all for depression, just like there is no magical cure-all for anxiety, but he can't help but want to make Dev feel better. To show him what he deserves. So he maybe did something *slightly* irrational in the service of cheering Dev up. Something Parisa had to fly to Cape Town to help him coordinate for the end of the week. Because fun facts alone obviously aren't going to do the trick.

The show has booked a top-floor suite at a hotel in Green Point with three bedrooms for Charlie, Dev, and Jules. Since Parisa was supposed to go home after Munich, she has to convince a production manager to let her sleep on the couch in their suite, promising to keep everything pristine for filming Charlie's confessionals the next morning.

"I'm not sleeping on the couch," Parisa says as soon as it's just the four of them. She drops her luggage in the first bedroom, and Jules claims the second, prompting a very awkward shuffle where Charlie and Dev pretend to be uncomfortable at the prospect of sharing the master. At least, Charlie's pretending.

Jules puts her hands on her hips. "It's a king-size bed. You'll be fine. If you're worried about cooties, build a pillow barrier down the middle of the bed," she suggests, and then she slams her bedroom door in their faces.

Dev responds to the revelation that they'll be sharing a bed for the next week by simply dropping his duffle on the floor and flopping backward onto the bed.

"*Shoes*," Charlie scolds.

Dev sighs and kicks off his filthy shoes in a pile on the floor. Charlie props his suitcase up on the stand. He hangs his shirts, then his slacks, then—

"Can unpacking wait until morning?" Dev asks with his head in a pile of pillows.

"That's how clothes wrinkle."

Charlie is also maybe stalling a little bit.

"That's what irons are for."

"I do not believe you've ever used an iron in your life."

When he's done folding his shorts into dresser drawers, Charlie goes into the bathroom to perform his nighttime routine. Thirty minutes later, he comes out of the bathroom, and Dev is still lying on top of the bed in his khaki shorts, scrolling through his phone. "Are you going to change for bed?"

Dev turns toward him, heavy-lidded. "Are you going to come over here and help me?"

Charlie crosses his arms and leans against the bathroom doorframe. "You're ridiculous."

"Can you promise me something?" Dev squints one eye. "Promise you will always blush like you are right now."

Charlie feels his face heat around the collar of his shirt. "I think I can safely make that promise, yeah."

"Good. Now are you going to come to bed?"

Charlie wants to climb into bed next to Dev, but he can't seem to unstick himself from the wall. They haven't slept in the same bed since the one night in Munich, haven't kissed since New Orleans, haven't talked about any of it at all. They're back to pretending like it never happened. And Dev—Dev is still so closed off. Charlie isn't sure what he's allowed, and if he climbs into bed next to Dev, he's going to want all of it.

Dev studies his not-so-casual lean. "What are you doing over there?"

"Just looking."

"Looking at what?"

"At you." Dev nervously knocks his glasses up his nose with his knuckle. Charlie likes having the power to make Dev nervous, so he adds, "I like to look at you."

Dev swallows, his face suddenly serious. "You shouldn't say things like that to me."

"Why not?"

"Because it makes it very difficult for me to keep my hands to myself."

Charlie smiles. "That's kind of the idea."

He slowly approaches the bed—*their bed*, the bed they'll be sharing for the next week. He feels as nervous as Dev looks. Nervous about the kissing, and about not talking about the kissing, not admitting what the kissing means. About what this *is*, about how it wasn't supposed to happen. About how badly he wants it to happen.

Dev meets him at the edge of the bed. "You're spiraling," Dev whispers as he brushes his fingers along the ridge of Charlie's twisted brow. Dev plants a kiss there, in the place where Charlie's eyebrows bunch in the middle. "Tell me what you need."

Charlie needs to kiss him, so he does. And when Dev kisses him back, the spiral loosens. Dev traces Charlie's bottom lip with his tongue, and when Charlie opens for him, everything shifts around the fixed point of where they come together. Hands in his hair and hands up his shirt, and Dev's tongue and Dev's teeth, falling back onto the bed, the beautiful asymmetry of their bodies. Moving quickly. Too quickly.

Charlie rolls off of Dev to catch his breath. Dev pouts petulantly in response.

"I was thinking," Charlie pants.

Dev pokes his ribs. "No thinking."

"*I was thinking* . . . you know what we haven't done in a while? Gone on a date. My skills are likely to atrophy at this rate."

"You think you have skills?"

"I'm serious." He sits up so he can look down at Dev, black hair matted and messy against a hotel comforter, glasses crooked on his nose. "Let me take you on a date tomorrow."

"For practice, you mean?" Dev clarifies.

"Sure." Charlie swallows down the lump forming in his throat. "For practice."

Dev

He couldn't say no to ten drunken seconds against a brick wall with Charlie Winshaw, and now Charlie's staring at him with those earnest gray eyes like he thinks Dev has the willpower to say no to this. To a date with him.

"We have to film your confessionals first thing in the morning," Dev says, impressed by his own professionalism, particularly in light of the fact that he had his hands up Charlie's shirt two minutes ago. "You have to tell the cameras all about how you could see yourself falling in love in Cape Town."

"Hmm," is all Charlie says about that. "After confessionals, then."

"I don't—"

Charlie interrupts his new excuse by reaching for the sides of his face. Charlie kisses him again, and it feels so different than when they kissed in New Orleans. There's no frenzy in it, no razor's edge of panic cutting between their lips. No fear that at any minute the kissing could end. The kiss feels steadying, solid, like something Dev can lean against. Something that isn't going to collapse beneath him.

Even though, rationally, he knows it will. He knows that wanting Charlie is self-destructive and stupid—that he'll probably end up back in the dark, drowning place—but he wants him anyway.

"Okay. Yeah. A practice date," Dev says when Charlie releases his mouth.

Charlie smiles, and Dev tries to hide the fact that he's smiling, too.

Dev takes off his jeans and changes one T-shirt for another before he finally crawls into their massive bed. Charlie lies down stiff as a board on the opposite side. It feels like there's an ocean of space between them. There's been an ocean of space between them all week.

"Good night, Charlie," Dev says as he clicks off the light beside the bed.

"Good night, Dev."

Dev tries lying on his back, tries turning onto his side, tries not to think about how epically fucked this season truly is thanks to him. Tries not to think about Charlie five feet away.

"Are you asleep?" he asks into the dark.

"It's been three minutes, so no."

Dev twists and turns uncomfortably. "You know in Munich . . . when you sort of . . . held me?"

Charlie slides across the bed without further prompting. Dev can feel his body heat between the sheets as he gets closer. His solidity.

Charlie begins to gather Dev up and pull him up onto his chest. "Do you want to be on top?"

Dev opens his mouth to retort.

"Oh, shut up, I heard it," Charlie snipes as he wraps his arms tighter around his shoulders.

"Are you blushing?"

Charlie doesn't respond. Dev wishes he could see his face

right now, but he settles for nuzzling himself into Charlie's warm throat.

"And now you're pretending to be asleep to escape your embarrassment."

"Please, Dev," Charlie says, but Dev can hear the smile in his voice, "just go to sleep."

So Dev does. It's the best sleep he's had all season.

It's winter here, fifty-five degrees with a cold breeze coming off the water, and early-morning clouds lingering over the mountain. Behind the clouds, though, Dev can see the sky is a perfect blue—as blue as the ocean, as crisp as the South African air, as beautiful as Charlie wearing a cowl-neck sweater and a pair of snug, dark-wash jeans.

"It's not too late to go back for real shoes," Charlie says as they climb into their Uber in front of the hotel. "We're going to be walking a lot. Victoria and Alfred Waterfront, please," he tells their driver. They've told the crew they're going to an undisclosed location to spend the day planning the rest of Charlie's romantic journey, and Dev has relinquished total control to Charlie to plan the entire (practice) date. So far, the date has only included Charlie being fussy about Dev's flip-flops.

"I can walk in these."

Charlie looks wholly unconvinced.

In his six years with *Ever After*, Dev's circled the globe numerous times, visited a dozen Caribbean islands, put his toes in almost every ocean; he's watched a proposal at sunrise over Machu Picchu, and he's written confessions of love on six continents. Cape Town is somehow better than all of that, better than *anywhere* he's ever been. The colors are brighter here, with Table Mountain rising massive above the city, and Dev is in love even before he discovers what bunny chow is.

He marvels at the metallic tray weighed down with curry. "It's Indian food. Inside a bread bowl."

"I thought you might like it."

"It's Indian food *inside a bread bowl.*"

"Yes, I know, Dev. I chose this place."

"It's Indian food inside a *fucking* bread bowl!"

"You're shouting," Charlie says, shooting an apologetic look at the street vendor ladling Charlie's vegetarian tikka masala. "Did you know South Africa has a large population of Indian immigrants?"

Dev did know this, because Charlie listened to a podcast on the way here and insisted on reciting the entire thing from memory.

After they eat an amazing lunch of Indian food served inside a bread bowl, Charlie leads the way to a giant market set up in an old warehouse where hundreds of stalls sell craft supplies and delicacies and little curios. The space is cavernous, echoing with sounds, stuffed with smells. Dev immediately loves it.

Charlie immediately does not. As soon as they step inside, his shoulders climb up toward his ears and his eyebrows twist into their usual snarl. "Let's take a quick minute."

Dev leads them over to a bench out of the way, and Charlie collapses onto it. Dev discreetly presses the Morse code pattern between his shoulder blades while he calms down. "Sorry . . ." Charlie exhales. "I wanted today to be perfect."

"Today already is perfect. Do you need to be reminded about the bread bowl?"

Charlie smiles feebly.

"We don't have to stay here," Dev offers. "We can go somewhere else."

"Don't you want to check out the stalls?"

"I just want to spend the day with you," he says without thinking. "I mean, since this is a practice date, I think it's good for you to practice speaking up for what you need."

Charlie takes a steady breathe and smiles. "I think I'm okay, actually. Let's look around for a bit."

"Great. I need your help getting my parents something classy for their fortieth anniversary this September."

Charlie lets himself be hauled off the bench. "I'll need to know more about Sunil and Shameem to be of any help in this regard."

Dev does not fixate on the fact that Charlie remembers his parents' names from one casual reference. "Well, imagine two Indian kids, coming to the US in the sixties, growing up in super traditional households, meeting freshman year at Cornell in the premed program. Then picture them getting arrested at various protests, becoming art history professors instead of doctors, and smoking a ton of weed, and you pretty much have my parents. Now they spend most of their time running a Raleigh art co-op and going on weekend yoga retreats run by white people."

Charlie stares at him, unblinking. "That all tracks."

They wander toward a stall selling gorgeous ceramics—very Shameem, very not in Dev's price range. A little plaque at the stand explains that half of all proceeds go toward a community school in a nearby township. "What about your parents?" Dev can't resist reverting back to their old dynamic, with Dev trying to weasel his way behind Charlie's layers.

Only Dev doesn't have to weasel. Charlie opens right up. "There's not much to say about my parents. My dad is a construction foreman. My mom stayed home to raise me and my brothers, who all played football and loved beating the shit out of me. No one in my house had the slightest idea what to do with a little neurodivergent kid who feared contamination and loved taking apart household appliances to learn how they worked. There is a reason I wanted to leave at sixteen."

It takes what little willpower Dev has not to reach out and kiss Charlie on his face in the middle of the market, and thankfully the artist steps out from behind the register at that exact moment.

"Can I help you find anything?" she asks.

"Your work is lovely," Charlie says. Dev studies a beautiful bowl and serving platter set, imagines the look on his parents' face when they discover he bought them something other than a cheap tea towel from his travels.

"Are you looking for anything in particular?"

"A gift for my parents," Dev answers. "They would love your pieces."

"Those ones were made by my wife, actually."

Charlie tugs on the edge of Dev's jean jacket. "You should buy them."

Dev subtly tilts the bowl so he can see the price tag on the bottom. He's fuzzy on the rand-to-US-dollar exchange rate, but he's not *that* fuzzy. "I think—sorry, I think we're going to keep looking."

Dev tries to slide around the end of the stall, but Charlie doesn't move. "Do you ship items to the United States?"

"Yes, although it usually takes three to four weeks."

"That's perfect. We'll take the bowl and the serving platter."

"Charlie, no. I can't. . . ." Dev leans in so the artist won't overhear. "I can't afford them."

"But I can. What's your parents' address?"

"You don't have to do this for me."

"I know I don't have to," he says plainly. "I want to."

Their shoulders press together for a second, but only a second, before Charlie pulls out his wallet to pay. Dev watches Charlie hand over his credit card and doesn't let himself fixate on Charlie's profound kindness, either.

By the time they get back outside, the clouds have melted away into a warm afternoon, and Charlie produces a pair of Fendi sunglasses from some unknown pocket and pulls off his sweater. He begins tying it around his waist.

"*No.* Absolutely not."

"What?" Charlie gestures to the double-knotted sleeves snug on his hips. "It's fucking hot, and I'm not going to carry it all day."

Dev shakes his head in feigned disgust. It's so quintessentially *Charlie*: looking like a cologne model from the shoulders up with his five-hundred-dollar sunglasses, and like a soccer mom from the waist down, with his sweater tied around him and his sensible shoes.

Dev has the sudden urge to take a picture of him, to document this day and this exact version of Charlie, so six months from now, when Dev is sitting on his couch at his El Monte apartment, with his three Craigslist roommates, watching Charlie's televised wedding to Daphne Reynolds, he'll have proof there is some version of Charlie Winshaw who buys other people's parents extravagant anniversary presents, who lets Dev eat off his plate, who says *fuck*. A version of Charlie Winshaw who belongs only to him, even if it's only for a minute, even if it's only for one practice date.

The urge is too great to ignore. He grabs Charlie by the elbow and drags him down to the pier where there's a pretty tableau of Table Mountain. "Take a selfie with me, Charlie."

Charlie doesn't resist. He puts an arm around Dev's shoulder, and he leans in close, the indent of his temple locking against the hard line of Dev's jaw, and all Dev can think about for hours afterward is how perfectly Charlie fits there, tucked beneath his chin.

Charlie

Charlie really wants to kiss Dev right now.

"Where to next?" Dev asks as their limbs come apart slowly like bits of Velcro. Charlie points vaguely toward Table Mountain, unable to concentrate on anything but Dev's mouth.

"The *sky*? Are we going for a helicopter ride? How very *Ever After* of you."

Charlie really, really wants to kiss him. With his head tucked under Dev's chin, he could have reached up and kissed him here, on the pier of the V&A Waterfront, with hundreds of tourists going about their own sightseeing as witnesses.

Which is, of course, why he couldn't kiss him.

"No, we're going to Table Mountain."

Dev narrows his eyes. "How do we get up there? By helicopter?"

"There's a cable car."

Dev nervously pushes his glasses up his nose. "A cable car?"

"Yes."

"That, like, goes up the side of the mountain?"

"Yes, logistically, that's how it will work."

Dev swallows.

"Are you afraid of heights?"

He throws his shoulders back with some kind of forced bravado. "I'm not afraid of anything. Except emotional intimacy and abandonment."

And heights. He is clearly afraid of heights. He fidgets in the backseat of the Uber on the way to the aerial Cableway, and when the red cable car comes into view, making its three-thousand-foot ascent, Dev has to wipe his palm sweat onto his skinny jeans.

"We don't have to do this."

"I mean, I'm sure it's worth it, once you get to the top."

"Yeah, but if—"

"If you can handle shopping, I can handle this."

They climb out of the Uber and get into the advance-ticket line. Charlie woke up at five in the morning so he could prebook their time slot before his confessional, and soon they're stepping into the giant car crammed full of sixty other tourists.

Dev tucks himself against a handrail with his back to the window. The car lurches forward. Dev loses his balance, reaches out for Charlie's hand as the floor begins to rotate for three-sixty views of Cape Town. Dev clenches his eyes shut. "Just tell me when it's over, okay?"

Charlie gives his hand a small squeeze, secretly grateful for Dev's fear and the justification it gives them to hold hands. They're two thousand feet up, trapped in a metal box, spinning their way up a mountain. Dev's hand is in his, and the view is too spectacular for fear.

"Dev," he whispers. "Open your eyes. It's beautiful. *Dev*."

Dev peels open one eye. Then another. Charlie watches the view register on Dev's equally beautiful face. "Whoa," Dev says when he sees the way the city melts into the lush green of rolling hills, the impossible blue of the ocean, the sharp juts of gray mountain appearing beneath them, Lion's Head peak puncturing the skyline.

"I know."

The cable car arrives at the observatory on top of the mountain, and as they spill out with everyone else, Dev pulls back his hand. Charlie understands. He's the star of a reality show, and he has six girlfriends, and any one of these tourists could recognize him and take a picture—a picture that could end up on any number of gossip sites. But for one glorious minute, Dev was holding his hand in public, and some things are too spectacular for fear.

He waits until they're past the observation deck, where the throngs of tourists lessen, dwindling down even more once they're on the hiking trail to the other side of the mountain. When it's just the two of them, he reaches out again to take Dev's hand. Dev intertwines their fingers, and Charlie had no idea such a simple gesture could feel so huge inside his chest.

The hike out is perfect, all breathtaking vistas and Dev's hand snug in his. The hike back to the cable car is less great. When the sun starts to go down, the temperature drops considerably, and Dev gets hungry, and then tired, and then plagued by foot pain.

"I told you not to wear flip-flops."

Dev collapses onto a rock. "I know, goddamn you!" He screams in agony, takes off a shoe, and throws it into a king protea bush.

"Okay, you are not Reese Witherspoon in *Wild*."

"I mean, we have similar cheekbones."

Charlie hunts down the rogue flip-flop and puts it on Dev's foot like Dev is a very cranky Cinderella. "I'm sorry I've planned such a terrible practice date and that you're so miserable." Dev rolls his eyes. "Now, come on. I'll carry you. Climb on my back."

"I'm not a child, Charlie."

"No, you are a grown man having a temper tantrum and throwing your flip-flops at innocent flowers."

"I have blisters!"

"Yes, I know, sweetheart. Come on."

Dev consents to be carried half a mile back to the cable car, at least until they're around other people again, his hipbones stabbing into Charlie's back, legs wrapped around his waist like the sleeves of his sweater, chin on his shoulder.

"This isn't a terrible date," Dev says into his ear. And maybe it's because they can't see each other's faces, but Dev takes a sharp breath. "It's maybe the best date I've ever had."

They promised to meet up with Parisa and Jules for dinner at a Caribbean restaurant called Banana Jam Cafe. When they arrive, Jules and Parisa are already there, lounging on a patio under a red umbrella, enjoying their second round of Jam Jars, which have turned their tongues electric pink.

"What did you boys get up to today?" Parisa asks, putting her feet in Charlie's lap as soon as he sits down.

"Charlie carried me down a mountain."

"Not down. More . . . *across*."

"Heroic and manly nonetheless."

"The two words my father most often used to describe me."

They order too much food and consume too many pink alcoholic drinks, and Charlie tries to pay attention to the story Parisa is telling about her misadventures with Jules exploring the other side of Cape Town, but Dev is here, and he said their date was the best he's ever had, and Charlie is struggling to focus on anything else.

"So, do you want to go?" Jules is saying. To him, it would seem.

"Go where?"

"To the party tonight," Jules clearly repeats. "The one we just told you about. We ran into those guys who are here filming some movie about pirates, and they invited us."

"I've decided it's a good networking opportunity for Julesies," Parisa says, "who is way too brilliant to still be working as a PA."

Jules beams at Parisa.

"You in?"

The last thing Charlie wants to do is sit in a hotel room while a bunch of Hollywood dude-bros get high and hit on Jules and Parisa, where he won't be allowed to touch Dev for another several hours. "I think not. I'm pretty tired."

"Dev?" Jules asks, shooting him a look that's half optimism, half already-accepted defeat. "Do you want to come to the party with us?"

"I have foot blisters. Horrible, monstrous lesions on my feet. Pustules, Jules, and I can't—"

"Enough. I get it. You're both losers."

"*Such* losers," Parisa says, nudging Charlie's stomach with her toe. "We're going to this party, and we're going to be out all night, and you're going to sit in our hotel suite, all alone, just the two of you, watching *The Expanse*."

Parisa winks at him, and the implication lands. They'll have the suite to themselves. *For hours.*

Dev will be in their room, in their bed, and Charlie will be allowed to touch him in whatever way Dev wants. He looks over at Dev, who swallows dramatically as soon as their eyes meet, and Charlie remembers his forgotten fantasy of tracing the distance from Dev's mouth to the hidden parts of him.

Fun fact: in South Africa, servers will never bring you the bill unless you ask for it, so you're allowed to remain at a restaurant for as long as you want.

Charlie asks for the bill.

Dev

They don't touch at all in the Uber, because Jules is sitting between them, with Parisa in the front, drunkenly flirting with their driver. And they don't touch in the elevator, and they don't touch once they're in the hotel room, sitting on opposite ends of the couch while Jules and Parisa change their clothes and pregame with a bottle of chenin blanc. Even when the hotel door clicks shut behind them—Parisa giving one last suggestive wave that seems to imply she's not quite as oblivious as Jules—they still don't touch.

So Dev cues up the next episode of *The Expanse* on his laptop for some ungodly reason, and Charlie's sitting three feet away, watching the beautiful man on the computer screen like he really does only care about the science. On the one hand: *good.* Dev's already let this thing with Charlie go too far, but there's a distinct difference between *kissing* the star of their show and *having sex* with the star of their show, and one will sound distinctly worse when it's reported by the gossip bloggers, who will use Dev's actions as further proof of *Ever After*'s inherent immorality.

But on the other hand: they have the entire hotel suite to themselves, and Charlie planned them a perfect date, and shouldn't a practice date end with practice sex?

Practice sex. God, that will sound terrible in the legal briefings.

Maybe it's best if they just watch television all night. Dev doesn't even know if Charlie *wants* to have sex.

"Um. Dev?" Charlie coughs from the other side of the couch.

Dev turns, and Charlie isn't on the other side of the couch at all. He's right there, leaning into Dev, pinning him against the back cushions, kissing him wildly. *And thank God.*

Dev twists his hands into Charlie's hair, his legs around Charlie's legs, because somehow, this makes the most sense. Not Charlie with the six remaining women, but Charlie here, with him.

Dev wrestles his way out of his jean jacket without breaking contact with Charlie's mouth and is pissed they can't do the same with Charlie's sweater. He's even more pissed that Charlie is so profoundly bad at removing clothing when it really counts, but then the sweater's gone, and his T-shirt, too, and Dev's not mad at all. He pulls off his own shirt, and then Charlie's enormous hands are roving his skin, touching every inch of him.

"Bedroom," Charlie pants into his collarbone. "I want you in our bed."

Dev's heart explodes like a glitter bomb inside him, and he's barely able to follow through with Charlie's request. They stumble from the couch to the bedroom, tripping over each other's feet, kicking off each other's shoes. Dev is dimly aware of the fact they maybe shouldn't leave a trail of their clothes through the suite, but he's distracted by Charlie's hair and Charlie's mouth—by pushing Charlie down onto the bed and falling to his knees on the carpet in front of him.

Charlie is flushed and pouting, his gray eyes delirious from alcohol and Dev. *This makes sense.* He reaches up and unfastens Charlie's jeans.

"Dev—" Charlie starts, but Dev already has Charlie's pants down his hips, revealing his gray boxer briefs and his erection straining through his underwear. "Wait a minute."

Dev waits, hands paused on Charlie's muscular thighs. "Is this okay?"

"Yes." Charlie exhales, and Dev watches the way that one small action creates a dozen ripples across Charlie's chest and abdominal muscles. "Yes, God, *yes*, but I need a minute. It's not that I don't want to, obviously. . . ." He embarrassingly gestures to his groin in a shy way that is *so Charlie*, and Dev's heart pole vaults up to his throat. "I really, really want to, but the thing is . . . I . . . I haven't . . . I haven't done this before."

Dev laughs a little and kisses the inside of Charlie's thigh. "Yes, love, I was able to guess you've never been with a man before."

"No, Dev." Charlie chokes on his words, coughs them out. "I haven't done this *at all.*"

Before Dev can fully process this revelation, Charlie flops backward and covers his face with his hands, breathing heavily into his fingers. Dev scrambles up onto the bed. "Charlie, look at me. *Charlie!*" He pries away Charlie's hands. "Are you telling me you've never been with *anyone*? Ever? Like, in any way?"

Charlie makes a gasping sound like a dying animal and curls himself into a tight ball.

"But you're twenty-eight!"

"*Jesus*, Dev, I know! I'm a freak!"

"You're not a freak. Come on." He grabs Charlie's shoulder and pins him on his back. "Stop. Look at me. There's nothing wrong with you. I just—I can't believe you came on this show. You realize you're expected to have sex with two women during week nine when we do overnight dates, right?"

"Well, that is not happening for a number of reasons!" Charlie shouts at the ceiling.

"The show loves to exploit a virgin, but usually they know about it going into the season, and—"

"Dev, please stop talking about the *fucking* show."

"Right. *Right.* Sorry." Dev rubs Charlie's stomach until they both calm down a little. "We don't have to do anything tonight."

"No, I . . . I want to." Charlie puts his hand over Dev's, pulls both hands tight against his stomach. "In the past, the emotions stuff, and the touching, and all the little social interactions it takes to get to this level of intimacy with a person. Even with people I've dated—it wasn't just that I wasn't attracted to them. I've never wanted anyone to see me that vulnerable. I . . . I'm *terrified* of letting you see me."

Dev knows Charlie is handing him something important, something he's never trusted anyone else to hold before. "*Oh, love,*" Dev says, leaning in to kiss the cluster of freckles to the left of his nose. "I already see you."

Charlie keeps his promise and blushes, and Dev wants to kiss every pink splotch. He's not sure he's ever wanted someone like he wants Charlie in this moment, and there's nothing Charlie could say to change that.

Dev pushes aside the sobering enormity of that realization

and reaches out for a pump of the lotion Charlie keeps by the bed. "I'm going to touch you," Dev tells him, like he did the first night of filming, like he's done a dozen times since. His fingers hesitate at the waistband of Charlie's underwear. "Tell me if you want me to stop, okay?"

"Okay," Charlie whispers. Charlie winces when Dev first strokes him, then settles into the touch. The feeling of Charlie against his palm makes Dev feel drunk and stupid, but he's slow and careful with Charlie, because slow and careful is what Charlie needs, and because Dev is a little bit obsessed with being what Charlie needs.

Charlie arches into his hand. He's quiet and shy the whole time, biting down on his lower lip, bunching his fists into the comforter, barely letting himself breathe. Dev's eyes never leave his face as he gets hard over the knowledge that no one else has ever been lucky enough to see Charlie like this. Only him. He watches every ounce of tension slowly melt out of Charlie and savors the exact moment where no part of him is pinched together.

Dev wishes he could take a picture of this version of Charlie, too.

Charlie

"Okay?"

Charlie nods, even though, no. He's very much not *okay*. He's something else entirely.

Dev slips off the bed, and Charlie stays on his back, unable to move. He feels like he's dissolved into the mattress, fused with the sheets, and he stares up at the ceiling, trying to remember how breathing works. It feels like when he took apart his family's

VCR when he was six so he could learn how to put it back together. *He* is the VCR—everything laid bare, the inside parts on the outside, wires exposed.

Here is this thing he put off for so long, that he never thought he would be able to share with another person without humiliation and shame, and now he's crossed the invisible barrier of his mind to find something surprising on the other side. *Himself.* More *about* himself.

He's not sure he could've experienced this with anyone but Dev. Dev, who *sees* him, who tried to connect with him, emotionally, from the first night. Who never accepted his stammering or his evasiveness. Who pushed and pushed and kept pushing until he bulldozed his way right inside Charlie's heart. He thinks about Parisa and her two-foot spectrum and what this *means* about him.

There's a pressure behind his eyes, building in his throat, but he fights off the inexplicable urge to cry. Happy tears, he thinks. Dev returns to the bed with his black skinny jeans and exposed chest as he leans over to kiss Charlie's temple.

"Where did you go?"

"I thought you would want me to wash my hands right away," Dev says in a low voice. "I grabbed your wet wipes, in case you wanted to—"

And then Charlie *is* crying. He can't help it, because Dev knows him so well. Dev knows him and understands him and wants him anyway, and Charlie has never been this attracted to anyone else.

"Oh, love." Dev takes his face with hands smelling like hotel soap, and surely he must know. Dev must see the way those two words tear down all of Charlie's defenses every time he says them. Dev says *oh, love,* and some dormant thing—some part of Charlie that has secretly always wanted to be *someone's* love—comes to life inside him.

"Why are you crying, Charlie?"

"Because you're perfect." And he sits up so he can do what he's been fantasizing about since night one. He licks Dev's Adam's apple. He follows the path toward his collarbone, his breastbone, the bottom of his rib cage—until Dev is beneath him, skinny and sharp and *his,* at least for right now. "You're so beautiful," Charlie whispers as he pulls off his jeans.

Dev laughs. "I'm really not."

"You are. You so, so are." The skinny jeans get caught around Dev's ankles, and Charlie tugs, almost falls off the bed with how desperately he needs these pants off. When he looks up, his eyes catch Dev's across the six feet four inches of Dev's body, and there's something shining in Dev's eyes that Charlie can't understand. He wants to understand every damn thing about him. "Can I please see you naked?"

There is victory in being brave enough to ask for what he wants. Dev makes a strangled sound of consent and lets Charlie undress him fully, and there is all of Dev.

Charlie can't wait another second to touch him. "Fuck," Dev says as Charlie frantically licks his palm. "*Fuck,*" he says again when Charlie wraps his hand around him. Dev says fuck *a lot* as Charlie makes a sloppy showing of the whole affair, too eager, too enthusiastic to remember to be self-conscious. Dev comes apart at his touch anyway, and after, Charlie doesn't want to wash his hands; he wants to kiss Dev until there is no space left between them.

So he does. He presses their slick chests together, pushes Dev back into the mattress, and kisses his mouth, his jaw, his throat, kisses him until his lips go numb. Then he places his ear to Dev's sternum and listens to the sound of his heart while Dev's fingers tease apart his curls one at a time.

He feels unlocked. Like he has nothing left to try to hide, no reason not to show Dev the rest of him. So Charlie starts talking into the low light of the room, saying things he's never said aloud, not even to Parisa. Talking about his childhood, about his brothers, about his parents. About sitting alone at lunch every day in elementary school because the other kids were afraid of his intensity and his differences, about the bullies at recess. About the high school therapist who told him exercise might help reduce his anxiety, about consequently becoming obsessed with exercise. About how the same classmates who called him names in the hallway and threw milk cartons at him on the bus suddenly wanted to talk to him after he became obsessed with exercising. About being so desperate to escape his small town and his small life and his small-minded family, only to arrive at Stanford at sixteen and discover there are small minds everywhere.

Dev listens and says nothing, and never stops playing with Charlie's hair. The sharing is even scarier than the sex because it's another barrier, another line he never thought he'd be able to cross with someone. It's the type of intimacy he's avoided the most strictly, convinced he could never trust anyone with these parts of himself. Dev accepts every part of him like it's nothing and everything. "I think I really, really like you," Charlie tells Dev's sternum.

The confession hangs between them for a second. "Two reallys?" Dev finally says, and Charlie can hear the smile in his voice. "And you haven't even seen what I can do with my mouth yet?"

Charlie laughs and Dev flips them over so it's Charlie with his back against the mattress and Dev looking down at him.

Dev isn't smiling anymore. Charlie stops laughing. Dev kisses his collarbone, bites at his nipples, licks the vertical line down the center of his abdomen like he did that night in New Orleans when Charlie stopped things from going any further.

Dev goes further, kissing the crease of his hip, the inside of his thigh until Charlie is hard again. "Please," Dev's voice strains, "can I?"

Charlie arches his hips in consent, too consumed with feeling to speak, and when Dev licks him again, he's not sure if he should laugh or swear or scream, so he maybe does all three. He doesn't censor himself at all, says exactly what he's thinking and feeling, and watches the way his words make Dev lose all restraint.

Charlie is a mess, but so is Dev, and he can't believe they found each other on this ridiculous show about fairy-tale love.

"So . . ." She smirks over her mug of coffee. "How was it?"

"Shush," he hisses. His eyes dart to Jules's closed bedroom door. "Don't be gross, Parisa."

"I'm not being *gross*. I'm being supportive." Parisa props a hip against the counter and reaches for a muffin. "I tell you about all my hookups."

"I never asked you to be so forthcoming and would actually prefer you stop."

Parisa has the decency to at least lower her voice. "I'm not asking for all the gory details here. Just—did you have sex?"

He sips his tea and tries not to blush at the memory. "I mean, we, um—but not *that*."

Parisa punches his arm. "Oh my God, Charles, work my pussy *out*."

He chokes on his lemon ginger. "*Excuse me?*"

"Sorry. You're not quite there yet." She dials it back. "I just mean I'm proud of you. I'm sure it took a lot of courage to let yourself be vulnerable like that with someone."

Charlie studies her across the kitchen and thinks about what Dev said last night, about already seeing him. He realizes Parisa already sees him, too. "Thank you."

"So why didn't you have penetrative sex? Do you need me to draw you a diagram of where things go, or—?"

"I seriously hate you."

"You love me."

"I'm sending you home now."

"But then who will help coordinate your special surprise for your boyfr—Good morning!"

Charlie is kicking Parisa's shin when Dev walks into the kitchen. Somehow, just the sight of him in black skinny jeans and a black T-shirt, his hair still damp from the shower, is enough to send a shiver across Charlie's bare arms. He can almost feel Dev's hands on his hipbones, keeping him pinned to the bed as he—

Charlie clears his throat. "Morning."

"Morning," Dev grumbles as he moves toward the French press without making eye contact.

Parisa just can't help herself. "Sleep well, Dev?"

He startles as he attempts to pour the coffee. He darts his eyes between Parisa's smug grin and Charlie's telling blush. "Slept okay, thanks."

Parisa rolls her eyes, clearly disappointed by her inability to fluster Dev. "Fine. I'll just go see if Jules is ready."

As soon as she's gone, Dev steps closer. "So, she knows—"

"Everything," Charlie blurts, biting his bottom lip. "She knows everything. I'm sorry."

Dev scrubs a hand across his freshly shaved face. "And she doesn't care?"

"No," Charlie says. "She doesn't think it's a big deal."

A sullen look flashes across Dev's face, and Charlie hears what he said. "Not like that." He reaches out for Dev's waist, pulls them together. "Parisa just wants me to be happy."

Charlie kisses Dev, tastes the first sip of morning coffee on his tongue. Dev deepens it, runs his fingers through Charlie's hair, until Charlie's on his tiptoes, and they're pressed against the hotel refrigerator, and Charlie is two seconds away from saying fuck it to today's Group Quest and the six women and this entire show because all he wants is to drag Dev back to their bed and get lost in his perfect body, and he didn't know, had no idea, it was possible to feel this way about another person.

When Dev finally releases his mouth, Charlie sighs. "You make me so fucking happy."

Three months ago, when he and Parisa agreed to do the show, the idea of getting fake-engaged to someone at the end of the process, as awkward as it sounded, didn't really matter. He knew he would have to appear on daytime talk shows with some woman who was only in it for the fame. They'd have to be photographed together, seen in public together on dates. He knew there would be a mandatory six-month engagement after the show ended, before they were allowed to end things amicably, but the uncomfortable inconvenience of it seemed like a fair trade for getting his old life back. It wasn't like he ever thought a real relationship was in his future.

Except now—now he falls asleep each night with Dev's arm around his waist and wakes up every morning to the sight of Dev's pillow drool, and suddenly, there are only twenty-four days left, and Charlie is having a hard time imagining how this all ends.

He tries to pay attention to the women on the Group Quests, but the show doesn't make it easy. Despite the fact that he's down to his top six, the women are still forced to compete in ridiculous challenges for his time and attention. Charlie cannot fathom how anyone actually falls in love on this show; he's spent maybe five hours with each woman individually.

Thursday, the show films at Kirstenbosch botanical gardens, where the women learn pseudo-botany and make love potions he's actually forced to drink. When Mark Davenport traipses out for his weekly fifteen minutes of work to announce Daphne as the Group Quest victor for the week, everything erupts into the same old drama. Megan locks herself in a bathroom, Delilah calls Daphne a con artist, and Angie jumps to her defense. Charlie is exhausted with all of it.

When they get back to the suite, Dev gets word that Megan is coming to speak to Charlie. The suite is quickly prepped for filming, and when Megan shows up an hour later, it's clear her handler has goaded her into this late-night visit. She's wearing next to nothing, and she immediately throws herself at him. It's week six, and Dev finally got approval from Maureen back in LA to send Megan home at the Crowning Ceremony. This is clearly Maureen's way of making sure Megan goes home as dramatically as possible. The other five women, back in their suite, are probably talking about Megan's desperate plan to seduce him for the cameras. Charlie has been doing this long enough to see the strings, which Maureen can somehow pull from ten thousand miles away.

"I just really needed to see you," Megan purrs into his throat. He diplomatically leads her to the couch. She clearly *is* here to try to seduce him. As soon as they sit down, her mouth finds his, her hands rove his body. He counts his Mississippis until it's an appropriate time to stop her.

She looks devastated by his sudden distance. Charlie studies the tight lines around her mouth, the purple bags peeking out beneath her eye makeup. He's been so distracted by Dev the past few weeks, he hasn't really paid attention to the women at all. Looking at Megan, he can see she's not in a healthy place. She's lost weight, and in her glassy-eyed expression, he can see his own struggles with anxiety mirrored back to him. She's been poked and prodded into fitting the villain narrative they wrote for her, and now she's about to snap from the stress.

"Megan," he begins.

"I love you," she blurts before he can say anything else. He briefly registers that this is the first time anyone has said these words to him. He wishes it weren't coming from a woman who just wants to win.

"Megan," he tries again, but this time he's interrupted by another knock on the door. It's Delilah, also heavily made up, with her handler in tow. "Charles, I'm sorry," she announces as she swans into the room, "but I had to come tell you that Megan is *crazy*."

Charlie flinches at the use of the *c*-word.

"She told me she was going to have sex with you tonight so you couldn't send her home."

Megan leaps off the couch. "Delilah is just slut-shaming me because she's an uptight virgin!"

"Because virgin-shaming is much better," Charlie says. No one hears him. Delilah and Megan are screaming at each other, and the cameras are gleefully capturing the scene. Delilah keeps throwing out words like *psycho* and *unstable*, and he's back at Win-Han, hearing the whispers in the hallways. It's offensive. Horrible.

Behind the cameras, Jules looks livid, but she holds Parisa back before she impales the producers on the heels of her Louboutins. Even Ryan Parker looks mildly ill. But when Charlie finds Dev across the room, he's watching the fight with cool detachment. He doesn't understand how Dev can just stand there and let this play out, let two women emotionally abuse each other for entertainment.

But that's what *Ever After* does. It exploits people during their most vulnerable moments, and a crew of mostly decent people lets it happen. Dev has stood by before—while the boyfriend screamed at Kiana, and while Megan bullied Daphne—and he shouldn't be surprised Dev is standing by and letting this happen now. It doesn't matter what they're doing behind their closed hotel door, in their shared bed, because at the end of the day, Dev will always put the show first.

Charlie can't believe, after everything, that he's only just now realizing this.

He's suddenly furious. He wants to defy Maureen Scott and her entire toxic franchise, but he doesn't know how, doesn't have any power over this situation.

Except—"Enough," he hears himself say. "I am done condoning this behavior."

"Charles," Megan starts, falsely apologetic.

He pulls himself up off the couch and tries to look confident. "I'm sorry, but I think you both should leave."

"You're right," Delilah says. She gets to play the role of the reasonable one. "We'll talk about this tomorrow when we've all cooled off."

"No, I think you should both leave the show. Permanently."

Both women break the fourth wall, staring at the cameras and producers, clearly confused. This isn't how they were told the night would end, but Charlie isn't going to back down. He knows that right now, somewhere in Los Angeles, an editing team is mining *thousands* of hours of footage—almost every minute of his life on this show has been documented so the whole thing can be trimmed down into eighty-minute episodes without commercials—and Maureen Scott is there, manipulating Megan's footage so this scene becomes the culmination of her villain arc. Charlie doesn't have power over much, but he does have the power to ruin this scene.

"I am sending you both home right now," he says, "because I have no interest in dating women who let their producers manipulate them into acting this way."

The room is painfully silent except for the sound of Megan's snivels.

"I'll see you both out."

Producers rush off to pack their things, and the cameras hurry downstairs so they can film the black vans whisking away the two women who've been dismissed. Charlie finds his team again. Parisa and Jules look proud. Ryan looks amused. And Dev, in the corner next to the refrigerator—the same refrigerator he pushed them against two days ago—looks absolutely pissed.

"I can't believe you did that," Dev seethes when the drama is over and they're back in their room, the door closed. "Maureen is going to be furious."

"I can't believe *you* did that today," he snaps back. "*I* am furious."

Dev peels off his sweat-stained T-shirt. "Me? I didn't do anything."

"Exactly. You did *nothing* while Delilah said all those horrible things to Megan."

Dev snorts as he pulls a T-shirt out of his unpacked duffle and has to sniff it to verify it's clean. "What was I supposed to do, Charlie? This is my *job*, and your little stunt referencing producers on camera made me look really shitty at my job."

Charlie sits down on the edge of the bed and tries to massage the tension headache forming above his eyebrows. "Your job?" he echoes. "Right. You're only my handler, and next season, you'll handle Angie instead when she's named the next princess."

"Angie will never be the next princess. She's starting med school in the fall."

"That's hardly the point." He takes three slow, deep breaths. They've never fought before, and Charlie doesn't know the rules. "Don't you think you tend to overlook the more insidious aspects of this show when it doesn't align with your ideas of fairytale romance?"

Saying this, clearly, was against the rules. Dev blinks at him. "What? No. I don't do that."

"Dev, the way this show treats mental health, and with your depression—"

"My depression has nothing to do with this show."

"You were depressed for a week, and no one in the crew did anything about it. They were happy to ignore you as long as I was performing for the cameras. And they work you to death during filming. Do you even have time for virtual therapy?"

Dev fidgets defensively in front of the bed. "I'm not in therapy."

Charlie's mind immediately flashes to the image of Dev curled up in a tight ball on the bed in Munich. "You're not?"

"Nope." He attempts a casual shrug, but his Fun Dev disguise is slipping in the corner. "I don't really need it."

Charlie is out of his depth. He doesn't know how to have a hard conversation with someone he cares about this much—with someone he is terrified of losing. "Your treatment is your choice," he starts, his throat dry, "but in Munich, things seemed not great."

"I'm okay," Dev says immediately. "I'm always okay. It's all good, dude."

"Did you seriously just call me *dude*?"

Dev puts his hands on his hips and stares Charlie down on the bed, like he's *daring* him to call bullshit. Dev's face is a perfect mask of calm. Charlie wants to rip that mask right off. He wants to grab Dev by the shoulders and shake him. *Stop. Stop pretending you're okay. You don't have to pretend with me.*

Charlie presses his fingertips against his closed eyes until he sees stars. He wishes he had the right words to make Dev understand; he likes every version of the *real* Dev. He wants twenty-four more days of Defensive Dev and Passionate Dev and Hangry Dev and Hopeless-Romantic Dev. Cheekbones and chin. Amused mouth and violin eyes. *Legs* and that patch of dark hair on his lower stomach. He doesn't want twenty-four more days with the version of Dev that Dev thinks he needs to be to please other people.

He stands up and takes a few steps closer to Dev and tries. "I care about you," he says. He reaches to take Dev's face in his hands, and for a minute, Dev lets him. "I just want you to be healthy."

Dev yanks back, severing their physical connection. "I *am*

healthy. I'm fine. I'm not some broken thing you need to fix. I'm not *you*, trying to prove to a bunch of tech douches you're neurotypical."

Charlie physically recoils. "Needing therapy doesn't mean you're broken. I've been in therapy for my OCD since I was twelve, and not because I want to prove anything to anyone but myself."

Dev snorts. "That's great *for you*, but I really am fine."

"I could never be with someone who isn't healthy, Dev."

"You're not with me," Dev snaps. "This is all just practice."

Dev told him four days ago the only things he fears are emotional intimacy and abandonment, so maybe Charlie should've seen this coming. Charlie has opened up to Dev in every possible way, and what has Dev given him in return? Nothing more than *dude* and *I'm fine*. The same old Fun Dev bullshit. He is so, so stupid to think this meant anything to him.

Charlie grabs his tennis shoes off the floor by the bed.

"What are you doing?"

"Going to the hotel gym," Charlie grunts as he shoves his feet into his sneakers. He doesn't bother tying them. He needs to get the hell out of this room before Dev sees him cry.

"It's the middle of the night."

"Then I'll go for a run."

"Wait!" Dev shouts as Charlie barrels out of the room. "We're in the middle of a conversation."

"I think the conversation is over."

Charlie pushes past Jules and Parisa, who are standing in the kitchen eating a midnight snack, pretending they haven't been listening to this entire argument.

"Charlie, stop!"

Charlie doesn't stop. He's out the door, down the hall, taking the stairs to the ground floor two at a time.

"*Charlie.*"

Dev reaches for his shoulder, and Charlie wheels around. He's angry and he's tired and he's so damn heartbroken he doesn't know what to do with himself except exercise away this horrible knot in his chest.

"You know what, Dev," he says, and he fails in his chief mission of not crying in front of him. "For someone who claims to love love, you're really good at pushing it away."

Then he turns and heads down the last flight of steps, knowing Dev isn't going to follow.

Dev

Charlie takes the last few steps two at a time, pushes through the door at the end of the stairwell, and vanishes. He's gone, and there is something about the *whoosh* and *click* of a closing industrial-strength door that feels final. It feels like twenty-four days, gone in an instant.

A creeping numbness starts in his fingertips. It claims his hands, his forearms, his elbows, until he's standing in a stairwell unsure of how to move. *What did he do?*

He was so angry with Charlie for screwing up the scene with Megan and Delilah, and still, Charlie was so utterly *Charlie*. Earnest and vulnerable and sweet. He took Dev's face in his hands and told him he cared, and Dev took Charlie's affection and smashed it at their feet.

For someone who claims to love love, you're really good at pushing it away.

But Charlie could never love him. Charlie's story ends with a Final Tiara, and maybe it's better he realizes that now and not in twenty-four days. Charlie unburdened his whole self to Dev, unwrapped himself like a present, gave himself away. Dev would have to be stupid to think that means he gets to keep him.

Dev never should've started this thing. He never should've let Charlie start this thing.

Dev shoves open the door to their hotel suite. He's not sure how he got back here. His brain is trying to do the breaststroke under twenty feet of water. Jules and Parisa are both standing in the kitchen. It's two in the morning, and they still haven't changed from today's Group Quest at Kirstenbosch. Parisa is wearing a bright yellow caftan that falls over her curves like honey, Jules in her corduroy shorts and a homemade Stormpilot T-shirt, Finn and Poe's screen-printed faces in a giant puff-paint heart. They're both wearing expressions his water brain can't understand.

"I'll go after mine," Parisa says. "You stay with yours."

Parisa floats out of the room, and Dev is somehow in his bed now. *Their* bed. The bed where Charlie opens up for him every night.

"Dev?" Jules asks, cautious. "What happened?"

She obviously knows. She heard them fighting.

He buries himself in blankets that smell like oatmeal body wash and tries very hard not to cry. "Go away, Jules."

He can feel the mattress shift slightly under her weight. "Come on. Talk to me."

He cocoons himself deeper into the bed, and he doesn't think about Munich, when Charlie grabbed onto the blankets and refused to let go. Jules goes with a different approach. She somehow weasels her way into the blankets, too, and slides down into the middle of the bed with him. "Dev, please. I care about you," she whispers into their blanket fort. He feels those words gather in the back of his throat like a sob. "Tell me what happened."

"You shouldn't care about me. I'm a monster."

"No, you're not."

Little light makes it through the hotel comforter, and he can only see the outline of her face, not her actual expression, when he says, "I'm sleeping with him, Jules."

For a second, she's quiet, a foot in front of him, their bodies angled like parentheses. "Am I supposed to be surprised you're having sex with the man who literally shares your bed?"

He curls himself into a tighter ball. "Jules—"

"Dev." Her hand reaches out for something in the dark and finds his throat. It's still comforting. "I know you and Charlie are hooking up. I've known since you first kissed in New Orleans. I mean, Parisa and I easily could've shared the king-size bed, Dev."

He groans into the mattress. "Why did you let me do this? I'm ruining everything!"

"First of all, I did not *let* you. You're an adult. And second, what are you ruining?"

"Um, the show. That we work for. Where we help hot people find love with someone of equal hotness."

"Honestly, after tonight, fuck the show."

"I can't." This conversation is somehow so much easier to have muffled by starched sheets. "You don't understand. The Delilah and Megan thing doesn't matter. It's a distraction from the love, which is what he *wants*. Charlie wants a happily ever after, and my horny ass is destroying his chance to have it!"

"Is that really all this thing is with Charlie? Just sex?"

"Of course not. It's . . ."

Shit, Dev doesn't even know what it is, but he feels like it's been happening the whole time, since the first night when they shook hands on their agreement and Charlie forgot to let go. In the beginning, he told himself it was about helping Charlie open up, helping him fall in love with one of the women, but when he thinks about Charlie with his two black eyes and Charlie on the curb after kissing Angie and Charlie in the kitchen the first time he let him tap Morse code onto his shoulder, Dev isn't sure that's true.

"The thing with Charlie is over," he eventually says. "I messed it up and pushed him away. It's for the best. Better to end things now than delay the inevitable."

Jules kicks her legs frantically until the blankets scrunch down toward the bottom of the bed and their heads are exposed to the soft light of the room. Dev blinks and realizes he no longer feels trapped underwater.

"Have you thought about, I don't know, apologizing to him?"

He covers his face. "What's the point? Charlie has to get engaged to a woman at the end of this."

"Then why did you kiss him in the first place?"

"Tequila shots," he says. But he isn't sure that's true either.

"Look," Jules says, sounding pissed. "I'm shit at this kind of stuff, but . . . you are kind of my best friend, okay? And I . . . I, like, love you or whatever."

"Wow, Jules," he says sarcastically. "That was very sweet."

"Fuck you, I'm trying. I just . . . Do you remember that day we moved you out of Ryan's apartment?"

He groans again. He's mostly tried to forget everything associated with their breakup, bury the memory of the depression that followed.

"We ate pizza on the floor of your new apartment, and I asked you why it took you *six years* to break up with someone who didn't make you happy. Do you remember what you said?"

He shakes his head.

"You said sometimes easy is better than happy." She pauses and stares at him across the bed in a way that makes him feel *too* seen. "And I couldn't figure out how someone who is so obsessed with all the fairy-tale bullshit we peddle on this show could think that. But I'm starting to get it."

"Get what?"

She reaches out to brush the unwashed hair off his forehead. It's a surprisingly tender gesture for her. "You're one of the funniest, smartest, kindest, most passionate motherfuckers I've ever met, Dev. And you deserve a happily ever after, too."

Dev coughs away the tears. "Wow, Jules," he says seriously. "That was very sweet."

Charlie never comes back to their bed, and the next morning, Dev doesn't see him until the crew is loading into four vans to drive to Franschhoek an hour outside of Cape Town for Charlie's Courting Date with Daphne.

Now that the villain is gone, the show has a narrative to sell, and that narrative is Daphne and Charlie. They need more footage of the couple deepening their relationship. Franschhoek is in the heart of South Africa's wine country, and the couple spend the day riding a wine tram between different vineyards for tastings.

Despite the fact that a wine tram is maybe the best idea Dev's ever heard, the date is torture for him to witness. Daphne and Charlie are wonderful together. They're just so *similar*: quiet and steady, closed off but opening slowly, like two beautiful flowers simultaneously coming into bloom. They are blond and smoking hot, and they look like every other *Ever After* couple. They look like Brad and Tiffany, the first prince and princess Dev watched fall in love on this show when he was ten years old.

Daphne and Charlie are endgame, and Dev was a brief side plot that would probably be cut from the film adaptation of Charlie's life.

At a vineyard called Leopard's Leap, Jules snatches a bottle of chenin from the crew's reserves, and they sneak outside to sit in the sun and get a nice workplace buzz going. Parisa didn't join them for the Courting Date—she insisted she had to stay back in Cape Town to work—so Dev can't even ask her what Charlie said about their fight. And he can't ask Charlie, because Charlie is refusing to talk to him.

After they're both feeling overserved and affectionate, Charlie and Daphne are taken to a restaurant in town attached to a B&B. They have an intimate conversation over a candlelit dinner, and the producer in Dev is thrilled. This will all be gold when the show airs. It's week six. There are only four women left. Everything is right on schedule.

"I, um . . ." Charlie starts stammering in front of the cameras. "I was given this card by the producers."

Charlie pulls a creamy envelope out from under his place mat, and everything inside of Dev drops. Charlie reads the card out loud. "'A romantic day deserves a romantic night. We have booked you a room at this charming B&B, and—'"

Dev doesn't need to hear the rest. He pushes past the key grip and the gaffer until he finds Ryan, the supervising producer in charge of this shoot. "What the hell? This is an overnight date? Why wasn't I told?"

Cameras are already moving for the next scene. "Because we thought you'd react like *this*," Ryan answers. "Look, Charlie's emotional connections with the women are great, but his physical connections are lukewarm at best, and after the shitshow with Megan and Delilah, we need something we can sell. A surprise overnight date will be good for ratings, and you can be a little bit overprotective of him."

Dev follows Ryan following the crew upstairs to the hotel room. "I'm overprotective of him because Charlie isn't ready for a sex date."

"We ran this all by him this morning," Ryan says calmly. "Charlie said he was fine with it."

Dev turns and sees Charlie and Daphne, arms around each other's waists, blissed out on good wine and good company. They stumble together into a staged hotel room with rose petals on the bed and a hundred white candles and a giant bowl of fucking condoms on the bedside table.

Dev has to watch as they fall together onto the bed, as Daphne straddles Charlie the way he usually does, as they kiss the way Charlie and Dev kissed in their own shared bed. His pounding heartbeat counts out each second of foreplay, and this, he thinks, is probably the reason you don't get involved with your star when you work on a reality dating show.

"Cut!" Skylar finally says in Dev's headset. The cameras have enough footage of the amorous couple. Everything else will be implied when they air the outside of a closed door.

On the bed, Charlie and Daphne untangle themselves, and as Charlie sits up, his eyes find Dev's among the line of crew members. It's like everything but Charlie's gray eyes blink out of existence. He's all Dev can see, and he wishes he could say something to change Charlie's mind.

What would he say? *It wasn't just practice. It was never just practice. Please don't do this.*

He has no right to say anything to Charlie.

Dev feels an arm snake around his waist, and he assumes it's Jules. He turns to find Ryan instead. "Come on," his ex murmurs low in his ear. "Let's go get a drink at the bar."

Charlie

As soon as the cameras and the crew members are gone, Charlie and Daphne spring apart like repellent magnets. He sits on one edge of the bed, trying not to think about the look on Dev's face, about Ryan's arm on Dev's hips. Daphne is perched on the other side of the bed. He has no idea what she's trying not to think about.

He knows why he agreed to this overnight date. After screwing things up with Megan and Delilah, this is the least he can do to appease Maureen and make Dev look like a good handler again. Looking at Daphne, seeing her body language, he isn't sure why she agreed.

Her thick blond hair is mussed in the back from their performance, and the sleeve on her blouse has fallen off her shoulder. He almost reaches out to fix it, but he can tell by her body language she's nervous, so he doesn't touch her. He studies her from three feet away.

She is so lovely. Her blue eyes sparkle in the dim light of the room and her pale cheeks are flushed from kissing. If he's honest with himself—if he lets himself acknowledge the secret compartment of his heart that has always wanted some form of companionship—Daphne is the kind of person he imagined himself with. For one awful second, he indulges that fantasy. He thinks about how much easier this would all be if he'd come on this show and fallen in love with Daphne Reynolds instead.

The thought churns his stomach. He's mad at Dev, but even thinking about Daphne feels like a betrayal. Not just of Dev, but of himself, of who he really is and what he really feels in the secret parts of himself. Maybe things with Dev were never real, maybe he's off hooking up with his ex right now, but Charlie knows nothing can happen with Daphne off camera. Now he just has to find a way to tell her.

"I don't think we should have sex!"

Conveniently, it's Daphne who blurts this in a blind panic from the other side of the bed.

"I just . . . I'm not ready for . . . sex," she fumbles. "I . . . I hope you understand."

"I understand." He puts his hand on the bed between them, an invitation for platonic closeness she can take or leave. "I don't think we should have sex either."

They are, however, trapped in this hotel room together until dawn without cameras. And she still seems uncomfortable about something.

"Daphne?" he tries. "Can I ask you something? Why did you come on this show?"

"For love," she says, almost too automatically.

"Yeah, but you don't love me, and you're still here."

She narrows her eyes at him. "You think I don't love you because I won't have sex with you?"

"No, I think you don't love me because you don't love me."

Quite frankly, he isn't even sure if she's attracted to him. He could feel it in every stiff touch earlier, every passionless kiss. Now that he has a point of comparison, he realizes he's not the only one who has been faking. Kissing Daphne is like kissing himself. The version of himself he's always been with everyone but Dev.

"I should be falling in love with you," she says after a tense silence. "If I'm ever going to fall in love with . . . It, uh, it should be you. You're perfect."

He snorts. "I am so far from perfect."

"Well, okay. Sure. No one is *perfect*. But you're perfect to me."

"Perfect looking, you mean?"

"Well, no, actually." She gestures to her shoulders. "Muscles don't really do it for me. I mean *perfect*. You're the smartest person I've ever met, and you're so sweet, and you make me laugh."

"Laugh *at me*?"

"No." She finally reaches out for his hand. "Charlie, you're so clever and witty. I wish I were as funny and comfortable with myself as you are."

Well. Now he's crying in a sex suite in Franschhoek.

"Oh, hey. What's wrong?"

"Your perception of me is what's wrong. Daphne, there is so much you don't know about me."

"Like what?"

Since he can't say *like hooking up with my producer*, he says, "I have OCD."

And all she says is, "I know."

"What?"

"I mean, I figured." She shrugs. "I thought maybe it was just severe anxiety."

"I have that, too."

Daphne smiles at him. "I'm sure that's been difficult to live with, but you don't really think that makes you any less wonderful, do you? I think you're perfect just the way God made you."

"Wow." He exhales. "I kind of wish I loved you."

She drops his hand. "I wish I loved you, too."

He can feel there is still something else she's holding back. "You know, I've watched this show since I was a kid. On Monday nights, my mom would let me stay up late, and we'd swoon over the princes together. It's what I grew up dreaming about. Carriages and candlelit dinners and happily ever after. And I haven't been able to find it in real life. With all of my boyfriends, it never felt right."

He can't help but picture little Dev, also watching *Ever After* past his bedtime, and all at once, he's not mad at Dev at all. He's just sad for him, for the little kid who fell in love with love stories where no one looked like him, no one thought like him, no one loved like him.

"I came on this show because I thought it might finally feel right," Daphne says.

"But it doesn't?"

She shakes her head. She's crying now, too. They make quite the sexy pair. "I want it so badly. Love. I don't know what's wrong with me that I can't find it."

He squeezes her hand as he repeats the words Dev said to him that magical night they had together. "There's nothing wrong with you, Daphne. I think you're perfect just the way millions of years of evolution and natural selection made you."

That gets her to laugh, at least. Charlie thinks about Dev and about deserving love. "Maybe you're simply chasing the wrong kind of love."

Daphne looks up at him. "What other kind of love is there?"

Dev

"I think we should order a whole bottle, right?"

Ryan slides onto the barstool and casually lifts a hand to get the server's attention. That's how Ryan always moves. Casually. Confidently. The opposite of Charlie in every way.

It's best not to think about Charlie or the way he moves at the moment.

Ryan orders a bottle of Shiraz, and Dev pours himself a full glass.

"Cheers," Ryan attempts, but Dev is already swallowing it down. "I've got to give it to you, D. He's a great prince. He's kind to the women, he's agreeable with the producers, he's fine as fuck. You've really been able to connect with him."

"Yeah, except for the hiccup the other night with Megan and Delilah."

Ryan smiles over his glass. "Honestly, that kind of made me like him more. I get what you see in him."

Dev doesn't say anything.

"I've been thinking about what you said a lot. Back in LA." Ryan clears his throat awkwardly. "I never should've said that stuff about him. Called Charlie crazy. I was being insensitive. I should've known how that would make you feel."

It's almost an apology, and an almost-apology is more than he ever thought he'd get from Ryan, but he's not feeling particularly magnanimous at the moment. "You were never the best at handling me when I wasn't Fun Dev."

Ryan bristles on his stool. "That's not fair."

No, he thinks. What's not *fair* is that right now, Charlie Winshaw is having sex with the world's most flawless woman, and Dev isn't even allowed to be upset about it, because this is his job. This is what he's wanted all along for Charlie. He's not allowed to be angry at Charlie for fulfilling his role as *Ever After*'s prince, but he *can* be angry at Ryan for never fulfilling the role of supportive boyfriend. "It feels fair. I seem to recall a lot of weeks when I couldn't get out of bed where you basically ignored me."

"Do you really want to do this right now?" Ryan chokes on actual emotion and pours more wine in an obvious attempt to cope. Dev does want to do this right now. He feels like shit, and the petty part of him wants to make Ryan feel like shit, too. "You wouldn't let me in."

"What is that supposed to mean?"

Ryan keeps his voice low. "You can accuse me of only wanting Fun Dev, but the truth is, Fun Dev is all you ever let me see. When things got bad, you would shut me out entirely."

"That's not—"

"Dude. Every time I suggested you try therapy again, you bit my head off. Every time I tried to reach out, you retreated further into yourself. It was like you wanted to preserve this idea you thought I had of you. You wouldn't let me love the real you."

Dev snorts into his Shiraz. "Says the man who doesn't believe in love."

"Just because I don't want to uphold the capitalist, heteronormative structures of matrimony and procreation does not mean I didn't love you. Is that what you really think? Of course I loved you. We were together for six years. I know I couldn't love you the way you wanted to be loved, but in my defense, the kind of love you want doesn't exist without a team of producers, a ton of editing, and a really good soundtrack."

Ryan pushes back from the bar and pulls a wad of rand out of his wallet. He throws it onto the counter before polishing off the last of his wine. "You love orchestrating big romantic gestures, Dev, but you're scared shitless of anything that's real. That is why you stayed with *me* for six years even though you knew we didn't have a future."

For someone who claims to love love, you're really good at pushing it away.

Ryan leaves. Shockingly enough, making Ryan feel like shit didn't help at all. Dev reaches for his wine again, then stops himself. He's tired of numbing himself with alcohol every time his heart feels too big inside his chest. He doesn't want to bury all his feelings and he doesn't want to keep hiding them from everyone in his life. He doesn't want to push away love.

What he *really* wants is to be as healthy as he says he is.

Dev crashes in a shitty Airbnb with Jules and five other producers, and the next morning, he gets up to watch a single camera film Charlie and Daphne emerging from their room hand in hand. They're both fresh-faced and sharing secret smiles. Jules hands him a box of Romany Creams cookies, and they sit in the back of a van eating Dev's feelings together.

With both Megan and Delilah gone before the Crowning Ceremony, the show is in a weird spot. They can't send any more women home going into week seven, but they also need Crowning Ceremony footage to round out the two-hour episode. In a production meeting when they get back to Cape Town, Skylar breaks down the plan. They're going to do a "super-special surprise" concert.

Usually around week five or six, the show brings in a musician to do a private concert. It's never that surprising, because they do it literally every season, and it's definitely not special, because the musician is usually some no-name country singer the cast doesn't actually like. Whoever they got this season has to be desperate enough to fly twenty hours one direction for ten minutes of publicity, so Dev is sure it will be particularly awful.

When he gets back to the suite to help Charlie prep for the night, everyone is acting weird, perhaps on account of the fact that Dev and Charlie were having sex, and now Daphne and Charlie are having sex, and everyone has to pretend like this is a perfectly normal situation. Still, Parisa is more aggressive than usual, taking angry phone calls in her room, and Jules is more placating than usual, constantly hovering around Dev to see if he needs anything. And Charlie, who hasn't spoken to Dev since the stairwell, looks at him before they leave for the music venue and snaps: "Is that really what you're going to wear tonight?"

Dev double-checks that he's wearing what he always wears: cargo shorts, an oversize plain T-shirt, his high-tops. "Uh, yes?"

Charlie disappears into their former shared room and emerges five minutes later holding a folded pair of khakis, a button-down shirt, and the jean jacket. "Can you put these on, please?"

Dev can't imagine why Charlie cares what he looks like, but he notices Jules has her hair down and is wearing the same outfit from the night out in New Orleans, and Parisa has changed into a floral jumpsuit, her breasts spilling out magnificently. "Y'all, what's going on?"

"Just put on the damn clothes," Parisa orders.

Dev puts on the damn clothes.

When the van pulls up to a small music venue on Long Street, the block is already barricaded for filming, and production vans are lined up out front. When the four of them stumble inside, filming has already started for some reason, and everyone turns to stare when they enter. Ryan and Skylar are off to the side looking more excited than this shoot should warrant, and when he turns, he finds Parisa filming something on her phone against *Ever After* rules. She's filming Dev, he realizes, and the crew and contestants aren't staring at Charlie. They're staring at *him*. What the hell is going on?

He turns to the stage for answers. A young man sits on a stool in the center of the stage, glowing under a soft yellow light. As soon as he has Dev's attention, he plucks at the strings of a guitar and starts singing into a microphone and *Holy Mary mother of God*, it's Leland Barlow.

Leland Barlow, in all his baby-faced glory, is sitting on a stage in a concert venue in Cape Town, South Africa, and Dev is having a stroke. Is he having a stroke?

He presses his hand to his heart, trying to figure out if this is real. If this is happening. *Ever After* somehow booked Leland Barlow, the silky-voiced love of his life? It takes him until Leland reaches the chorus of his first song for Dev to look around and realize everyone is still watching him. "What the hell is this?"

"Surprise, bitch!" Parisa shouts.

Dev turns to Charlie, who is blushing nervously by the door. And he understands there is no version of *Ever After* that has Leland Barlow in its season budget. "Did you do this?"

Charlie brushes his hair out of his eyes and stammers, "Yes, well, I, uh—"

"Did you do this *for me*?"

"You missed the chance to see him in concert last Christmas, and after Munich, I thought you could use some cheering up, so Parisa reached out to his manager, and—"

Charlie cuts off when Dev launches himself into his arms, hugging him so tight, neither of them can breathe. He's not sure if the cameras are filming this, and he doesn't care. Charlie squeezes his back, tension unspooling in his arms, and for a second, it feels like they've turned back time to before the fight, to those blissful days of sharing a single pillow on a bed big enough for three.

Dev is laughing and crying and dying all over even before Leland comes down off the stage after the first song so Dev can shake his hand. In person, Leland is almost as tall and almost as skinny as Dev, his skin the same dark brown. Dev shouts, "I'm obsessed with you!" in Leland Barlow's face. "But like, not in a creepy way."

Leland Barlow looks him up and down and smiles. "You can be obsessed with me in a creepy way."

It is officially the greatest moment of Dev's entire life.

Skylar steps in because, incidentally, this is a *show*, and they're pretending the Leland Barlow private concert is for the four remaining women, not Dev. So Charlie dances with Daphne, Angie, Sabrina, and Lauren L. each in turn while the cameras film them and Leland Barlow croons in the background. As soon as that's done, though, Skylar gives the crew permission to join in, and it becomes an unprecedented crew-cast dance party. Parisa and Jules rock back and forth in each other's arms, and Dev temporarily forgets to be jealous of Daphne Reynolds. He gyrates ridiculously against her until she laughs so hard she cries. Then Angie steals her away, and Dev is sing-screaming all the lyrics with Jules, and Jules spins him into Charlie, and Charlie—

Charlie's hand brushes his shoulder, and time rights itself: the fight, and the door closing, and Charlie belonging with Daphne, not him, at the end of all of this.

They dance together carefully, some overtly hetero arm-flailing thing, with absolutely no hip movement. Chest to chest, two feet between them, they lock and unlock their knees in rhythm with the song, and Dev returns to his old trick of only looking at Charlie's ear.

"I can't believe you did this," Dev says to the ear and the ear only. "Even after I was such a dick to you."

"Well, you were a dick *after* I decided to do this, so." Charlie bobs his head. "Do you like it?"

Dev stops fake-dancing. "Charlie." His voice snags on the second syllable. He wishes they could dance for real. He wishes he could go back and erase the stupid fight so they could have twenty-three more days of kissing and not talking about it.

He wishes they could kiss and talk about it.

"I love it."

Charlie takes a step closer, his fingers brushing Dev's forearm, and Dev pulls back. "Sorry, I . . . I need to get some air."

He pushes his way outside the venue, leans against a wall, and attempts to breathe through the shock of this entire night.

It shouldn't surprise him that Charlie spent obscene amounts of money to fly his favorite pop star to Cape Town. Charlie Winshaw held him all night when he was depressed; he bought his parents their anniversary present and hauled Dev's cranky ass across a mountain; he read Dev's script and he always carries Dev's duffle and all he wants is for Dev to be healthy. That's who Charlie *is*. He's a beautiful, kindhearted nerd with big eyes and perfect hair and a stupid face, and he was smiling tonight. Not the shy smile, but the bigger one—the one he usually saves for when they're alone together, like he invented a new type of smiling just for them. Dev loves that smile.

And he loves the way Charlie blushes whenever he touches him (or looks at him, or says words in his general direction). He loves the way Charlie pushes past the Fun Dev façade and doesn't get freaked out by what's on the other side; the way Charlie makes him work for every laugh; the way Charlie's body feels beneath his hands, and the way Charlie's hands feel on his body. He loves the clumsy way Charlie kisses when he's excited, and the way it feels when Charlie is tucked up beneath his chin, and the way Charlie's face softens after, and it's fucked up and unfair, because this was never supposed to happen.

"What are you doing out here?" It's Jules. She props herself against the wall next to him. "You okay?"

He feels like his heart is scrambling uphill. "No. I'm really super *not* okay."

She presses her head against his arm. "What's wrong?"

"Jules . . ." He swallows through the pressure in his throat, because not saying it seems so much worse than saying it at this point. "I'm in love with him."

Jules snorts. "No shit, dumbass."

He laughs, and then he sobs. "No, *really*. I *really* love him." He tries in vain to mop away his tears. "What am I going to *do*?"

Jules reaches over to scratch his arm. "Have you considered just letting yourself love him?"

Charlie

For a second, it seemed like maybe he was wrong. Like maybe he wasn't stupid to believe they were something. Dev was right here—right where Charlie wanted him to be—and he was looking at him like he mattered, like Leland Barlow had fixed everything he was supposed to. But Charlie pushed, and Dev pulled away. Dev always pulls away.

He tries to anchor himself to this moment, to this wonderful, chaotic, impossible moment, with Leland Barlow singing for the crew. Daphne's smile is so big it might break free of her face, and Angie is grinding on him during all the slow songs, and Parisa is here beside him, for two more days. He wants to stay here, in this venue, in the tangle of limbs and the smiles of people he considers friends. But Dev isn't here.

He sneaks away from a dance circle forming around Skylar. Outside, he finds Dev and Jules leaning against a wall. Dev is crying.

"Oh, hey, Charlie," Jules says in the soft voice she usually saves for Dev. "I was just about to go back inside."

"You don't have to leave."

"Actually, I do. The two of you should talk." Jules pushes herself off from the wall. The door clicks shut behind her, and it feels like Charlie and Dev are the ones trapped inside a tiny, claustrophobic room. Dev's standing there, eyes on his feet.

Charlie licks his lips. "Was this too much?"

Dev looks up at him. "Not too much. Just the right amount of much. Charlie, I am so sorry."

Charlie takes Jules's spot against the wall. "Sorry for what?"

"For the other night. For being a dick about Megan and Delilah, and an even bigger dick about your concerns about my depression. It turns out that according to Ryan, I have a history of pushing people away when they express concern for my mental health."

At Ryan's name, Charlie feels everything sour inside him. He doesn't want to think about Ryan and Dev in Franschhoek. "I shouldn't have pushed you."

"No, it was good that you did." Dev angles his body toward Charlie, so Charlie turns, too, two parallel lines leaning against this wall. "You were right. I've been neglecting my health for a long time, and when we get back to LA, I'm going to find a new therapist."

"I'm happy for you." He means it, but the words sound hollow. All he wants is to reach out for Dev. He always wants to reach out for Dev, no matter how hard Dev pulls away. He wants to reach and reach and keep reaching.

"I'm happy for you, too," Dev quickly adds. "For you and Daphne. I hope you know that."

It takes him a minute to figure out why they're talking about Daphne right now. "Do you . . . do you think Daphne and I had sex last night?"

"Didn't you?"

"*No*, Dev." Charlie laughs. "That was just for the show. Daphne and I spent the night doing Korean face masks and watching *You've Got Mail*."

"Oh." Dev's shoulders slump with relief, and a little bit of hope creeps in. Charlie reaches out and grabs the edge of Dev's jean jacket.

"And . . . you and Ryan?"

Dev leans forward and butts his head against Charlie's. "Of course not."

Charlie knows he's smiling like an idiot with his forehead pressed against Dev's, and he knows the best-case-scenario of this whole thing is twenty-three days. A handful of nights in private hotel rooms and a handful of days of pretending. At the end of this, he'll fake-propose to Daphne. They'll be seen together, and he won't ever be allowed to be seen with Dev. As long as Dev works for *Ever After*, and as long as Charlie wants America to believe he was the perfect star, no one can ever know about *this*.

But Charlie needs to know if any of it was real. "It wasn't practice," he confesses.

"Huh?"

"Can we just be honest with each other for five seconds?" Charlie catches the sharp point of Dev's hip. "It was never practice for me."

Dev wraps his arms around Charlie's shoulders, and for a second, Charlie imagines they're slow-dancing together to a Leland Barlow song. "It wasn't practice for me either."

Dev tilts his head down until their mouths find each other, and Charlie feels parts of himself realigning, slotting into place. He can't worry about getting caught outside the concert because right now, all he cares about is absorbing Dev's body heat and the smoky-sweet smell he wants between his sheets.

They come apart breathlessly, and Dev pushes his glasses up his nose with two fingers. "Charlie, we only have twenty-three days until the Final Tiara."

"That's twenty-three more days than I ever thought I'd have with someone I care about," Charlie says. He grabs the front of Dev's jean jacket and pulls Dev close again. "Let's just give ourselves twenty-three days without pretending it's just practice."

He thinks Dev will fight him on it. He's prepared to beg, prepared to argue all the reasons they shouldn't feel guilty for doing this behind the show's back. But Dev just kisses him one more time and says, "Okay. Twenty-three days."

Charlie holds out his hand. "Will you dance with me?"

This question earns him his favorite Dev smile in response. It's not the full one he does when he's passionate about something, and not the crooked amused one Charlie fell in love with first. It's the small one Dev fights against, so he won't give himself away entirely. It gives him away every time.

Dev takes his hand, and for a few minutes, they dance in the cool night, Dev's hands laced behind his neck, Charlie's hands on Dev's waist, Charlie tucked beneath Dev's chin while the faint sound of a Leland Barlow song swirls around them. It's "Those Evenings of the Brain."

They dance, and Charlie pretends one more time—pretends they're inside the venue, dancing where everyone can see them.

Story notes for editors:
Season 37, Episode 7

Story producer:
Jules Lu

Air date:
Monday, October 25, 2021

Executive producer:
Maureen Scott

Scene: Daphne returning to Cape Town after her overnight date in Franschhoek

Location: The contestants' suite

[*Establishing shot of Daphne entering the hotel room.*]

Angie: Uh-oh, look who's returning from her sleepover [*Wide shot to include Angie doing a body roll.*]

Sabrina: Bowchicawowow.

Lauren L.: Isn't it weird to celebrate Daphne having sex with our shared boyfriend?

[*Close-up reaction of Daphne bursting into tears.*]

Angie: Oh no, what is it, Daph? What happened?

[*Some unsteady footage as Angie embraces Daphne, then all four women hug and stumble over to the couch. Angie holds Daphne's head in her lap, Sabrina rubs her back; Lauren attempts to smooth out Daphne's hair.*]

Sabrina: Was the sex bad? I had a feeling it was going to be bad. You can tell by how he kisses.

Daphne: W-we didn't . . . we didn't have sex.

Lauren L.: Is it wrong that I'm relieved?

Angie: Why didn't you have sex with him?

Daphne: Because it didn't feel right. Because it never, ever feels right.

[*Stay on the wide shot as the other three women comfort Daphne while she cries.*]

Maureen's notes to the editor: Why the fuck would we include this scene? Cut the whole thing and expand on the Megan/Delilah fight instead.

WEEK SEVEN

Charlie

They say goodbye to Parisa at the Cape Town airport before she gets on a flight to Los Angeles and they get on a flight to Bali. Everyone cries, except Parisa, who looks them all in the eye and says, "I'm not crying." She dares them to question her as tears smear mascara all down her face.

"Hot-Ass." She sighs as she hugs Charlie goodbye last. She takes his face in her hands and kisses both his cheeks. "I am so glad I got to share this experience with you."

Then she reaches into her purse and pulls out a brown sandwich bag with a sharp crease across the top. "A parting gift."

Charlie peels back the crease to find . . . "What is *wrong* with you?"

"I included some diagrams, too, just in case," she says breezily.

He shoves the bag into the front pouch of his carry-on. "Goodbye, Parisa. Leave now, please."

She cackles. "I love you, Hot-Ass," and even with the epithet, it feels so much realer than it did when Megan said it.

"Tell me you love me back, Charlie," she demands, punching his arm.

"I love you, Parisa."

"Bitch, I know." She smirks. And she's gone.

Bali is the textbook definition of paradise. It takes a day of airplanes and chartered vans to arrive at their villa for the next week, but it's worth the travel time. Palm trees fringe the property, giving way to the undulating brown mountains rising behind the house. Bali is all songbirds and bright Hindu shrines thick with incense and blue skies and *Dev*.

Dev next to him on the plane and next to him in the van. Dev in his bed at the villa they share with Jules—who knows, and who also doesn't care. Dev when he falls asleep to the sound of tokay geckos croaking, and Dev when he wakes up to the sunlight pouring through the windows, still tucked against his chest.

"Good morning," Dev says as he rolls over in his arms on Monday. His left eye is crusted shut and his breath smells like dirty socks. Charlie kisses him anyway. They have the day entirely off from filming, so they lounge in bed for hours, and only get up when Dev's stomach demands it. They eat a late breakfast with Jules on a patio in the sun.

"Should we go explore town today?" Dev asks as he polishes off his second jaffle.

"Actually," Jules leans back in her chair, "I took the liberty of planning something special for the pair of you."

It turns out she planned them a Courting Date, minus the cameras. Jules rents them a scooter to drive into town, and they spend the afternoon snorkeling in Jemeluk Bay. They eat dinner at a rooftop restaurant, and at sunset, a *jukung* takes them out into the Indian Ocean, where they watch the sun dip low beside Mount Agung. Charlie has been on a lot of romantic dates during his time on *Ever After,* but this date is the most stupidly romantic of them all.

The jukung is narrow, so they sit with Charlie in front and Dev behind him, knees slotted against hips. Bali is religiously conservative, so they have to be careful not to touch in front of their boat guide as the sky ignites fiery orange, dissolves into bright pink. But when it softens to a rose-colored haze, Dev leans forward and props his chin on Charlie's shoulder. "That, right there," he whispers, pointing to the sky. "That is the color of your face when you blush."

Charlie's heart is hot butter, seeping through his body, warming his chest, his stomach, his arms. In describing the ridiculous dates on this show, Dev once said it is impossible not to fall in love on a boat.

Charlie should have known better than to doubt him.

Dev

"That is the color of your face when you blush," Dev says, and Charlie *blushes*, dusty pink splotches along his throat. They have to be careful here, not just because Bali is conservative, but because the town is small. Crew members could be anywhere, could see anything.

But when Charlie melts back into him, Dev can't help himself. He grazes his unshaved cheek against Charlie's smooth one, wraps one arm around Charlie's waist.

"Do you want a picture?" their jukung captain asks in nervous English. "Of the two of you?"

"Yes," Charlie says before Dev can say no. He hands over his phone, and they swivel their bodies toward the back of the boat. Charlie throws an arm over Dev's shoulder, and they smile, cheek to cheek.

"You are very beautiful," the captain says. Dev isn't sure if *you* means Charlie, or if *you* means Charlie and Dev together. He wants to believe it's the latter.

"Lady Gaga!" Charlie shouts suddenly as they're headed back to the villa. He pulls Dev into a restaurant where a trio of young men are singing a pitchy rendition of "Shallow." Tourists awkwardly dance around the bar, and Charlie—maybe emboldened by the boat captain's acceptance—grabs Dev's hand and twirls him around the way they couldn't dance together in front of Leland Barlow.

Charlie sings along, quite terribly, to the song as they dance. The equatorial sun has brought out new freckles on his shoulders, and the humidity makes his clothes cling to his abdominal muscles, and Dev can't believe how much he loves him.

"This will be our song," Charlie murmurs low and close.

"This absolutely will *not* be our song."

But when Charlie glares, Dev comes in on the chorus with the Bradley Cooper harmonies despite himself.

Charlie lifts their joined hands and presses a kiss to the back of Dev's, and the gesture feels so natural, almost like he's done it a hundred times before. Almost as if they're a normal couple, not two people playing at happily ever after for three more weeks.

As soon as they're alone back at the villa, Dev kisses Charlie's shoulder, swallowing the constellation of new freckles before traveling up toward Charlie's mouth.

Charlie tastes like peanut sauce, and they kiss and kiss and kiss, until Charlie hooks his hands around the back of Dev's thighs and hoists him up. Dev scrambles to wrap his legs around Charlie's waist, and somehow, Charlie holds him there, suspended, like he weighs nothing. "How are you doing this? I feel like Rachel McAdams in *The Notebook*."

"If I'm a bird, you're a bird," Charlie says. Dev gapes at him. "Yes, I've seen the movie. I didn't grow up under a rock. And *The Notebook* is a prime example of the problematic tendencies in popular romantic media, and—"

Dev smashes his face against Charlie's, just to shut him up, and they kiss and kiss and kiss again, with Dev's arms twisted around Charlie's neck.

"Any other problematic romantic fantasies I can fulfill while we're here?"

"Unless you have a pottery wheel or the prow of a ship stashed away in your meticulously organized luggage, I'm not sure what you can do for me."

Charlie grins. "I think there are a few things I can do for you."

He carries Dev into the bathroom and sets him down on the closed toilet seat with such impressive muscle control, Dev is positive it's the sexiest thing that's ever happened in human history. Charlie turns on the shower and pulls off his shirt.

"To be clear, mixing cleanliness with sex is *your* romantic fantasy."

But then Charlie undresses him with painstaking care, folding his shirt, his shorts, his underwear, all in a neat little pile he sets down beside the sink, and *that* is somehow the sexiest thing that has ever happened. Dev gives Charlie full control, lets him haul them both into the shower, lets him position his body under the warm water, lets him lather his hands with organic oatmeal body wash and send those hands up Dev's chest, covering them both in suds.

Charlie is naked and on display, and Dev can't believe he gets to look. Charlie is carved from marble and meant to be showcased at some Italian museum, but it's Dev's body he treats like a precious antiquity. Charlie scrubs his forearms, his shoulder blades, his kneecaps. He scrubs the inside of his thighs until Dev has to remind himself to breathe. No one has ever touched him as tenderly as Charlie does, as lovingly. It's never been this good, this natural with anyone else. No one else has ever seen this much of him.

Charlie kneels down in front of him.

Breathe, he reminds himself. *Just breathe.*

Water sluices down Charlie's nose, across his clavicle, traveling the horizontal fault line of his abdominal muscles, and Dev hunches forward to protect Charlie from the water as he takes Dev in his mouth.

"Oh, love," he says involuntarily. Everything he says and does becomes involuntary, his other hand sweeping through Charlie's hair and holding on tight. He says please and thank you, and he falls into Charlie's lap when it's over, sitting on the floor of their hotel shower, wrapped up in wet limbs.

Charlie pulls him into a rough kiss, and when Charlie mutters, "I love the way you taste," Dev bursts out laughing. The sound is wet, echoing off the shower walls, and Charlie looks both offended and pleased with himself.

They only dry off and don't bother with clothes as they spread out on the cool sheets in their bed. They rock-paper-scissors for who gets to choose what they watch, and Dev wins and still chooses *The Expanse*, even though he doesn't understand the plot. Charlie props himself against the headboard and Dev props himself against Charlie. It's never *ever* been this good.

Dev toes his laptop a safe distance away and reaches up to kiss Charlie—a heady kiss that's more hands and teeth than anything else. But when they pull apart again, he does something new. He tries talking, tries opening up for Charlie the way Charlie opened up for him.

He tells Charlie about his perfect childhood: vacations in Europe and summers in the Outer Banks, every material need met. Parents who loved him and supported him, always; a brain that never stopped and a heart that was too big.

He was always a happy kid, quick to make friends, a natural performer, which made it all the more confusing when he started going through phases where he became sullen and withdrawn, phases where he'd cry at the smallest things and fake being sick to avoid going to school for days at a time. His parents would worry during these phases and argue late into the night about doctors and medications and specialists who studied chakras and energy flow. They loved him, and he hated that he was causing them pain. So it just became easier to pretend to be Fun Dev all the time, to put on a smile so he wasn't such a burden. After all, he had no reason to be sad. Everything was always fine.

He tells Charlie about the boyfriends whom he knew could never really love him back, the boyfriends who never bothered to find out what exists on the other side of Fun Dev, and the boyfriends who never called him beautiful, and Charlie takes

Dev's face in his giant hands and pulls him close. "You are the most beautiful man in the world."

"I'm really *not*."

"You are," Charlie says, brushing kisses along his cheekbones. "You're so good at seeing other people. I wish you could see yourself."

Charlie

"An entire Group Quest based around *touching*? Whose idea was this?"

It's Wednesday morning, and Dev is screaming at a field producer. Unfortunately, the field producer is screaming back, so neither of them hear Charlie quietly protesting, "It's fine."

"It was Maureen Scott's idea to have the contestants learn Balinese massage, and if you have a problem with it, Dev, why don't you call her yourself?"

"It's really fine," Charlie tries again, but Dev is already screaming back, "You should've caught this! Have you been sleepwalking through this season? Charlie doesn't like to be touched, and—"

"It's fine, Dev," Charlie says loud enough this time. Dev stops, turns, and looks at Charlie. Well, he looks at Charlie's ear. For their day of Balinese massage, Charlie and the contestants are all wearing sheer robes over their underwear. Charlie's robe is decorated with pink frangipani flowers, and it cuts him across the upper thigh. He looks. Well. He looks very gay, and when he first stepped out of the changing room, Dev turned very pale and stopped looking at anything south of Charlie's chin.

"You don't have to say it's fine," Dev says. "It's in your file. This is *his* fault."

The field producer smiles beatifically at Dev while flipping him off with both hands.

"What the fuck is this?" Ryan shouts at everyone and no one as he comes stomping onto set. "Didn't you dickweeds read his file? Why are we doing a massage Quest? Charlie doesn't like to be touched!"

Charlie can hardly believe this is the same man who screamed at him seven weeks ago while he attempted to ride a horse. "It's fine, Ryan. Really. I don't mind."

Ryan claps a hand on his shoulder. "Dude, you sure?"

"*Dude*. I'm so sure."

Ryan shrugs and hurries off to prep the contestants, and the field producer returns to debriefing the camera crew. Only Dev still looks angry about the situation. "I really appreciate you standing up for me," Charlie says quietly. "But if you remove every potential trigger from my path, I will never develop coping strategies. It's okay to let me struggle sometimes. I'm okay with this Quest."

Dev stubbornly tucks his chin against his chest, and Charlie understands so plainly, so quickly. Dev's anger has nothing to do with Charlie and his triggers.

"Are *you* okay with this Quest?"

"Why wouldn't I be okay with it?" Dev pushes his glasses up his nose.

"I don't know. Maybe you're . . . *jealous*?"

"I am not jealous," Dev huffs, sounding unmistakably jealous. Charlie brushes his knuckles across Dev's hand as he passes by, trying to reassure him with the one small gesture they're permitted on set. It's odd to return to this world of pretend when things with Dev off camera feel so real.

"Hello, I am Wayan," says the petite Balinese woman once the cameras are all in place. She instructs the women on the art of massage, explaining different oils and techniques, before Charlie is forced to strip down under a thin towel so the women can give him semi-seductive massages one at a time. They mostly fail in this endeavor. Daphne acts like she's more terrified of germs than he is, Lauren L. giggles the entire time, and Angie massages him like she's kneading very stubborn dough. He'll probably bruise. In their defense, there is truly nothing erotic about erotic massage with an audience, and he almost falls asleep while Sabrina rubs his calves with a disgusting amount of oil.

He wakes right up, however, as Sabrina creeps closer to massaging something else entirely.

"Sorry. So sorry. Sorry!" He says as he half falls off the massage table, feebly trying to conceal himself behind the towel. "I'm so sorry!"

"I lied," Dev hisses five minutes later as Charlie struggles to put on the rest of his clothes in a back room. "I was really jealous."

"Sweetheart, I know."

"Be honest with us, Charlie: was that your first time?"

Dev throws the rest of his fried banana at Skylar's face. "Leave him alone."

"You got to give it to Sabrina, though," Ryan says. "It was a bold move at the eleventh hour. A real Hail Mary."

"Do I have to *give it to her*?" Charlie borrows Jules's signature head tilt. "Do I *really*?"

The whole poolside patio erupts with laughter. Jules spills a tiny bit of red wine onto her pajamas from her position at the foot of Dev's lounge chair. The blooming stain doesn't bother him in the slightest.

Charlie holds the sweaty neck of his third lemon radler. "Poor Wayan was still standing right there, holding the massage oil. I'm pretty sure she got an eyeful of my dick."

"Charles, *I* got an eyeful of your dick," Skylar clarifies.

"Can we all please appreciate the fact that Charlie just said the word *dick* out loud without hyperventilating?" Dev says, and he raises his soda water into the air to toast. "To corrupting Charlie!"

"Hear, hear."

Skylar, Jules, and Ryan all raise their glasses high in the air. "That's the heart and soul of *Ever After*, right there," Ryan says. "Getting innocent tech millionaires to expose themselves on national television."

Dev leans across his lounge chair to clink his can against Charlie's bottle.

Charlie takes a long drink. "The real problem is, I was planning to send Sabrina home on Saturday, but would it be . . . *untoward* . . . to reject a woman two days after she offered me a hand job?"

The entire pool patio thoughtfully considers this moral quandary. Jules answers first: "Would we call it an offer, or would we call it attempted sexual assault?"

"I think her hand really did slip," Skylar says, probably to prevent Charlie from suing.

Dev looks grim, reaches over, and puts a hand on his shoulder. "I think you know what you have to do."

Charlie sighs. "Marry her?"

"Exactly."

"Wait, wait, *wait*!" Skylar leans forward so enthusiastically she spills half her beer and almost herself onto the concrete patio. "If you know you're sending Sabrina home this week, does that mean you know who you're going to *choose*?"

Dev tenses on his chaise, his joking mood swallowed in an instant, an edge of darkness cutting across his face. Charlie wishes he could tell him, *Don't worry. It's you. It's only you.*

He takes three deep breaths and answers carefully. "I know who I would *like* to choose, yes," Charlie says, and he shoots Dev the briefest glance before he returns his attention to Skylar. "But I am not quite sure how it's all going to play out yet."

Skylar's drunk face melts into a scowl. "Are you going to choose Daphne? Of course you're going to choose Daphne. It's what we've been planning all season. It's going to be such a boring and predictable season."

"If I had it my way, Sky, it would be neither boring nor predictable."

"When did you come out to your parents?" Charlie asks hours later, after he's managed to undo Dev's bad mood with a second dinner, a fashion show involving a stolen frangipani robe, and lots of kissing.

"God, I love when you talk dirty to me," Dev says, nipping at his ear. They're tangled up on top of the bed, the ceiling fan whirling, an empty plate of midnight chicken satay on the bedside table.

"Dev."

Dev sighs, sits up, crosses his legs. "My sexuality wasn't much of a mystery to my parents. When I was five, I told my mom I wanted to marry Aladdin, and my parents just gave me space to be exactly who I was without making a big deal out of it."

Charlie hugs a pillow tight against his chest.

Dev pushes his glasses up his nose. "Do you . . . Have you thought about coming out? As bisexual? I mean, in like two years, after the show airs and everything settles down?"

"Well, I don't think I am bisexual, actually," Charlie mumbles. Dev props himself back on the pillows and stares at Charlie expectantly. He's not sure why, after everything else he's shared with Dev, this still feels hard to talk about. "I . . . I don't experience sexual attraction very often. I mean, almost never. Present company excluded." Dev does a charming little bow at that. "And I'm not really sure if that's because the way I was raised taught me to repress the fact that I'm attracted to men, or if it's because I'm maybe"—he pushes his hair off his forehead—"maybe on the asexual spectrum? Or, I don't know. Parisa used this word *demisexual*, and I think maybe that could be me? Or maybe graysexual, which I googled, and it means you only rarely experience sexual attraction. I mean, I know I enjoy both giving and receiving sexual pleasure, but I don't know what that means."

He catches himself mid-spiral and takes a breath. "I guess I'm saying, I still have a lot to figure out about all that, so I don't think I'm ready to come out as anything."

"That's okay." Dev reaches over to touch his knee. "Sexuality isn't always a straight line from closeted to out-of-the-closet. You can take time to explore and evolve and figure out exactly what kind of queer you are, if that even matters to you."

The room is silent except for the whorl of the ceiling fan.

"Sorry, do you not like that word?" Dev backpedals. "What letter of the *LGBTQIAP*+ alphabet are you?"

"No, *queer* is fine. It's just—you wouldn't care if I didn't have it all figured out?"

Dev nudges Charlie's shin with his toe. "Why would I care?"

"I'm twenty-eight. Shouldn't I already know?"

"Some people know at five, some people know at fifty. It's not a race."

"And it wouldn't bother you? If we were together?"

Dev stills on the bed across from him. "*Together?*"

Charlie feels his face flush. It's been a long day, and he shouldn't cross the invisible demarcation of time by referencing *the future*. He only just got Dev to agree to three weeks. "Like, hypothetically. In an imaginary alternate timeline where we could be together after the show."

Dev scratches his unshaved jaw. "In a hypothetical, imaginary, alternate timeline would I be bothered by your sexual ambiguity?" He makes a show of considering. "Um, no."

Charlie's already humiliated himself enough with this conversational tangent, and he should move on, but this line of questioning suddenly feels like a stain of bourbon on Dev's shirt. He's got to get it out—all the way out, right now. "Would it bother you that I don't have any other sexual experience?"

"It hasn't bothered me so far," he teases. Charlie can feel his face frozen in its pinched expression, the tension headache appearing above his brow. Dev's voice softens. "Oh, hey, okay. You're serious."

Dev pushes up imaginary sleeves like he's getting down to business, ready to follow Charlie's spiraling thoughts down whatever paths they need to take. "In a hypothetical, imaginary, alternate timeline where we're together, would I be upset by the fact that you're sexually inexperienced and questioning?"

Dev is smiling. Laughing *with* Charlie, always.

"Hmm. I imagine in this hypothetical, imaginary, alternate timeline, we are living together?"

"That was fast."

"Believe me, you would never step foot in my current apartment."

"I absolutely do believe you."

"So, we own a home in Venice Beach."

"Well, that sounds expensive."

"Well, you're paying."

"And a long commute to Palo Alto."

"You're working from home," Dev retorts, raising his voice over Charlie's logic. "So, we have this house, which probably always smells like disinfectant with bleach and oatmeal body wash. And you'd obviously have your own bathroom, because you need lots of space for all your primping."

"And because you never clean the toothpaste out of the sink."

"Oh, no. Never." Dev shakes his head solemnly. Charlie laughs, but there's also a lump of something gathering in the back of his throat. "And presumably, some Saturday nights, we stay home and puzz and watch space-themed shows full of hot men who don't date each other. And some Saturday nights, we go out to restaurants where you secretly bring your own fork, and after, we come home and watch something about real housewives."

Dev's voice catches, and Charlie wonders if the joke of the hypothetical, imaginary, alternate timeline has clogged his throat a little, too. "And I think," Dev says quietly, "if that were my life, then no, Charlie. I wouldn't care that you've never had sex with anyone else, and I wouldn't care if you weren't sexually attracted to anyone else. It would be pretty wonderful, knowing you'd chosen me."

Dev shakes out his arms again, shaking off that beautiful version of their lives they can never reach. But Charlie wants to reach it. He wants to reach and reach and keep reaching. He grabs Dev by the front of his T-shirt, gathers him onto his lap, and kisses him because he can't help himself. Dev's fingers in his hair, and Charlie's arms around Dev's waist, and the beautiful simplicity of kissing someone who always accepts him, who understands his brain, who doesn't want to change him or put him in boxes, who only wants him to be more of himself.

Shit, he loves Dev. Fully. Stupidly. Maybe irrevocably. He thinks about the first night, about Dev's arrogant little smirk. *I know I can make you fall in love.* Charlie laughs into Dev's mouth at the memory. "What's so funny?" Dev asks, poking him in the ribs.

Charlie shakes his head and kisses Dev's throat until he's jelly again in Charlie's lap. "Can I show you something?"

Charlie climbs off the bed, and Dev does a little pout at his absence. He goes to his carry-on bag and pulls out the brown lunch sack Parisa gave him at the airport.

"What's this?"

"It's Parisa's parting gift."

Dev peels back the corner of the bag just a bit before he rolls over in hysterical laughter. "Condoms and lube! Parisa gave you fifty condoms *and lube?*" Dev pulls out three index cards. "Oh, and she drew you some pictures—*sweet Jesus*. Parisa has a rather graphic artistic style."

Charlie flops onto the bed and tries to cover his face with his hands to hide his blush. "I know. She's awful."

"Why did you want to show me this?"

He squints at Dev through a slit in his fingers. "Um . . ."

"Oh, Charlie," Dev says in a voice that's half-sweet and half-patronizing as hell. "You know I don't need to do the things Parisa vividly depicted on these index cards to feel satisfied, right?" Dev reaches over and rubs soothing circles on Charlie's stomach. "I meant what I said. I don't care about your lack of experience. I am *very* satisfied. I don't need anything else."

Charlie takes a deep breath and tries to remember the rewards of being brave enough to ask for what you want. "But what if *I* wanted to try something else?"

Dev stills again, and Charlie reaches up and carefully removes Dev's glasses, sets them next to the chicken satay. "Charlie," Dev starts, his throat coated with something. There is a question in those two syllables, and Charlie answers it by straddling Dev and sliding their bodies together. He spreads his hand across Dev's chest, his fingers wide, and wishes his hands were larger, so he could always be touching all of Dev.

"Charlie," Dev tries again, succeeds this time. "We don't have to—"

"I know, but I want you to. Do you, um. Do you want to . . . with me?"

"Good God, yes." Dev arches up and makes a mess of trying to find Charlie's mouth, clutching at the waistband of his sweatpants and catching his teeth on Charlie's chin.

"I might be awkward, though," Charlie warns him.

"You better be awkward. The awkwardness is what does it for me, honestly."

Charlie laughs. Dev reaches up to take Charlie's face in both hands.

"I mean it." His voice goes soft, coaxing. It's the voice he uses on set when Charlie's freaking out, its pitch and melody perfectly tuned to Charlie's anxiety. "That first night, when you were nervous sweating and you had vomit in your chin dimple . . ." Dev lowers his hands to Charlie's shoulders, then traces them down over the contours of his chest. "Damn, you were beautiful."

Charlie falls headfirst into a long, hot kiss that doesn't end until they're both naked and breathless and hard. Dev holds him impossibly close before he shifts on the mattress and tells Charlie exactly what he needs to hear. "I mean it, Charlie. I don't like you despite some of your characteristics," Dev says, and it feels like he's talking to himself as much as Charlie, like the words are caught in an echo chamber made for two. "I like all of you. You know that, right?"

Hearing Dev say what Charlie knew in his heart—he didn't know it was possible to love Dev *more*, for love to become a bottomless well inside of him he could spend his whole life filling. Coming together with Dev in this new way makes the well inside of him pour over. It feels like an unzipping of his skin, as if he's stepping outside this costume version of himself to become his actual self—that he's discovering something true buried so deep he thought he would never reach that person, but there he is, and Dev is with him, holding his hand, guiding him through.

In the middle of the night, he wakes up reaching out for Dev, but he's already there, arms wrapped up tight around Charlie. "I would choose you," Charlie whispers into the darkness.

Even though Dev's eyes are closed, Charlie's pretty sure he hears him.

Dev

I would choose you.

That's what Charlie said. *I would choose you.*

But today, Charlie is not choosing Dev. Bali went by too quickly in a haze of incense and Charlie's skin, and now they're at another Crowning Ceremony. Tonight, Charlie will choose three women to continue onward to Home Kingdom dates, and after Home Kingdom dates, Charlie will choose his top two, and at no point in the next fifteen days is Charlie going to hold out a tiara and ask Dev if he's interested in becoming his prince.

Across the set, Charlie picks up a jeweled tiara. "Daphne," he says, and the woman steps out of the lineup to approach him. "Are you interested in becoming my princess?"

"Of course." Daphne beams, and Charlie smiles shyly as he puts the crown carefully in her hair.

Dev has always known how this story will end. Now he has two weeks left to figure out how to accept it.

Story notes for editors:
Season 37, Episode 8
Story producer:
Ryan Parker

Air date:
Monday, November 1, 2021
Executive producer:
Maureen Scott

Scene: B-roll, post-massage Quest (post–Handie Crisis)
Location: Shot on location at the villa, Amed, Bali

Charlie [muttering, barely audible]: I know.

Producer [voice off camera]: Are you okay? With what just happened with Sabrina?

Charlie: Mildly embarrassed, but that's standard operating procedure.

Producer: [*Steps into the shot.*] What Sabrina did was not cool. You shouldn't feel embarrassed about that. It was not your fault. You should, however, be embarrassed about how you look in this tiny robe.

Charlie: I'd happily burn it along with the memory of this entire day.

Producer: Now let's not do anything too hasty. . . .

WEEK EIGHT

Charlie

Coming home doesn't feel like the right way to describe it.

For Charlie, it feels like the past and present collide inside his chest when their connecting flight from Taipei arrives at the San Francisco airport. This is where his journey started eight weeks ago, when Parisa put him on a plane to Los Angeles to become the *Ever After* prince. This is where he used to fly in and out of when he worked at WinHan, he and Josh in adjacent business-class seats to London, Singapore, Tel Aviv, Mumbai. And now this is where he lands for Angie's Home Kingdom date, Dev's carry-on duffle over his shoulder, Jules drooping against him while they wait for the equipment on the baggage carousel. He watches Skylar and Ryan pound espresso shots from Peet's Coffee so they can meet with the travel team to debrief the plans for tomorrow. He watches Dev play some stupid game on his phone. And he thinks about who he was when he left San Francisco and who he's going to be in two weeks when this is over.

A fleet of vans carry the exhausted crew to a hotel in downtown San Francisco, driving past Charlie's apartment building on the way, the one he's lived in for almost three years now, the one that's been empty for two months. He looks up and searches for the window on the twentieth floor, south corner—his window—and realizes he misses it. Not so much the apartment itself, which was cold and sterile, but what it represented. About him, about his life, about how far he'd come from the bullies at school and the bullies at home. On the twentieth floor, it always felt like the past could never reach him.

He could have that again. In two weeks, he'll propose to Daphne. She's already promised to say yes when he asks. The show will air, and they will pretend to be in love on the live finale special, and thanks to Dev, he'll come across like the perfect prince. He'll be famous again; he'll get a job again; he'll be allowed to sit at a desk and do work befitting his brain again. He'll be allowed to *contribute* something again. It's the whole reason he came on this show.

He could have everything he's ever wanted. So why can't he stop thinking about a little house in Venice Beach that smells like oatmeal and bleach? Why can't he get this lump out of his throat?

"I truly did not think it was possible, but I stand corrected."

"You didn't think what was possible?"

"For you to be unattractive. But behold"—Dev flourishes his hands—"the power of the hat."

Charlie rips the beanie off his head and is immediately assaulted by the icy breeze coming off the water. They're at Golden Gate park to film his reunion with Angie, and there's still a morning fog hanging over the bay. It's late July, and Charlie has to put the hat back on despite Dev's mockery.

"You look bald," Dev observes. "Like, I knew your hair was one of your best features, but I'm not sure I realized just how much it was doing for your face."

"You are aware of the fact that you're also wearing a hat, right?"

Dev cocks his head to the side. "Yes, but I happen to look incredible in a hat."

Charlie takes a risk and discreetly reaches out for Dev's hand. "You look incredible all the time."

"I thought I could say the same about you before today." Dev doesn't pull his hand away, and Charlie marvels at this moment, holding Dev's hand in a park, in public, almost like normal people (if you ignore the cameras, lights, and production crew). The lump in his throat is golf-ball size.

"You boys seem like you've really *bonded*."

Charlie turns and sees Maureen Scott wading across the park in her heeled boots, her silver bob completely unrumpled by the wind. Dev takes a giant step back until Charlie's hand is only holding empty air. Charlie knew the showrunner was scheduled to rejoin them again at Home Kingdom dates for the final two weeks of filming. He also conveniently tried to block this fact from his mind. Set is immediately different under her watchful gaze; Skylar is back to popping antacids while she screams at PAs; Ryan's decisions seem a little more calculated; Jules's movements seem a little more nervous, her eyes constantly darting between Dev and Charlie, then flickering to Maureen.

Dev's change is the worst. He's stiff and formal and always so eager to please her. "Charlie's ready for the intro shot whenever Angie is, Maureen."

Maureen cuts her eyes between the two of them and flashes a smile. "Wonderful."

When Angie appears on the other side of the park, Charlie does exactly as Dev instructs: he runs toward Angie, scoops her up, and twirls her around in delight. "Good to see you, too," she says in his ear, surprised and confused.

Charlie cuts his gaze over to Maureen Scott, hovering behind Skylar's shoulder. Angie follows his gaze. "Ah. Got it," she says. Then she grabs the back of his neck to pull him into a kiss. "Then let's sell it, boo."

Angie certainly sells it. She hangs all over him as they eat lunch at her favorite burrito place in the Mission. She holds his hand as they tour the UCSF School of Medicine, where she'll be starting in the fall. She kisses him at the top of Lombard Street and, in a heartfelt moment, confesses she's in love with him. At first he feels guilty, but when the cameras are off, Angie winks and presses a friendly kiss into his palm.

"She's good," Dev says once they're in a town car together driving out to Berkeley to meet Angie's family. "It's too bad she won't be our next princess. Even if we could convince the network, Angie actually wants to be a doctor and not a reality television star. Go figure."

A phone buzzes, and Dev stares down at the screen in his hand. "You got a text." Dev's voice is vacant as he pushes the phone into Charlie's hands.

Charlie glances down at the screen and sees the name right there in bold letters. *Josh Han.*

His hands sweat as he struggles to swipe open the text. The words swim and it takes his brain a few minutes to arrange them in their proper order, to parse out their meaning. He hasn't talked to Josh in over a year, not since the midnight emergency vote of no confidence removed him from his own company, and he wasn't even allowed to pack up his office. Strangers came to his apartment with a moving van carrying his leather chesterfield, his antique chess set, his books.

Hey, man. The first text says. *I heard you're in SF for filming.*

A second text. *Did you want to meet up? Brunch tomorrow at LD?*

A third. *We can talk work stuff.*

He's robbed of breath. This is everything he hoped for. It's *more* than he dared to hope for, because it's Josh. His company. The company they built together. *Brunch with Josh.*

"It looks like everything is working out," Dev says from the other side of the car. Charlie can't stop staring at his phone screen.

Unfortunately, he's an anxious mess even before meeting Angie's parents.

"Welcome! Welcome!" Angie's mother booms when they arrive. She pulls Charlie into a hug without asking, and then he's introduced to Angie's entire extended family—parents and grandparents and aunts and uncles and siblings and cousins and three text messages from Josh Han and it's just too damn much.

Ryan and Jules are both already screaming at the travel team about crowd-size limitations when Charlie makes a beeline for the nearest bathroom to ride out a panic attack, his first in weeks.

Angie follows him. "Shit. I'm so sorry. I should've known better than to invite so many people, but Maureen wanted it to be special."

Of course Maureen did. The boyfriend from back home on the first night, the wool suit, Megan and Delilah, the massage Quest—sometimes it feels like Maureen Scott is intentionally trying to provoke him. "No, it's okay. It's just . . . I'm so sorry I'm embarrassing you in front of your family."

Angie kneels down in front of the toilet where he's cradling his head in his hands. "You're not embarrassing me because you have anxiety, Charlie. And it's not like you're actually my boyfriend."

He looks up at her then and tries to take a deep breath. "I'm sorry," he says, and he means it, so profoundly. Angie doesn't deserve to be used on national television. None of the women deserved it. "I'm sorry none of it was real between us."

"Oh, baby, that's okay. I know. I know." She gives his leg a pat, tries to tap out the pattern on his knee without knowing it. "I was always just along for the ride, and I have no regrets. I got to travel to some amazing places with some amazing ladies. Besides, everyone knows the female friendships are the only relationships on this show that actually last."

The bathroom door opens, and Dev slides his skinny frame through the crack. As soon as Angie sees him, she backs away so Dev can take her spot at Charlie's feet. "Hey, how's it going?" Dev immediately starts tapping Morse code onto Charlie's leg in the correct pattern. "Ryan beat up some aunties, so the place is mostly cleared out at this point."

Charlie puts his hand over Dev's. "Thank you."

Dev holds his gaze a little longer than he should in front of Angie. "Of course."

As Dev helps Charlie up off the toilet seat, he looks up and sees Angie watching them. She smiles softly. "I know," she says again. And Charlie understands now. *She knows.* She's maybe known the whole time.

Angie doesn't break character for the rest of the night, and when dinner's over, she walks him out to the black Suburban waiting to whisk him back to his hotel. She kisses him deeply, says she can't wait to see him in Macon at the end of the week for the Crowning Ceremony. But right before he gets in the car, she pulls him in close and whispers too quietly for the mics to hear, "It's not too late to stop playing by their rules."

Dev

The next morning, Charlie vomits twice, and his hands are shaking so badly, he asks Dev to knot his tie.

"Why are you wearing a tie to brunch?"

"I . . . I want Josh to remember I can be . . . professional."

Dev bites his tongue to refrain from saying anything about where Josh Han can shove his professionalism. Charlie's sweating too profusely for humor. "You're coming with me, right? I . . . I can't do this alone."

"I said I would come," Dev calmly reassures him.

Charlie nods frantically. "I need you there, to coach me. To stop me from saying the wrong thing."

Dev pulls Charlie in close by the knot on his tie. "You never say the wrong thing, love."

Of course, Josh Han is dressed like every Silicon Valley tech bro Dev has ever met when they get to the restaurant twenty minutes later. He's wearing hiking sandals and a Patagonia vest over his moisture-wicking shirt. Josh probably spent a lot of money to look like he doesn't give a shit, and Le Délicieux is definitely not in Dev's dining budget. It's hard to remember that this is Charlie's normal life—ties with Windsor knots and business brunches at overpriced restaurants in downtown San Francisco. They've only ever known each other within the incubator of *Ever After*, but Josh Han and the waitstaff at Le Délicieux—who all seem to take issue with Dev's choice in cargo shorts, based on their stares— are good reminders Dev wouldn't belong in Charlie's real life, no matter what Dev tries to imagine otherwise.

"Chaz!" Josh shouts when he sees Charlie. "Bro, it's been too long!"

Josh hugs Charlie. Charlie tenses.

"Still weird about touching, huh?" Josh chuckles and gives Charlie's arm the most patronizing pat. "That's my Chaz."

There is no version of Charlie Winshaw that would willingly consent to a nickname like *Chaz*, and Dev is pissed about this whole thing before he even sits down.

"And who's this?"

Charlie turns awkwardly to Dev, his brow a jumbled mess of anxiety. "This is my . . . producer. Dev."

My producer.

Josh looks momentarily confused as to why Charlie brought his producer to a business meeting, but he eventually shrugs, as if to say *only Charlie.* They sit down, and Josh has already ordered a round of Bloody Marys to get them started. Dev ignores his.

Josh begins talking about second-quarter earnings and Nasdaq and some summit in Tokyo while Charlie nervously sweats all over his linen napkin. Dev studies the man who humiliated his boyfriend and iced him out of an entire industry.

Sorry. *His talent.*

Josh Han is as handsome in person as he always is in product launch videos. His thick dark hair is perfectly styled, and he has a gorgeous jaw Dev would like to stroke before he punches it.

Except Dev can't punch Josh Han, because this is Charlie's chance to get everything he wants.

"Honestly, I couldn't believe it when I heard you agreed to do that show," Josh is saying, stirring his celery around his empty glass. "But the hype for the season is *insane*. It's all anyone is talking about."

"Oh, well, I . . . um . . ." It's like someone flipped a switch to turn him back into that version of Charlie who fell out of the town car on night one.

Under the table, Dev puts a hand on Charlie's knee to calm him. "We are so lucky to have Charlie as our star. He's honestly been one of the best princes we've ever had. I think the season will be fantastic."

Josh laughs, and it's clearly at someone's expense. "You should've seen him in college. Girls used to follow him around campus, but he was totally oblivious," he says, speaking about Charlie like he isn't right here. "I don't even think he kissed anyone until— What was her name? Senior year? Remember, I had to arrange it for you, and you still managed to fuck it up."

Josh laughs again, and Charlie becomes smaller, shrinking in his gray suit.

"Ha. Ha." Dev makes those two syllables as cutting as possible. "It's so humorous when you mock him for not conforming to your hypersexualized notions of masculinity."

"Whoa, dude." Josh Han holds up two hands. Next to him, Charlie shoots Dev a look.

"You, uh, said in your text you might . . . work?"

A server comes to the table, and Josh takes the liberty of ordering for everyone before he deigns to offer Charlie a glance. "Yeah, I might have a gig for you, actually," and even this is so laced with condescension Dev has to clamp his jaw shut to stop himself from screaming. "We've acquired this new startup for their dating app—great concept, runs like TikTok—but our engineers are having problems integrating the app into our existing codebase, and we've run into a ton of problems. No one knows the WinHan codebase like you do."

Dev can feel the way every muscle in Charlie's body seems to be holding its breath. "You're offering me a job?"

"Unless you've already got something else lined up when you're done with the whole fairy-tale thing."

Josh knows Charlie doesn't have a job lined up, knows he has effectively prevented his college best friend from working anywhere. Charlie was a liability with investors before, but now that Charlie is about to become one of the most famous men in the country when his season finally starts to air—now that WinHan *needs* him—Josh is going to act like none of that ever happened.

"You want me to run this startup?" Charlie asks. He sounds so damn hopeful.

"Well, not *run* it, no. I just need you to integrate the code. We'd hire you as a contractor. I know it's been hard for you since everything went down at WinHan, and I figured you need this. And who knows? If this goes well and you've got your little quirks under control, maybe we can even talk about bringing you back into the office."

And then Dev has to say something, or else he truly will punch Josh Han in his chiseled jaw. "Are you kidding me right now?"

Charlie manages a warning "*Dev*" under his breath, but Dev is already too far gone, only dimly aware that one shouldn't shout in a restaurant with four different crystal chandeliers.

"How can you sit there and insult him like this, offer to hire him as a contractor when his name is still half the company title? You built your fortune on his brain, and now you want him to beg for a chance to be let back in the building? Fuck you."

"Hey, now," Josh says, scanning the room to see which important people are witnessing this little blowup. Even in humiliation, Josh is handsome and poised, and some part of Dev's brain that isn't overwhelmed with rage wonders if some part of Charlie's brain loved Josh Han before he knew what it meant to have feelings for another man. Is that why Josh has the power to make Charlie feel so powerless?

The thought only intensifies Dev's anger. No wonder Charlie came on the show believing he doesn't deserve love the way he is. Every single person he's ever loved has only reinforced his conviction that he's not enough.

"And he doesn't have 'little quirks,' and there is no part of his personality he needs to learn to control to appease you. Charlie is compassionate and brilliant and funny and sexy as hell"—that last detail, perhaps, could have been omitted, but he plows onward—"and quite frankly, if you can't accept him as he is, then you don't deserve him. And that's your fucking loss."

At some point during this performance, Dev stood up, and now several servers wait in the wings to escort him out. He'll escort his own ass out, thank you very much.

Quickly, he turns to Charlie, who's flushed and sweaty and—he stands by it—sexy as hell. "I'm sorry. I support you no matter what, but I could not sit here and watch you be disrespected. I'll wait for you outside."

Then he turns on the heel of his Converse high-tops and storms out of the restaurant.

Charlie

He watches Dev stomp past the baby grand piano attempting to drown out the previous fight with calming music. The business brunchers either turn to glare at Dev or turn away, embarrassed, pretending not to notice the absurdly tall, absurdly skinny man in the absurdly oversize jean jacket throwing a fit.

"What the hell was that?" Josh snaps.

Charlie swivels back to face him and feels the anxiety grind through his lower intestines alongside the ever-expanding lump of something caught in his throat, tennis ball size now. Ever since he got the texts from Josh yesterday, he's been sick over the thought of seeing this man again—his former dorm mate, his former best friend, his former business partner. The man whose opinion and esteem he always held in the highest regard.

The thought of seeing Josh again was overwhelming, but this is what he wants. A chance to work in tech again. It was all for this. The potential national humiliation, the cameras and kissing women and hot-air balloons and so much damn touching all boils down to *this*. Now he stares at Josh across the table in this lavish restaurant, and suddenly, he can't even remember what he liked about his old life.

Except that he liked how the work was a shield against living—he liked how the world inside his glass-and-chrome office kept him from thinking about the world outside of it where he felt alienated and disconnected. He liked how the productivity made him feel worthy, and he liked how being busy never left him time to think. He liked how the twentieth-floor apartment made him successful in the eyes of other people; it meant the measure of his life was something, even if beneath the surface, everything felt empty. *That* is what he lost. *That* is what he is fighting to get back. Glittering *nothing*.

"I cannot believe I just got chewed out by someone who works in reality television." Josh angrily reaches for Dev's untouched Bloody Mary. "What even was that, Chaz?"

Maybe it's the way he dismisses Dev, or maybe it's the sound of the old, ironic nickname for him, but the clog in Charlie's throat now feels like certainty. "Sorry, but I have to go." He rises and nearly upends the table with his knees. "Actually, no, I'm not sorry. I'm just going."

"Wait. You're leaving?" Josh asks even as Charlie's already moving away from the table. "But what about this app? We could really use your help."

He doesn't look back. "I'm going to pass."

He's outside where the fog has cleared, and he blinks in the sun until he sees Dev leaning against the building, staring down at his phone like a sullen teenager. At the sound of Charlie's footsteps, though, he looks up. His violin eyes are almost molten amber in this light, and the sun hits his cheekbones, the sharp point of his chin. Charlie feels so absolutely *certain*.

Dev frowns. "I know, I know. I screwed up. I shouldn't have lost my temper, but he was a dick to you, and I couldn't just—"

Charlie takes three steps toward him, fists the front of his jean jacket, shoves him back against the wall, and swallows the rest of Dev's sentence. He tries to kiss him with the sureness he feels blossoming inside him, new feelings he's only beginning to understand, still fumbling to process. It's Josh always laughing at him and Dev always laughing with him. It's the difference between a twentieth-floor apartment and a house in Venice Beach. It's the dawning realization that Charlie could spend the rest of his life grabbing Dev by the front of the jean jacket and kissing him against every brick wall.

Charlie knows he loves him. He knows he would choose him if he could. But until now, he hasn't really let himself consider what choosing Dev would mean. A life together. A future. Dev in his bed from now until forever. His brain can barely fathom it. He's always been alone, has always been prepared to be alone, has no idea how you build your world around someone else or with someone else or what that even means. But he knows, in the back of his throat, in the pit of his stomach, in the consistent pumping of his heart that a life with Dev would be a glittering *something*.

Dev pulls back. "Charlie, we're in broad daylight on a busy street."

Charlie simply yanks him back down with his teeth, kisses his *thank you* against Dev's mouth, Dev's jaw, Dev's throat, like Morse code. "So you're not mad I screamed at him, then?" Dev asks as Charlie nuzzles himself against the curve of Dev's neck.

"Not mad."

Charlie is something else entirely, and he doesn't know what to do with all this certainty.

According to the show, Daphne and Charlie will reunite after their week apart in a sun-dappled park in downtown Macon, running toward each other, Daphne leaping into his arms.

In reality, they reunite in an empty hotel gym at six in the morning without cameras or crew members. The contestants aren't allowed to stay with their families during Home Kingdom dates—Dev explained that it has something to do with access to the outside world, but Dev also had barbecue sauce on his chin at the time, so Charlie wasn't really listening. Daphne and Charlie are staying at the same Courtyard Marriott, and they clearly have the same restless need to exercise before their staged date.

"How was Dallas?" Daphne asks from the elliptical, her blond ponytail swishing behind her. She's wearing a sports bra and a pair of spandex shorts, and she is undoubtedly the most beautiful woman he's ever seen. Which resolves some of his sexual ambiguity, at least. He's unequivocally not attracted to women.

"Dallas was awful," he says from the free-weight bench. "I feel terrible that Lauren doesn't know the truth. She seems to genuinely think our relationship is working."

Daphne considers this for a moment. "We all sort of knew the truth coming into it, though. Anyone who has seen this show knows people always have ulterior motives for coming on *Ever After*. And we knew the risk of getting our hearts broken."

"I suppose."

Dallas was also awful because of Dev—because Dev is slipping away again, not all at once like before, but incrementally. There are moments when his voice hollows out, moments his gaze goes somewhere Charlie can't follow. Then he'll snap back, laughing at something Charlie said, or lip-syncing to the Proclaimers in their Dallas hotel room, kissing Charlie until they both forget everything else.

When Daphne finishes her thirty minutes on the elliptical, she comes to sit beside him on the bench. "It's weird, isn't it? That you're going to meet my parents today?"

"Do you feel guilty about lying to them?"

Daphne gathers her ponytail and begins to weave it into a braid. "Honestly? No. Does that make me a bad person?"

Before he can reassure her, Daphne plows on. "I'm sort of *relieved*. My mom and dad constantly pester me about getting a boyfriend. Even though it's fake, my parents will be so happy to see us together. And I want to—"

"Please them?" Charlie tries. Daphne bites her lip, and Charlie thinks about Josh Han. He thinks about trying to please other people and trying to please himself. "Will it make *you* happy, though? When we're lying to people about our engagement?"

She doesn't say anything, but he already knows the answer. Daphne wants fairy-tale love, but she also simply wants other people to see her with it, to have them approve of her normalcy. They really are so fucking similar.

"Will it make you happy?" she finally asks. "To be able to work in tech again?"

He stares up at a television screen mounted to the wall playing the news on mute. Daphne reaches over for his hand. "You still want that, right? To propose to me at the end? To make people think we're in love?"

The glass door to the gym opens before he can answer—before he can figure out what his answer even is—and Dev is standing there in his ratty basketball shorts and Charlie's Stanford T-shirt. He's silent for a second, staring at Daphne and Charlie close together on the bench, their fingers intertwined.

"Oh," Dev fumbles, and Charlie quickly drops Daphne's hand. "Sorry, I just, uh, you weren't in your hotel room, and we need to go over the schedule for today," he says.

He means, *I woke up in our bed and you weren't there.*

Charlie stands up and tries to match Dev's professionalism. "Yes, of course. We should do that."

He takes a step toward Dev, but Daphne rises from the bench and grabs Charlie's elbow. "Hey," she says in a low voice, pulling him close, unaware of how their closeness will affect the man standing by the door. "It's almost over. Soon you'll have everything you want."

She stands on her tiptoes and kisses his cheek.

"I'm sorry," Charlie says as soon as he's alone in the elevator with Dev.

"Don't be. It's fine."

"Dev." Charlie reaches out for him. "We were just talking about—"

"It's totally fine."

But it's not totally fine.

Dev

"Are you ready to meet your future in-laws?"

Charlie tries to grin, but grimaces instead.

"Take it again," Maureen orders from behind the cameras, "and this time, try to sound excited."

Charlie and Daphne trudge back to the beginning of the path leading up to the Reynoldses' house. "Are you excited to meet your future in-laws?" Daphne asks with more gusto, her arm threaded through Charlie's.

Charlie stares down at her lovingly. "I'm so ready," he says before he leans down and kisses her once, reassuringly, on her pretty mouth.

And Dev needs a drink. Or a package of Oreos. Or a lobotomy. Something to ease the pain of watching Charlie kiss Daphne.

Last night, when they landed in Macon, Charlie dragged Dev back to their hotel room. He undressed Dev chaotically, stared at his naked body in the glow of a single bedside lamp, and held him tight against his chest. He fucked him slow and deep, like he was saying goodbye, and when Dev woke up this morning, Charlie wasn't there. His absence in their bed ripped a hole through Dev's chest, sent him stumbling through the hotel half-dressed in search of Charlie, only to find him holding hands with Daphne.

He has to accept that soon, there will only be mornings without Charlie.

Charlie raises a fist to knock on the front door, but Daphne's dad flings it open before he can. "NeeNee! And Charlie! Welcome! Come in, come in!"

Charlie and Daphne step inside the house. Dev can't follow.

He sits in an equipment van and watches a relay of the footage on a portable monitor, and when no one is looking, he pulls out his phone and stares at the selfie they took back in Cape Town, Charlie tucked under his chin.

"Let's hope Reverend Reynolds brings some drama," Maureen says. "We need some creepily possessive old-fashioned dad confrontation to spice up this snooze-fest."

Reverend Reynolds disappoints in the best kind of way. "An atheist app designer?" Richard Reynolds chuckles. "Not exactly what we expected, is it, Anita? But honestly, we're just so happy our NeeNee finally brought a man home."

"*Dad!*" Daphne blushes down at her plate of apple pie.

"Well, sweetheart, it's just, you've never brought a boy home to meet the family. We were starting to worry."

Charlie reaches over and takes Daphne's hand. "I feel honored to be the first," he says, like a perfect prince. Daphne's blush deepens.

Dev slides out of the van. "I'm going to take a walk," he tells Jules. Her voice hitches with worry. "Should I come?"

"I'm fine." He flashes her a breezy Fun Dev smile of reassurance before he disappears into the night. Daphne's childhood home is on a sprawling acre outside of Macon, woods fringing the boundaries. He heads past the golden glow of the floodlights on the back of the house, toward the tall, dark trees and the silence. Out here, his feelings have more room to breathe.

"Dev," a familiar voice calls behind him. "Wait up!"

He pauses against a beech tree as Ryan's shadow advances in the dark.

"What's up?" Ryan asks. "Why'd you bail?"

He lifts his shoulders in a half-assed shrug Ryan probably can't see. "You know how it is. You've seen one Home Kingdom date, you've seen them all."

Dev tilts his head back against the bark and looks up at the sky through the fragmented branches. He can't remember the last time he could see this many stars.

Ryan clears his throat. "I imagine this is all a lot harder now that you're fucking the star."

Dev jerks his head. He must have misheard. Misunderstood. "W-what?"

"It must be harder," Ryan says, his tone as indifferent as ever. It gives nothing away, even as Dev feels his insides slide down to his feet in panic. "You're watching the guy you're sleeping with meet his future in-laws."

Ryan knows. Dev's brain seizes painfully around this realization and its fallout. He'd thought they had more time. He'd parceled out the remaining days with Charlie like chocolate in an Advent calendar, and he'd thought they had *more time.* He thought the clock would end with Charlie proposing to Daphne; he didn't think it would end with people finding out.

Dev can't decide what to do or what to say or how to move his arms. Should he deny it? Own it? Beg? Barter? *Please. Please don't tell. Please let us have just a little more time.*

"How . . . ?" he tries. "What . . . *why*?"

"Come on, Dev." There's nothing gloating or vindictive in Ryan's words, just the usual self-righteous calm. "You flew his best friend to set, and he flew your favorite pop star to South Africa."

He says it like it's the most obvious thing in the world. Maybe it is.

"I've done that job. Before this season, I was the prince's handler for four years, and do you remember me ever spending my days off hanging out with the guy? Do you remember me happily sharing a living space with him for two months? Of course not."

"Please don't tell," Dev blurts when he finally finds his sentences again. "I know I am ruining the show, but—"

"The *show*? Dev, I don't give a shit about the show. I give a shit about *you.*"

He thinks about Franschhoek, when Ryan didn't tell him about the overnight date; he thinks about Ryan trying to talk to him about Charlie at the bar; and he thinks about their fight all the way back in week two. He realizes this is a conversation Ryan's been trying to have with him for a while.

"Dev, what are you doing, hooking up with the talent?"

"I'm in love with him," he says without thinking.

"So at the end of this thing, is it going to be you accepting that Final Tiara, or is it going to be Daphne Reynolds?"

Dev flinches. "Don't be cruel."

"I'm not," Ryan says. And he's really not. His tone is tired and a little sad, but it's not cruel. "I'm being practical. What's going to happen, Dev? In a week, is Charlie going to get engaged to Daphne?"

"I mean, he's under contract, so—"

"So you're going to let a man who's been having sex with you behind the cameras get engaged to a woman on national television? And then what?" Ryan pushes. "Are you and Charlie going to continue dating in secret while he goes on talk shows with his new fiancée? Are you going to go in the closet for this dude? Are you going to live right off camera in Charlie Winshaw's life forever?"

"I don't know!" Dev takes three deep breaths, holding each one in for three seconds. Everything is spinning. It's a humid night, suffocating. He hasn't thought about any of this yet, and he doesn't want to troubleshoot his future with Ryan Parker of all people.

But if he thinks about it, if he considers it for even one second, he knows. He would do it. He would live off camera in Charlie's life if Charlie would let him. If Charlie wanted him, he would do just about anything for that little house in Venice Beach, including hiding away there like a gay Rapunzel, waiting for the moments when Charlie could come to him in secret.

He's always known how this story ends, because it has ended

the same way for thirty-six seasons. Dev doesn't get the happily ever after, but he would settle for less if it meant being with Charlie. Because the alternative—*losing Charlie*—is going to destroy him.

"Charlie and I—we know we don't have a future," he tells Ryan when the silence stretches too tight between them.

"But you said you love him," Ryan says quietly. He reaches out for Dev's hand and gives it a squeeze—a squeeze that reminds Dev he and Ryan were friends once, before everything else. "Is this why you were depressed? In Germany?"

"I'm going to get back into therapy when we're back in LA." The words come quick. Automatic.

"Yeah. I've heard that one before."

He wants to tell Ryan it's different this time. Who he was with Ryan isn't who he is with Charlie; *Charlie* isn't Ryan, and when Dev pulls away, Charlie reaches, and when Dev slips under, Charlie stays.

But Charlie can only stay for ten more days, so what's the point of explaining?

"Are you going to tell Skylar?"

Ryan snorts and drops Dev's hand. "Skylar already knows."

"She doesn't. She can't."

"She definitely does, and she definitely can. She's not an idiot, and you're not subtle."

"But . . ." Dev is spinning again. Or maybe the entire world is spinning? Either way, he needs to sit down in the dirt. The earth is so warm and his body is so weak, he sinks. "If Skylar knew, she would fire me. I've destroyed the season."

"You really didn't. This show is about the drama, and Charlie's delivered that."

"This show is about love," Dev counters.

Ryan shakes his head. "D, love is the unintentional by-product of this show."

Dev pulls his legs against his chest and buries his face in his knees.

"Skylar doesn't care if you're sleeping with Charlie," Ryan says calmly from above him, "so long as Charlie delivers her the hetero fairy tale the network demands. And thanks to your amazing job as Charlie's handler, they're going to get it. But you—you deserve better than being someone's dirty secret, Dev."

Dev drums out the Morse code for "calm" against his shins and tries to remember how to breathe. Tries to remind himself he survived losing Ryan, once. He can survive losing Charlie, too. Even if those two things don't feel equivalent on a humid night in Macon, Georgia.

"Besides," Ryan says before he turns back to the house, "it's not Skylar you should worry about. It's Maureen."

Dev wraps his arms tighter around his legs and feels himself collapse inward, like a dying star.

Charlie

His fingers clumsily fidget with the bow tie on his tux, and he watches himself in the mirror, the sweat gathering on his brow. They'll have to redo his makeup before the Crowning Ceremony. Assuming he can figure out how to properly dress himself first.

Skylar pops her shaved head through the dressing room door. "We need you in five. Everything coming along in here?"

"Have you seen Dev?" Charlie tries to keep his voice steady

around this question, but instead the words convey the panic grinding through his internal organs.

"Ryan asked him to lock up the set. Anything I can help with?"

"The t-tie," he stammers as his fingers slip through the fabric again. "I can't get it."

Skylar comes closer and places her steady hands over his trembling ones. "Let me."

The head director is shorter than he realized, standing on her toes to get a good angle on the bow tie. She seemed larger than life, indomitable, when he first met her two months ago. "Big night," she says. "How are you feeling?"

He's sweating and shaking and barely able to form cogent sentences. "I think you can tell exactly how I'm feeling."

She smiles up at him as her hands deftly arrange the fabric into a perfect bow. "Do you know who you're going to send home?"

He nods. The anxiety isn't about sending Lauren home tonight. She is the obvious choice, the only woman remaining who doesn't know it's all a ruse. He's anxious because of what sending home Lauren *means*. He'll be one step closer to the end of this journey, and he still hasn't figured out what to do about the certainty and the glittering something and the fact that Dev is already pulling away.

She steps back and admires her handiwork. "Then what are you worried about?"

Something in her tone suggests she's not asking as *Ever After*'s head director; she's asking as the woman who taught him the dance moves to "Bad Romance" in a New Orleans club. As the woman who got drunk with him on a patio in Bali.

"I never thought it would feel real," he starts. He can't answer her as anything other than the star of her show, so he quickly adds, "with Daphne, I mean. I never thought I'd develop real feelings for anyone on the show, and I'm not sure what to do. How do you know when you're going to love someone *forever*?"

Skylar stares up at him, her face an unknowable mask. She takes two steps backward and collapses onto a folding chair. "Did you know I was married to a man for ten years before I met my current partner?"

He obviously did not. Skylar never talks about her personal life outside of the show. For all he knows, she doesn't have a life outside of this show.

"Mm." She reaches into the pocket of her jeans and pulls out a roll of Tums. "Diego. He was a good man. He treated me really well, and even though I wasn't attracted to him, and even though I was repulsed by the idea of having sex with him, I was pretty happy."

Charlie shifts uncomfortably on his feet but doesn't let himself break eye contact with her as she carefully unfolds her private self to him in a slow, rhythmic voice.

"I was aware of the fact that I was more drawn to women, but I didn't particularly want to have sex with them, either, so I swept it aside for years and years, until finally, I decided to try a support group for questioning adults. That's where I met my current partner, Rey. They were the first person I ever heard use the word *asexual* as anything other than the punch line of a joke."

Skylar pauses, and Charlie drops his gaze to the floor. "Why are you telling me this?"

She ignores his question and continues on with her story. "I went up to Rey after the group session, and we started talking. For a long time, we were just friends. They were the person who helped me figure out I'm biromantic, the person who helped me feel okay about being sex-repulsed. They see me exactly as I am while also helping me become a truer version of myself."

Charlie thinks about Dev and about the beautiful simplicity of being *seen*.

"I'm telling you this, Charlie, because you asked how you know you're going to love someone forever, and the truth is, despite what we tell people on this show, forever is never a guarantee. I don't know if I'm going to love Rey for the rest of my life, but I know right now, I can't imagine a future where I don't love them. And for me, that's enough."

Charlie fidgets with his tux jacket and wishes he could find a way to thank her for sharing herself with him, find a way to tell her what it means.

Skylar swallows an antacid. "I think you have to decide if you love him enough right now to try for forever."

Charlie chokes. "*Him? Her*. Daphne. I . . . I love . . . Daphne."

Skylar rises from her chair and approaches him again, reaches up to brush the errant curls off his forehead so he's camera ready. "Son, I know everything that happens on my set."

She doesn't say it threateningly, doesn't sound angry. She says the word *son* the same way Dev says the word *love*—as if Skylar knows he's always wanted to be someone's son, too.

"But what if," he asks the head director of *Ever After*, "I don't know how to choose him?"

"We're almost at the end of our quest to find love," Mark Davenport intones for the cameras, "and tonight, Charlie will make the most important decision of all."

Charlie stands behind the small table bearing only two tiaras. Across the room, Daphne, Angie, and Lauren L. are lined up, awaiting his decision.

"Are you ready to choose your final two?" Mark asks. Charlie clears his throat and reaches for the first tiara.

"Wait!"

He looks up to see Daphne stepping out of formation, her blue eyes wild. "Can I . . . Charlie, can I speak to you for a minute? Before the ceremony?"

Charlie tries not to seek out Dev in the producer lineup along the back wall as he crosses the room. Daphne leads him and the cameras out into a little alcove. "What's wrong?" he asks, because it's clear something is. Daphne is wringing her hands and worrying her bottom lip.

"I think," she starts, "I think you should send me home tonight."

Charlie tries to temper his reaction for the cameras. He doesn't know how he's going to keep Dev, or if it's even possible for them to be together when this is over, but he knows the only way they stand a chance is if Charlie gets engaged to Daphne. They all need this season to be a success. "What do you mean?"

Daphne squares her shoulders. "You don't want to get engaged to me," she says, "and I don't think a fake engagement is going to make either of us happy, really."

Charlie involuntarily looks at the cameras. "It's not, uh, fake."

"It is. We agreed to a fake engagement, but I think we were wrong."

"I thought you wanted people to see you in a relationship?"

She reaches up to tuck her hair behind her ears. "I've been thinking about it . . . and I don't know. Maybe what you said in Cape Town was right. Maybe I'm chasing the wrong kind of love. Maybe I need to figure out what I *really* want, and I can't do that if I'm engaged to you for the next six months. I can't do that if I keep pretending to be someone I'm not." Daphne takes his hand. "Don't you want to figure out what you really want?"

He *knows* what he really wants. He just doesn't know how to get it. "I—"

"Cut!" Maureen Scott stomps in her high heels into the alcove, shoving a camera operator out of the way. "Cut! Turn off these cameras! What the hell are you doing?"

Charlie shrinks at Maureen's anger, but Daphne stands firm. "I'm sending myself home."

"Like fucking hell you are," Maureen snaps. Charlie feels the panic creeping up his esophagus and wishes he could see Dev through the glare of lights. Maureen is screaming at various crew members and Skylar is trying to salvage the scene and somewhere, beneath the steadily increasing thrum of his anxiety, is the creeping realization that everything is about to fall apart.

Dev

It's all falling apart.

It's been slowly falling apart for days. Ryan knows and Skylar knows and now Daphne Reynolds is talking about fake engagements in front of the cameras. The season has been hanging on by a thread, and now Daphne has chopped that thread with a machete.

"Production meeting! Now!" Maureen shouts, and Jules has to grab Dev by the elbow and guide him behind Skylar and Ryan as Maureen cuts a path toward the cramped room where Charlie changed before the Crowning Ceremony. Daphne and

Charlie are here, too. "What the fuck is wrong with you?" Maureen asks Daphne. "Are you truly as stupid as you look?"

Daphne backs herself into a makeup mirror.

"You can't send yourself home," Maureen continues. "You signed a contract. We've built the entire season around you!"

"But we don't . . . we don't love each other," Daphne mutters.

Maureen Scott throws her head back and laughs. "No one gives a shit if you're *in love*. This show isn't about love."

Something sinks inside of Dev, and then he's sinking, sitting on the bottom of the pool with the pressure of nine feet of water pushing down on him. He looks across the room and finds Charlie, and he tries to use his blond curls and gray eyes and chin dimple to anchor himself.

"Maureen, maybe we could discuss this calmly," Skylar tries. She's holding up both hands between Daphne and Maureen.

"There's nothing to discuss. Our perfect princess is going to get engaged to our prince. That's the story we've been telling, and that's how it's going to end."

Dev stares at his boss and watches her silvery bob swish elegantly around her mean face.

"If Charlie proposes to me," Daphne says, her voice surprisingly clear, "I will say no. You cannot force me to say yes."

"And you can't force me to propose to her," Charlie adds. Dev feels a weird mixture of pride and dread at the sudden certainty in Charlie's voice. "Daphne is right. I'm done pretending to be something I'm not."

Maureen points an angry finger at Charlie's face. "You're not done pretending until your contract is over."

"Maybe Charlie can propose to Angie instead," Jules tries in a soft voice almost muffled by the screaming.

Maureen wheels around to face her and scoffs. "I've already told you we are not going to have a bisexual win this season."

Dev watches the way this statement registers on Daphne's face, watches the way her mouth slides open in horror. Charlie looks equally stricken. He meets Dev's gaze, and his expression asks a simple question. *Did you know?* Did he know that his boss refused to let a bisexual woman become the next star or the winner of this season?

"Oh, don't look at me like that," Maureen snaps at the pair of them. "None of this is about me or what I believe. I'm a Democrat. I support gay rights. I hired all of you," she says, gesturing to Dev, Skylar, Ryan, and Jules. Dev has never felt more like a prop, like a checked box. Maureen plows on. "But this show hinges on appealing to a wide viewership. I'm giving America what it wants, and it does not want a bisexual princess."

For a minute, the dressing room is quiet, seven adult bodies packed together in horrified silence.

"What America wants?" Daphne echoes slowly.

"What if *I* was gay?" someone asks at the same time.

It's Charlie's voice that slices through the tension in the room like a felled tree in the forest. Everyone looks at him. No one breathes. Especially not Dev.

"What if I told you I was gay?" Charlie says again, his gray eyes steady as they fix on Maureen. "What if I told you I can't get engaged to any of the women at the end of this season, because I'm gay? What if I told you I was in love with a man—"

Charlie has never said that word before. *Love.* Dev wants to bask in the sound of it sweeping past Charlie's lips, but Skylar and Ryan both turn to look at him while Daphne's tongue gets caught on a vague sound of disbelief. "You're . . . *what?*"

"What if I told you I was in love with a man," Charlie pushes forward, like the brave, beautiful, *naïve* man that he is, "and I wanted to choose him instead?"

Maureen puts her hands on her hips, stares down the man Dev loves, and says, "You do not want to play that game with me, Charles. You think we've never had a gay prince before? Of course we have! I don't give a shit what you do or with whom when the cameras aren't rolling, but when they are, you're going to pretend to be head-over-heels in love with *her*." She points angrily at Daphne.

Charlie looks around the room—at Dev, at Jules, at the people who know the truth and are saying nothing out of fear. "And what if I refuse?" Charlie asks, each word clipped.

Maureen is still for the length of one shallow breath. "Then I'll give you a terrible edit and let the entire world see just how crazy you really are."

All the air is pulled from the room by Maureen's words, and Dev's brain doesn't have the oxygen it needs to understand. But it tries. The boyfriend on night one. The wool suit. Daphne throwing herself at him at the ball. Megan and Delilah. The massage Group Quest. The entire season, Maureen kept putting Charlie in situations to exploit him (because she knows about his mental illness, knows about WinHan, *of course she does*) and now she's standing in a back room using that footage to blackmail him.

All Dev can think is *six years*.

He made so many excuses for Maureen—justified so many of her actions—for so long and somehow only now does he understand the truth. Maureen was never his ally, never his friend, and this show was *never* about love. He threw away six years of his life.

Charlie looks around the room at the silent producers who still aren't sticking up for him. At the producers he thought cared about him. He looks at Dev. "Well," he says, and Dev can hear it in his voice. He's trying so hard to be strong. Dev wishes he could help, but he doesn't have any strength left in him to give to Charlie. He's hollowed out, emptied of feeling, a husk on the bottom of a pool. "I guess we'll have our happily ever after, then."

Daphne is the only person who calls out for him as he shoves his way toward the door.

Charlie

"Charlie, *wait!*"

Charlie doesn't wait. He storms down the hall and out into the ballroom where Angie and Lauren L. are still waiting with confused looks on their faces. He should feel anxious right now—he waits for the panic to take over—but the anger is taking up too much room inside him at the moment. He's so *fucking* angry.

He's angry at Jules, who only supported his and Dev's relationship when it was convenient for her to do so. He's angry at Skylar, who knotted his bow tie and told him to choose Dev and still didn't speak up for him. He's angry at Maureen, obviously, for being exactly who he thought she was.

And he's so damn angry at Dev.

He has virtually no awareness of Daphne returning from the back room, her makeup redone, taking her place between Angie and Lauren, but he knows it must have happened. He knows he picks up a tiara and calls her name, and that she steps forward. When he asks, "Are you interested in becoming my princess?"

Daphne Reynolds says yes, despite everything. He knows he gives Angie the second tiara and sends Lauren home, but he can't recall any of the particular details of that or anything else, because the anger is ringing too loudly in his ears.

After, Ryan tries to talk to him. Skylar pulls him aside. Jules apologizes. The anger drowns out all their words.

He ends up in the back of a town car. He ends up in an elevator. He ends up outside of his hotel room door. When he fumbles with his card key and gets the door open, he finds Dev there, sitting on the edge of the bed they wrecked together the night before. And Charlie is angry, but he's also hurt, and he can't quite help himself from falling into Dev's arms as soon as they're alone.

"That was awful," Charlie cries into the crook of Dev's neck.

Dev runs his fingers through Charlie's hair, teasing apart the curls like he always does, but when he speaks, it's with his hollow voice. "I know, love. I know. I'm so sorry."

Charlie lets himself cry a bit longer, lets himself enjoy the feeling of Dev's arms and Dev's body before he pulls back. "What are we going to do?"

Dev's eyes are glassy. Faraway. "There's nothing we can do. We all signed contracts. You'll propose to Daphne and get engaged, and the show will air, and then you'll finally get everything you want."

"I want *you*," Charlie says. Because he does. Even though Dev stood there like a coward while Maureen threatened him, and even though Charlie is angry right now, he understands. Dev spent six years—hell, Dev spent most of his *life*—thinking this show was the perfect fairy tale, and he only just witnessed the ugly truth of it for the first time. Charlie understands why Dev couldn't stand up for him, couldn't stand beside him.

What he doesn't understand is why Dev is pulling away right now.

"We both knew how this was going to end, Charlie," he says, as he slides out from beneath Charlie's weight. He walks over to the hotel desk and rubs his finger along the edge of a Courtyard Marriott notepad. "We both know this has an expiration date."

"What if I don't want it to end? What if I want"—he almost says forever, but Dev is standing in front of the desk with his closed-off posture, and the word can't make it past his lips— "more."

Dev folds his arms across his chest. Charlie sees it for what it is: a feeble attempt on Dev's part to protect himself. "There isn't any *more* to have. We want different things."

"I thought we both wanted that house in Venice Beach?"

"That was a fantasy!" Dev erupts. "It would never work!"

"Because of me?"

"Because of both of us! Because you're a reality television star and I'm your producer!"

"Only for another week."

Dev rakes his fingers violently through his hair.

"Do you want kids, Charlie?"

It's the last thing he expected Dev to ask him, and any attempt at an answer gets sealed off inside his dry throat.

"Because I want kids. Four of them. And I want marriage. I want to walk down the aisle wearing a heinous white tux that would embarrass the shit out of you, and I don't want to spend another six years with someone who doesn't want what I want."

It's all spinning so far out of Charlie's control. He thought, stupidly, that their uncertain future was something they could

step into together, but now it feels like they're pulling in opposite directions, a dysfunctional team in a three-legged race.

He tries to find a clear thought, a clear emotion, a clear string
of words, and offer it to Dev. He wants to find a way to make
Dev understand. "Two months ago, I came on this show believing I wasn't worthy of love, and now you want to know if
I've thought about marriage and kids? Dev, I haven't. I never
thought any of those things were an option for me. I'm not saying they *aren't*—I'm just saying I don't know right now. I need
time to figure myself out."

Dev looks down at him, pushes his glasses up his nose with
two fingers. "I don't want time, Charlie. I want to walk away
before we both get hurt."

"I'm already hurt."

"*Charlie.*"

"Dev . . . " He reaches out in the only way he knows how, in
the only way he has left. "I love you."

Charlie expects to feel better once he's said it. Instead he feels
naked and exposed on the bed. He's handed Dev something del-
icate, and Dev's got this look in his eyes like he might smash it
just to see what happens.

"You don't love me."

"Don't tell me how I feel. *I love you.*"

Dev shakes his head dismissively. Charlie might punch him.
He might grab onto his ankles like a little kid and never let go.
When he sees the silent tears gathering behind Dev's glasses, he
does neither of those things. "I love you, Dev," he says again.
He'll keep saying it until Dev believes it. "I love everything
about you."

Charlie pulls Dev's face down so he can kiss his tear stained cheeks.

"I love you because you try to understand my brain even though you're terrible at being patient, and because you're passionate about the stupidest things, and because you're the most beautiful person I've ever seen. I love how you make me laugh. I love your ugly cargo shorts, and I love how cranky you get when you're hungry, and I love how stubborn you are, and I don't love you despite those things. I love you *because* of those things."

Dev releases a sob at hearing his words paraphrased back to him.

"I get that you're in pain right now," Charlie continues. "I know that this show isn't what you want it to be, and I get that you're pulling away because you're scared of how much it's all going to hurt, but I love you. I love you so much right now, I can't imagine ever not loving you. And it's okay if you don't love me back yet. I can love enough for both of us. Just please stop pulling away."

"*Charlie.*" They are the two loveliest syllables in the whole world when Dev says them. Dev reaches down and kisses his mouth, his chin, his eyelids, his ears, like he's creating a sensory map of Charlie's face. "I love you. How could I not love you?"

Charlie grabs his wrists to hold him in place. "Then let me *choose* you. Choose *us*. Please."

Dev desperately clings to the front of Charlie's tux. He buries his face deep in the fabric, and his words struggle their way out. "We both knew we weren't going to get a happily ever after."

"We could." Dev is floating away, and Charlie believes that if he holds tight enough to Dev's hips, he can keep him. "Just stay, Dev. Just choose to stay."

*   *   *

The next morning, it takes Charlie a while to understand why Dev isn't in bed. Why his luggage is gone. Why Charlie's jean jacket and his oatmeal body wash are missing. Why there is a torn-out piece of notebook paper on the pillow next to him, neatly folded into thirds.

Charlie reads the letter. Once. Twice. He reads it ten times. He doesn't cry—at least, not then, not when he first understands Dev is not coming back. There's no panic, no anxiety, no spiraling. There's only the aching sense of sureness about who he is and what he has to do.

He climbs out of bed and walks three doors down the hallway of a hotel in Macon, Georgia. He knocks, and Skylar Jones answers, bleary-eyed and still wearing sweats. "Charlie? What is it?"

Charlie takes exactly three deep breaths. "Can we talk?"

Story notes for editors:

Season 37, Episode 9

Story producer:

Ryan Parker

Air date:

Monday, November 8, 2021

Executive producer:

Maureen Scott

Scene: Confessional with Lauren Long during her Home Kingdom date

Location: Shot on location in Dallas

Lauren L.: I can't believe Charlie's here! I've dreamed about this day for so long! It's all I've ever wanted—to have someone like him to bring home. He's everything I've always pictured for my future, and now it's real! I'm about to introduce my future husband to my parents!

THREE MONTHS AFTER FILMING

Raleigh, North Carolina—Monday, November 8, 2021

Dev

On a Monday night in November, the second-to-last episode of Charlie Winshaw's season of *Ever After* airs to twenty-three million viewers. Dev Deshpande is not one of them. Monday nights are when he schedules his appointments, and it's dark outside the office in east Raleigh where he sits, waiting, while his therapist brews two mugs of peppermint tea.

Dev reaches into a box full of fidget spinners and other stimming toys and pulls out a neon purple squishy ball. He knows now that his need to stay busy, to never stop moving, was a way to avoid confronting the parts of his life that weren't working, but he also knows having something to do with his hands makes those confrontations a little bit easier. He's learned a lot about himself in this office these past three months.

Alex Santos steeps the tea leaves into the twin mugs, then crosses the room to their wingback chair. "So," Alex asks, their head cocked to the side in a way that reminds Dev of Jules. He doesn't want to think about her tonight but forces himself to confront the too-big feelings in his chest. "How are you doing?"

Dev squeezes the purple ball. "I'm okay."

His therapist gives him a searching look, and Dev understands. He knows *okay* was his refrain for a long time.

"I really am okay. I'm mostly relieved. It's almost over."

Alex shifts in their chair. "How will things be different once the season is finally done airing?"

"Well, presumably the crew will stop trying to call me and text me and email me every five seconds," he starts. Not that he's talked to anyone since Macon. He deleted all his social media, and he deletes every text message sight unseen. Even the ones from Jules, until she stopped trying to reach out altogether. He's built a small life for himself here—living at his parents' house, writing every day in his childhood bedroom, leaving the house only for biweekly therapy sessions and walking his mother's Maltese around the park—but at least it's a life without *Ever After*. Without the toxicity and the pretend.

"And once the hype dies down, I won't have to worry about seeing his face on magazine covers in the grocery store checkout line."

"Is it still hard to see him?"

He squeezes the purple ball harder. "You know, Alex, one of these days, you're going to make a declarative statement, and that will be when we really level up in our therapy-ship."

Alex purses their lips disapprovingly. "You want a declarative statement? You are using humor to deflect from your very real emotional pain."

"Touché."

Alex smiles and gets up to fetch the tea. It took Dev *weeks* to get a smile out of his therapist, but it turns out someone gruff and no-nonsense was what he needed after upending his entire life. He needed someone who wouldn't be charmed into thinking he was okay. Alex always sees through his bullshit and *always* calls him on it.

"Fine, yes, I'm deflecting. And yes, it's still hard to see him on magazine covers. I still . . . love him. I think I'll always love him." He sets down the stim toy so he can take the cup of tea Alex passes him. He wraps his fingers around the warm mug.

"If you still love him, why aren't you with him?"

"Because love isn't enough!" He doesn't mean to yell, but Alex, used to his outbursts of emotion, barely flinches. "Love does *not* conquer all. Charlie was our *star*. I was his producer. Even if everything hadn't gone to shit with Maureen, we never could've been seen together in public. It was stupid to think our story was going to end any other way, and I hope, after the show is over, I'll finally feel like I made the right choice."

Alex takes a sip of their tea. "In leaving?"

"I mean, I *know* I made the right choice. I chose *me*," he says, retreading a conversation they've had a dozen times across this office. "I couldn't work for a show that treated people that way any longer. I couldn't watch Maureen Scott force"—he almost works up the nerve to say his name and swerves at the last second—"her fictional ending. *Ever After* is problematic, and I had to leave to get healthy. And I *am* healthier."

He really is. He didn't even realize how unhealthy he was until he started digging into all the things he'd been ignoring. His depression, yes, but also his dreams of writing, which he pushed aside for the show. His fundamental belief that his existence wasn't worthy of the spotlight. His dependency on alcohol to numb his emotions when things got hard. His need to please others above pleasing himself. His chronic fear of letting anyone see anything but Fun Dev. The quiet resentment he carried toward his parents for trying so hard to understand, but never understanding.

But he's here, confronting those things. He's completely sober, for the time being, anyway. He takes meds for the depression, and he's focusing on his own career, and he's doing the hard work to learn to love himself. He knows it's hard work he will probably have to do for the rest of his life. None of that could have happened if he'd stayed enmeshed in the show.

"I know you think a full *Ever After* blackout wasn't the best way to cope, but I don't think I would be doing this well if I'd spent the past nine weeks watching him fall in love with Daphne Reynolds on a wine tram."

Alex steeples their fingers beneath their chin. Dev has this theory that his therapist is a secret member of the Fairy-Tale Family; whenever Dev mentions a plot detail about the show, their upper lip twitches. Of course, if they *are* watching *Ever After* week to week, they would never mention it.

"When the season is finally over, I think I'll be ready to move back to LA and be able to move on entirely from this whole part of my life."

"Do you think not really knowing what happens on the season makes it harder for you to move forward?"

"Nope." He shrugs. "I know what happens. I lived it."

Alex doesn't say anything for a few minutes, both of them sipping their tea and staring out the window. It's starting to rain. "Do you think you'll be ready to start dating again then, too?"

He takes three deep breaths and taps his fingers against the ceramic mug in the familiar pattern he can't seem to unlearn. "I . . . I don't know. I think maybe my ideas about love have been all wrong."

"How do you mean?"

"Fairy tales aren't real. Happily ever afters aren't *real*. I've been clinging to these false romantic ideals—these *heteronormative* romantic ideals about marriage and monogamy and domesticity—my entire life, and maybe it's time I stop basing my ideas about love on these fabricated narratives. I'm happy now. I'm healthy. I've signed with an agent for my script. I'm pursuing my goals. Why have I let the world convince me I'm not enough without romance?"

Alex leans forward and sets their mug on the table between them. "I'm not sure I agree," they say slowly, "that happily ever afters aren't real, or that romantic ideals are inherently heteronormative."

It's the most definitive statement they've ever made, and Dev's eyes dart to the wedding band on Alex's finger. He wonders, not for the first time, who waits at home for his therapist during these 7 p.m. sessions. "But you're right, Dev. You don't need romantic love to be complete or to be happy. If you don't want those things, then"—Alex waves their hands as if they're casting a magic spell—"you don't want them. But I want to make sure you're giving up on your old romantic ideals *because* you don't want them. Not because you think you don't deserve them."

He imagines a house, a puzzle on the coffee table, plants by the windows. The mug has gone cold against Dev's fingers. "If I ask you something, will you answer it honestly?"

Alex's mouth tugs down at the corners, but they nod.

"Do you watch *Ever After*?"

"My wife does," Alex says honestly, and Dev's surprised. "Every Monday night. She has a whole watch party. There are brackets involved. And a lot of wine."

Dev smiles. "Sounds right."

"If I ask *you* a question, will you answer it honestly?" Alex quirks an eyebrow at him from across the office.

Dev nods.

"Do you still fall asleep listening to his old voicemails every night?"

He's healthier, but he's not perfect, and he slips back into humor when it's all he can do to keep his heart from breaking. "You know, Alex, sometimes you make it very difficult for me to love you."

When the session ends, he exits through an empty waiting room, walks past a stack of magazines on a corner table. He knows not to look. He looks anyway. The *Us Weekly* right on top has a picture of his face, and Dev feels the familiar pain in his ribs as his heart pushes past the boundaries he's built for it. The face on the cover is tired, pained. The caption reads, "Will Charlie Winshaw Get his Fairy-Tale Ending?"

He knows not to pick it up. He picks it up anyway. There, in the corner, is a small photo inlaid with a white border. Him and Daphne, shoulder to shoulder, huddled under a polka-dotted umbrella, smiling at each other. A second caption: "Happily Ever After?"

One picture, three words, and it cuts through all his feigned indifference. He sobs in his therapist's waiting room, then sobs in his car, then drives in circles around Raleigh until he can go home without looking like he sobbed at all.

When he walks into his parents' house a little after nine, they're both sitting on the couch trying too hard to be natural. The fact that they're both reading books is a dead giveaway, but there is also the bottle of wine on the coffee table, the remote control askew on the arm of the couch, his mother's flushed look of guilt as proof. They were watching. They watch every Monday night when he's out of the house. His best guess is they do it out of some mixture of curiosity and a desire to protect him, but he's too wrung out at the moment from crying to care.

His dad looks up from his book as if he were so engrossed in it, he didn't hear Dev come in. "Oh. Hey, there. You're home."

"Devy," his mother says, "how was therapy?"

"You know, the printer is making that noise again," his dad cuts in. "Do you think you could take a look at it?"

"Do you want dinner? There are leftovers in the fridge."

Living with his parents at twenty-eight is exhausting, but they're both trying so hard. And Dev is trying so hard to accept their efforts.

He promises to look at the printer tomorrow, heats up the leftovers and eats them over the kitchen sink, then kisses his mother on the cheek before he goes to bed.

In his room, he imagines he'll close the door and somehow feel stronger than he actually does. He'll feel indifferent to what night it is and to the photo on the magazine cover and everything else.

He doesn't, though, and instead he pulls the jean jacket out of the closet where he keeps it tucked away. He climbs into his bed, curls himself into a tight ball, and pulls out his phone.

In the first month after Dev left Macon, Charlie called every day, leaving short messages. Small, sad, desperate pleas.

"Please call me back. I just want to talk."

"I love you, and you love me. It's that simple, Dev."

"I am trying to respect your health, but I can't walk away from us."

"Hey, it's me. Just reaching out. I'm going to keep reaching, Dev. I will never stop reaching."

Even though Dev deleted every text message without reading it and ignored every phone call from the crew, he would listen to five-second bursts of Charlie's voice every night before bed. He would play them over and over again, bathing in the sound of each syllable sweeping over Charlie's tongue.

The messages were never more than ten seconds, except the last one, which Charlie left five weeks ago. That one was one minute and forty-two seconds—a rambling mess of a voicemail that cuts Dev open every time he thinks of it. Charlie hasn't called since.

Dev wants to be strong enough not to listen to it now. He also wants to be strong enough to not use the oatmeal body wash he orders from Amazon by the crate because smelling like Charlie is a way for those few weeks they had together to feel real. He's come so far with his mental health in the past three months, and he thought as soon as he started to get healthy, he would realize Charlie was a giant, self-destructive mistake. He thought getting healthy would naturally mean the Charlie-shaped sinkhole in his chest would go away. He wants to let go of all those stupid romantic notions.

So why does he still miss him? Why was Charlie the first person he wanted to call when he signed with an agent to represent his script, and why is Charlie the first person he wants to talk to whenever he has a breakthrough in therapy? Why can't he resist hitting the play button and pressing the phone to his ear?

"Uh, hey. It's me. Again. I know you probably don't listen to these messages, and I know you probably don't care, and I know I should probably stop. The healthy thing to do is *stop*. Jules thinks I should get on a plane and show up at your parents' place and tell you how I feel. She said that's what Prince Charming would do. I told her that's what a stalker would do."

Here, Charlie laughs, as he always does, and the sound pokes at all the holes in Dev's heart.

"If you wanted to see me, then we would have seen each other. You would've come to LA. Except, did I tell you I'm living in LA now? I mean, we don't talk, so I guess I probably didn't. I have so many imagined conversations with you—in the shower, on the way to the gym, while cooking dinner—I sometimes forget we haven't actually spoken since Macon. But yeah, I bought a house. It's out in Silver Lake, and my neighbors are all hipsters, so you'd probably hate it, but it was the only place for sale that could do a quick closing.

"It was so weird—after I bought it, I kept walking into rooms and feeling this overwhelming sense that something was missing. So I filled every room with furniture, and I let Parisa hang art on every wall, and I bought plants to put in front of every window, and it took me days to realize you were the missing thing. I kept expecting to see you standing by the window, or in the third bedroom at the desk working on your script, or in the kitchen burning pancakes. I guess I really liked the idea of you being in my future, and I haven't quite figured out how to not have you in it."

And here, the seconds stretch out in silence, static and the faint sound of three slow breaths. "That was selfish of me to say. This . . . this whole message is selfish. I'm glad you never listen to these. I just needed to say it, I guess. So I can learn to let you go."

*　　　*　　　*

Dev listens to the message over and over until he falls asleep to the sound, and when he wakes up Tuesday morning before seven, he has thirty-six missed calls, some from the crew, but most from numbers he doesn't recognize. There are dozens of texts and emails, and he shoves his phone under his pillow. He climbs out of bed, hides the jean jacket in the back of his closet, and goes downstairs for coffee. He has half a mind to ask his parents what happened on last night's episode to prompt this unprecedented deluge, but when he comes into the living room, he's taken aback by the presence of people who are not his parents in his house first thing in the morning.

He's so shocked, it takes him a good minute to register it's the *Ever After* crew. In Raleigh, North Carolina. A week before they film the live finale.

"What. The actual. *Fuck?*"

He isn't sure if he's asking this question of his parents, who are shuffling around the kitchen getting coffee for their guests, or if he's asking the guests. Skylar Jones is staring at his baby pictures on the wall. Parisa Khadim is helping herself to coffee creamer in his parents' refrigerator. Jules Lu is asking his mother where she got her house slippers. Ryan Parker is sitting in front of his parents' desktop computer.

"It's the printer-connection thing," Dev's dad is saying. "You fixed it last time you were here, but then the flashy light started flashing again and it keeps making that noise."

"It's fine, Mr. Deshpande," Ryan says patiently. "I can fix it."

Dev is going to lose it. "Seriously, what are you all doing here?"

They all stop what they're doing and turn to face him for the first time in three months. For the first time since Maureen Scott threatened Charlie and he snuck away in the middle of the night to leave them to clean up the mess.

At first, no one moves. Then Jules—with her baggy jeans and her topknot and her *NSYNC concert T-shirt—walks across the room like she's going to embrace him. She punches him in the arm. "Some best friend you are. You wouldn't answer any of our calls, you asshole."

"*Ouch*. So, you flew to Raleigh to punch me?"

"No," Ryan says as the printer runs its test page. "We flew to Raleigh to make you watch."

It's then that Dev realizes the first episode of *Ever After* is cued up on his parents' wall-mounted TV. It's frozen on Mark Davenport's cheesy grin as he stands in front of the castle fountain.

"No."

"We don't want to hold you down for the entire thing, but we will," Jules threatens.

"I actually brought rope in my carry-on," Skylar adds.

Dev doesn't understand why they're doing this—why they flew three thousand miles to make him watch a season that is over and done. Why can't they let him move on from this?

"Watching is the least you owe him," Parisa says angrily. She quite obviously flew here to murder him. He doesn't really blame her.

"I'm sorry, but I can't watch."

His mother crosses the kitchen in her silk pajamas with his dad's robe thrown over the top, confidently entertaining Hollywood producers and publicists in her kitchen like she does this every day. "How about this, Devy . . . why don't I make frittatas for everyone, and we'll put on the first episode. If you hate the first episode, we don't have to watch the rest."

His dad does his best attempt at a stern face. "Your friends did fly all the way from LA, and it would be rude to make that all for nothing."

"Okay, fine." He consents, if only because he'll go to therapy again tomorrow, and he'll be able to tell Alex he stopped avoiding it, and maybe then, maybe after watching Charlie date the women for nine episodes, Dev will finally stop missing him.

Dev settles onto the couch between Skylar and Jules, and everyone else finds a seat. The sweeping theme music fills the room, and Mark Davenport is on the screen, looking ageless and dashing. "Are you ready to meet your Prince Charming?" he asks cloyingly. Dev's heart constricts in his chest, knowing he is going to see Charlie on the screen soon. Jules takes his left hand. Skylar takes his right. They both hold tight.

"You're in for one wild ride," Mark says on-screen. "This season is quite literally like nothing we have ever seen before. It's a game changer."

"We say that every single season," Dev mutters. Jules punches him in the leg to shut him up.

Mark Davenport continues the voice-over. The first shot of Charlie is him blurry on a horse at the infamous shoot that led to Ryan's job reassignment. Then the camera cuts to Charlie standing on a cliff looking windswept and lovely, and Dev chokes on all the old feelings. It barely looks like his Charlie—his limbs are stiff, and his posture is too good, and his face is twisted into a grimace. He is still the most beautiful man Dev has ever seen.

Mark wraps up the show's intro. "Are you ready for a new quest for love, America? This is *Ever After*."

They go to the title card, and this is usually where the show begins in earnest. Instead, it cuts back to Mark Davenport, this time in the studio where they'll film the live finale, pacing elegantly. "Now, before we dive in, I should warn you . . . our prince this season isn't polished. He isn't always camera ready. This season of *Ever After* is different. We're going to peel back the curtain for you a little bit, give you unprecedented access to what really happens on set. Nothing is off-limits."

Dev knows several things are off-limits, but he's still sucked in by the time the show truly begins. A commercial break, and then Daphne Reynolds is stepping out of a carriage, and Dev is thrown back into that night, embarrassed for Charlie all over again. Charlie's interaction with Daphne is cringey. He's wooden and uninteresting, and the secondhand humiliation is so extreme, Dev's about to insist they turn it off when something *truly* unprecedented *does* happen.

Dev is on-screen. He steps into the shot and waves his hands at the cameras. The boom picks up the words *give me five* before he darts across the shot into the limo.

"Wh—"

"Just watch," Jules hisses.

He watches, and he sees something he didn't see that night while he was in the limo convincing Angie to dance with Charlie. Mark Davenport steps over to Charlie and puts a hand on his shoulder. "I know you're nervous, but don't worry. Dev, your handler, is the best. He's going to take really good care of you. He won't let you look like an idiot in front of twenty million viewers."

Mark laughs, and Charlie kind of squawks, and then Dev is out of the limo again bounding over to Charlie. Dev reaches up and his fingers are in Charlie's hair, adjusting his crown. Charlie blushes at Dev's touch, and it's right there for viewers to see. Charlie, an hour after they met, falling over himself because of Dev instead of Daphne.

"You can do this," Dev says, and Charlie gives a shy little smile, twisting something inside real Dev's chest on the couch. "I believe in you."

Dev steps out of the shot, and the normal show starts up again, with Angie getting out of the horse-drawn carriage.

"You guys, what is this?"

"This is what we've been trying to get you to watch," Jules says smugly. "This is *Ever After.*"

Back on-screen, they show what happens after the carriage exits are over, after Skylar calls cut. "You're doing *bleeping* spectacular!" Dev tells Charlie. Charlie smiles back, earnest and huge, and it feels like watching part of Charlie open for the first time.

When the second episode starts up instantly, Dev doesn't move from his seat. There's so much footage of Charlie and Dev he didn't know existed: footage of Dev sitting beside Charlie the day Megan faked her injury at the jousting Quest; footage of Dev trying to calm him down later that night after Charlie kissed Angie for the first time; footage of them laughing on set, footage of them joking between takes, *so much footage* of Dev fixing Charlie's hair.

Through it all, it is still a normal season of *Ever After.* There are still Group Quests and women gushing about Charlie, and Charlie gushing about the women. All the drama unfolds like it's supposed to, with the women fighting back at the castle, and Megan's perfect turn as the villain, and the suspense of the Crowning

Ceremonies. The editing team has simply gone through and expanded the scope of the show just a little to make room for Dev.

The episodes are flying by. When Charlie has his panic attack with Daphne at the ball, and he runs into Dev's arms, it's so obvious on Dev's face that he cares in ways he shouldn't. Watching himself fall in love with Charlie is like falling in love with him all over again.

Dev sits in the living room where he first discovered *Ever After*, and he doesn't move, doesn't get up to go to the bathroom, only eats when his mother directly inserts food into his mouth. He watches a scene with Charlie and Angie in Germany he didn't know existed. "I just want Dev to be okay," Charlie says, sounding pitiful.

"Sweetie, I know. I know," Angie says in return, and America must know, too.

Dev watches the Leland Barlow night. There are interviews he never saw. Daphne, looking giddy: "He told me about the plan the other night! I think Dev is going to be really surprised."

Angie, looking knowing as hell: "I think this might be the sweetest thing anyone has ever done for their producer."

Then Charlie explains for the audience: "Dev, my handler, went through a difficult time in Germany, and I wanted to do something special to cheer him up. The show was going to fly this country singer down to Cape Town, but I was able to change their minds."

They show Dev losing his damn mind over Leland Barlow, and then they show the dance party with the contestants and crew. Jules twirls Dev into Charlie's arms, and they do their awkward dance together on the night Dev realized he was in love with Charlie.

And then he's watching that last night.

At the Crowning Ceremony in Macon, Daphne asks to speak to Charlie, and the cameras follow them to the alcove. Right there, on his parents' television screen, Daphne tells Charlie she's done pretending until Maureen Scott calls cut and steps viciously into the frame.

The show abruptly cuts to Charlie sitting on a bed in a hotel room. It takes Dev a second to recognize it as *the* hotel room. At the Courtyard Marriott. The last place he saw Charlie Winshaw.

"It is time for me to be honest," he is telling the cameras in a confessional. "I came on this show for the wrong reason. I wanted a chance to rebuild my career, and I know now that what I did was unfair—to the women who came on this show for love and to the people who work here. But the thing is . . ." There are tears filling his beautiful gray eyes. "I didn't think it was possible to find love on this show. And I was wrong."

They cut back to Mark Davenport in the studio. He stands onstage, wearing his bespoke suit, his face somehow grim and optimistic at the same time. "It's been quite a journey up to this point, and I'm sure it hasn't been the journey you were expecting. To be honest, we weren't expecting it either. But that's the thing about love, isn't it?" he says with a glimmer in his eye. "Sometimes it comes when you least expect it. When it comes down to it, this show is about helping people reach their happily ever after. Will our star find that? Tune in next week for the heartbreaking finale you won't want to miss."

And that's it. It's over. There is nothing more to watch, because they don't have the live finale. It hasn't happened yet.

Dev leaps up out of his seat, unable to contain the nervous

energy inside of him. His body explodes with shooting pain from sitting in the exact same position on the couch for an entire day. He looks around the room. At his dad, sitting at the kitchen table. At Ryan, asleep in his dad's recliner. At Parisa, sitting on the love seat with his mother, and at Jules and Skylar, still flanking him on the couch. They never left his side. Not once, for twelve hours straight.

Everyone looks back at him, and Dev isn't quite sure where to start, so he starts with the obvious. "How did you get Maureen to do this?"

Skylar answers. "Maureen Scott is no longer affiliated with *Ever After*."

Dev sits back down. "Wait, what?"

"Funny thing about discriminating against someone based on their sexuality," Parisa says humorlessly. "It's illegal. Maureen forcing Charlie to get engaged to a woman after he came out to her was illegal. Charlie called me after what happened in Macon, and we lawyered up."

"Maureen thought that because Charlie signed a contract, she could force him to stay closeted," Jules adds. "But the network saw things differently when Parisa filed a discrimination lawsuit. They quickly decided it was best to sever their working relationship with Maureen."

Parisa does a little mock bow when she sees Dev's mouth swing open.

"Maureen got a ten-million-dollar buyout, so it's not exactly a win for social justice, but once she was gone, the network had no problem adapting the narrative to reflect the truth of the season. We were able to do a quick reedit of the first few episodes and then a total overhaul of the back half."

"We had the waiver you signed to release any footage of you, but we still tried to contact you before the show aired. Unfortunately, you did this really cute thing where you refused to talk to any of us for three months," Parisa says, her tone suggesting genuine hurt hiding somewhere beneath her usual bravado.

"*We?*"

Parisa smooths out her ponytail. "You know I love a good public relations clusterfuck, and *Ever After* is the biggest clusterfuck there is. They hired me as the new head of PR during their transitional rebranding."

He never thought that any of this was possible. Never thought this version of *Ever After* was possible. Couldn't envision this ending. "I . . . I can't believe this. I can't believe you *aired* this."

"It was the truth," Skylar says with a little shrug. Dev studies her. No antacids, no stress. Her hair is even starting to grow back. Slowly. But still. "But to be honest, the season wouldn't have happened if Charlie hadn't fought for it. We all made mistakes working for Maureen. Let things slide we shouldn't have. Stayed quiet when we should have spoken out. I'm sorry I wasn't a better boss to you, Dev. I should've spoken up when I knew you were having a hard time."

"I didn't want you to know about my depression," he says plainly. "I didn't want anyone to see that side of me."

Skylar shakes her head. "We all have stuff, Dev. You think I'm not in therapy for my anxiety? You think I don't need meds sometimes, and help?"

They never talked about it on set, so he honestly didn't know. With Maureen in charge, the mantra was *work hard and shut up about it*. There was no room to discuss emotions. No room to *breathe*, because that was the cost of making the kind of television people demanded to see.

"God, if the show was in trouble before . . . how did the Fairy-Tale Family react to this season?"

"There were some tough parts." Skylar puffs out her cheeks. "Not everyone in the Fairy-Tale Family wanted to stick with the show when it became clear that we were promoting a gay relationship. Of course, they didn't say that outright. They claimed to be upset that we let our star hook up with his producer off-screen, but it was obvious what it was really about. There were some . . . boycotts."

"But," Ryan cuts in, suddenly very awake, "we also brought in a ton of new advertisers and new viewers. Honestly, breaking the rules might be the thing that saves *Ever After*."

Dev's busy brain keeps spinning around these revelations, stacked like Jenga pieces. "What about *Us Weekly*? The photo of Daphne and Charlie?"

Parisa rolls her eyes. "You've been in this business a long time, Dev. Shouldn't you recognize a publicity stunt when you see one?"

"Daphne is our next princess," Jules explains, "and we need to keep her relevant in people's minds before we make the announcement at the finale."

Dev shoots Parisa a look. "*Ever After* is in transitional rebranding, but you chose vanilla Daphne Reynolds as your next star?"

The four of them all exchange weird looks. "Things with Daphne got"—Ryan searches for a vague enough word—"*interesting* after you left."

"We were so sure there was no way you didn't know about this season," Jules cuts in. Dev thinks about his therapist, who definitely knew and respected the boundaries he set. He thinks about his parents watching in secret every Monday night. He's not sure if he's grateful or furious they kept this from him.

"And then I reached out to Shameem, and we discovered you've been living in a social-media-free hole," Ryan continues, "and we figured we had to try to show you, to see if there is any chance you might—"

"Any chance I might what?"

"Dev," Parisa says. "Charlie put it all on the line. He fought for a season of television that tells the truth, and the last thing the world saw was you leaving him in Macon without a word. He had his heart broken." She sounds so hurt, and he understands it's because he hurt the person she loves most in the world, and loving someone means carrying around their hurt, too. "But the season isn't over. There is still the live finale, still a chance for you to make this right."

The real reason they flew across the country is finally clear. They have a show to make, a story to wrap up, a fairy tale that needs its happy ending. Dev thinks about the season he just watched and about the Charlie-shaped sinkhole in his chest. He thinks about the house in Silver Lake, the plants by the window, Charlie in a soft sweater. He thinks about a bed where the sheets always smell like oatmeal body wash and a life that's always filled with *him*. On an end table in his parents' living room are a serving platter and bowl, flown halfway across the world by Charlie Winshaw.

Then he thinks about who he was three months ago and who he is now and who he wants to be and—

"I'm sorry, but I can't."

And he turns and walks out of the living room.

*   *   *

It's Jules who comes, Jules who finds him sobbing into a jean jacket on his childhood bed. She sits down on the corner, and he waits for her impassioned speech about why he should risk everything to profess his love for a man on national television.

"You left me, too, you know," she eventually says, with no sympathy and all bite. "So that sucked."

Since he'd rather be yelled at than cajoled at the moment, he sits up and reaches for her hand.

"Jules."

She stops him. "I don't want you to apologize, okay? I get it. You weren't in a healthy place, and you had to do what was right for you. And the reality of our friendship is, you always kept me at a distance. You never really let me in. I've been talking to my therapist about it—"

His right eyebrow shoots up.

"Yes, I have a therapist. Everyone has a fucking therapist," she snaps. "I'm not exactly good at letting people in, either. I don't like to be vulnerable with anyone, but I'm worried you never let me see the real you because you were afraid I wouldn't love all of you."

Jules's words cut as deep as the image on the magazine cover, exposing the fear he carries around with him, always. Still.

"In case I'm right, I want to make sure you know that I love you for who you are, even when you're a cowardly asshole who bails on his friends for three months," she says in a very Jules Lu–like fashion. Then she does something very un-Jules. She reaches for both of his hands, gathers them to her heart, right over the face of J. C. Chasez. "You are deserving of my love just as you are, and you're deserving of his love, too."

He starts crying again, but Jules doesn't let go of his hands, doesn't let him hide the evidence of his tears. "You deserve the love you've been orchestrating for other people for the last six years. You deserve a happily ever after."

"A happily ever after?" he snorts, and an unseemly wad of snot gathers on his upper lip. Jules kindly pretends not to notice while she lets him reach for a tissue. "You don't believe in happily ever afters. You think our show is stupid."

"Our show *is* stupid. We once made women downhill ski in Switzerland while wearing bikinis. In the dead of winter. People come on our show so desperate for marriage, they delude themselves into thinking they're in love. Barely half the couples make it past six months."

"What about Brad and Tiffany? They've been married for fifteen years, and they have three kids."

"Yes, we parade them around a lot."

"Or Luke and Natalie, or Greg and Jane, or Brandon and Lindsey—"

"The point is," Jules interjects, "most people don't fall in love in two months. But sometimes you meet someone, and you just *know*. And then we put them on a boat in Bali, because who can resist falling in love on a boat?"

"Don't quote me to me."

She squeezes his hands impossibly tight. "That list you just recited of our rare successful couples . . . do you notice any patterns?"

"They all have names you can easily find on a souvenir license plate?"

"They're all white, yes. White and passably straight and middle class and Christian and *incredibly hot*."

Dev laughs, narrowly avoiding another snot situation.

"*Ever After* is good at selling one very particular kind of love story. Most of the people who come on our show are all the same, but Charlie—"

Just the sound of his name makes Dev's heart punch into his throat.

"Someone like Charlie never should've come on our show, but he did. He's so special."

"I know he is." Dev bristles. "He's the most incredible person I've ever met."

She looks like she wants to slap him across the face. "So what's the fucking problem?"

"What if I'm like our naïve contestants? What if . . . what if the love I've wanted my whole life isn't real? What if there are no happily ever afters?"

Jules takes their knotted hands and drops them into her lap, but still, she refuses to let go of him. "I don't think happily ever after is something that happens to you, Dev. I think it's something you choose to do for yourself."

Story notes for editors:
Season 37, Episode 10
Story producer:
Jules Lu

Air date:
Monday, November 15, 2021
Executive producer:
Ryan Parker

Scene: Interviews with Angie Griffin, Lauren Long, and Daphne Reynolds at the live finale
Location: Studio in Burbank

Mark: Are you disappointed at all with the way things turned out?

Angie: Disappointed? Ha, hardly. Look, I auditioned for this show on a dare. Don't look at me like that, Mark. I've done worse things for free alcohol. I figured best-case scenario, I'd get to travel to some cool places with some cool people before starting med school. And I was right—that part was amazing. But I never believed any of the couples on this show *actually* fell in love. I guess I still don't, since we were all faking the whole time, but also, the truth is, I did fall in love on this show. I fell in love with Charlie. I fell in love with Daphne, who has become one of my closest friends. It's not romantic love, but I think it matters just as much.

Mark: What have you learned from this process, if anything?

Lauren: I've learned it's possible to be so in love with an idea of something, you can be blinded to the reality. And I've learned I want something real.

Mark: If you could go back and give advice to the version of yourself that started your journey on this show six months ago, what would it be?

Daphne: I would tell her to stop chasing someone else's idea of love. And I would tell her she deserves the kind of love she truly wants.

THE LIVE FINALE

Burbank, California—Monday, November 15, 2021

Charlie

"Can I please, *please* take off this fucking crown?"

Jules smooths out a crease in his purple tie, then tilts her head up at him. "Absolutely not."

"I'm not even a prince anymore," he argues. "I'm just a man, about to talk to another man, about how a third man broke my heart on national television."

"You can do that in a fucking crown." She stops grooming him long enough to fuss over his emotional state instead. "Are you going to be okay?"

"Yes, Jules."

"Did you rehearse the questions I sent you?"

"I did."

"And you know if at any time, you're feeling uncomfortable, or need a break, all you have to do is—"

"I know."

"You're really okay?"

"I'm really okay."

He really is. In five minutes, Charlie is going to sit on a couch in this Burbank studio across from Mark Davenport in front of four cameras, a studio audience, and twenty million live viewers to debrief the season that has aired for the past nine weeks. He will be forced to rehash it, and he'll be forced to relive the heartbreak. He's had three months to cope with what happened in Macon, but for the people across the country who tuned in, it *just* happened when the episode aired last week. He'll have to reopen all those old wounds for the sake of entertaining reality television, but he really is fine. Totally fine.

Charlie can see from his position tucked behind some risers that things are about to get started. The studio lights are all in place, and Mark's assistants have positioned him in his chair. He can hear Skylar's voice announce, "We're live in thirty!" Then she counts it down, swallowing the last three numbers as Charlie's heart pummels against his chest.

Three . . . two . . . one . . .

"Welcome, Fairy-Tale Family, to the live finale of the most unusual season of *Ever After* in the show's history." The studio audience applauds on cue, and a makeup artist quickly touches up Charlie's face. "Tonight, we are going to sit down with our prince and see how he's been doing since filming ended unexpectedly in Macon. We know he came on this show with less-than-noble intentions in terms of finding his princess, but in the end, our prince found something much better. Take a look."

On a monitor in front of him, Charlie watches as the show plays a supercut of every scene he and Dev appeared in together. Their entire relationship, set to a Leland Barlow song, arranged in a beautiful montage. Charlie imagines turning his entire body to stone, to something implacable, so the memories can't penetrate him.

"Let's bring him out. Charlie Winshaw everybody!"

Jules gives him a quick pat on the back, and he steps out into the lights. The audience goes *nuts*. He can't see them—the studio lights generously paint everyone in silhouette—but he can hear their screams. A high-pitched voice shouts, "Charlie, we love you!" A deeper one: "I'll be your prince!"

He does a shy, double-handed wave in the direction of the darkened crowd. He knows he looks awkward. For once, he doesn't care. "Oh, wow. Thank you, everyone! Thank you so much."

He trips over the single step leading to the platform where Mark is waiting. The audience laughs, but he knows this time they're laughing with him.

"Well, I'd say they're excited to see you," Mark Davenport jokes as they take their seats.

Charlie unfastens the button on his blazer and leans back casually on the couch. "Uh, are they?"

His nervousness is met with more applause, and isn't it wild that his true self is the version of Charlie Winshaw people like the most?

"Welcome back to the show after being away for a while. How's it been for you since the show finished filming?"

"It's been . . ." Charlie starts. He takes a second, inhales three times. On the third exhale: "Well, for a while there, it was pretty shit, wasn't it?"

Some of the audience members laugh. The rest make sounds of sympathy.

"It was tough in the beginning," he admits honestly, because honesty is what the audience wants, and because being his most honest self is all Charlie wants. "Having your heart ripped out on national television kind of sucks. But thankfully, I made some amazing friends on this show. Angie and Daphne, but also crew members who've helped me get through it. Ultimately, I wouldn't trade my experiences on this show for anything."

Mark nods knowingly, because of course, he does know. Charlie emailed him his answers beforehand. "Talk to us about that."

"As you all now know," Charlie starts, gesturing to the audience, "I came on this show because I thought I had something to prove to the world. I was diagnosed with obsessive-compulsive disorder when I was twelve and diagnosed with a panic disorder in my late teens, but I grew up with a family that didn't recognize, honor, or validate those parts of me. My family always made me feel like those aspects of my identity made me less worthy of happiness.

"When I started my journey on this show, I wanted to convince the world I was someone that I'm not, but ironically, my time on *Ever After* helped me become my more authentic self. I learned I deserve love—both platonic and romantic."

The audience erupts in another round of boisterous applause. The feelings are his, but the words are mostly Parisa, who sat on his living room floor with him three nights ago, helping him find the right way to express what it's all meant to him, being given permission to be himself.

"I know your goal was to work in tech again," Mark asks, flawlessly rehearsed. "Has that happened?"

"I've had a few job offers, yes, but the truth is, my desire to work in tech stemmed from my belief that my profession was the measure of my worth. It never made me happy. I've realized the work we're doing at the Winshaw Foundation is important, so I'm not looking for any other job opportunities at the moment."

"Everyone in the Fairy-Tale Family is very proud of you, Charlie," Mark says, transitioning smoothly. "But now let's get to the stuff we actually care about." The audience laughs. "Have you talked to Dev at all since filming ended?"

He feels his throat catch fire around the collar of his shirt, feels his chest constrict. He takes three deep breaths, drums his fingers against his knee, and answers. "No, I haven't. I don't think he wants to talk to me, but honestly, I think it's for the best."

Mark doesn't say anything, and Charlie knows he's supposed to keep talking to fill the silence, but he didn't script this part. It was too hard to sit across from Parisa and imagine telling her about the voicemails, about the imagined conversations with Dev, about walking into rooms and still expecting him to be there. That despite all the evidence to the contrary, he truly believed he could reach out for Dev and hold on.

"The thing is, sometimes this show—and I mean no offense, Mark. You know how much I've grown to love *Ever After*. But sometimes this show makes you believe a relationship can help you fix yourself. As much as I grew over the course of the show, that growth was dependent on Dev, and when he left, I realized my happiness can't be contingent on another person. I've been learning how to be healthy on my own, and wherever he is, I hope Dev's doing the same thing."

"If you could talk to Dev again, though," Mark goads, leaning across his chair. "What would you say to him?"

"I . . . I don't think I can talk to Dev again," Charlie says. It's the kind of honesty that surprises him, the kind of honesty that leaves him breathless. All he does is talk to Dev in his mind, but the idea of seeing him again—the idea of learning to say goodbye *again*—hurts too much. "It would be too hard to talk to him. I think maybe Dev and I are two people who were meant to enter each other's lives very briefly. We weren't meant to have a happily ever after, but that doesn't mean the happiness we had was any less important or any less real. I think—"

Behind him, a producer is yelling, and Charlie breaks off, thinking they're finally going to commercial break. Maybe he'll finally have two minutes to rush behind the risers and cry in private, because no matter how honest you're trying to be, some things should only belong to you.

Skylar doesn't call cut, though, and the producers keep screaming, keep cursing at a volume the studio microphones will definitely pick up. When Charlie turns toward the sound of the commotion, he sees someone rushing onto the stage. For a moment he's terrified. While most people responded to his season with an outpouring of love, there are still some dangers to being a queer person who discusses their mental illness on the internet, even for extremely privileged white men like him. He knows Angie and Daphne both had to deal with much worse after the show aired.

"Well, this isn't quite how we planned to do this," Mark says with an edge of annoyance as he studies the man on set. The gate-crasher stops on the edge of the platform, and Charlie squints through the studio lights, sees black skinny jeans and a ridiculously oversize jean jacket.

It's Dev.

Dev

I don't think I can talk to Dev again.

That's what Charlie said. That's what Dev feared. As he got on a plane, as he sat in the backseat of a town car on the way to the studio, as he sat in a greenroom watching the man he loves talk about how happy he is now without him. Why would Charlie want to talk to Dev again? After everything, why would Charlie ever want to see him?

Charlie said those words—*I don't think I can talk to Dev again*—and Dev stormed out of the greenroom. Part of him wanted to run outside and call a Lyft. He ended up onstage instead.

He's never been on this side of things before. This side of things is horrifying.

The lights are too hot and too bright. Dev squints, trying to adjust. The audience is painted in shadows, and he stumbles two steps forward, freezes. Skylar is just off camera, swearing at him.

The audience reacts to Dev's unexpected presence with a collective gasp, and Charlie slowly rises from the couch. He looks different. His hair is shorter in the front, and he's lost some weight, but it's more than that. It's the way he stands, so confidently, so unshakable, so certain of what to do with his arms.

They are thirty feet apart, separated by the glossy studio floor and two months of memories and three months of not talking.

"Hi," Charlie says, breaking the silence first.

"Hi," Dev says back.

Everything is too silent and too still, and it turns Dev's brain to microphone static. He forgets everything he meant to say. He's scripted this scene a dozen times for other people, but he has no idea what he's supposed to say as himself. When it's *real*. He says: "I know I fucked it all up."

Then: "Shit, you can't say 'fuck' on live television. Oh *fuck*."

He rams his fist into his hair and tries to take three deep breaths. He looks up and sees Charlie smiling from thirty feet away, and that smile feels like encouragement. He takes a step forward.

"What I'm trying to say is, I'm sorry. I know you don't want to talk to me, but I feel like I owe you an apology at the very least."

Dev takes another step forward, watches Charlie tense, and pauses. "I'm sorry I left without telling you, but I felt like there was no way for you to ever truly choose me, so I chose myself instead. I didn't think there was room for me—for us—in the world of *Ever After*, but you rewrote all the fucking rules. *Freaking* rules."

Dev stops talking and looks at Charlie, looks at all of him. He gives himself a minute to appreciate the exquisite beauty of this man in a gray suit, in case this is his last chance. The minute stretches. Dev doesn't move, and Charlie doesn't move, and it feels like there are no cameras. There is no audience. No Skylar swearing into a headset or Mark Davenport looking gleeful in his chair. There is just Charlie. Just Dev.

Charlie shatters the moment. "This sounds more like an excuse than an apology."

"Can't it be both?" Dev shrugs sheepishly, hopes he can somehow charm his way out of this public embarrassment. Then again, he embarrassed Charlie publicly when he left, so maybe this is exactly what he deserves. "I'm sorry I gave up when things got hard. I'm sorry I didn't see another way for the story to end. But I'm not sorry I left, because I needed to learn to take better care of myself."

"I know," Charlie says. He takes a step forward, so Dev takes a step forward, and now Charlie's only about two Devs' lengths away. "So is that the only reason you came to speak to me in front of twenty million viewers? To apologize?"

He wants to say yes. He wants to smile and laugh it off and be Fun Dev. Charlie doesn't want to talk to him, and it would be so much easier to slip into that old way of being like he slipped into this jean jacket, to hide his heartbreak behind an indifferent smile. Because there is nothing more terrifying than standing up in front of the world and declaring that you deserve love.

But then he thinks about what Jules said. Maybe this show is bullshit. Maybe (okay, *definitely*) fairy-tale love is not real. Charlie Winshaw is not Prince Charming, but he's still pretty damn special, and maybe Dev deserves to be on this stage anyway. Maybe they both do.

"No," Dev says. "I came here to tell you I love you, Charlie. I don't think I know how to *not* love you, and I am even more in love with you now than I was three months ago. I want the house and the puzzles and the plants by the windows—if you still want all those things, too."

Charlie's face transforms into the one Dev fell in love with first, the snarl of his furrowed brow, the sheen of nervous sweat on his forehead. "Are you going to pull away again?"

"No, I won't."

Charlie takes three certain steps forward. As the distance fades, so does everything else, and this conversation shrinks down to the two of them, a foot apart. Charlie doesn't speak, and Dev doesn't know what else he can say. He doesn't have the perfect words, because he's not perfect, and Charlie's not perfect, and this whole thing is so utterly imperfect, Dev snorts.

"I still want kids," he blurts.

Charlie smiles. "Hmm, yes. I think you've mentioned."

"And marriage."

"Also sounds familiar."

Charlie is right here, and Dev knows it's his turn to reach out. So, he reaches. He takes Charlie's hand, intertwines their fingers, and when Charlie lets him, it fills Dev with a stupid kind of hope.

Charlie bites down on his bottom lip. "Is the white tux a negotiable though?"

Dev shakes his head grimly. "It is not."

Charlie grabs the collar of Dev's coat. "Unfortunately," he starts, and Dev holds his breath, "you look so damn sexy in this jean jacket, I can't resist you."

The tension breaks in his chest, and Dev laughs, truly and fully, for the first time in three months. "That is the reason I wore it, obviously."

Dev is so hopeful, he feels like he's choking on it, and he leans forward an inch, the smallest of tests. Charlie meets him more than halfway, pushes himself up on his toes, and kisses Dev on this show about fairy-tale love. In front of Mark Davenport and a live studio audience and twenty million viewers. He kisses Dev with hands and with teeth and with tongue, and Dev kisses him back with *I'm sorry* and *I love you* and *I promise*.

Kissing Charlie is like all the pieces of himself coming together, confident and sure. Kissing Charlie is like the scene at the end of the movie, and it's nothing like the scene at the end of the movie, and he wants to spend the rest of his life telling Charlie what he needs and being what Charlie needs. "I love you, Charlie." He tucks the words into the hollow base of Charlie's throat, just for the two of them. "All of you."

Charlie leans back so he can see Dev's face. "I love all of you, too." Then he kisses him again, deeply, then tenderly, then like he did in the shower in Bali, as if Dev is something precious and rare.

"Well, Fairy-Tale Family," Mark Davenport interrupts, probably to keep the kiss on this side of prime-time television standards. "There you have it. Our Prince Charming did manage to find love, and now there's just one thing left to do."

Mark Davenport reaches for something beside his chair, then rises and moves toward them. He's holding a royal blue pillow with something glistening atop it in the studio lights.

Dev covers his face in his hands. "*Oh my God.*"

"There is only one way this season ends," Mark Davenport says, and he hands Charlie the pillow holding the crown, a twin of the one on Charlie's head. It's the Final Tiara, the Crowning Ceremony that never was, here, on this stage, in this studio, with two men. Dev knows it's all stupid—grown adults, playing at fairy tales—but he feels ten years old, watching for the first time.

"Please don't laugh," Charlie says, his tone serious even as his face breaks into a ridiculous grin at the absolute absurdity of it all. Not just the show itself, and not just this moment, but every moment from the first, when Charlie fell out of a car at Dev's feet. Practice dates and real dates and New Orleans and Cape Town and maybe, maybe, other places, too. Places they'll visit together, side by side in adjacent first-class seats. Food to eat and mountains to be carried across and a house to come back to, always.

"Dev Deshpande. Are you interested in becoming my prince?"

If happily ever after is something you choose, then Dev decides to choose it for himself. "Yes," he says.

THE PREMIERE

Dev

"Are you ready to meet your princess?"

Mark Davenport stands in his signature spot in front of a gurgling fountain with the castle in the background, perfectly framed on their fifty-inch television screen. "Last season of *Ever After* broke all of the rules, and we ended up with a new couple in our Fairy-Tale Family."

"Woot-woot!" Dev shouts at the television. Charlie responds by burying his face in ten throw pillows. Here, in the privacy of their own home, *he blushes*. Dev constantly marvels at the fact that Charlie somehow survived two months of filming and the last six months of unrelenting media attention.

"After last season aired, we saw an overwhelming outpouring of support, particularly from members of our Fairy-Tale Family who were so honored to see themselves represented in the love story on our show," Mark is saying. "And no one was more moved by what she saw than our very own Daphne Reynolds. Take a look."

The show cuts to a package on Daphne's journey last season, which is primarily footage of Charlie and Daphne making out.

Dev's totally fine watching it. It doesn't bother him at all. But on the off chance that it *does* bother him, Charlie reaches out and takes his hand. To remind him how this story ends.

There are other moments, too. Moments of Megan harassing Daphne back at the castle, moments of Angie and Daphne sneaking away together to escape the drama, moments of Daphne struggling to process in front of the cameras during her confessionals.

The package jump-cuts to the interview they did with Daphne on the live finale after Dev and Charlie's reunion. She sits on the couch in a knockout of a silver strapless dress and reflects on her experiences with Mark Davenport.

"The truth is, I was never in love with Charlie. I was trying to force myself to have feelings, because I thought if I could fall in love with him, it would solve what I thought was a major problem in my life."

"And what problem is that?" Mark Davenport asks leadingly.

Daphne sighs, and there is the faintest hint of tears in the corners of her blue eyes. "I grew up in a deeply religious family. That's not to say my family isn't tolerant and supportive—" The show inlays a small box in the corner of the television screen, showing Daphne's adorable Southern family cheering her on from a greenroom. "It's just, since I was a little girl, playing with Barbies and watching Disney movies, I always thought my future had to be me walking down the aisle toward my prince. I pursued that future, and I dated men, and I never let myself question why none of those relationships ever felt right."

Daphne sighs again, and the audience hangs on her every word. "Then I came on this show, and I met so many people who come from different backgrounds, and have had different life experiences, and I started to suspect maybe there was a different kind of love story, too. Something I hadn't let myself consider. When Charlie tried to come out in Macon, it all sort of . . . *clicked*. The truth I'd been hiding from myself. I'm a lesbian."

A very raucous group of butch women in the front row scream in wild approval, and Daphne smiles shyly. "I came out to my family, and I feel like such a weight has been lifted off me. I don't think I ever would have gotten to this point without my journey on the show."

"Honestly, who even cast last season?" Dev asks from their couch. "Was the network *trying* to make it a queer party?"

"I do not remember it feeling like a queer party when we were filming it," Charlie says, and Dev prepares himself to be outraged. "Except for you, love. You are always a one-man queer party."

"Damn right I am."

The show cuts back to the castle, to Mark Davenport standing by the east gate in a prepackage. "Fairy-Tale Family, without any further ado, allow me to introduce to you our new star: Daphne Reynolds!"

Daphne comes riding onto set atop a white horse, her posture perfect in the saddle. She's wearing tan riding pants, black boots, and a billowing white shirt like a real-life goddamn prince. Daphne takes off her helmet and shakes out her long blond hair.

Charlie squeezes his hand tighter. "Do you wish you'd been there?"

Does he wish he were part of the first (intentionally) gay season of *Ever After*? Of course, he does. Part of him will always love *Ever After*. Love the magic, the energy, the way romance plays out in front of the cameras. He loves a perfect make-out session against a brick wall. He loves the drama, the heartbreak, the tears, the music, the first kisses.

And yeah: the show is kind of trash. It asks people to compete for love. It sometimes exploits them at their most vulnerable moments. It heightens everything to absurdity. But isn't that kind of the point? Isn't that why people watch reality TV? To escape from reality?

Without Maureen, the show will be a lot more progressive, but it's still *Ever After*, and Dev is happy to be watching it play out right here, from the comfort of his couch, with Charlie sitting beside him.

"No, actually." Dev leans over and kisses Charlie. "I think I'm good."

Charlie opens his arms, and Dev settles in against his chest.

Mark Davenport smiles directly at them from the television screen. "Over the course of the next ten weeks, Daphne will embark on a Quest to find her fairy-tale princess. Are you ready, America?"

Dev is so ready.

ACKNOWLEDGMENTS

To go full pretentious gay for a minute here, Oscar Wilde said life is far more likely to imitate art than art is to imitate life. In the case of this book and my writing process, he was absolutely correct. When I started writing this book in 2019, I hadn't come out as gay yet, and it was only through writing Charlie's journey toward self-love that I was also able to write my own. In 2019, I also wasn't in therapy and had been ignoring the gravity of my mental health needs for years by overworking myself. Once I realized Dev's story could only end with him choosing to get emotionally healthy, did I accept that I needed to make the same choice for myself.

So thank *you* first and foremost, for reading this book, for embracing these characters, and, by extension, for embracing me. It means so much to me, and I hope you found something here—some joy, some laughter, some love—that you can take with you into your own story.

This story never would have been told without the help of so many people. Thank you to my extraordinary agent, Bibi Lewis, who believed in this book from the beginning and who "got it" from the first early-morning phone call. Thank you for your compassion, your care, and your patience with my neuroses at every stage in this process.

To my editor, Kaitlin Olson, who made this book so much better with every insightful question, every thoughtful suggestion, every un-italicizing. Your understanding of these characters and this story helped me understand it better. You turned this into something I can be proud of, and words cannot fully capture my gratitude.

Thank you to everyone at Atria Books who dedicated time to bringing this story to life. In particular, Polly Watson (copy editor extraordinaire, who made line edits one of my favorite parts in the process), Jade Hui (for answering my intense emails), Isabel DaSilva, Megan Rudloff, Jill Putorti, Sherry Wasserman, Libby McGuire, Lindsay Sagnette, Dana Trocker, Suzanne Donahue, and Sarah Horgan and Min Choi for the most perfect cover ever!

Thank you to Hannah Orenstein, for your generous support of other writers, and your commitment to building a supportive community. To all the other writers and early readers who supported this book—I'm so humbled.

Thank you to my family, for supporting me in my writing long before this book came into existence. To my dad, Bill, who gave me his love of writing and taught me how to dream. To my mom, Erin, who is legitimately the single greatest human who has ever lived. To my stepdad, Mark, who built me a desk and bought me a computer that ran on DOS at a garage sale so I could write books in my bedroom at fourteen. To Kim and Brooklyn, who immediately jumped on board. To Grandma O'Reilly, who will never know I accomplished this dream, but whose fingerprints are on it all the same. And to Grandpa Coch-run, who raised us with stories and filled my heart with words.

Biggest family thanks of all to Heather, the best travel part-ner and sister-friend this triple-water sign could ask for. Thank you for sitting with me through so many cryfests, for trying to reassure me that my anxiety is an unreliable narrator, and for al-ways asking what you could do to help. You're the *second* greatest human who has ever lived. None of this would exist without you.

Thank you to Michelle Agne, who read it first, and Meredith Ryan, who read it most—you both brought me back from so many spirals as I navigated publishing a debut novel during a pan-demic. I dedicated this book to both of you because not only did you help *The Charm Offensive* become its best self but you also help me become my best self every day by teaching me what it means to be vulnerable, be brave, and love unconditionally.

A special thank-you to Andie Sheridan, for their support, and for all the writing sprints and conversations about radical queer love. I treasure the feedback you gave me and the time you put into helping Charlie and Dev say what I needed them to say. You're my writing role model, and I can't wait to hold one of your books in my hands someday soon.

Thank you to everyone who answered my questions and let me bounce around ideas, but a special thank-you to the fol-lowing people: Bryan Christensen for your amazing writerly wisdom and for sitting outside with me for five hours in the freezing cold to talk through revisions; Peter Lu for respond-ing to my computer science questions so generously (any errors about CS are entirely my fault and unintentional); thank you Skylar Ojeda for your insider information into the life of a tele-vision producer (any errors are entirely my fault and probably intentional, to be honest); Thamira Skandakumar and Shrisha Menon, for your thoughtful conversations about representation and the emotional labor you put in; thank you to everyone who helped me brainstorm Group Quests and contestant jobs and possible titles, and a special thank-you to Leanna Fabian, who put up with being my roommate the summer I wrote this and tolerated all manner of odd questions. Thank you, Hayley Downing-Fairless, for being my pandemic photographer and capturing author photos I don't hate.

Thank you to the group of amazing 2021 debuts who let me experience this journey alongside them, and all the writers who let me slide into their DMs to ask questions. Thank you to all the booksellers, librarians, bloggers, Bookstagrammers, and reviewers. Thank you to all the ace and aspec content creators who have helped me find my truest self by sharing theirs with the world.

Thank you to my therapist, Karen, because even though I *could* have done this without them, I am very glad I didn't have to. Thank you for reminding me to stop and appreciate all the beautiful moments along the way. Queer-affirming therapists save lives, and the work you do for our community is valued beyond measure.

Finally, thank you to every Mountain View High School student who has sat in my classroom for the past eleven years. I hope you didn't read this book (seriously, it's not for children), but on the off chance you're reading *this*, I want you to know it's never too late, you're never too old, and your dreams are never too big. And if your dream is to write, please know I believe in you. Your story fucking matters. Only you can tell it.

ABOUT THE AUTHOR

Alison Cochrun is a high school English teacher living outside Portland, Oregon. When she's not reading and writing queer love stories, you can find her torturing teenagers with Shakespeare, crafting perfect travel itineraries, hate-watching reality dating shows, and searching for the best happy-hour nachos.